Praise for Jessica Hall's novels

Into the Fire

"My kind of book! [It] kept me reading well into the night. A fast-paced serpentine of high tension, steamy sex, and just the right touch of romance." —Lisa Jackson

The Kissing Blades

"A nonstop action romantic thriller." —*Midwest Book Review*

The Steel Caress

"Sharp romantic suspense . . . [an] action-packed tale. Jessica Hall provides a wonderful romantic thriller." —*Midwest Book Review*

"Once I started it, I couldn't put it down until I finished. What more can I say—do *not* miss this riveting, passionate novel. It's fantastic!" —The Best Reviews

The Deepest Edge

"If you like Paris, swords as old as time, a soul-deep love story, and wild adventure, *The Deepest Edge* is for you." —Catherine Coulter

"An amazing thriller that is exotic, passionate, and exhilarating. Don't miss this book!" —*Romantic Times* (4½ Stars, Top Pick)

"Keeps the reader's interest from start to finish." —*Booklist*

"A taut romantic suspense thriller." —*Midwest Book Review*

HEAT OF THE MOMENT

Jessica Hall

AN ONYX BOOK

ONYX
Published by New American Library, a division of
Penguin Group (USA) Inc., 375 Hudson Street,
New York, New York 10014, USA
Penguin Group (Canada), 10 Alcorn Avenue, Toronto,
Ontario M4V 3B2, Canada (a division of Pearson Penguin Canada Inc.)
Penguin Books Ltd., 80 Strand, London WC2R 0RL, England
Penguin Ireland, 25 St. Stephen's Green, Dublin 2,
Ireland (a division of Penguin Books Ltd.)
Penguin Group (Australia), 250 Camberwell Road, Camberwell, Victoria 3124,
Australia (a division of Pearson Australia Group Pty. Ltd.)
Penguin Books India Pvt. Ltd., 11 Community Centre, Panchsheel Park,
New Delhi - 110 017, India
Penguin Group (NZ), Cnr Airborne and Rosedale Roads, Albany,
Auckland 1310, New Zealand (a division of Pearson New Zealand Ltd.)
Penguin Books (South Africa) (Pty.) Ltd., 24 Sturdee Avenue,
Rosebank, Johannesburg 2196, South Africa

Penguin Books Ltd., Registered Offices:
80 Strand, London WC2R 0RL, England

First published by Onyx, an imprint of New American Library,
a division of Penguin Group (USA) Inc.

First Printing, October 2004
10 9 8 7 6 5 4 3 2 1

 REGISTERED TRADEMARK—MARCA REGISTRADA

Printed in the United States of America

PUBLISHER'S NOTE
This is a work of fiction. Names, characters, places, and incidents either are the product
of the author's imagination or are used fictitiously, and any resemblance to actual persons, living or dead, business establishments, events, or locales is entirely coincidental.

Every day police officers, fire fighters, and paramedics work long hours to rescue us from dangerous situations. They often must risk their lives while trying to protect ours, and yet they are always there when we need them most.

This novel is dedicated to these men and women. They are the bravest and best of us.

1

The night didn't chase the summer's twin demons, mid-July heat and humidity, out of the French Quarter. It curled its immense dark arms around them and pulled them in close. It made buddies of them, and lured them from the wharves and the swamps into the streets, so the trio could carouse and carry on together.

In New Orleans, even the weather was expected to raise a little hell on a regular basis.

The three worked their way through the bars. They beaded the outsides of plastic go-cups and the flushed skin of hot faces. They wilted clothes, hair, and spirits like lettuce under a heat lamp. They pressed against the out-of-towners and hugged them around the lungs and dogged them until they trudged, shoulders hunched, back to their nice, bland, air-conditioned hotels.

Tourists were so easy.

After midnight, only the thin-blooded locals had enough backbone to ignore the dark, smothering heat and slip into their favorite watering holes, where the air-conditioning might be pitiful but the music was pure magic and the bottles were kept packed in ice.

The locals all knew that a decent jazz quartet and a cold beer could make up for just about anything.

Douglas Simon wanted more than a drink when he entered Maskers Tavern and paused to mop his face with a handkerchief. His appearance earned him only brief glances from the handful of patrons scattered along the bar.

Not that Douglas Simon was someone who attracted a great deal of notice wherever he went. He was of average height and weight, and his features were unremarkable. His washed-out-brown short hair and matching eyes mirrored his quiet, unassuming demeanor. The suit that he wore was just as bland.

The bartender, however, zeroed in on Douglas and turned to press a security button on the wall by the cash register.

A moment later a well-dressed, black-haired man emerged from the manager's office. "Doug."

"Mr. Belafini." Douglas held out a hand that was ignored. *So this is how it will be. I'm still not good enough for a handshake.* "I do hope I'm not late." He'd just discovered that three years in prisoners' personal effects storage at Angola had killed his watch's battery.

"You're right on time." Stephen Belafini gestured toward a private party room set off to the left of the bar. "Shall we?"

Douglas followed Stephen into the room and swiftly scanned the empty tables. No hit man waiting to escort him out of the bar and take him for a final ride. The walls and door were paneled in glass, too, so everyone could plainly see them.

"I am glad to see you." When the other man gave him a sharp look, Douglas added, "I thought perhaps your father might be here, and he can be somewhat intimidating."

"Prison has made you a little paranoid, Doug." Stephen smiled, showing perfect teeth. "I couldn't say this when I visited you at Angola, not with the guards listening in, but my father wants you to know that your loyalty to the family is deeply appreciated."

How appreciated remained to be seen. "Thank you."

"In fact, my father would have sent a car to pick you up tonight," the other man continued, "but we didn't know where you were staying."

"I rented a room over at the Big Easy Sleep Motel." He wasn't ashamed of it. "I couldn't afford anything better."

"You will after tonight."

Did Belafini think that he was a fool? "Was there any problem with obtaining the agreed-upon amount?"

"Not at all. Don't worry about the money. As far as I'm concerned, you've earned every cent. Sit down." Stephen drew out a chair by the corner table. "I have to get the cash out of the safe." He nodded toward the manager's office. "You want anything to drink?"

Douglas sat down carefully. He couldn't relax, not until he walked out of this place with what he'd been promised. "A gin and tonic, please."

"Gin and tonic it is." Stephen went out, spoke to the bartender, and then disappeared into the manager's office.

The last man to leave Maskers Tavern alive did so at a normal, unhurried pace. He left by a side door, crossed the street, and walked down to a small hotel. Despite the rapidly descending digits on his watch, which he had set to countdown mode, he didn't rush. Although he'd done his work a little differently this time, he'd performed several field tests beforehand. He knew to the second exactly how much time he had left.

Four minutes.

In the hotel, he made his way through the lobby, nodded to the yawning desk clerk, and then took the elevator to his room on the third floor. Once inside his room, he threw the dead bolt and removed his jacket.

Three minutes.

He paused by the bed to pick up his binoculars and the carefully folded white silk scarf he had left there. He shook out the scarf, pressed the delicate fabric against his face, and breathed in deeply. He had stolen it from the woman to whom it belonged some time ago, and the faint scent still clinging to it brought tears to his eyes.

The woman—his woman—always smelled of lilacs.

She would have been appalled to see him now, in this room. The A/C rattled, and recycled the air like a wet-cold sneeze. The industrial-grade carpet was an overblown paisley design in red, green, and yellow, while the machine-quilted coverlet on the bed featured avocado, gold, and blue cartoon fireworks. In the bathroom, which was approximately the same size as a shallow linen closet, he had found a dented plastic ice bucket, cellophane-wrapped glasses with the ghost tinge of soap residue, and wrapped across the toilet seat a band of paper that read SPARKLING CLEAN FOR YOUR CONVENIENCE!

He would never have taken a room in such a dive, either, but for the view from the street-side window, which was incomparable. With the binoculars he could see from St. Louis to Canal Street to the west, and to Pirate's Alley to the east. That window was where he went now, to push the double set of hinged panes out and let the night air in.

Two minutes thirty seconds.

What the man had done at Maskers, he had done many times before. He had become something of an expert in the field, so to speak. He had never lingered near one of his jobs, and had never watched the results of his labors, but this particular situation was special.

This time, it was personal.

It had cost him to make this happen: money, time, and no small amount of pride. Some would say he was jeopardizing his future, perhaps even his life, to defy the very specific orders that he had been given regarding this job. In his business, however, a man didn't rise to the top unless he took risks.

This night would be a Declaration of Independence and his Ascension, rolled into one.

The nuns who had taught him in Catholic school wouldn't approve of his choices, but they had in part helped to instill in him a burning need for self-determination. Sister Mary Thomas had made him memorize verses from the Bible, such as the one from Leviticus that had been echoing in his head for weeks: "You shall neither sow nor reap what grows of its own accord, nor gather the grapes of your untended vine."

Two minutes.

Tonight he would tend to his future, his pride, his destiny. Tonight he would tend to Cortland Gamble.

He didn't see himself as a desperate man, only a righteous one. After this night, he would take what was his; what should have always been his. He would punish Gamble, the man who had dared to take that away from him. Killing his rival had been an often-repeated fantasy, but murder would be too quick, too easy. Gamble needed to understand what it was like to live in plain view of a heart's desire held just out of reach, like a starving fox lusting for the grapes of an untended vine.

Gamble had tried to reap what he had not sown. The marshal had to be made to suffer, as he himself had suffered.

One minute.

Calmly he waited and watched. When there were only thirty seconds left, a taxi pulled up to the front of Maskers and stopped. The driver actually got out to open the door for his passenger, a thin, elegant woman in a pretty floral dress.

"You're going to regret that big tip," he murmured as he watched the woman hand the cabbie a wad of bills.

Twenty seconds.

The woman turned toward the hotel for a few moments as she scanned the street. She was hunched over slightly, her shoulders rounded, her back a parenthesis. The streetlight under which she stood revealed her long black hair and narrow, frightened face. Her hair shifted, and a glint of gold sparkled.

The scarf he held slipped from his fingers and floated unnoticed to the floor.

The woman pulled the cobweb-fine ivory shawl she wore closer around herself, and then hurried into the bar.

Ten seconds.

He ran out of the room, down three flights of stairs, and made it out onto the street in time to witness the first explosion. The ground shook, and windows up and down the street shattered as a huge fireball exploded from the bar's entrance. It was so huge, so loud that it drove him back against the front façade wall of the hotel, concrete slamming into his spine.

A woman staggered by him, her hands clapped over her ears, her mouth stretched into a silent scream.

He couldn't move. *It wasn't her. It couldn't have been.*

She had no reason to come here. No reason, unless she'd been the one passing information to Gamble . . .

Sister Mary Thomas had made him memorize so many verses. Perhaps it hadn't been Leviticus. It may have been something from Galatians. Something about *what a man sows.*

The sound of distant sirens made him fumble for the cell phone in his jacket pocket. He had to try four times before he could dial the number correctly.

A discreet voice answered with, "Crescent City Hospice."

"Is Mrs. Belafini there?" he asked, his voice hoarse and trembling.

"No, sir, I'm sorry, she's not. May I take a message?"

What was that verse? *What a man sows . . . whatever a man sows . . .*

"Sir?"

A huge waft of heat and smoke reached him, permeating his clothes, stinging his eyes. "Where is she?"

"She had me call a cab and checked herself out about thirty minutes ago. I don't know where she was going." The nurse's voice grew concerned. "Is everything all right, sir?"

He didn't hear her. He only heard the gentle voice of Sister Mary Thomas as she read from Galatians to her sixth-grade students.

Do not be deceived, God is not mocked; for whatever a man sows, that he will also reap.

The cell phone fell to the pavement and shattered.

New Orleans's historic French Quarter didn't have many fires, and Channel Eight's Live Spot van arrived on the scene two minutes after the first fire truck. Other trucks, the narrow street, and billowing flame and smoke kept back tardier news teams, and so only one camera captured the firefighters as they went into a synchronized attack on the burning tavern.

Burning embers fell, fiery snowflakes from red-tinged black clouds. The attractive redheaded woman in a pale lemon suit seemed oblivious to them as she posed near the bumper of the closest fire truck and spoke to a remote-feed camera being aimed at her by a middle-aged bearded man with three still cameras slung around his neck.

"Like so many oversized bees in their thick yellow protective jackets, black boots, and hard hats," Patricia Brown said, turning to glance at the burning tavern before facing the camera again, "our brave firefighters must *swarm* around this lethal inferno to combat the terrible flames. As you can see, the full complement of Company 21 has responded to this very serious three-alarm blaze."

She made a gesture, and the cameraman panned to the red-and-silver trucks and the firefighters working in concert to unreel and position the heavy hoses and hook them up to the street hydrants. Patricia clicked off the mike and used the time to touch up her lipstick and have a look in the van's side-view mirror.

"Settle down and stop making insect analogies," she told her reflection. "Look steady but concerned. Gravely concerned. If it bleeds, it leads."

She checked her teeth to make sure the fresh lipstick hadn't rubbed off on them. When the camera was once more focused on her, she was in position and had her gravely concerned expression back in place.

"As soon as the fire can be driven back, these dedicated men will be entering the building to search for survivors. We'll bring you more updates as the situation develops. From where I'm standing, however"—she briefly glanced over her shoulder—"it does not look promising. Patricia Brown, Live Spot Eight News."

"You sound a little raspy, babe," her cameraman said as he stopped filming and began snapping some still shots. "Get some water from the van."

"It's all this damn smoke, Dave. I can barely breathe." Patricia saw a familiar silver SUV pull up to the curb and forgot her respiratory problems. "Here's Gamble. Come on."

"He won't talk to you," Dave predicted. "He never does."

"He might this time." She discreetly fussed with her hair. "Roll on me when I get to the curb."

"He isn't going to like that, either."

"Just do it." As she reached the SUV, she produced her concerned smile. "Fire Marshal Cortland Gamble has just arrived at the scene of the fire at Maskers Tavern here in the Quarter." She paused for a moment to let the tall, broad-shouldered man climb out before she came around the door to corner him. "Marshal Gamble, do you have any idea what started this deadly blaze?" She extended the microphone she held toward his face.

"Not yet." Cort motioned to David to stop filming. When he did, he looked down at her narrow yellow leather pumps. "You're standing in my crime scene, Tricia."

"Was it a crime? Could this have been the Torcher's work?" When he didn't respond, she clicked off her microphone, lowered it, and made her blue eyes go round and helpless. "Cortland, please." She placed a manicured hand on his arm and her Southern accent went from the discreet hint she used for broadcasts to a honey-thick drawl. "My producer is screaming for details, and you know what a cast-iron witch she can be. I'd be *really* grateful for anything you can give me."

A year ago Cort might have been tempted to find out exactly how far her gratitude would extend, but lately he'd steered clear of beautiful, polished women like Patricia Brown. Actually, he'd been avoiding the whole gender as much as possible since Mardi Gras.

Cool, brown-green eyes gleamed through the foggy memories of one night, almost six months ago. He had been using his mouth on her, her thighs taut under his hands, her hips lifting and twisting with impatience and urgency. He had kept teasing her until she said, *Do I have to get the gun again?*

"You'll get a statement." He nodded toward the other reporters being herded outside the line of patrol cars parked to serve as a temporary barricade. "The same time everyone else does." He went around her.

Before Tricia could follow, a uniformed patrolman blocked her path. "You heard the man, lady. Walk it over there."

Cort checked in with the fire chief on the scene but otherwise stayed out of the way. His men were among the best-trained firefighters in the country, and they knew how to handle a blaze. The blast of thousands of gallons of water from the hoses drove back the fire an inch at a time, soaking everything that had been feeding it, transforming flames into thick, gray smoke.

As soon as it was safe to enter the building, the men went in and almost immediately began carrying bodies out. Reporters surged forward, eager to take shots of the victims, but the uniformed cops herded them back. Three teams of paramedics rushed forward to check for signs of life before their steps slowed and they exchanged frustrated looks with the fire crew. The body count soon passed five, and eagerness and frustration turned to silent shock and horror.

While the fire chief went to address the media, Cort quietly directed the men to carry the dead around the corner of the building, away from the press's avid lenses. The paramedics soon ran out of body bags and brought sheets to cover the rest until the morgue van arrived.

Cort noticed one of the younger men standing and staring at the shrouded bodies. He had the wide-eyed, wild look the more experienced men learned to keep from their faces, so he walked over to him. Closer, he saw the firefighter was the son of his senior investigator.

"How are you doing, Jack?"

"This is totally screwed." John McCarthy seemed oblivious to the fact that he was speaking to his father's boss as he gave the line of bodies a jerky nod. "Know where we found five of them?"

From the lacerations on the hands and necks of some the victims, Cort could guess. They had likely beaten their hands bloody, trying to get out, and then had clawed at their throats as the smoke smothered the life out of them. "By an exit door."

"The back one. Piled by it. It was chained and locked." He looked down at one covered victim. "That girl there, she can't be more than eighteen, nineteen. I got a cousin her age."

Cort saw tears in the younger man's fierce, bloodshot

eyes. Words of sympathy would not remove the burden, would not erase the fact that no matter how hard they fought, they couldn't save everyone. Sometimes, they couldn't save anyone.

That was the job.

The sound of a motorcycle diverted Cort's attention for a moment, and he saw a tall, skinny youth in a black leather jacket and black helmet drive up into the center of activity. The fire chief moved to chase off the kid, but some hoses tangled and he changed direction to deal with that first.

The biker parked, dismounted, and stepped up onto the sidewalk in front of Maskers.

"I've got to run interference for the chief," Cort said to Jack. "I need someone here to keep the press and the bystanders away. Are you up for it?"

The firefighter peered at him as if seeing him clearly for the first time. "Damn, Marshal, I—I mean, yes, sir."

"Good." Cort tapped the two-way radio clipped to his belt. "Call if you need help." He headed straight for the biker.

Fire fascinated people. When Cort had first joined the department, seeing how many were drawn to watch buildings burn had appalled and disgusted him. But over the years he had learned that for most it was a reluctant, horrified compulsion, the same they felt when they passed the scene of a bad auto accident and were unable to look away.

That still didn't give biker boy the right to drive up in the middle of a dangerous blaze.

Cort came up from behind the biker while he was releasing his chin strap and clamped a hand on the kid's left shoulder. "Hold it."

The biker stopped in his tracks before removing the helmet and turning around. A NOPD detective's gold badge hung from a narrow black cord around a pale throat. A flare from overhead illuminated a thin, clever face, spiky brown hair and long, narrow hazel eyes. The black leather bomber jacket covered a wrinkled plain white blouse and the faint bulge of a shoulder holster.

Cort dropped his hand. "Detective Vincent."

"Marshal Gamble." The faint smile that curved Terri Vincent's lips was almost as cool as her voice.

Terri's mouth was one reason he'd been avoiding her. The other was knowing what she could do with it. "Why are you here?"

"Homicide snagged the call, and it was on my way home." She batted some drifting ash away from her face before studying the building. "Bad one, huh?"

"Yes."

Cort hadn't been anywhere near Terri Vincent since Mardi Gras, and he noted there had been some definite changes. She was thinner and her tan had deepened. Her hair looked shorter, but when she had turned her head he realized that she'd grown it out, and now wore it scraped back and clipped up off her neck. There were deep shadows under her eyes. As she took out a notepad and pen, he saw she had cut her nails down short and squared.

So she won't bite them, he thought, *when she can't have a cigarette.*

As usual, the homicide detective didn't wear a speck of makeup on her face. A little dent in her lower lip told him that she had been smoking too much again. Her plain brown trousers were too baggy and had deep wrinkles, as if she'd worn them for a week. If not for the tortoiseshell hair clip and the slight rise of breasts under the leather jacket, she wouldn't even look female.

There wasn't a damn thing about her that he liked, and still Cort wanted to drag her to the nearest wall, pin her there, and use his hands to find out what else had changed. Then do it again, with his mouth.

Terri's gaze shifted as two more covered litters were carried out of the building. "How many inside?"

"We don't know yet." He nodded toward the litters. "That makes twelve bodies."

Her expression didn't change, but he didn't expect her to react. Like his brother, J. D., Terri had seen a lot of death. "Another Torcher job?"

"Could be." So she had been following the case. Probably so she could crow over Cort's inability to catch the serial arsonist. "You're not to say a word to the press either way."

"You mean I can't give Tricia Brown an exclusive? Shit, there goes my bribe." She tugged off her jacket and tied it by the sleeves around her waist. "I'd better talk to the uniforms and have a look at the bodies. See you around, Marshal."

The way she so casually dismissed him had always gotten under his skin. After what had happened between them during Mardi Gras, it was a slap in the face. "I don't want you here."

Something flickered in her eyes. "Then you should file another grievance with my boss." She went around him.

Terri Vincent was tired. She'd put in a double shift, trying to clear some backlogged paperwork before her transfer came in. It had taken nine straight hours of two-fingered typing on her ancient typewriter, a full bottle of liquid correction fluid, and six aspirin to plow through it. When she'd clocked out all she'd wanted was to go home, fall someplace flat, and sleep until she was twenty-nine.

The only thing that truly sucked about being a cop was the paperwork.

She'd told Cort Gamble the truth; the French Quarter call had come in when she was on her way out. Homicide ran a skeleton crew on graveyard shift, and the supervisor was a thirty-year veteran who preferred watching Howard Stern to taking a call. It was three a.m., so she had thought it a safe bet that Cort Gamble wouldn't be there.

I'm never going to Vegas, she thought as she walked away from him. *I'd lose my pants and end up walking around wearing a barrel.*

As Terri checked in with the patrolmen providing crowd control, her gaze kept drifting back to the fire marshal as he briefed the scene investigators. She had schooled herself not to pay much attention to Cort—masochism wasn't her thing, and he always seemed to catch her looking—but now he was busy, so she could ogle him as much as she wanted.

Where Cortland Gamble was concerned, there was plenty to drool over.

Terri had always liked big men, and the marshal was a solid six-four, with wide shoulders and long limbs. Another man his size might have lumbered around like an ape, but he moved easily and efficiently. He kept his brown hair cut short and his square jaw clean-shaven, and his clothes were so pressed and immaculate that he could have been posing for a *GQ* cover shoot.

Of course, everything about Cort Gamble was always perfect. He would settle for nothing less. She sometimes wondered if he ironed his boxers.

The marshal also worked out religiously, running every morning and benching free weights. Terri knew because they were members of the same gym, although she had made a point to learn his routine so she wouldn't be there when he was. He must have upped his weights since spring, because everything on him had gotten a little tighter, a little more muscular. Even the veins on his arms looked more prominent, she saw when the heat made him shrug out of his jacket.

Too bad all that strength and physical beauty don't make up for the fact that you're still two hundred and twenty pounds of walking, talking jerk.

As if he'd heard her thoughts, Cort glanced across the road at her.

Before he could give her the "you bitch" look, Terri casually turned to one of the uniforms and instructed him to begin canvassing the crowd. As she spoke, the back of her neck felt weird, as if all the short hairs were standing on end, and her chest went tight. A glance over her shoulder confirmed that Cort was still watching her. With something a little more fierce than the "you bitch" look.

Why, she had no idea. Like the man said, he didn't want her here.

She'd known Cortland Gamble for ten years, since she'd graduated from the police academy. His brother Jean-Delano had been in her class, and the entire Gamble clan had come to the ceremony. Since J. D. and his brothers were three of the finest-looking men in the city, every woman at the commencement had zeroed in on them.

Terri had liked J. D., even when they'd tied for class marksman on the firing range. When he'd called her over to introduce her to his family, she'd been prepared to like his big brother.

And look where that got you, cher.

A microphone appeared in front of Terri's face. "Detective Vincent, can you tell our viewers any details about the victims of this terrible tragedy?"

"Not with you sticking that thing up my nose, Trish."

Patricia backed off, but not much. "Come on, Detective, you wouldn't be here unless those people were murdered. Give me something."

"Okay." Terri leaned in and dropped her voice to a murmur. "Yellow's really not your color."

She left the fuming reporter behind as she crossed the street and went around the building to the alley where they had laid out the bodies. One young-looking firefighter stood watch as two forensic techs worked on bagging the remains. The watcher's hands were in fists, and his smoke-blackened face had irregular, clean patches around the eyes.

Terri went to him first and lifted her badge. "Detective Vincent, Homicide." She checked the name tag on his jacket: MCCARTHY. The same name as one of Cort's lead arson investigators; like being a cop, firefighting tended to run in families. "You related to Gil McCarthy?"

"My dad." He eyed her. "How can I help you, ma'am?"

"You can stop calling me ma'am. It's Terri." She crouched down in front of the body furthest from the techs and lifted an edge of the sheet. The face of the young man beneath it showed some minor burns and lacerations, but the cause of death was evident from his flushed skin and soot-blackened mouth and nostrils. His wide dark eyes held the flat, frozen stare of the dead. "They all like this?"

"Only five. The last two down there"—he nodded toward the other end of the line—"they were burned up pretty bad."

Terri heard a tearing, liquid sound and one of the techs

swore softly. *Body coming apart.* She took out her cigarettes and offered the pack to the young firefighter. "You want?"

"Yeah." He had been looking in the direction of the sound, and took one in a trembling hand.

"Let's step down here." She led him to the corner where she lit his cigarette and then her own. "I ran into your dad last summer on the lake. He was driving a pretty Aquamaster, wide open and hauling ass. That his, or did he rent it?"

"He bought it." He took a drag off the cigarette and let out a shaky stream of smoke. "My mom about killed him, but he said it was that or a bike."

"Good boat for the Gulf. I'll have to bug him for a weekend swap." She nodded toward her Harley.

"Oh, man." Brief lust appeared in his eyes. "How fast does she go?"

"I've had her up at ninety so far, but she tops out at one-twenty. She runs ultra-quiet, too; I had her specially outfitted with more baffle plates in the mufflers." She casually looked around, saw the techs were finished. "When's your next day off?"

"I got the weekend coming."

She pulled out a dog-eared business card and wrote an address on the back. "This is my place down at the lake, if you and your dad want to use it." She handed him the card. "Key's under the geranium pot."

He looked uncertain. "You sure, Detective?"

"Just tell Gil to replace the beer." She met his gaze. "It's good to get away sometimes. Clears the head."

"Yeah." He tightened his hand around the card. "Thanks."

Terri left him on guard and went back to the bodies. After checking with the forensic techs, she unzipped the first bag and carefully searched the body. The contents of the victim's charred wallet were still readable, and she made note of the name and address before replacing the ID where she had found it and moving on to the next body.

Facing brutal, untimely death was part of Terri's job, but she never got used to it. The day she did, she'd quit the force.

Three more victims were carried out to the alley as Terri worked her way down the line. Maskers had drawn a lot of youngsters; most of the victims were barely into their mid-twenties. Two of the least-burned girls had fanny packs with fake driver's licenses; they looked young enough to be teenagers. Six carried no ID, and they and four others were charred too badly for Terri to even make out their features.

She pulled up the last zipper and straightened, taking a moment to clear her own head. She'd been a homicide cop for seven years, and she'd never seen so much death all at once. Here, with so many, it was almost suffocating. Especially now that she knew most of their names, where they lived, what photos they carried. At least three of the men had been fathers of young children.

So much life, gone, just like that.

It wasn't her case yet. There were no signs of foul play, no evident gunshot wounds, nothing that would indicate that murder had been committed. It could have been a tragedy of accident or neglect: faulty wiring, a kitchen fire, a carelessly discarded cigarette. But it felt wrong. Something inside her was already twisted up and snarling, eager to track down the sick bastard who had done this and snuffed out so many young lives.

Not if Cort Gamble has anything to say about it.

"Bastard."

Terri turned around to see who was reading her mind, and saw New Orleans's Medical Examiner Grayson Huitt crouched beside the first body. The pathologist was a tanned, blond former surfer and had the easygoing personality to match. Now, however, he looked as happy as she felt.

"Hey, Doc."

The shaggy blond head lifted, and the hard lines around his mouth vanished as soon as he spotted her. "Detective Vincent." He rose and came to her. "You moonlighting?"

"Got the call coming off shift." She stepped back from the line of victims. "I've found licenses on most of them but I'll still need headshots of the unburned faces for the families." Notifying the next of kin was the only thing she hated more than paperwork. "I think you'll need dental records on a few of them."

Gray eyed the line of bodies. "We can cover the notifications."

"No, you've got enough to do. Let us handle it." She rolled a hand over the back of her neck. It came away damp with sweat. "Fifteen. Jesus Christ, Gray, most of them were just kids."

"I know." He slipped a friendly arm around her waist and gave her a squeeze. "Go on home, get a couple hours' sleep. We'll look after them."

He smelled of the exotic coffee he drank by the potful, and it felt nice to rest her head against the side of his arm, just for a moment. Gray was a good guy, the kind you could lean on and trust when things went bad. It was too bad that was all they'd ever be—pals.

"Is there a problem, Detective?"

Cort Gamble's chilly voice made Terri close her eyes for a moment. *Why, Marshal? Don't you have enough of your own?*

"Nope." She pulled away from Gray and faced him. The fire marshal stood two feet away, water and soot stains on his jacket but otherwise still perfect.

Terri knew she looked like hell, but she didn't need to see the disgust in Cort's eyes. She'd seen that there once too often. No, what she really needed was a cigarette, a beer, and a dark quiet corner to enjoy them in.

A dark corner in, say, Toronto.

"Gray, I'll be in at seven," she said, still looking at the marshal's cold eyes. "Call me when you've got the head-shots ready for pickup." She walked out of the alley and headed for her bike.

Cort followed. "What are you doing, working nights?"

He made it sound like she'd pulled the duty simply to piss him off. "I work when I'm assigned, Marshal. Like every other cop in town."

"This isn't your case yet."

He didn't want her here. Didn't want her anywhere near him. Like she needed telling. Did he honestly think she hadn't noticed the way he'd been dodging her since his mama's Mardi Gras ball? The man had practically put it on the front page of *The New Orleans Tribune,* in twenty-point type: STAY AWAY FROM ME, TERRI.

She'd stayed away. It didn't break her heart to know how he felt. Her heart was already in too many pieces for it to do that.

"Did you hear me? This isn't—"

"I heard, and God willing, I won't be around when it's assigned." She picked up her helmet. "See you later."

He put a hand on her bike. "What are you talking about? You're still working Homicide."

J. D. must not have mentioned her transfer request. Then again, J. D. was off on his honeymoon. He had married Sable Duchesne, the love of his life and the woman who had nearly gotten him kicked off the force. He had better things to do than think about his brother and his partner. Like chase his new bride around the beach.

"Either you want me, or you don't, Marshal." Nudging his hand away only took an elbow. "Try to make up your mind." She eased the helmet over her head and fastened the chin strap.

When she straddled the bike, he leaned in. "I don't want you."

She flipped up her face shield and gave him one last, long look. She didn't have to imagine him naked. She knew, thanks to one long, sultry night when he'd gotten drunk and come looking for her.

I trusted you, and you talk to me like this. Like I'm trash.

It had taken Terri a while—hope did burn eternal—but she finally realized after a few weeks why Cort Gamble had been treating her like a bleeding AIDS patient: He regretted the night they'd spent together. The night when he had fulfilled every fantasy she'd had, rocked the foundations of the world, and then left her to wake up alone in a cold, empty bed.

Leaving her to face the morning after solo wasn't the worst. She'd been there before. Neither was the way he'd treated her since; everyone did things they regretted. She should know. He was one of them.

No, Cort was entitled to his feelings. Terri was a big girl; she could handle it. She'd never once felt that he owed her anything.

But this—this rubbing his contempt in her face—this she really didn't need.

This was the worst.

"Not a problem," she said, very softly, before she started the motorcycle and rode into the night.

2

The fifteen fatalities at Maskers Tavern hit the AP wire and overnight became headline national news, served up on CNN in minute detail and filling the primary crime slot on every morning news show across the country.

Patricia Brown's prediction had been very accurate: *If it bleeds, it leads.*

Cort left the Quarter only after he had his arson task force in place and the scene was secured, and then he had to go around through the back entrance to his office building to avoid the press staking out the front.

Cort's assistant, Sally, a pleasant and efficient former 911 dispatcher, was waiting inside with a steaming cup of coffee, a stack of messages, and a handwritten schedule.

"The mayor wants to see you in his office at ten with a prelim," she said, handing over the coffee. "Don't ask about the calls from the papers and the TV stations. You don't want to talk to Dan Rather or Peter Jennings, do you?"

"No." Cort glanced at his watch and saw it was barely seven a.m. "Who dragged you in this early?"

"Night-shift supervisor. He hates the phones, and evidently they haven't stopped ringing since five a.m." She followed him into his office and placed the paperwork on his desk. "Anyone you *do* want to talk to?"

"Gil McCarthy. Anyone from the task force." He drank some of Sally's excellent brew and then reluctantly added, "Detective Vincent from Homicide."

"J. D.'s partner?" Sally's eyebrows elevated. "She's still speaking to you?" She made that sound on the order of a divine miracle.

Which, in retrospect, it likely was. "Just put her through."

"Aye-aye, Cap'n." She closed his shades on her way out.

Cort switched on his computer and began to type up the preliminary report the mayor would be demanding on his desk in two hours. As fire marshal, Cort had the responsibility to monitor all the fires that occurred within the city limits, evaluate the different types of outbreaks, and assess if there was a pattern that could indicate deliberate or malicious intent.

He had precious little to go on with Maskers, other than the high body count and the rapid burn of the structure. Whatever had started the fire had been fast, powerful and efficient. Judging from the distribution of the window-glass shards and other exterior damage, the bar hadn't just caught fire.

Something had detonated inside the building.

There was only one active arsonist in New Orleans who might have pulled off this job, and Cort had been tracking him for months. If Maskers was the Torcher's work, he was going down. Fifteen counts of first-degree murder would earn him Angola and, after his appeals were exhausted, a lethal injection.

His cell phone rang, and he answered it. "Gamble."

"You didn't come home last night," a man said, his French accent on the heavy side. "Your mother sees you on the TV. She calls me. She is upset with you. Now I am supposed to yell."

Hearing his father's voice made Cort sit back in his chair. "I'm not fifteen, Dad."

"I tell her this, she yells at *me*."

"I have a bottle of Maison Surrenne."

There was nothing Louis Gamble liked more than French cognac, except perhaps a fine cigar to go with it. "The forty-six?"

"The forty-six."

"So I have yelled." His voice went from brisk to gentle.

"It was not a good night, eh? I'll bring over some lunch for you."

Louis Gamble was the owner of Krewe of Louis, the most celebrated French Creole restaurant in New Orleans. He was also the best chef in the city, and food was his cure-all for everything.

"No, thanks, Dad. I won't be here." Cort sat back in his chair and rubbed his eyes. Temporarily living with his parents while hunting for a new apartment closer to work had been convenient, but worrying them—at their age—wasn't. He'd have to step up his search and move out soon. "I'm sorry that I forgot to call."

"Your mother will want to fuss when you get home. You will let her."

His mouth hitched. "I will."

"Lache pas la patate, mon fils."

Don't let go of the potato. Cajun-speak for "Don't give up," which Louis had picked up from Sable, J. D.'s new wife. Cort suspected his father's recent penchant for swamp slang was both to show affection for his new daughter-in-law and to aggravate Cort's mother a little. *"Oui, père."*

He ended the call and finished the lukewarm coffee in his cup before glancing at his top right desk drawer. He didn't want to take out the unmarked, unsealed envelope tucked under his business stationery. He never wanted to.

Yet as he had nearly every day since Mardi Gras, Cort opened the drawer, lifted the stack of paper, and took out the envelope. He turned it over in his hands, wishing he could toss it in the trash can next to his desk. Knowing he never would.

Cort opened the flap and removed three photos. They had been taken ten years earlier, at his younger brother's graduation from the police academy.

The first showed a younger version of J. D. in his patrolman's uniform, standing with his arm around Terri Vincent. Back then she had been just as tall and skinny, but her dark hair had been pulled back in a long ponytail. J. D. was the only one smiling.

Terri, in contrast, had looked at the camera—at Cort, who

had been holding the camera—the same way she might regard a junkie with a knife in a dark alley.

Cort could look back now and acknowledge that maybe she'd been justified. He certainly hadn't been friendly toward her that day. He'd been polite, but the hostility at first sight had been clear and mutual.

To be honest, he'd treated *her* like an armed drug addict on that day.

Not without good reason, naturally. Cort had watched her kid around with the other graduates and listened as she told one joke after another, some of them fairly crude. He'd discovered that she smoked cigarettes, a habit he had always personally detested. No boyfriend showed up, and none of the female graduates appeared to be friends with Terri. She'd seemed content just to hang out with the guys. Cort had known girls who had been tomboys when he was a kid, but they'd all grown up to be fine, attractive women.

Terri Vincent evidently had never made that transition, or had never cared to. It had irritated him on one level and angered him on another. He preferred confident, feminine women who didn't try to compete with men. Yet not one of the girls he'd been with had made him feel the sort of intense, unshakeable attraction he'd instantly felt for Terri.

The second photo was a candid group shot, showing J. D. talking with Terri and a group of friends from their class. Cort's mother, Elizabet, had borrowed the camera to take that one, and the lens had caught Terri's profile as she grinned at his brother. She wasn't beautiful or what Cort would consider even pretty, but in that photo, the sun had been full on her face and her tawny skin had glowed. So had her smile.

She'd never smiled that way at Cort, of course. Not once in ten years. But he'd seen her glow again. That one night, he'd made her do it.

Something clenched in his gut before he shoved away that particular set of memories and moved on to the third and final photo, which showed Terri Vincent sitting by herself at the end of a row of empty chairs. That had been just after the Gambles had left to take J. D. home and celebrate.

Cort remembered his brother inviting Terri to come along, but she had refused, claiming her family was somewhere around waiting for her. Cort had stayed behind to talk to one of his friends, which was how he'd discovered that she had lied to J. D.

Her family wasn't there. No one had come to see Terri graduate.

Cort didn't know why he'd taken the third picture, or why he hadn't gone up to her and insisted she come home with him. He'd wanted to, but she was J. D.'s friend, not his. He also hadn't trusted himself to keep his hands off her.

He'd watched her refuse several other offers to celebrate, and then she'd slipped away from the ceremony, the same way she had arrived: alone.

Later Cort had the film developed and had given his mother duplicates of all but the third shot. He'd kept the negatives, and he had never shown the one of Terri alone to anyone, not even his brother. Of course it made him feel adolescent and obsessive. He should have tossed the pics years ago, and yet each time he tried, he found himself doing just as he did now, carefully replacing them in the envelope and putting them away.

Sally knocked twice and stuck her head in. "I've got some fresh coffee made. Homemade muffins too, if you want."

He closed the drawer. "You angling for a raise?"

She grinned. "Oh, always."

Sally kept him supplied with coffee as he finished the prelim and called Gil to check on his progress. His chief investigator already had his men combing through the scene, photographing the damage and bagging evidence.

"From the smell, kerosene had to be the accelerant," Gil told him. "The whole place stinks of it. No containers or ignition devices so far. It's not like anything we've seen before, but this guy was a pro."

"Keep looking." His cell was ringing again. "I'll talk to you later." He switched phones. "Gamble."

"My son was in that bar last night," a deep, rasping voice said.

The voice was unmistakable. "I'm sorry to hear that." Cort knew mob boss Frank Belafini only had one son, Stephen, and had been grooming him to eventually take over his operation.

"No, you're not, but you're going to be."

The office phone was hooked up to a recorder, but there was no way for him to tape a conversation on his cell. "What do you want, Belafini?"

"I want the son of a bitch who murdered Stephen."

Spoken by a man who had ordered more murders than either of them could count. "You already know that's not going to happen."

"You find him and bring him to me, Gamble. Or I will, and you can watch my boys tear this city apart, one block at a time."

"Come on, Detective, can't you at least confirm that it was murder?" Tricia Brown pleaded over the phone.

Terri doodled on her desk pad, drawing a noose out of the cable attached to a microphone. "What part of 'no comment' don't you understand, Trish?"

"We've got fifteen dead bodies," the reporter told her, sounding as if she had the Maskers Tavern victims parked right there on her desk. "Someone has to be held accountable for those deaths, and the public has the right to know who."

She drew a bug-eyed stick figure hanging from the noose. "You mean someone should be crucified for it, and you want to hammer the nails in personally. Think that'll get you a spot on 'Good Morning America,' or 'Regis and Kelly'?"

"I'm a newswoman." Patricia abandoned righteousness and segued into outraged dignity. "I report the *facts.*"

"You're a ratings hound, Trish." Terri picked up a red pen and drew a stylish helmet of hair on the stick figure. "Nail an exclusive on this one, and you won't have to play weather girl anymore whenever Charlie Boudreaux goes on vacation. Unless that station manager you're bopping decides to make good on his promises."

A sharply inhaled breath. "I'll have you—"

"Only if you kiss me first." Terri released the line button, which ended the call, and pressed another for the main switchboard. "Unless she wants to confess to a murder, route all future calls from Patricia Brown to the public-relations officer."

"Yes, Detective."

"Vincent."

Terri hung up the phone and looked up to see Homicide Captain George Pellerin standing over her desk. Her boss's broad, ugly-interesting face wasn't red, which generally meant he *didn't* want to chew her out for something. "Sir?"

"Pack it up." He handed her a white envelope. "Your transfer came through."

She resisted the urge to cheer as she looked over the new assignment orders. She'd be working on temporary assignment in the Organized Crime Unit; the first choice she'd listed on the app. "Thanks, Captain."

"Don't look so goddamn happy about it," he grumbled. "You're back here as soon as Gamble is through sunning himself and that new wife of his in Jamaica."

Which would be in three weeks. Plenty of time for Cort to work with another cop on his bar fire. He'd be happy and she wouldn't have to cramp her face with any more fake smiles. "Yes, sir."

"Hazenel is taking over your open cases, so bring him up to speed before you go." Pellerin eyed the other detective across the squad room before giving her a sharp look. "You took the Maskers call last night."

"It came in pretty late; I thought I'd spare Jerry the run." She nodded toward the report in her typewriter. "I'm just wrapping up the next-of-kin reports."

"Copy me on those. And Vincent."

"Sir?"

"Don't get comfortable." He tapped the edge of her desk. "I want you back here in three weeks."

Coming from Pellerin, that was definitely a compliment. "Yes, sir."

Lawson Hazenel wasn't happy to see Terri or the pile of

folders she dropped on his desk an hour later. His plain, blunt face turned distinctly sour as he eyed them, then her. "Thanks a lot, Vincent. As if I don't already have enough to shuffle."

"Whine to the Captain, Haze." She took the top file and tossed it in front of him. "This one is still pending; bar fire down in the Quarter last night. Fifteen dead, maybe more. Check in with Gray Huitt, he'll have the latest on the body count."

"Now *I* want a transfer." He flipped open the folder and scanned the top page. "FD confirm it as arson yet?"

"No, but she went up awfully fast. Like the place was built out of cardboard." She removed the pages from her notepad with the victims' IDs and handed them over. "I've done the prelim reports and a victim-support unit is handling the home calls. Marshal Gamble should issue a statement by the end of day."

"*Marshal* Gamble." Law added the notes to the file. "Correct me if I'm wrong, but the last time you referred to him, wasn't it 'that stone-faced prick who busted me down to the typing pool'?"

"He improves on closer acquaintance," she lied.

"That's not what I hear tell from your cousin." He cocked his head. "Caine said Gamble nearly broke his jaw when he mixed it up with him during Mardi Gras."

Cort had gotten into a brawl with her cousin, Caine Gantry, back when they were investigating Caine for the murder of gubernatorial candidate Marc LeClare. Terri still wasn't sure what they'd fought over.

"My cousin was being a world-class idiot that night," she said. "*I* nearly took a shot at him."

The other cop looked skeptical. "If you're suddenly so tight with the marshal, then why are you sashaying over to OCU?"

"I just wanted a change. J. D.'ll be back next month, so will I." She liked Lawson Hazenel, but she wasn't about to have a heart-to-heart with him. "Let's go over the rest of these so I can get out of here."

After briefing Law on the remaining open cases, Terri

packed up what she needed from her desk and carried the box
to the elevator. Because it worked closely with several different federal agencies, the Organized Crime Unit had recently
moved its offices to the courthouse building down the block.
Terri drove over, reported in at reception, and was escorted to
her new desk in OCU's version of the Homicide squad room.

Discreet cubicles formed a labyrinth of tidy desks, busy
computers and plainclothes detectives. She nodded to the
few she knew as she stowed her personals. The computer on
her desk was off, but the sight of it made her smother a
groan. She was the least computer-literate person in the
NOPD, one reason she'd still been using a typewriter over
in Homicide.

"I hope you come with a manual," she told it.

"They all do." A tall, dark man appeared in the gap between her cubicle walls. He was either a deeply tanned
Caucasian or a light-skinned African-American. It was impossible to tell from the smooth-shaven head and intense
unreadable black eyes. "You would be Therese Vincent."

"Terri. Hi." She held out her hand.

"Sebastien Ruel. Welcome to OCU." After a brief handshake, he gestured toward the big corner office. "Let's talk."

Terri followed her new boss to the office, where his name
along with CHIEF INVESTIGATOR was spelled out on a discreet
Formica sign beside the door. She'd heard of him, of course.
An FBI special agent turning cop always spread a lot of ru-
mors. Word was he'd left the agency under a cloud, but Terri
doubted it. Internal Affairs had been on an anti-corruption
bent for the last decade, and dirty cops weren't welcome in
the NOPD. The police commissioner would never have
hired anyone with a tarnished rep to take over as director of
OCU, either.

Ruel invited her to sit down and offered her coffee, which
she refused, before he took a seat behind his desk. On it was
a single file, which he opened. "You've been assigned to
Homicide for the last seven years."

He had a smooth, even voice without the slightest trace
of an accent. It matched his expression, Terri thought.

Maybe it was something they taught up at Quantico. *Feature Control 101.* "Yes, sir."

"*Chief* will do." He flipped a few pages. "You have exemplary performance reports, several citations for casework and community service, and top ranking out on the range."

She felt a little embarrassed by the praise. "I like competing. I like shooting things, too."

"Word is that you're the best marksman on the force. It says here that you turned down a couple of offers to join SWAT." He glanced up. "I'd have thought that an ideal assignment for someone with your weaponry skills."

Her father had wanted her to apply for a SWAT assignment after graduation, back when they had still been speaking to each other. "I'm a marksman, Chief. Not a sniper."

He closed the file. "You requested OCU on your transfer application. Any particular reason?"

"I'm interested in learning," she said. "Your department has an excellent case-solution rate, and I'm sure anything I learn here will help me when I go back to Homicide."

"Over the last several months you've been making a number of inquiries into the Belafini family." Ruel smiled at her startled reaction. "We've been investigating them for two years, Detective. Any interest shown in that direction is always brought to my attention. Would the Belafinis have anything to do with your transfer request?"

"I was hoping to check out a theory I've been working on." She hoped her face wasn't as red as it felt. "Related to an ongoing arson investigation. It's nothing, really."

"Please." He made a casual gesture. "I'd like to hear about this."

"You're familiar with the Torcher arson case?" After he nodded, she said, "I think this guy may be involved with the mob. At least four of the seven fires attributed to him happened to single owners with long-established, successful businesses in prime locations. Three of the four owners in question sold their properties at a loss immediately after the fires. The fourth died in a suspicious car accident and his heirs immediately sold out. The four properties weren't bought outright by the Belafinis, but I'm betting the new owners are either working for the family or willing to pay protection."

"That's quite a theory." He didn't look doubtful or impressed. "Evidence?"

"I don't really have any. Yet," she tacked on. "I'd hoped to look over your case files on the Belafinis and see if there was anything that could help me identify who the Torcher is."

"So you've been chasing a firebug instead of murderers."

"What I did on this case, I did on my own time," she said, trying not to sound defensive. "If the bar fire last night was his, the Torcher just picked up fifteen counts of murder or manslaughter."

Ruel was silent, long enough to make her wonder if she should have bothered getting her box out of the car. Then he smiled. "Well, Terri, I think you'll fit right in here. Your first assignment happens to be directly related to the Belafinis and mob activity."

"There is something else you should know." She might as well get the rest of it over with. "About my father, and why he left the force."

"I've already reviewed your father's case file." His flat black eyes studied her. "If I thought it was a concern, you wouldn't have gotten past the receptionist."

He was the first cop in eight years besides J. D. who hadn't evaded the subject. "I appreciate your confidence in me, Chief."

"You've earned it." He removed a folder from his desk drawer and handed it to her. "This is everything we have on the suspect you'll be investigating. He's well known, long-established in the local community, and has excellent connections all over the city. We believe he's been on the Belafinis' payroll for several years, and it's likely that he is involved in the Torcher arson cases as well."

Terri opened the folder. The photo and stats inside made her frown. "I'm sorry, sir, I think you gave me the wrong file. This information is on Cort Gamble."

His dark eyebrows elevated a notch. "Marshal Gamble *is* our suspect, Detective."

*   *   *

Sebastien Ruel liked Terri Vincent.

He watched her read over the information in Gamble's file. He'd had some hesitancy toward her at first, until he'd investigated her. Outside of a minor infraction over the Le-Clare case, her record was pristine. He'd attended the last department range competition and had been impressed by the focus and precision she had displayed.

Terri was also well liked and respected throughout the NOPD, even by most of the good old boys who still considered female officers suitable only for traffic- and parking-violation duty. That, in itself, was a sizeable accomplishment. Women in the department were still fighting upstream against decades of gender bias.

Ruel studied her face. She wasn't pretty, and did nothing to make herself more attractive, which had probably helped.

Meeting Terri Vincent reinforced everything he had learned about her. She possessed all the qualities of a good cop: She was friendly and established rapport quickly; she was an attentive listener, yet refreshingly upfront and honest, inviting reciprocal candor. She also had enough professional savvy to know how and when to put on a cop's face and watch her mouth.

Ruel liked her far more than he had expected to, but he had absolutely no qualms about using her to get to the fire marshal. He would have used his own mother if it meant he could bust Cortland Gamble, and through him, the man who had murdered his partner.

He also hadn't lied to her, but he had abbreviated the truth somewhat. Ruel's investigation of the Belafini family had started ten years earlier, a year after a disastrous assignment he'd taken as an FBI special agent out of the Baton Rouge field office.

Back then Tom Matterly had been his partner, and a royal pain in his ass. The old man had been five years short of retirement and he triple-checked everything Ruel did.

"You can screw up your pension, boy," Tom had told him. "You're not screwing up mine."

At the time they had been investigating a racketeering

ring working out of Baton Rouge that had been burning out anyone who wouldn't pay protection money. Tom had been positive that a minor mob thug named Faducci was running the ring, so they set up a sting operation, using a business front as bait.

Faducci had fallen for it, or so Ruel had thought. Tom had called him at two a.m., sounding nervous and excited.

"They want me over at the warehouse in thirty minutes," his partner had told him. "Bring backup."

Ruel had brought two other agents with him to the meet. When they arrived, they found Tom tied up inside. The old man had been stabbed in the abdomen and left to bleed out.

"Run," was the last word Tom uttered before he died.

Ruel shouted to the other agents and ran for the nearest door. There was a tremendous explosion, and his memory ended there. A week later he woke up in a burn unit with second- and third-degree burns that nearly cost him his legs.

His supervisor had been the one to tell him that the other two agents had died in the warehouse, which had burned to the ground. The next day Faducci and most of his operation had vanished.

Ruel had recovered, slowly. It had taken another eight months before he could pass the physicals to return to duty. Bureau policy prohibited Ruel from working on the Faducci case, and the agents assigned to it had never found any productive leads.

The agents assigned to the case didn't know that Tom's widow had come to see Ruel in the hospital. That she had begged Ruel to make sure the men responsible for murdering Tom would get the death penalty. One of the agents had come to the hospital the day after her visit, to tell him that Marianne Matterly had killed herself.

It had taken years of painstaking work to untangle the web of corruption and lies and false identities, but finally Ruel had tracked down Tom's killer. Faducci now resided in New Orleans and was using his real name.

Frank Belafini.

He already had enough evidence to put Belafini behind

bars for ten to twenty years, but it was nowhere near enough to get the murder conviction and a death sentence. Belafini's network of corruption in New Orleans had to be shut down as well, or the mob boss would simply run his operation out of a prison cell.

According to Ruel's informant, he'd have no problem doing that, seeing as Cort Gamble was in Frank Belafini's back pocket. It made sense, too—who better to falsify reports and cover for the mob than the man in charge of all of the city's arson investigations?

After learning that Gamble was Belafini's man inside the fire department, Ruel had abruptly shifted his strategy. With enough evidence, he could take down the marshal. The man had a lot to lose, and would likely beg to cut a deal. All Ruel needed was Belafini on tape, admitting to Matterly's murder. He intended Gamble to be the one to get him that confession.

As soon as Terri Vincent nailed Gamble for him.

"You'll be reporting directly to me," Ruel told Terri when she was finished reading. "Your cover assignment is as acting OCU liaison to the fire department on the Maskers fire. I want you with Gamble's arson task force, every step of the way."

Terri closed the file. "Murder investigations are run out of Homicide."

"As far as the FD is concerned, we're looking into this one as a possible protection-racket hit." Which it was. "If anyone questions your involvement, that's your cover. If they push you on it, you refer them to me."

"Chief, I've known Marshal Gamble for ten years. His brother is my partner." She paused as if searching for the right words. "With all due respect, there's just no way he's working for the mob."

Ruel admired her sense of loyalty, too. Some might think that because of it Terri would try to protect Gamble, but he was counting on her relationship with her father. Given the right amount of motivation, Terri Vincent would want to prove the marshal was innocent. Given her history, he also knew that she would also not hesitate to bust Gamble when she discovered otherwise.

It was time to give her the first push. "We've already gathered a substantial amount of evidence against the marshal." He pulled up the financial files on his computer and turned the monitor around for her to view. "Three days ago, an anonymous deposit was made to Gamble's bank account, in the amount of fifty thousand dollars. We also have a statement from a reliable source who witnessed Gamble and Frank Belafini meeting in a back room at the Italian-American Club downtown."

"Did the witness overhear what they said at this meeting?" When he shook his head, she looked slightly relieved. "One meeting and an anonymous deposit don't prove that he's working for Belafini."

"I know. That's your job now. I want hard evidence linking Gamble to Belafini. You should have ample opportunity to get it now, while he's investigating this bar fire." He noticed how pale she turned. He'd expected her to get angry and protest the allegations. "This a problem for you, Terri?"

"Did you bring me over here because Cort Gamble's brother is my partner?"

She was a bit more intuitive than he preferred, but he could use that as well.

"It was a consideration, yes." Simply not the main one. Idly Bastien wondered how she would react if he showed her the time-stamped photos he'd taken of Gamble walking in and out of her duplex back in February. "You know the fire marshal's family and his friends. You've worked with him in the past on the LeClare case. All of that gives you an in that I don't have. Gamble would never expect you to be investigating him."

"No, he wouldn't." She met his gaze. "This assignment puts me in an impossible position, Chief. The conflict of interest with work and my personal involvement with the suspect . . ." She paused and cleared her throat. "I'm going to have to pass on this one."

She needed another push, it seemed; this time from the

opposite direction. "We could be wrong about Gamble. Perhaps someone is setting him up."

"Someone is." She looked sick now.

"I can't take your word for that. I need evidence." He leaned forward. "You do this, Terri, and you could clear his name."

The new hope in her eyes was all the answer he needed.

3

Cort arrived on time at the mayor's office, which was a madhouse of aides, advisors, and PR reps. He found out why when he was told that a press conference was scheduled to begin within ten minutes.

"You'll issue a statement about the investigation and answer whatever questions they have," Mayor Jarden said as he buttoned up the dark jacket cut to flatter his narrow shoulders and pear-shaped proportions. "You can expect plenty of them. Miriam, I think I need a dusting."

The mayor's assistant, a rail-thin black woman who had once been Miss Baton Rouge, hurried up and tied a short plastic cape around his shoulders before whisking baby powder over Jarden's face with a blush brush.

Louis Gamble had always said that anyone could be elected mayor of New Orleans. Cort was beginning to believe it.

"I don't have anything for them, sir. The incident happened only eight hours ago." He wondered what the mayor's reaction would be if he told him that on average, it took his men six to eight months to solve an arson case.

"Be sure you blot me, or I'll look like I've been snorting coke." Jarden kept his eyes closed as Miriam plied the brush over his wide, low forehead before dabbing a tissue at his upper lip. "My aides tell me this is another Torcher fire."

The mayor's aides were spending too much time watching the local news. "I can't confirm that yet, and neither should you."

"There," Miriam said, stepping back. "Now don't sweat."

"Turn the thermostat down, then. Gamble, I'm not confirming a goddamn thing." Jarden tugged off the cape and walked over to a wall mirror. After a leisurely inspection, he made a minor adjustment to one wave of his hair and the tilt of the American-flag pin on his lapel. "This is all yours."

Cort watched as the mayor's assistant applied a lint brush to Jarden's sloping shoulders. "I can't issue any kind of a statement to the media until we finish processing the scene. Even then, we may not have sufficient proof that it was arson."

"Then I suggest you do your best imitation of a White House press secretary." Jarden gave his assistant a troubled look. "Should I change this tie, Miriam?"

"No, sir." She tightened the silk knot beneath his sagging chin. "Blue projects confidence and authority."

Confidence the mayor had, Cort thought. Authority, too, and probably more than was wise. It was brains that he needed. Intelligence had never been a prerequisite to holding political office in the state of Louisiana.

"Excuse me for a moment." Cort stepped out of the office to call his investigator at the scene. "Gil, I have to talk to the media. Right now. What have you got?"

"We've recovered some thin rubber fragments, fuse cord, and traces of ammonium nitrate granules from a wall niche under a collapsed roof-support beam," Gil told him. "Haven't figured out how he delivered the kerosene, though. The scene is saturated with the stuff."

"Any witnesses?"

"Delivery guy drove past fifteen minutes before the explosion. Says he saw a man carry in a bunch of balloons and some gift boxes. I need to set up my screens."

Now that the fire was out, Gil would sift through the layers of the burned-out building to recover evidence, a painstaking process that took days. However, the presence of the fertilizer granules virtually ruled out the possibility of the Torcher being the setter. In all his previous fires, the arsonist had used a very specific, handmade gasoline-and-gunpowder device. "Keep me in the loop."

Three of the mayor's advisors escorted them to a city hall conference room, where every seat was filled and dozens of reporters stood in the aisles. The cameras began flashing as soon as the men entered the room.

After being introduced, Mayor Jarden stepped up to the row of microphones clipped to the podium. "Good morning, ladies and gentlemen. As you're aware, a deadly fire broke out last night at Maskers Tavern in the French Quarter. At this time, we have fifteen confirmed dead."

The reporters all began shouting questions, and the mayor held up both hands for quiet. When he had it, he added, "I am here to personally assure the people of New Orleans that justice will be swift and immediate. I have mobilized a fifty-two-member interagency response team to investigate this incident and apprehend those responsible for this cowardly and monstrous crime. The team will be headed up by New Orleans Fire Marshal Cort Gamble. As Marshal Gamble is the expert here, I'll turn this over to him now." The mayor stepped to one side.

Voices exploded from the floor as Cort reached the podium, forcing him to talk over them. "Ladies and gentlemen, this investigation has just begun, and it would be irresponsible of me to speculate at this time. As soon as my department has had the opportunity to process the scene, I'll be in a better position to brief you on the facts."

"Was it the Torcher, Marshal?" one particularly loud reporter called out.

"I can't confirm or deny that at present," he replied.

Another, female reporter shot to her feet. "Was the fire set deliberately?"

"We have recovered evidence that indicates this may have been arson, yes." More shouted questions, over which he said, "Until the evidence is properly catalogued and processed, I cannot classify this incident as a case of arson."

Cort fielded a dozen more questions before the mayor stepped in and called the press conference to a close. "Marshal Gamble and his response team are committed to bringing a swift resolution to this case, and they will have full support from my office. Thank you, ladies and gentlemen."

The mayor's aides cleared a path for the two men to leave the conference room. As soon as they were out of camera range, the mayor's genial expression disappeared. "You've been working on this Torcher case for how long?"

"Five months."

The mayor grunted. "You haven't pulled in any solid leads yet, have you? What am I paying you for, Gamble?"

Cort reined in his temper. "We have hundreds of leads that we're still following up, Mayor. But no, nothing solid has come to the surface yet."

"Give us a minute," the mayor said to his aides, and led Cort into his office. When he shut the door, he asked, "Everyone on your payroll aboveboard?"

"Yes, sir."

"That fire captain out in California, John Orr, is serving four life terms for the fires he set. He was"—he made a vague gesture—"what do they call it?"

"Orr was a serial arsonist." Like the Torcher, only slightly more twisted. It was believed that Orr had set fires so he could successfully investigate them. He'd even written a novel based on his own crimes, making himself both the hero and the villain.

The mayor gave him a sharp look. "This Orr was also an arson investigator."

It seemed that the mayor had been watching a little too much television as well. "Every man on my payroll has been checked and rechecked. We run annual backgrounds, psychs, and financials. They're all good men, career investigators with a minimum of ten years of consistent, outstanding service to the department."

The older man grunted. "You'd better be right, Marshal. I want progress on this case, real progress, and quick, or the first announcement at my next press conference will be about accepting your formal resignation."

*   *   *

"You can't buy those shoes. They're all wrong for those lovely feet."

"My feet know they are." Elizabet Gamble sighed as she put the chestnut suede cutout pump back on the display cube. "My heart, however, still insists that my arches have not collapsed *that* much." She glanced sideways at the elegant, silver-haired man in the pale cream suit beside her. "What do you think, Andre?"

"You can never go wrong with the Italians." Alexandre Moreau swept a hand toward a display of imported footwear. "Softer leather, a more attractively defined toe, and vastly superior construction." He lowered his voice to a confidential murmur. "That and no cutouts, so you can wear your Dr. Scholl's gellies without anyone ever suspecting a thing."

Elizabet laughed. "I do believe you've prevented yet another fashion disaster."

"Darling, I live for nothing else. Come now." He held out a gallant arm. "Let's have tea and trade war stories."

The old gentleman escorted her to a tearoom three doors down from the shoe boutique, where they were ushered to one of the best tables. Elizabet Gamble was a well-known society figure, but Alexandre Moreau was a New Orleans institution. The tearoom's proprietor knew having the two of them in clear view of the front windows was better advertising than taking out a full page in the *Tribune*.

Once they had been served a fresh pot of oolong tea and a platter of tiny, hot butter-pecan scones, Elizabet sat back and relaxed. "I don't know why I'm looking at shoes. I believe I own more pairs than that particular shop keeps in stock."

"Shoes are like good manicures. One can never have too many." Andre added a dollop of cream to his cup before testing it. "Scalding but not over-brewed. Quite nearly perfect, in fact. I shall have to collect a business card on my way out."

Elizabet knew that Andre hosted a number of functions and was always on the lookout for new caterers. "Are you busy this summer?"

"Eternally. The Edwinsons finally found someone willing to marry that odious son of theirs; the McElroys are entertaining minor British royalty at the lake, and the Ladeaux twins turn seventeen next month." He rolled his eyes. "To think, I agreed to manage this party when I barely survived their sixteenth."

Andre was always busy. Although he came from one of the oldest Creole families in New Orleans, his parents had made a number of unfortunate investments before they died. The last stock-market disaster had decimated the family's assets, and Andre had been forced to liquidate the entire estate to satisfy creditors.

Undaunted by the reversal in fortune, Andre relinquished his life of leisure, turned to Creole society, and went into the business of refining the youngest members of it. As a personal family consultant, he groomed young men and women in proper manners, dress, and attitude. He planned their social calendars, coordinated many of their families' events, and often presided over these events. He also provided parents with advice on suitable matches; more than one society family owed an excellent marriage to Andre's discreet guidance.

Andre was one of the few men who truly understood the demands as well as the pleasures of society, and the need to preserve it. Elizabet considered him one of her dearest friends.

"I thought I would miss the curls, but I much prefer this sleek look." He nodded to her new, shorter haircut. "You're looking quite splendid."

"Stop lying; I look tired." She made a wry face. "I couldn't sleep last night. Cortland had a late call and never called or came home."

"The bar fire over in the Quarter I saw on the news this morning?" When she nodded, he reached over and patted her hand. "You know he's fine, Eliza."

"I know, he's a grown man, it's his job, and I shouldn't worry. Louie already lectured me once." She rubbed her temple. "It's just that . . . Cort has been so distant lately. He works all these outrageous hours and has completely abandoned any sort of social life. He hasn't attended a single function since his brother's wedding last month."

Andre produced a theatrical, horrified look. "Obviously the boy is in desperate need of comprehensive therapy."

She chuckled. "Oh, you know what I mean."

"Have you spoken to him about it?"

"I've tried, but I haven't pushed." She had learned her lesson on that score with her youngest son, J. D. "The distance is what bothers me most. He hardly speaks to his father and me—or anyone—these days. When he does, he's monosyllabic."

"I don't recall Cortland as being the most verbose of your sons," Andre said.

"He's always been my quiet one, but not like this. Something is definitely wrong." She frowned. "I've never had to worry about him before, Andre, and now I find that's all I do."

"Could he be lonely? Is he perhaps between *amours?*"

She gave him an ironic look. "I'm afraid that Cort has never had a problem in that department."

"No, I imagine not. Half the female population of Louisiana would leap at him, if he stood still long enough." Andre warmed her tea and refilled his own cup. "I wish Magda and I had had children, so I could give you some well-intentioned paternal advice." His expression turned faintly sad, as it always did when he referred to his beloved wife, who had died after a long battle with breast cancer. "Alas, I must keep to what I know. I suggest you throw a party."

"What sort of party?"

"Nothing too formal. A summer fete would be perfect." He added a sugar cube to her cup. "Invite all the eligible young women in the neighborhood—I can give you a list, if you like—and surround him with the nubile young lovelies. One will catch his eye and then all your worries will be put to rest."

"That's rather more obvious than I want to be, Andre." She also didn't want to make the mistake of trying to meddle too deeply in her son's life. She had done that with J. D., and had nearly driven away her youngest son.

"The mayor's wife is obvious, my dear." He made an airy gesture. "You are rescuing Cortland from a case of overwork or depression or whatever it is that he's suffering." He gave her a shrewd look. "That is better than lecturing him when he comes home tonight, don't you think?"

She pursed her lips. "It would have to be small. Soon, too, before he finds an apartment and moves out. Once he has his own place he'll simply make excuses not to attend."

"Then we shall get to work immediately. A guest list of fifty should do. You can have it at the house; your gardens are so lovely this time of year. My services are at your disposal." He took out a wallet-sized planner and consulted it. "In say, three weeks, after the ACS dinner?"

"J. D. will be back from his honeymoon by then. I can make that the official cause for celebration, and even if Cort does move out by then, he will want to be there." She beamed at him. "You're a genius, Andre."

"Of course I am," he said, his smile complacent. "I am French."

Grayson Huitt positioned the head of Jane Doe Number Four above the film plate. His hands were as gentle as if she still breathed. "Here we go, sweetheart." He walked over to stand behind the shield and flicked the switch to take the X-ray.

"Do you always talk to them?" his assistant Lawrence asked, giving Jane's charred features an uneasy look.

"Absolutely." Gray smiled. "It's when they answer that you have to start worrying."

The shorter, pudgy man rubbed a thick finger against the sparse mustache he had been trying to grow. "I guess."

"They still have plenty to tell us. Come over here." He went out to the table and picked up the corpse's blackened hand. Only two fingers remained intact. "The blobs on the fingernails have white edges. This lady liked French manicures. Her hair is gone, but you can still see traces of the lipstick and eye makeup she wore."

"So she was big into makeup?"

"She definitely cared about how she looked." Carefully Gray transferred the remains to the waiting gurney. "Maybe a little too much."

Lawrence frowned. "Every girl I know gets her nails done."

"No, look at the condition of the torso under the burns. The sunken abdomen and muscle loss, and the fact that she has no fat layer to speak of. The skin layer here isn't charred as it is on the extremities, so we know the fire didn't do this to her. She might have had an eating disorder." As Gray draped the dead woman's body with a plastic sheet, he heard the outer door sensor beep. "Develop this plate for me, will you?"

Terri Vincent was waiting outside in the main pathology lab. She was studying the rows of shrouded bodies that filled all of Gray's tables and the gurneys lining two walls.

She looked much worse than she had last night. Her face was shock-white and her whole body tense. In the five years they'd been friends, he'd never seen her like this.

"Terri?"

"Gray." She jumped a little, startled out of some deep thought. "Any more victims come in from the bar fire?"

"No, thank the Lord." He heard the strain in her voice and opened the door to his office. "I just made some fresh coffee, come on in."

She refused a cup and wouldn't sit down. "I've been re-assigned to Organized Crime, but I'll be working on the Maskers case." She was pacing, as much as his small office would allow her to. "I'm going over to see what the ATF picked up from the scene, and I thought I'd stop in, see how you're doing."

That wasn't the entire reason that she was there, but Gray could bide his time until she was ready to tell him all. If she did; Terri could be remarkably closemouthed when she wanted. "We've identified all but four of the victims. We're working off dental with Missing Persons now. Shouldn't take too long."

She went to the window and looked out through the blinds at Lawrence, who was wheeling in Jane Doe Four.

"Can I get copies of the autopsy reports as soon as they're done?"

"Of course, always."

She glanced back at him. "Why are you so decent to me?"

It was charming, how Terri had no idea of her own appeal. She probably thought that because she was tall and lean and small-breasted that it made her unfeminine. Her dancer's body and the modesty were a potent combination.

That and the fact that she looked more than a little like Sigourney Weaver didn't hurt.

"It's actually a subtle form of sexual harassment," he said in a mild tone. "You just haven't caught on to that yet."

"I'm that slow, huh?" She didn't laugh, as she normally would.

"I could be more obvious. Starting right now, if you like." He gave the top of his desk a pat. "Come here, sweetheart."

"Oh, man." She turned and banged her head into the glass three times.

"Keep doing that and you'll get a great big lump where everyone can see it." There was a time for kidding around, and Gray decided that this wasn't it. "Hey. Tell me what's wrong."

"I need some very specific help, but I feel like a complete idiot asking you." The hand resting on the windowsill curled into a fist. "I don't like using my friends to fight my battles."

"No one does." She was so tense now that he was becoming concerned. "So what's the battle?"

"It's complicated." She sighed and dragged a hand through her hair. "This is a real favor, a huge one. You're the only guy I can ask."

Read ask as trust. He nodded. "As long as it doesn't involve a felony, I'm good for it. I accept all forms of bribery: coffee, sex, food of any kind, backrubs, sex, foot massages . . . did I mention sex?"

She glared now. "You don't even know what I need you to do."

"You wouldn't ask unless it was important, and I trust

you. If it involves you and I getting naked, I'll even thank you." Her reaction made him set aside his coffee and go to her. "Ter, you know I'm joking." He nudged up her chin. "It can't be that bad."

She looked miserable. "Oh yeah, it can."

"Well . . ." He tried to think of what could be upsetting her this much. "You won't be giving me more work, right?"

"All I can tell you is that a truckload of shit is going to hit a room-sized fan very shortly," she said, "and I'm standing right in front of it."

"Sounds nasty. Cop stuff?"

"Mostly." She looked up at him, her eyes troubled. "Some of it's personal."

"Personal as in . . ." He rolled his hand.

"Cort Gamble."

He thought back over the scene at Maskers. Cort Gamble had treated Terri as if she'd been the one to set it. An internal lightbulb finally lit up. Gray had known that he'd never had a chance with Terri, sensing early on that she was already taken. He'd just never figured on Gamble being the one in possession.

He had to be sure, though. Sometimes women said one thing and meant another. "You and the fire marshal were lovers?"

"No. We sort of had a one-nighter a few months ago." Her voice strained on the words, and she wouldn't look at him now. "I don't want a repeat, but he and I . . ." She shook her head.

A spike of jealousy nailed itself through Gray's heart, and for a moment he considered throwing all his efforts into stealing her away from Gamble. Terri Vincent had interested him for a long time, and all subtlety aside, Gray liked getting what he wanted.

But Terri seemed truly unhappy, and Gray suspected Gamble had it just as bad, judging by the way he had acted at the fire scene. Gray wanted Terri, and he was as driven and competitive as the next man, but wrecking two people's lives was not his idea of fun.

He could be a pal, though, and watch her back. "I'm in."

He took her hand in his. He liked that she had long, strong hands. "What do you want me to do? Make ugly, manly threats? Arm wrestle him? Beat him senseless?" He might do the latter anyway, for his own gratification.

She laced her fingers through his. "I need a lover."

4

Terri left the morgue and walked to the fire marshal's office. She felt like a jackass for dragging Gray Huitt into the middle of her personal life, but she needed him if she was going to pull this off. She had to put something between her and the marshal, and Gray was big, solid, and safe. And cute. If she had to parade around a pretend boyfriend, he might as well be a good-looking one.

The fact that Gray already pretended to lust after her would help, too.

Terri had never trusted herself around Cort, and if she wanted to clear his name, she couldn't afford any distractions now. Ruel wasn't telling her everything, she sensed that much. He'd been far too casual about the case, and far too pushy about having her investigate it.

Cort, on the other hand, had to think that she wasn't available. Just in case he had any lingering fond memories of February. Her drooling over him from afar was getting old, too. Having Gray as a buffer would help her recover some of her dignity and self-respect.

Okay, and some pride, too. Cort didn't have to know how much his rejection had hurt her. As it was, she'd probably be carrying around the wounds until she hit menopause.

Terri stopped at a corner and bought a cup of iced coffee from her favorite street vendor.

"You want sugar today?" the heavyset black woman asked as she filled the cup.

"No. Got any Valium, Irene?"

"Sorry, baby." She grinned, showing gold-wrapped teeth. "Only chemicals I push are Equal and Sweet'n Low."

"Don't believe her, Detective," a doorman waiting in line said. "That lemonade she sells didn't turn pink because it was shy."

Irene scowled. "I don't know why the good Lord created man."

"Because She knew a vibrator couldn't mow the lawn," Terri suggested.

While everyone in line laughed, Irene handed Terri her drink and made change. "You gone over to the mob busters, I hear."

Terri never understood exactly how the downtown vendors got their information. The speed and efficiency of their personal grape vine made an AMBER Alert look sluggish. "Yeah, I'm there for a couple of weeks."

Irene moved her gaze from side to side before she leaned over the cart. "Watch out for that Ruel fella," she muttered. "He got those witchy eyes, see everything."

Terri sipped her coffee and waited until the line disappeared before she asked, "You know the fire marshal, Cort Gamble?"

"I seen him on the news. Got a nice ass, don't he?" Her laugh was belly-deep.

"That he does." Terri tried not to remember how many times she had grabbed it, that night back in February. "Hear anything about him lately?"

Irene considered that for a moment. "Couple of firemen talked about him getting them better equipment. His assistant, girl named Sally, she's been getting a lot of overtime. Don't mind it, though." She cocked her head. "You need me to ask around?"

"Don't be obvious, but yeah, whatever you can find out." Terri took out her wallet.

Irene became indignant. "Shit, girl, put that away. You been buying coffee from me practically every day for going on eight years; I can do a little digging."

Terri grinned. "Then you got my business for life, *cher.*"

A number of news vans were still parked outside the NOFD administration building, so Terri went around to a side delivery entrance. She was stopped and checked for identification three times before she was directed to a briefing room. The interagency meeting was in progress, so she slipped in and took a chair in the back beside Lawson Hazenel.

"I thought you were off to chase wiseguys," Law said as he handed her a copy of the prelim report.

"Me, too." Terri spotted Cort sitting at a table at the front of the room. He appeared to be in deep conversation with one of the fire captains. Her throat went tight. "You like iced coffee, no sugar?"

"Free caffeine?" Law perked up. "Hell, yeah."

"Enjoy." She shoved the cup into his hands.

The ATF's chief investigator was giving a rundown of what they had found at the scene. "Firefighters found the sprinkler system disabled, and the exit doors at the north, south, and east ends of the tavern chained and locked. Fire blocked the victims from getting to the west windows and main entrance, which were the only exits left. Not that they had a lot of time. Flashover was probably within the first sixty seconds. I've got a couple layouts to show you." Gil left the podium to man an overhead projector.

"What's flashover?" a man Terri recognized as a local fed asked.

"It's the last stage in a fire's development," Cort said. "Flashover occurs when all the combustible material within the affected area begins to burn." His gaze shifted, and then narrowed.

Terri sank down a little in her seat.

"The lighting failed almost immediately, and there were no emergency lights, so darkness contributed to the confusion," Gil said as he put up a transparency showing Maskers' floor plan. "We don't know yet how the fire burned as fast and as hot as it did. We can speculate that the tavern's open layout allowed smoke and heat to spread very quickly and was, in part, the cause of the bottleneck by the east exit door, but it had help. A lot of help."

Cort was still watching her, Terri realized, and cursed Ruel for the hundredth time. It wasn't going to be difficult to keep Cort from becoming suspicious. It was going to be downright impossible.

Law raised his coffee cup to catch the investigator's attention. When he had it, he asked, "Were all the victims found by the exit?"

"No." Gil took a moment to consult his notes. "They found three bodies in the bar area and two in the manager's office. From the damage to the last two bodies, both of which were partially dismembered, my guess is that they were in close proximity to the point source of one explosion. They may have actually triggered a device or just had the bad luck to be standing next to it."

Terri felt her stomach clench as the investigator described what the victims had endured. "The two in the manager's office died immediately. The eight in the bar were likely incinerated instantly during flashover; they suffered severe body and lung burns. The last five made it to the exit door but died shortly after. None of the bodies showed signs of being trampled, so they likely cooperated. Two were found holding hands."

She looked at Cort, whose face was completely impassive. She'd taken on some horrific cases in Homicide, but murder was hardly ever random. Most were single-victim crimes. Fire was like the wrath of God, sweeping down to consume everyone and everything in its path. *How do you stand this?*

"Who does this kind of demented shit to innocent people?" Law demanded.

"Basically, Detective, we deal with four kinds of motives," Gil told him. "They are vandalism, criminal intent, malicious intent, and psychological disorder. Kids and youth offenders are responsible for most of the vandalism fires. Criminal intent is arson committed for the purpose of financial gain or to cover another crime. Fires set for revenge purposes, like the churches and synagogues we've seen burned in hate crimes, are done with malicious intent. It's the psychological ones that are the most dangerous. They're set by people who are usually obsessed in some way with fire, and who get off on setting it and watching it burn."

"So which kind is this one?" the fed asked.

Gil glanced at Cort. "I'll let Marshal Gamble make the call on that."

Cort came up to the podium. "Thanks, Gil. Ladies and gentlemen, I know most of you already had heavy caseloads before you were dragged over here, so I'll apologize now for the mayor. As you know, he won't." He waited for the subsequent chuckles to die down. "We'll be doing this in four teams: evidence, witnesses, victims, perps. I'll tell you right now that most arson cases aren't solved overnight, so if you've got vacation time coming up, you'll want to reschedule it."

Several groans echoed around the room.

"This bar fire is a serious arson for several reasons," Cort continued. "We have multiple focus points, and audible detonations, not just window blowouts. Sophisticated explosives and high-temperature accelerant, or HTA, were likely used."

"Was it this Torcher nut?" a man in the front row asked.

"We don't know yet. The fire was timed, well organized, and set to burn fast, which fits the Torcher's profile. On the other hand, it was very, very hot and a lot of people died, which doesn't. The incineration devices were also constructed differently this time in comparison to the Torcher's past work. They were possibly delivered to the bar in gift-wrapped boxes by the perp himself a few minutes before the blaze began, and making a personal appearance is also not part of the Torcher's m.o. Exit doors may have been deliberately locked and the sprinkler system tampered with just prior to detonation."

"This wasn't just to burn the tavern, then," Law said. "It sounds like he wanted to dust everyone inside."

"In fires like this one, Detective, a victim generally has less than thirty seconds to get out." Cort's voice went low and flinty. "He knew when he planned it that he would be executing these people."

One of the female inspectors from the code enforcer's

office frowned. "You're assuming the arsonist is a man, Marshal?"

"Most arsonists, like serial killers, are male. Only a tiny percentage are women." Cort came around the podium and stood in front of room. "Whether this arsonist is the Torcher or not, he is intelligent, resourceful, and cool under pressure. The events of last night tell us that he has no regard for human life. The intent may have been criminal or malicious, but I'm betting this guy has an underlying psychological disorder."

"The psych jobs are repeaters, right?" Law asked.

"Yes. If the act empowers him, he'll be setting more. If this fire isn't big enough, he may come back again. He'll make each new blaze bigger to inflict more damage and create more of a spectacle. He'll want more attention from the media, and he'll only get that with a higher body count, so he'll go for places with higher occupancies and larger crowds."

"What sort of places?" one of the city inspectors asked.

"Large hotels, shopping malls," Cort said. "Even elementary schools."

"Jesus," someone behind Terri breathed.

"Gil has your team assignments. We'll have morning briefings at eight a.m. every day. If you've got a problem, see me. And one more thing: this isn't about headlines or the mayor running for reelection next year. It's not about who gets the collar. This is about saving lives. What I expect from you is simply your personal best." He looked directly at Terri. "If you can't give that to me, then don't waste my time."

Cort watched Terri throughout the briefing. After the way she'd talked last night, and what he'd learned this morning, she shouldn't have showed up. She couldn't have been given the assignment from Pellerin in Homicide; he'd called there earlier to speak with her and had been told about her sudden transfer to OCU.

The call from Frank Belafini hovered at the back of his mind. The mob boss didn't waste his time with idle threats.

He made promises, and he kept them. Killing Stephen Bela-fini could be the first move by another faction that intended to take over Frank's operation. If that were the case, then Maskers would only be the beginning. OCU would be most likely to know if there was a power struggle brewing, and might have sent Terri over to gather evidence for its own purposes.

Everything was moving just a little too fast for Cort's liking. Someone was pulling strings and it was looking more and more like Terri wasn't the one doing it.

He caught up with her in the corridor outside the briefing room. "I'd like to see you in my office, Detective. Now, if it's convenient."

"Certainly, Marshal." She turned to the pale-haired cop she'd been talking to. "Catch you later, Law."

Cort waited until they were behind closed doors before he spoke to her again. "I didn't expect to see you here." He hadn't wanted to see her for the rest of the summer. Or his life.

"Same goes." She pulled the chair in front of his desk back a foot before sitting down. "I got assigned to the case an hour ago."

He went to his desk and pulled up the agency roster on his computer, for appearance's sake. "You're over at OCU now?"

"Yep."

"As of today."

"Uh-huh." She tucked her hands in her trouser pockets and studied the certificates on his wall. They seemed to fascinate her.

Cort picked up the phone. "I'm calling Ruel."

"Okay." She got up and started for the door.

"Sit down, Detective."

She sighed and trudged back to drop into the chair.

All Cort got was the OCU chief's voice mail, on which he left a terse message before hanging up. "Did you request this assignment?"

"You mean, like to piss you off? No." She leaned back

and rolled her head from side to side, as if her neck felt stiff. "Seriously, I did try to get out of it."

"How hard did you try?"

That made her stop her isometrics. "Marshal, you've got fifty some-odd people working this one. I seriously doubt that we'll be brushing shoulders much."

He didn't want to brush her shoulders. He wanted to pin them to the floor. "Why is OCU involved? Are you sitting on something I don't know about?"

"We're looking into the fire as a protection-racket hit." Her voice remained bland. "I'm sitting on your chair."

"So Ruel assigned you to the case. On your first day in the department."

"OCU looks to be a pretty busy place." She drummed three fingertips against the armrest. "I guess as the rookie, I was the one he could spare."

He could sense the building tension underneath the act. She was hiding something. "Does he know about you and me?"

"You and me?" She gave him a mock-bewildered look. "Why, Marshal Gamble, there is no *you and me*."

No, there wasn't, and still he wanted to snatch her out of the chair and peel off her too-large jacket and rip open her ugly blouse to see if her breasts were still as perfectly shaped as his unreliable memory claimed. "Does Ruel know that you and I were intimately involved?"

"*Intimately involved.* Now that's a polite phrase for what we did." She tilted her head. "Your mama teach you to talk that way, or do you just read a lot of romance novels?"

He studied the long line of her neck and for a split second imagined wrapping his hands around it. "Does. He. Know."

Her lips flattened. "No, Cort. Ruel doesn't know. Your brother doesn't even know. I don't brag about my one-night stands."

He relaxed a little. "All right."

She wasn't finished. "I hate to dent your ego, but it really wasn't that big a deal. You got drunk, we screwed, end of story." She crossed one leg over the other. Her trousers hadn't been pressed, and the knees were wrinkled. "Try to get over it, will you?"

This was what he had to look forward to for the next two months or better. Her mouth, every day. "I need OCU's input on this case. I don't need to be blindsided. I don't need you."

"Request another body when you talk to Ruel." She glanced at her watch. "I've got to go check in with my team leader and get my assignment list."

"I'm not finished." Cort was standing over her, his hands clamped on the edge of the desk, before he could think better of it. "You're good. Really good."

Her chin elevated a notch. "One night in my bed doesn't qualify you as a judge."

"You're not over it."

Instead of going on the defensive, she grinned. "And yet, *I* haven't been running in the opposite direction every time I see *you.*"

She had noticed. That meant she had been paying attention. She was also trying a little too hard to sound nonchalant about it. "I'm not afraid of you."

"But you don't like me. I got that message, loud and clear." She seemed bored now. "It was a mistake, Marshal. We all make 'em. No hard feelings. Accept it, forget it, and move on."

Forget it? He'd dreamed of her so often that he'd developed insomnia, trying to stop. There was two feet of space between them. Twenty-four inches he could eliminate in a heartbeat. His door locked. His desk would work. So would the chair. And the floor.

"Move on." He gripped the edge of the desk until his hands ached. "Have you?"

"Yeah, I have."

Her only mistake was taking seven seconds to think up those three words.

Terri always tried to be so tough. Especially when he was close, like he was now. The matter-of-fact comeback didn't mask the fact that her pupils had dilated, or the new, faint sheen of perspiration springing up on her forehead and temples. Under the right side of her jaw, a tendon strained; the tips of her short-nailed fingers were pressed so hard against the chair arms that they were white. She was fighting to keep still, to keep up the nonchalance she didn't feel. To keep the twenty-four inches of emptiness hanging between them.

The hell she had moved on. She still wanted him. Still smoldered with it.

He was surprised by how acute his senses had become, with her so close. He could smell the coffee she'd drunk and the shampoo she'd used. No perfume—she never wore any—but he liked that. He was tired of women who smelled like florist shops and spice canisters. He could almost taste her mouth. Another twenty inches and he would.

Her lips parted, a silent taunt. Then something came out of them, something that he hadn't expected. "I'm seeing Grayson Huitt now."

"What?"

"Gray and I are together." Her smile was sharp and edgy. "Like I said, I'm over it."

"Excuse me, Marshal," Sally said over the intercom.

Cort straightened and turned to punch the button. "Hold my calls until I'm finished with Detective Vincent."

"I'm sorry, sir, it's Councilwoman Carter. She's just arrived and is waiting out here to speak with you." Sally's polite delivery indicated that the city council member was likely hovering in front of her desk.

"Two minutes, Sally." He switched off the intercom and swiveled around to see Terri going out the door. "Therese."

She stopped.

"We're not finished."

"We're not starting anything." Out she went.

The man who had killed fourteen people and the woman he loved in the Maskers fire didn't bother checking out of his hotel.

God is not mocked. God is not mocked.

He had the presence of mind to collect his belongings and wipe down the room before leaving his room key on the bedside table and walking out. Even if they suspected his abrupt departure, they would never locate him. The credit card and identification he had used were untraceable.

Do not be deceived, God is not mocked.

He bypassed the lobby and took the back entrance to a side street. He strode away from the sounds of the shouts and the hoses and the sirens, his mind refusing to acknowledge them.

He wandered for hours, up and down the streets of New Orleans, not thinking, only walking. When he grew tired, he found a bench and sat until he was rested enough to walk again. At one point he was on one of the street cars passing the Garden District. An hour later he was sitting in a café, being served a chicken-salad sandwich. He tried to eat, but it tasted of ashes.

His world was back in the French Quarter. The world he himself had reduced to ashes and death. He had killed. Murdered. That didn't matter. He had done it for her.

Whatever a man sows.

"You okay, hon?" the waitress asked when she brought his check and saw the untouched plate.

He looked up. She was thirty pounds overweight, she had dyed her hair a ridiculous shade of magenta, and she stank of grease and sweat. He considered shooting her in the chest simply for having the temerity to breathe when his beloved no longer could.

That was not her fault, however. It was his. *Whatever a man sows, that he will also reap.*

"I'm fine." He left her a generous tip.

He always carried a weapon, and the weight of it beneath his left armpit comforted him. He reached into his jacket several times to run his fingertips over the polished metal surfaces. It represented something more important than business or self-defense now: a swift, merciful end.

It was more than he deserved. More than he had given her.

Word of the fire spread like the flames had burned. Everyone around him was jabbering on about it; he could not escape it. He had always believed in God, but never more than he did now. There was no one better at twisted vengeance than the Almighty.

God is not mocked.

He found himself standing in front of a newspaper stand, staring at the front page of an afternoon edition printed specially to cover the disaster at Maskers. There were photos of the ruined building, close-up shots of some shrouded bodies. The plan, as expected, had worked superbly.

That he will also reap.

Another man stopped to put coins in the slot and took out a paper. After a momentary hesitation, the stranger removed a second and handed it to him. "Here ya go, buddy. On the house." He chuckled.

"Thank you." He unfolded the single section and saw two photos on the bottom half that had been hidden in the machine. One was of the mayor, addressing a press conference. The second was of a tall brown-haired man and a petite blonde woman.

The caption read, "Fire Marshal Cortland Gamble and Miss Ashleigh Bouchard at the National Fire Safety Board dinner at Krewe of Louis in January."

He stared at the photo until his eyes burned. Gamble had his arm around the woman, and was smiling down at her. Obviously he had been caught off guard by the photographer; he even looked happy. What man wouldn't, with a beauty like that beside him? What man would want a pain-riddled, dying woman when he could have Miss Ashleigh Bouchard, so young and healthy and full of life?

Gamble was regularly photographed escorting beautiful young women. He always had his pick of them. He had chosen this lovely creature to be the one he would hold and cherish and kiss and fuck back in January. Maybe he had even bullshitted her into believing that he had fallen in love with her.

Or perhaps he truly loved this one. Loved her body and soul, the way a man did when he found the one woman he was meant to be with, the woman who was everything. *Wouldn't that be something?*

It was a dangerous business, love. Far worse than his

former occupation. Love was so delicate and beautiful and fragile. As she had been. One never knew when it would envelop a heart, or when it would be burned alive while you watched.

Cortland Gamble didn't know how that felt. He had never suffered. He had never known true deprivation. He took the love he was offered—and even ignored it—without realizing what a treasure it was, or how quickly or irrevocably it could be ripped away.

There was so much he could teach Gamble about that now, given the benefit of his experience. Perhaps that is why God had done such an obscene thing to him. So that he would know, to the bottom of his soul, what pain a man could feel. He could see now that his grand plan had been only a pitiful farce. It was certainly nothing compared to what he knew now.

God hadn't simply instructed him, he had opened his eyes. He understood what real love was now. The marshal did not. A sense of peace settled over him as he saw his new path.

He had been chosen by God to teach Cortland Gamble.

He who sows sparingly will also reap sparingly, and he who sows bountifully will also reap bountifully. So let each one give as he purposes in his heart, not grudgingly or of necessity; for God loves a cheerful giver.

"You okay, buddy?" the man who had handed him the free newspaper asked.

"Yes." The Torcher smiled. "You have inspired me, my friend."

5

Elizabet decided not to press the issue of the summer fete when Cort came home that evening.

He didn't enter the drawing room but stood in the doorway, looking in. "Mother, I'm sorry that I caused you concern last night. It won't happen again."

"Of course it will." She set aside the letter that she was reading and regarded her son. "I know that with your job, being on call twenty-four hours a day is a necessity."

He shook his head. "Upsetting you isn't."

"I know you're not a child, Cortland. It may not seem like it at times, but I truly do." She patted the cushion beside her. "Will you come and sit with your old, fussy mother for a moment?"

He came and sat, the dutiful son. "You're not old, and the fussiness was earned."

"By you, or me?"

"Me."

She saw that the lines of strain around his mouth and eyes had deepened; he looked as if he had existed on nothing but coffee for the last twenty-four hours. Which he likely had, as she knew how caught up in his work her son could become.

It was more than exhaustion, however. Cort might think he could conceal everything behind a stern mask, but it never fooled her. A mother knew her child in ways the rest of the world couldn't.

No one knew how hard Cort was on himself except Elizabet, because in that they were exactly alike.

"I was so sorry to hear about that fire in the Quarter last night. So many people." She covered his hand with hers. "Is there anything I can do, other than to skip the usual nagging?"

"No." Cort leaned back and closed his eyes. "I need to get some sleep."

"Then perhaps you should avoid walking the floors until four a.m." She smiled when he peered at her. "That isn't nagging. That's a maternal observation. There *is* a difference."

"I didn't know I was disturbing you and Dad."

"Your father can—and has—slept through a hurricane. I imagine it's the cognac I'm not supposed to know that he's drinking." She picked up Wendy's letter and showed it to him. "Evan's wife wrote that Jamie took his first steps last week. Your brother, who apparently wants to kill my only grandson, bought him a pony to celebrate."

His mouth quirked. "J. D. and I never got a pony."

"You never stayed on the ground long enough. I think you spent half your childhood up in that tree fort of yours." She looked over at the family portrait hanging over the mantel. It showed a much younger version of the Gambles with their three sons. "J. D., on the other hand, was born running. *I* needed the pony to chase after him."

"I don't think so," Cort said, and put an arm around her shoulders. "All you had to do was give us that look."

She frowned. "What look?"

"That one." He leaned over and kissed her forehead. "I'm going to bed."

Elizabet wanted nothing more than to put her arms around him, press his head to her shoulder, and coax him into telling her what was wrong. But Cortland really wasn't a child any longer, and she wasn't sure how to handle the man he had grown to be. So she settled for a brief, affectionate hug and held in her sigh until he had left the room.

She rose from the settee and walked over to the portrait she had had painted when the boys were young. All three of her sons appeared healthy and happy—J. D., her baby, looked ready to leap out of the frame—but even in those days, Cort's expression had been so serious. "You're going to make me buy Mylanta again, aren't you?"

"You mean, I have not yet?" Louie Gamble said as he walked into the room.

Elizabet tried the look on her husband.

"That only works on the boys," he told her as he came over and tugged her into his arms. The kiss he gave her was passionate and completely inappropriate for two people who had been married for nearly thirty-five years. "Me, you must chase down and jump on."

She had never done such a thing. Well, not outside of their bedroom. "I will not."

He nuzzled her hair. "Then you must say the magic words."

Laughter bubbled out of her. "You're utterly shameless. You do know that."

Louie grinned up at her. "This is why you love me."

They were such an odd couple, Elizabet thought as she rested in her husband's embrace. Louie was six inches shorter than her, had always been twenty or thirty pounds overweight, and had started losing his hair in college. When she had first seen him at her parents' Mardi Gras ball, she had thought him one of the caterers. In fact, he had been arguing with one of the servers about overheating the gumbo.

"This is not soup you make with water and the can," Louie was informing the older man manning the hot table. He shook a silver spoon over a turret of bubbling gumbo. "It was made with filé, so it cannot be boiled on and on for hours. It must be only kept warm."

"Sir, if I turn down the heat it will grow cold," the server protested.

Elizabet walked up to him to tell him to stop bothering the help, but when she politely cleared her throat, Louie turned, grabbed her wrist and hauled her forward.

"Here, this lovely angel will tell you that it is perfect now," Louie said, and brought a spoonful of gumbo to her lips. When she hesitated, he leaned over and whispered against her ear, "Back me up on this, *ma belle fille,* and I will marry you."

Ma belle fille. My beautiful girl.

Elizabet opened her mouth to scold him for being so forward, and Louie promptly fed her the spoonful. Spices sizzled over her tongue and she closed her eyes to enjoy what was the most delicious gumbo she'd ever tasted in her life. When she could speak again, only one word emerged from her lips. "Perfect."

"You see?" Louie beamed, tossed the spoon onto the table, and put his arm around her waist. "You have to dance with me now. We are engaged."

Elizabet started to point out that they certainly were not, as well as that dancing was impossible, due to the ridiculous difference in their heights. She took one look into his intense dark eyes and completely forgot what she was going to say. Three minutes later she was dancing with him, much to the amusement of her friends.

"I am taller than you," she murmured, her cheeks hot.

"Yeah, you are." He pulled her closer and trailed his fingers over her cheek. "Taller and much better looking. People are saying I'm a lucky guy."

Elizabet's skin tingled where he touched it. "People are laughing at us."

"I don't care about them." He pressed his cheek to hers, and his French accent became much more pronounced, the way it had sounded when he was arguing with the server. "Do you know what I care about, *ma belle fille?*"

Did he really think she was beautiful, with her thin legs and long nose? "Gumbo?"

"When I can kiss you." He looked into her eyes and his expression turned deadly serious. "It will be soon, yes?"

Three dances later, Louie sat down on a bench in her mother's rose garden and pulled Elizabet onto his lap.

Embarrassed again, she tried to stand up immediately. "I am too big."

"Never for me." He was stronger than he looked and held her easily. "The more of you I can hold, the more of you I can love."

She wondered if her mother would spot them from the windows. Seeing Elizabet sitting on a strange boy's lap would cause the grand old lady to have a stroke on the spot. "Why were you arguing about the gumbo?"

"Did you like it?"

"It was heavenly," she had to admit. "I've never tasted better in my life."

"Now I *am* in love with you." He grinned as she stiffened. "You see, I made it."

"You made the gumbo." *Oh, God, he is a server.* "Are you with the caterers?"

"My father owns the restaurant, and a few others. I like to cook." He touched her dark hair. "I'm Louis Gamble. Tell me your name."

The Gambles were an old family, and she relaxed a little. "Elizabet Cortland."

"*Non, non.* Elizabet Gamble." He smiled. "It sounds good, *oui?* When can we change it?"

Her jaw sagged. "You're out of your mind."

"About you? *Mais oui.*" The next moment he was kissing her breathless.

Two weeks later Elizabet was married to him, and nine months after that their son Cortland was born.

All those feelings welled up in her as she caressed the fine, silky silver fringe of hair at the back of his head. Their marriage had never been an easy one. Her family and friends had disapproved of Louie, and Elizabet herself had often been proud and foolish as a result. She had nearly driven him away, a dozen times. He had stayed, not out of stubbornness, not for the children, but because he truly loved her.

It had taken her over thirty years to realize how rare and precious that kind of devotion was.

If only Cortland could find such a partner. Elizabet kissed her husband. "I do love you, my darling."

"The magic words, you see? This works, every time." He swung her up into his arms, still as safe and strong as they had been thirty-five years ago, and carried her over to the sofa. "Say them again, *ma belle fille.*"

*   *   *

Terri used a contact at a credit bureau to obtain copies of Cort Gamble's credit record, which was immaculate. Cort's bank flatly refused to turn over his account statements at first, until Terri offered to subpoena all their records and make a call to the state banking commission to suggest a comprehensive audit. That had flip-flopped the branch manager's attitude, to the point where he nearly tripped over his own feet, hurrying to bring her the computer printouts.

"Mr. Gamble is an excellent customer," the manager assured her. "He keeps his balance in the high five figures, and never writes an overdraft."

"Be still my heart." Terri scanned the printout, but the bank records weren't going to help. The fact that they were as pristine as his credit report might make it appear as if he were trying to hide something. "I need the details on the last deposit made to his savings account."

"What sort of details?"

"How it was made, who made it, and where."

The manager sat down at his computer and pulled up the account file. "It was cash, deposited by envelope in our drop box."

"Drop box?"

The manager nodded. "Some of our established clients prefer not to use ATMs. We maintain a drop box at all our branches."

She checked the statement. "All of his previous deposits are marked with an *E*. What does that mean?"

"Those are direct electronic deposits." He scrolled up on the screen. "Mr. Gamble's employer uses electronic transfer for his weekly paychecks."

"So only this fifty thou came in through the drop box?" When he nodded, she asked, "Do you need the account PIN number to use the drop box?"

"No, Detective. All you need to do is write the account number on the front of the envelope." He showed her one of the deposit envelopes.

Terri knew three dozen different anonymous ways to get a bank account number. Whoever had spiked Cort's account had probably obtained the number from a bank statement stolen from the mail or taken from the trash. "Thanks."

She drove home from the bank and saw the old Impala parked at the curb in front of her duplex. It was old, ocher-yellow, and spotty with rust. She seriously considered driving to a motel before she pulled around it into her short driveway. She'd lost track of time, or she would have remembered that she was about due for a visit.

Hopefully it wasn't for the quarterly "You suck as a daughter" lecture.

Jeneane Vincent was sitting on the front step beside a beat-up cardboard box. As soon as Terri climbed out of the car, the older woman rose and smoothed the skirt of her cotton dress. Like her daughter, Jeneane was a brunette, but that was all they had in common. Terri had taken after her tall, lean father, while her mother was short, plump and very feminine. Jeneane wore her hair long and curly, and pulled it back from her face with fancy little combs. Although her dress was home sewn, she wore bright red lipstick and her best earrings and necklace. Terri could even smell perfume.

Which meant her father was at it again.

"What did he throw out this time?" Terri glanced at the box.

Her mother picked it up and handed it to her. "Your trophies."

Her marksmanship trophies had always been displayed on the top two shelves of her mother's china hutch. There were six of them, one for each year she had competed in the top ranks. Five of them were first place.

She could let the rejection hurt later. "Did he smash everything into junk, or just dump them in the garbage like he did my pictures?"

"He asked me to pack them up. I was real careful with them and wrapped them in newspaper." Jeneane lifted her chin. "You know how it hurts him to see your things 'round the house."

Probably not as much as it pained Con Vincent to see his only child in the flesh. Terri didn't want the trophies any more than she had wanted the crumpled-up photographs her mother had brought to her the last time. However, any refusal on her part would only give her father another victory.

She was done with being the family loser.

"You didn't have to wait." Terri parked the heavy box on her hip and unlocked the front door. "You could have left it here."

Her mother hugged herself with her arms and looked up and down the street. "People 'round here steal things." She had never liked Terri's neighborhood, or any part of the city, for that matter.

"I'm a cop. People around here generally leave my stuff alone." It was too bad that her father wouldn't. "Nice seeing you, Mama. Drive safe, huh?"

"Wait." Her mother caught the door before she closed it. "We got to talk, Therese."

"You and me talking always ends up with you crying, me getting a tension headache, and us not speaking for three months." She set the box inside. "Why don't we just pretend we've done this already, save the tissues and aspirin, and you call me around Thanksgiving?"

Her mother's mouth became an upside-down, red *U*. "Don't you snap at me, *cher*. I ain't the one done this thing between you and your daddy."

"My daddy." Terri made a sound of disgust and strode into the duplex.

"If he had the cancer, you wouldn't treat him like this." Her mother followed, pausing only to shut the door with a small bang. "You'd be right there for him like a good child oughta be. You'd give him the love and respect he deserves from his daughter."

"Mama, your husband doesn't have cancer. He's a liar, a thief, and a felon. He has you for the love and respect, he doesn't need me." She went into her tiny kitchen and took a beer from the fridge. "You want something to drink? I've got Michelob, iced tea, and some real old red wine a neighbor gave me last Christmas that I use to get the smell out the drain."

"No, thank you. Your Tanta Rose sent some candles." Her mother took two paper-wrapped glass jars out of her purse and set them next to the others Terri kept on a shelf. "They're blue for healing and forgiveness."

Terri twisted off the beer bottle's cap and threw it across the room. It landed in her trash bin. "I'll light them the next time I fuck up."

"Watch your mouth, girl."

Girl. To her mother, she was forever thirteen. "What do you want, Mama?"

Her mother came into the kitchen and set her purse on the table. "I want you to come and see your daddy, *cher.*"

"Why?" Terri sipped from the bottle. "To thank him for trashing my trophies? That what he expects now?"

"He don't expect a thing." Jeneane's brown eyes shimmered. "It's been more than a year now. He makes like this because he's suffering."

Terri wanted to throw the bottle across the room, but she didn't feel like wiping up the beer later, so she set it down beside her mother's purse. "I'm busy, Mama, and we said all we had to say to each other the last time."

"He don't mean what he said. He says those things outta temper and then he's always sorry. You know that, baby."

Con Vincent hadn't said anything. He'd shouted. *You think you're better'n me? Look at you, you look like some kinda dyke in that getup. When you gonna start dressing and acting like a woman? You think that fools anybody into thinking you're as good as a man?*

She'd nearly punched her father out that day. It was the reason she'd stayed away from her parents' house for the last year. Her father's fragile ego might be able to tolerate an unfeminine cop for a daughter, but one who could kick his ass as well would drive him over the edge.

She sat down on one of the kitchen chairs. "No, Mama. I'm sorry you drove all the way here but I don't want to see him."

Some of the soft, cajoling tone left her mother's voice. "He's your father, Therese."

"Then let him come to me." She jerked out one of the chairs around her kitchen table and sat on it. "Let him apologize to me for a change."

"You know he won't do that." Jeneane put a hand on her shoulder. "He's a man, Therese. Men are proud."

"Women are, too, Mama. Pity you never learned that." The kitchen chair rocked and Terri's head snapped back as her mother slapped her. She slowly lifted a hand to her burning cheek. "You know, I like it better when you cry."

"I'm sorry." Jeneane stepped back, horrified. "I didn't mean to, *cher,* I swear to God. I only wanted—" she groped in her purse for the handkerchief she always carried.

"To see if Tanta Rose's candles work?" Terri swung a hand toward the living room. "Go light one, I definitely could use some of her mojo now."

"I told him I wasn't going to be put in the middle of you two no more," her mother sobbed. "I *told* him."

"I can see whose side you're on, no problem." Terri picked up her beer and took another long swallow. "Maybe you should wait until Christmas to call."

The handkerchief lowered from Jeneane's streaming eyes. "You won't be happy 'til you've destroyed this family."

She ran her fingernail along the beer bottle's label. "I'm not the destructive one, Mama."

"I can't come here no more." Her mother carefully folded the damp square of cotton into fours. "He don't want me to, and he's my husband."

"Better you than me."

"Whatever he's said or done, *cher,* he's your father, and you are just like him." She walked with great dignity out of the duplex.

Terri listened as the sound of the Impala's engine started up and then dwindled away before she put her arms on the table and rested her head against them. Her mother wouldn't come back, that much she could count on. Jeneane was nothing if not loyal to her husband.

None of the relatives—and there were plenty of them— had approved of the break between Terri and her father. Among Cajuns, loyalty to one's own came before anything, and Terri had violated that unspoken rule once too often. Like when she had arrested her cousin, Caine, back in February. Half the family had stopped speaking to her. As soon as Jeneane told everyone about this little visit, that would finish the job.

Terri would no longer be welcome among the clan. She was, unofficially, all alone in the world now.

She poured three-quarters of the beer down the sink and went in to take a shower. Everything she did was automatic and unthinking. When she was clean, she put on her robe and went to sit down on the side of her bed. She opened the drawer to the nightstand and took out the gun she kept inside. It was her backup piece, a nine-millimeter with an empty clip.

Terri turned it over in her hands, remembering the last time she had held it. She only let herself remember little moments from that night. Snapshots of the actual events. Never the whole thing. Never all the details.

In the single frame of memory she allowed herself to bring back, Cort had been between her thighs. He'd looked up, his mouth wet from her. *You want me to stop?*

She had taken out the nine-millimeter and pointed it at his head. *You want to die?*

For the six thousandth time, she wondered what she had done wrong that night. There were plenty of possibilities. Cort likely never had one of his deb girlfriends threaten to shoot him in bed. Or maybe it was the sex. Terri had been with a few guys, so she wasn't a virgin, but she had really been too shocked to do much for him the first time. As she recalled, most of what she had done was lie there and be stunned by her first experience with multiple orgasms.

He had, too. Her hand tightened around the weapon. She might have been like a rag doll during round one but she had made up for it after. She'd lost count of her own orgasms— the entire event had been pretty much a continuous climax for her—but she had made him come that night, too. Three times.

He could ignore her and shove her away. He could ridicule her, but he couldn't take that away from her.

Cort's aversion to her wasn't all that mysterious. They were from completely different worlds. He'd grown up in a mansion among the cream of Creole society. He'd enjoyed all the privileges of a kid whose parents didn't have to worry about the price tag of anything. J. D. had told her once that his mother traced their family roots back to some French king.

There were no kings in Terri's family. She'd grown up on the bayou, part of an extended, multiracial Cajun clan. She'd gone to public school, disdained tea parties and dolls for the excitement of hunting and fishing. She'd worn her cousins' hand-me-downs, chopped off her hair whenever she could sneak her mother's scissors from her sewing basket, and sworn so much Jeneane had gone through at least five bars of soap washing her mouth out. Terri had only had one hero as a girl, and one dream. Someday she was going to be a cop like her father.

That dream, like the one about Cort falling in love with her, hadn't come true. Maybe it was for the best. She wasn't good enough for Cort, and she was too good for her father.

Terri might have thrown a beer bottle across a room a time or two, but she never abused her weapons. She carefully placed the gun back in the drawer and closed it before she curled over and buried her face in her pillow.

There were no tears. She had no one and nothing left to cry for.

Cort skipped the morning briefing and went straight to the Quarter to check on the progress at the crime scene. ATF and forensic technicians were still searching for evidence and remains, and because of the amount of destruction had staked out the site in a grid for sifting.

"Marshal." Warren Akers, one of his senior lab techs, brought him a hard hat and gloves. "We've moved out most of the ceiling supports and structure rubble." He nodded toward a high pile of charred wood and scorched wall panels stacked to one side of the building.

Cort spotted a tall, blond man crouching beside one of the forensic techs. "What's the medical examiner doing here?"

"Looking for some body parts. One Jane Doe came in

pretty torn up. Guess they're having trouble with the ID."
Warren checked his clipboard. "Yeah, there's still one Jane
Doe listed on the vic list."

"Find Gil for me, will you?" Cort walked in on the
visqueen runner laid out to protect the scene from contami-
nants carried in on anyone's shoes.

Grayson Huitt had moved into what had been the manager's office and was peering under a partially melted filing
cabinet when Cort stepped in to talk to him. He didn't know
the pathologist very well, but from all accounts he was a
competent ME. Seeing Huitt's arm around Terri the night of
the fire had annoyed him, but the fact that they were involved justified it.

It was good that Terri had someone in her life, Cort decided, even if he was some West Coast pretty boy who cut
up dead people for a living. Cort didn't have to like it; he
only had to accept it.

"Something I can help you with, Dr. Huitt?"

"I could use an arm, two legs, and three fingers, Marshal." Gray shook open a red biohazard bag and reached into
the gap. "Although it looks like I've got part of a hand here."
He took out a small, shriveled object and held it up for
closer examination.

"Your Jane Doe?" The lingering smell of kerosene
seemed stronger this morning, and Cort turned his head and
breathed in.

"Unless there's another body we haven't recovered, I
think so. Now see, she's wearing wedding rings"—he
showed the dismembered hand to Cort—"but there was no
missing-persons report filed on her." He bagged the blackened hand. "Really strange."

"Did you ID a Stephen Belafini yet?" Once Cort had a
confirmation, he could talk to Sebastien Ruel and find out
what investigations OCU was running on Frank.

"Just this morning." Gray rose to his feet and gave Cort
his full attention. "You know him?"

"No." He eyed the red bag and felt a surge of pity. "How
are you going to ID her?"

"Fingerprints are gone, so we use dental. I'll check with

the families of the other victims, see if someone is missing a wife or girlfriend." Something apparently caught his eye, and he smiled a little. "Excuse me."

Cort watched Huitt as he intercepted Terri Vincent on her way into the building. She seemed surprised, then happy, to see him. A few moments later they walked out together, deep in discussion over something.

Huitt and Terri probably swapped jokes and laughed a lot together, but Cort couldn't see the attraction. Terri was a passionate, intense lover; Huitt was too laid back for her. The pathologist might be good-looking but he'd bore her to tears in bed.

Was she sleeping with him? Had it gone that far already? Cort measured the other man. Huitt was in shape and almost his height and weight, but he didn't have the reach or the aggressiveness. West Coast guys never did. Cort felt fairly sure that he could take him down in two moves. Maybe one.

"Marshal?"

"What?" He turned his head and saw Gil hovering. "Sorry, I was . . ." *Thinking about kicking some Californian ass.* He made a conscious effort to relax the hands he had tightened into fists. "Anything new for me?"

"We're taking it down, a layer at a time, but we've got kerosene everywhere. I'm going to check out the mechanical room," Gil said, and showed him the room on a diagram of the tavern's layout. "We figured the sprinkler system had to be tampered with, but the weird thing is, all the head valves out here are open. The system did come on."

"When was the last time it was checked?"

"Believe it or not, only two weeks ago. City water performed an inspection after a break in the main two blocks over. At the time they checked the sensors and pumps, and the report they faxed me certified that everything was operational. It was just installed five months ago; it had no reason to fail."

"Maybe it didn't." Cort felt his blood run cold as he looked around the site. The one thing wrong about this fire was how fast and hot it had burned. As if someone had used rocket fuel. The smell of kerosene suddenly seemed much stronger. "You check the feed equipment in the mechanical room?"

"Why check the . . ." Gil's eyes bulged. "Oh, shit."

"Clear the site out and call for a truck." Cort left the manager's office and headed for the mechanical room.

"Everyone, listen up," Gil shouted behind him. "We have a potential hazard situation and we're evacuating the building. Please proceed outside immediately."

6

"I copied you on all the reports I sent Homicide," Gray said to Terri as they walked out to his van. "I'm holding one on the last Jane Doe, but everyone else had been IDed. Your pal the marshal seemed interested in Stephen Belafini."

Terri frowned. Cort didn't need to be asking about Belafini's son, not when Ruel was looking for any connection. The damnable part of this was that she couldn't warn Cort not to. "He likes to stay on top of the details."

Gray unlocked the van and reached inside for a large envelope. "I got the feeling that he'd also like to knock my teeth down my throat, every time I open my mouth."

She shrugged. "He's like that with everyone."

"Not everyone, just your new boyfriend." He grinned and handed her the envelope. "I assume you've already brought me up in conversation."

"Yeah, I kind of had to. You know, to establish boundaries." She gave him a sideways glance. "You really okay with this, Gray? I know it's total adolescent bullshit. We can drop the act any time if you get second thoughts."

"Are you kidding?" He gave her a burlesque leer. "I live in hope. And I'm polishing my desk daily."

"Mistake." She shook her head. "Ruins the traction."

As Gray laughed, Terri tried not to look for Cort. She'd caught a glimpse of him inside but had backed out before making eye contact. He always made her feel awkward, but now she felt as if she were still in braces and a training bra.

Still, she'd been right about needing Gray as a buffer. After what had happened in Cort's office, it was absolutely imperative. She had never felt so intimidated by her body, or the way it wanted to adhere itself to the fire marshal every time he got within two feet of her. Even when, as he had yesterday, he was pushing her away.

That was fine. She'd just keep Gray and *three* feet of space between her and Cort.

Excited voices drew Terri's attention to the front of the tavern, where streams of techs were hurrying from the site. Gil McCarthy appeared and began directing people to clear the sidewalks.

Cort didn't come out.

"Something's wrong." She thrust the reports back into Gray's hands. "Hang on to these for me, will you?"

"Sure. Terri." He waited until she gave him a quick look. "Be careful."

She nodded and went first to Gil. "Why are you clearing the building? Where's the marshal?"

"We've got a problem. The marshal's handling it." A group of ogling teenagers distracted Gil, who strode in their direction. "You four aren't supposed to be in front of those barricades. Yes, young man, I'm talking to *you*."

Terri shouldered her way in around two techs carrying an air analyzer and scanned the site. She didn't see anyone or anything that constituted a threat, but she could hear a hissing sound and smell something like gas.

If this fire isn't big enough, he may come back again.

She removed her weapon and held it ready as she followed the hissing sound through the scorched bar to a door that had been closed. When she opened it the gas-like smell hit her like a slap.

Not gas. Terri had grown up with too many hurricane lamps to mistake the odor. *Kerosene.*

Terri replaced her weapon, stepped inside, and closed the door behind her. The fumes were so strong that she had to cover her nose and mouth with her sleeve.

"Cort?" she shouted. "Are you in here?"

He coughed several times before answering. "Get out!"

His voice was coming from behind a large piece of equipment, and when she went around it she found him standing on a box, hunched over and rubbing his face with a rag. A fine mist was erupting from a joint in the pipe and had sprayed down all over his jacket and trousers.

"Dear God." She grabbed the back of his jacket and tried to haul him down. "Get down."

"No." Using her as a brace, he coughed. "Leaking." He lifted the wrench and then turned his face and coughed again as the kerosene mist hit him in the face.

"Don't breathe." She grabbed a piece of discarded cardboard, climbed up beside him and held it like an umbrella over their heads, to block the spray.

Unsteady as he was, Cort carefully slid the wrench around the hissing joint and turned it until the mist stopped spraying. As soon as it did, Terri tucked her shoulder under his arm and dragged him off the box, out of the equipment room, and into unpolluted air outside. They both paused to drag in deep, cleansing breaths, and Cort coughed uncontrollably.

He was covered in kerosene, Terri realized. Soaked with it. "What the hell was that?"

"That was me . . ." He coughed again. ". . . Preventing another explosion." He wrapped his fingers around her upper arm. "Come on."

He escorted her out through the side entrance and into the alley, beside a pile of rubble. There she leaned against the wall while he stripped off his jacket and threw it to the ground.

"Where did all that kerosene come from?" she demanded. "And why the hell were you taking a shower in it?"

"I was checking the pipe. Someone rigged the sprinkler system." He leaned against the wall and his sides and chest heaved as he dragged in more air.

"Rigged it with what?"

"Kerosene." He turned on her, his eyes fiery red, his voice like ice. "He didn't use HTA. He drained the water from the sprinkler system and replaced it with a pressurized stoichiometric mixture."

Terri smelled her hands. "It still smells like kerosene."

"A stoichiometric mixture contains optimal ratios of fuel and oxygen, in this case, kerosene and oxygen. It spreads in a mist over a wide area and, when ignited, explodes. The pipes are full of it. That's what sprayed out of the sprinkler heads that night."

"The whole place would have been doused." It didn't seem possible. "It must have been like . . ." There were no words for it.

"The lake of fire."

She frowned. "I'm sorry, what?"

"Sinners. We're supposed to burn in a lake of fire for eternity." He stared at the pile of scorched wood. "That's what it was like in there. I couldn't understand why their lungs were burned as well as their bodies. There was no air to breathe. Only flames. He drowned them in fire."

Before Terri could say anything, he drove his fist into the nearest object, one of the burned ceiling supports someone had left propped against the wall. The beam snapped and fell to the ground in two pieces.

"Whoa." She stepped between him and the wall. "You hit the building and you're going to break your hand."

"Fuck my hand."

He was swearing. That was really not a good sign; Cort was the most controlled, polite man she knew.

"If you hit the wall, you will. Besides, casts are ugly, they itch like a mother, and everyone wants to write or draw something stupid on them." She looked up into his eyes and saw the pain behind the rage. "We'll find him, Cort. We'll get him."

He looked down at her, still seething, and then walked away. He stopped at one of the portable water coolers the techs had set up, stripped off his shirt, and washed the kerosene out of it with the cold water.

Terri had absently followed after him, intending to get a drink herself, but the sight of his naked back made her come to a screeching halt.

Damn. He had been working out. *A lot.*

Cort lifted the shirt to his face and scrubbed, and then

squeezed it out over his head. The streams of water that
soaked his hair and ran down all that toned, hard muscle
made her mouth dry, but not as much as the sight of his chest
as he faced her. The first time she'd seen him naked from the
waist up, she'd compared him to a god.

Now Cort made the gods look scrawny.

Terri had to make an excuse and get away from him, but
her mind blanked. "I'd better go . . . do . . . something."

"Stay." He wiped water from his face with the back of his
hand before he moved toward her. He held out a cup.
"Here."

She took the water and rinsed the taste of kerosene from
her mouth before drinking. "Thanks."

"Why did you come in there after me?"

"I'm a cop. Protect and serve and, uh, whatever." She
backed up a few steps and looked for an avenue of escape.
The only way out was back through the tavern, and there
were firefighters in there now, dealing with the kerosene. "Is
there a doughnut place around here? I'm starving."

He kept coming, and her back finally hit the brick wall.

"You know what kerosene smells like." Cort braced an
arm on her right side. "Don't you?"

"Uh-huh." His god-envied chest was almost in her face.
"I should really go find my team leader, huh?"

"One spark and the whole room could have gone up."
Cort slung the soaked shirt over his shoulder before he
propped the other arm on her left side, trapping her. He
ducked his head so that their eyes were level. "Don't you
ever do anything that stupid again, do you understand me?"

She started to nod but something else rose up inside her.
"Just curious, I was stupid, but you were, what? Saving
Gotham, Batman?"

"I was doing my job. I know the risks." He bent his head
a little closer. "You don't."

"Then you knew you shouldn't have been in there by
yourself. You should have waited for some backup." She
had crumpled the paper cup, dropped it, and was now jab-
bing him in the chest with her finger. She had no idea why.
"You might have passed out or gotten burned."

"Terri." He caught her hand and pressed it under his, against his heart. "Don't do that again."

Now she was confused. The way he was looking at her, that couldn't be right. "Do what?"

"Risk your life for me."

He had to stop staring at her mouth like that. It was making her think things that weren't possible. "Is this your way of saying thank you?" she asked. "Because if it is, you suck at it."

"Terri?"

She looked over his arm and saw the medical examiner standing at the entrance to the alley. "Right here, Gray." She ducked under Cort's arm and practically tripped over her own feet, hurrying toward him.

"Everything all right?" Gray glanced over at Cort before breathing in and frowning down at her. "You smell like a space heater."

"Valve problem; I caught some gas spray." She tugged at her jacket. "I just need to go home, shower, and change."

"The guys with the hoses want us out of here." He leaned over and brushed his mouth over hers. "Come on, I'll give you a ride back to your place."

"Don't let me smoke on the way over, we'll blow up," Terri said as she walked away with him and ignored the phantom sensation of furious eyes boring into the back of her skull.

"You need a room, Mister?" the young girl asked, not looking up from the small black-and-white television set. On the small, dusty screen, three teenaged cartoon girls were arguing about fashion while rappelling down the side of a building.

Douglas studied the prepubescent desk clerk. She had a pencil in her hand, and was working out of a pre-algebra textbook. The equations she had solved on the notebook paper covering the right side of the page went from one to eleven, with a blank line after number twelve.

She had barely given him a glance. Just like everyone else.

"I've already checked in, thank you." Douglas set down the plastic shopping bag that contained everything he owned in the world. Most of the bag's contents had been doled out to him that morning by the church-lady volunteers at the St. William Homeless Mission down the block. "I seem to have misplaced my key, however."

"That'll be five bucks."

"I beg your pardon?"

"The replacement key. My dad charges five bucks if you lose your key." The girl took the five singles he removed from his wallet. "You're in Room Eight, right?"

"Yes." He accepted the key, which had a triangular tab with a barely discernible number EIGHT etched into the purple plastic. "Aren't you a little young to be working as a desk clerk?" His own daughter would be about the same age now.

"Yeah." The girl chewed on one of her fingernails as she stared at the TV. "My dad's the manager, but he got wasted last night."

He'd done the same, last night. After three years of being a model prisoner, he'd lost all his tolerance for alcohol. The hangover had been ferocious and had killed his desire for a repeat performance. "What's your name?"

"I'm really not supposed to talk to the guests." She rolled her eyes. "Sorry."

"That's okay." He nodded toward her math. "The answer is forty-two, by the way."

"Huh?"

"The problem you're stuck on." He had read it upside-down. "If John has a balance of one hundred ninety-seven dollars in his checking account, and two hundred thirty-nine dollars after he deposits his paycheck, he makes forty-two dollars per week." Which was more than Douglas Simon made.

Her mouth dropped open. "How did you do that?"

"Subtract one ninety-seven from two thirty-nine."

"No, I mean, you just like looked at it."

"I've always been good with numbers." Once his own wife and daughter had surely gazed at him with such admiration. Not that he knew where they were now, or could even clearly remember their faces. He took out the photo he carried in his mostly-empty wallet and studied it often. "Thank you for the room." He picked up his charity bag and walked to the door.

"Hey, Mister." When he looked back, she smiled. "My name's Caitlin."

It was a small kindness, the first he'd been shown in a very long time. "Thank you, Caitlin."

Room Eight was a dismal box with a closet-sized bathroom, a TV with rabbit-ear antenna that received exactly three channels clearly, and a single surprisingly comfortable bed. Douglas put away the two sets of clothes he had bought from a thrift store and hung up his jacket before loosening his tie and sitting down on the edge of the bed. The cheap coverlet was furry with little white fabric pills and had faded stains overlapping the bold paisley pattern.

He hadn't lied to Caitlin about being good with numbers. Douglas always had been, from the time he was her age. He could look at a row of numbers and understand them in ways other kids couldn't. He learned to do equations in his head faster than most people could read. Numbers were really the only constant in the world. They were logical, steadfast, and dependable.

Unlike his former wife.

He picked up the phone, called information, and dialed the number of his parole officer. The auto-answering system put him on hold, during which time Michael Bolton demanded to know how he was supposed to carry on. Douglas didn't know, but he didn't mind listening. He had nowhere to go and nothing to do for the next week. He supposed that he had chosen this motel because it was close to St. William's, where he had been getting his free—and only— meal of the day.

Today's dinner would be watery jambalaya and undercooked rice. The men he sat with would be filthy and paranoid, and smell of cheap scotch or red wine. A tired preacher would read something from the Book of Job.

Like Douglas, Job had made some very financially unsound choices.

Michael's soaring voice was cut off in mid-note, and a shriller, female voice answered, "Marcia Dayton."

He squinted at his shoes. They were also from the thrift store, and badly needed a polish, but they were so old that they might fall apart if buffed too hard. "Ms. Dayton, this is Douglas Simon, case number three-oh-nine-seven-eight-three-five-six," he repeated from memory. "I could not remember if I called to let you know about where I am staying at present."

He imagined her at a messy, crowded desk. Marcia Dayton sounded as if she were bone-thin and wore huge spectacles and a pink hand-crocheted shawl over her scrawny shoulders. She probably had the ringless hands and pictureless desk of a dedicated spinster.

"Simon. Simon. What was that case number again?" There was a sound of paper being shuffled as he repeated it. "Okay, got you right here. No, you didn't call, and you're two days late getting in touch with me. Where are you, Doug?"

No one had called him Doug except Stephen Belafini, and he didn't want to think about him. "I am currently residing in Room Eight of the Big Easy Sleep Motel." He recited the address and room phone number.

"That's a real dive. You find a job yet?"

"No, ma'am." And he wouldn't. He knew making the rounds of the insurance firms was useless. No company, reputable or otherwise, would employ a former property adjuster turned arson-conspirator embezzler.

His parole officer let out a gusty sigh. "Doug, you gotta get a job. You still have seventy thousand dollars in restitution to be paid."

Seventy thousand dollars written off as a loss and for which his former employer had already been reimbursed. Seventy thousand dollars no one needed, that no one wanted, but that Douglas still had to pay back. Such was the justice system. "Yes, ma'am." It was a shame he had not been able to get the money out of Stephen.

Stephen, who had tried to kill him.

"Look, my calendar is full this week, but stop by next Wednesday. I'll take you over to Job Core and get your name on the labor-pool list." She sipped something. "It's the best we can do."

He looked at his hands. They were still pale and smooth. The warden had made him the payroll clerk's assistant and Douglas had done nothing but bookkeeping during his incarceration. "I appreciate that, ma'am."

"Nine-fifteen a.m. next Wednesday, then. Don't be late, Doug." She ended the call.

He replaced the receiver on the telephone. That was the only call he had to make; there was no one else who would speak to him or wanted to hear from him. There was no one to whom he wished to speak, except perhaps his daughter, and that would never happen.

This was it. This was what his wife had predicted he'd hit, if he'd continued on his path.

This was rock bottom.

He turned on the television to watch the news at noon. When he saw the live coverage at the site of the French Quarter bar fire, he switched channels, but the story was being played on every local station. The news anchor switched from the live feed to a taped press conference given the previous day by the mayor and the city fire marshal.

Douglas turned up the sound and listened to Cortland Gamble dodge questions. The man had moved up in the ranks; three years ago Gamble had only been a senior arson investigator. In fact, when Douglas had first met him, he'd dismissed Gamble as just another ex-firefighter/jock who was too stupid to be a threat to his little operation.

Instead, Gamble had spent months quietly investigating Douglas. Despite a complicated paper trail, he had gathered proof that Douglas had been falsifying arson reports and filing accidental fire claims in exchange for a portion of the insurance settlements and to cover Belafini's protection racket. Gamble had used the proof to persuade some of the insured conspirators to testify against Douglas, and then the police had come and arrested Douglas on twenty-nine counts of conspiracy and fraud.

The investigation had been meticulous, and Douglas's well-paid lawyer could do nothing about the charges. When Douglas refused to turn state's evidence against the Belafinis, the district attorney withdrew the offer of a deal. A grand jury was convened, and Gamble was brilliant and immoveable on the stand. Douglas's life crumbled around him as the verdict was read: guilty on all counts.

He lost everything—his job, family, home, even his freedom—thanks to Cort Gamble.

Douglas turned off the television and lay down on the bed. He had disconnected himself from the past. What was done was done. He needed to take a nap before he walked down to the mission for dinner.

The sound of a man's voice woke him up several hours later, and he felt groggy as he sat up. "What is it?"

"Get up, Doug."

Automatically he sat up and straightened his tie. "Who's there?" He didn't see him standing on the other side of the room until he rose off the bed. "What are you doing here?"

"I need your help."

The man didn't look familiar, but the look in his eyes made Douglas' stomach knot. "What do you want me to do?"

"Do you know the saying about casting stones when you live in a glass house?"

"I do." He looked away from the other man's face. "What does that have to do with me?"

"Cortland Gamble was the investigator who put you in prison."

"He was." While Stephen and his father were the ones who had let him go in their place. "What is your point?"

"What if I could give you proof that Gamble is no better than you? That he is, in fact, working for Frank Belafini right now?"

Douglas blinked. A chance to get even with Belafini and Gamble. He couldn't think of what to say.

"Meet me at the Blue Primrose Café in the Garden District

tomorrow afternoon at two p.m. and I'll give you everything I have on Gamble, and the money you were promised."

"How do you know about the money?" That confused him even more. "Why not give it to me here and now?"

"I didn't bring it with me." The man thrust his hands into his pockets. "I had a hard time tracking you down."

"Why give it to me at all?"

"Because what you have suffered, *he* must suffer," he told him. "Or there is no true justice in the world. Wouldn't you agree?"

"Justice," he said hoarsely. "Yes."

"I give this to you cheerfully, Doug. God loves a cheerful giver, did you know that?" The other man strolled out of the room.

"Well." Douglas stared at the closed door. "I suppose I do now."

"Ash, orange is *not* the new pink," Moriah Navarre said as she studied her friend.

Ashleigh Bouchard reached into the sides of her designer overalls to push her bra and the C-cup breast implants it protected a little higher. "Is too."

"No, it's not." And God willing, it would never be. "Orange is just orange. Like the fruit. Like the juice."

"It's not orange, it's tangerine. It's Todd Oldham tangerine *silk,*" Ashleigh Bouchard said as she slowly turned from left to right, examining her reflection in the full-length mirror. "Does it make me look thick in the waist?"

Moriah snorted. "You could be nine months pregnant and still look like a wasp."

Ashleigh was on the cutting edge of every fashion trend. Her dirty-blond hair had artful white streaks scattered through it, à la Kelly Clarkson, and she had the new black-and-silver dagger-nail manicure that was so popular among the twenty-something elite. The carrot-colored silk overalls she wore had been purchased on a recent shopping trip to Texas. They had been designed to mimic a garage mechanic's overalls, complete with glass buttons bearing the Oldham logo and black faux oil stains on the legs and bib.

If she carries around a pillowcase with that getup, Moriah thought uncharitably, *people are going to drop candy in it.*

Moriah wished she had never agreed to come over to the Bouchard house. She was much happier staying at home than she was sitting and watching Ashleigh try on every outfit from her three walk-in closets. But the Bouchards' only daughter was one of her oldest friends from college, and she had called Moriah the moment she'd heard about Elizabet Gamble's summer fete.

"The Gambles are throwing a little party for J. D. when he comes home from his honeymoon," her friend had told her. "I have to be the most gorgeous female present."

"J. D. is married." And Ashleigh had apparently forgotten that he had also dumped Moriah shortly before marrying his college sweetheart.

"I'm not interested in J. D., goose. I want *Cortland.* Come over as soon as you can and help me pick out something."

Now she sat on the edge of the ivory-lace-canopied bed and, between giving opinions on Ashleigh's wardrobe, wondered what sort of an excuse she could offer the Gambles. They would invite her, of course. In Creole society, everyone always invited the ex-girlfriend.

The ex-girlfriend was also expected to refuse.

She didn't want to go, but not because she was ashamed of her breakup with J. D. She had dated all three of the Gamble brothers at one point or another, and she had never been in love with any of them. She was genuinely happy that J. D. had been reunited with Sable, because she had long suspected the Cajun girl owned his heart.

What she couldn't bear, what she wouldn't face, was the pity. *Poor Moriah,* her friends whispered. *She's got everything but a man, and she can't ever keep one longer than a few months.*

The problem wasn't with the men, either. Moriah had dated plenty of nice, presentable men. Some of them had been handsome beyond belief. Others had been clever, witty, amusing. A certain few had even been all of those things. But none of them touched her heart, and in the end, she had turned them all loose. Now she had the rep of two near misses with the Gamble boys and a dry run through the rest of the social register—and still no ring on her finger—people were beginning to talk. She agreed with them. Whatever was wrong, the blame definitely rested on her own head.

"Maybe if I wear the legs tucked in my new suede boots." Ashleigh whirled around. "What do you think? The black suede, I mean." She frowned. "Shoot, I think I took them to be re-heeled last month."

Moriah climbed off the bed. "I think you need a new outfit. You should go shopping."

"Oooo, you're right." She began unfastening the glass buttons anchoring the silk straps to the top of the bib. "Let me change and we'll grab some brunch on the way."

"I can't go with you, Ash. I've got some calls to make and this dinner my mother is planning . . ." Moriah trailed off, tired of hearing her own excuses. "No, that's not true. I just don't feel like it."

"You don't feel like shopping." Ashleigh made this sound as if Moriah had contracted a terminal disease.

"That's right. I also don't feel like talking about Cort Gamble, or his family, or his brother J. D. who, until February, was dating *me*."

Ashleigh's pink lips rounded. "Oh, Moriah. I'm such an idiot. I am so sorry."

Ash was self-absorbed, but she wasn't vicious, so now Moriah felt depressed *and* as if she'd just kicked a puppy.

"It's okay. Everybody forgets." *Everyone but me.* "Call me next week and we'll go out on the lake." She slipped out of the bedroom and walked down the long, curving staircase to the first floor.

The Bouchards' butler waited by the front door. "Leaving so soon, Miss Moriah?" he asked as he offered her the straw hat she had carelessly left on the foyer table.

"Yes, Charles. I have O.D.ed on Oldham and orange." She gave him a wan smile. "Miss Ashleigh will probably want her car brought around in about ten seconds. Or, if she decides to freshen her makeup, two hours."

Ashleigh's voice rang out above their heads as if on cue. "Charles, bring my car up, I'm going out."

She checked her watch. "Make that five seconds."

"Your accuracy, as always, is formidable, Miss." He kept his dignified expression but gave her a fond wink. "Have a pleasant day."

As Moriah drove away from the Bouchard house, she was nearly sideswiped by a driver in a dark van on the narrow two-lane street.

"Hey!" The near miss jolted her out of her bleak mood. As the van passed, she hit the window control, turned her head, and shouted, "Watch where you're going, you moron!"

The driver, a man in dark glasses and a ball cap, simply gave her a little wave with the cell phone in his hand.

7

"I need to know if OCU is running an independent investigation connected with the Maskers fire," Cort told the mayor's aide. "I can't work blind, and if Belafini's involved, it will change things."

The aide seemed unconcerned. "Ruel told you himself that he wasn't, didn't he?"

Sally walked in before Cort could reply. It surprised him, because she always used the intercom or, in an emergency, knocked.

"Look, Marshal, if you've got a beef with OCU—"

His assistant wouldn't barge in without a good reason, so he interrupted the aide. "Just a moment. Sally, what is it?"

She looked at him, as dazed as a woman who had just been clubbed over the head. With visible effort, she pulled herself together and said, "Marshal, we have an eleven-seventy-one on a car in the Garden District."

A car on fire usually wasn't enough to rattle his assistant.

"Excuse me." He left the aide in his office and stepped outside with Sally, who was shaking so much now that her teeth were clicking together and her entire body trembled. "What happened?"

"Call came in." She swallowed. "There's a woman trapped inside a car, and she said it's burning. She said the doors and windows are jammed and she can't get out."

"Did you route the call to dispatch?"

His assistant nodded.

"Leslie." Cort gestured for a passing secretary. "Stay with Sally." To his assistant he said, "It's all right. I'm going to check on this now."

"You don't understand." Sally grabbed his arm and dug her fingers in. "She asked for you. She was crying and she called you Cort. Then she started . . . screaming."

Terri. "Who was it, Sally?"

"I don't know." His assistant covered her face with her hands. "God forgive me, but I didn't recognize her voice."

Cort left her with the secretary and ran down the hall to Central Dispatch.

The shift supervisor met him halfway there. "Marshal, we've got a situation over in the Garden District."

"I know. Who's in the car?"

"Plates are registered to an Ashleigh Bouchard," the supervisor told him. "We've sent two units and they're at the scene. The car is right in front of the Bouchard residence."

Ashleigh Bouchard was the daughter of his parents' friends and, until a few months ago, had been his escort to half a dozen social functions. She drove a brand-new 2004 Mercedes-Benz convertible.

"Radio ahead and tell them I'm on the way." He headed for the parking lot.

"Marshal, wait. You should know . . ." The supervisor looked the same way Sally had. "They didn't get her out in time. I'm sorry."

Ashleigh had been his lover. Four weeks after he took her to bed, he'd had his fill of her bright, empty chatter. He'd escorted her one night to her favorite restaurant and had—very gently and with great tact—told her that she'd be better off with someone younger and more attentive. She'd been a little tearful by the time dessert arrived, but she hadn't created a scene.

"You'll be sorry that you let me get away," she assured him, tossing back her mane of streaked blond hair. "I'm a huge catch, you know."

Cort rarely resorted to his lights and siren, but he used them now. On the short, fast drive to the Bouchards' home, he tried to imagine how Ashleigh had gotten trapped. When they'd been together, he'd driven her car a few times, and it had been in perfect condition.

There were two fire trucks and an ambulance at the scene, as well as half a dozen black-and-white units. Billowing, oily black smoke still rose from the Mercedes, which was being foamed down by three firefighters. Someone had tried to use the Jaws of Life, which now sat discarded a few feet from the car.

Cort called over a nearby patrolman. "I want an ID list on everyone here. Check licenses, confirm addresses and phone numbers. On everyone."

"Yes, sir."

He scanned the clusters of onlookers, but they weren't behaving in the usual manner. They weren't looking at the car. They were clutching each other. Some of them were openly weeping. Uniformed officers weren't moving them back, they were comforting them.

Terri Vincent was standing next to the wreck, talking to one of the female firefighters. She spotted Cort, put her hand briefly on the other woman's shoulder, and strode over to him. She had on her darkest pair of sunglasses and her mouth was a flat, grim line.

"Detective."

"Marshal. You get the girl's call?"

"My assistant did." Through the foam and smoke he could now see that the firefighters had smashed out the front windshield of the Mercedes. "Was it Ashleigh Bouchard?"

She took off her sunglasses. "Yes, it was," she said, her voice gentle. "I'm sorry, Cort."

He looked at the burning wreck for a long time. "Who identified her?"

"The family's butler, Charles. As far as we know, she was alone in the vehicle."

Cort searched the surrounding faces until he located Charles. The older man was sitting on the lawn. A paramedic was giving him oxygen and wrapping his hands in burn packs.

Charles had been with the Bouchard family since Ashleigh was born. Soft-spoken and quite venerable, he had always treated the Bouchards' daughter with subtle affection. Now he sat, a dazed old man, staring at the grass.

"He tried to get her out, didn't he?"

"Yeah. Him and two teenagers from next door. They took Ashleigh's body and the kids over to the ER, but he won't leave. Her parents are on their way and I think he wants to be the one to tell them." Terri watched a news van that was parking at the end of the block. "And here come the ghouls."

"Over here." Cort led her onto the property and behind a concrete wall that would shield them from the cameras. "What else?"

"Charles was able to tell me some of the details." She took out her notebook and flipped it back two pages. "Ashleigh drove from the driveway down to the street. Charles was closing the front door and heard a sound like a couple of muffled bangs close together. He walked out and saw the Mercedes where it is now, next to the curb. It was already burning."

"Did someone hit her from behind?"

"He didn't see any other cars. He saw black smoke and heard Ashleigh shouting. He ran down the driveway and saw flames inside the car. He tried to open the doors, but said that the car was locked up tight. She was trying to open them from the inside, too, and couldn't."

"The fire started *inside* the car?"

"According to Charles, and seven other witnesses, it did. Both the front and back seats were burning around her."

He looked back at the wreck. "Did he try to smash a window?"

"Yeah, and broke his hand in the process. The glass on the windows is reinforced. One of the neighbors told me that the family was evidently nervous about carjackers and special-ordered it that way. The two teenagers managed to pull Charles away just before the gas tank blew. She was alive until it went." Her gaze shifted to the bystanders. "All these people could do was watch."

Most car fires began in the engine, where short circuits, leaking flammable fluids, and damaged components were at fault. The exhaust system was also vulnerable, especially in the manifold, where temperatures reached high levels. Fires rarely started in the interior unless a lit cigarette or other flame source was dropped.

Ashleigh didn't smoke or, to Cort's knowledge, use drugs, so she had to have had something else flammable in the car with her. That still didn't explain why she couldn't get out. "This wasn't an accident."

She nodded. "That's my thinking."

"Anyone seen near the car?"

"According to one of the maids, when not in use, the Mercedes was kept locked in the garage at the rear of the house, there." She pointed to it. "About twenty minutes ago, Charles went to the garage to get it for her and drove it to the front of the house. If there was a firebomb, it wasn't hooked up to the ignition."

He surveyed the property. "We need to cordon off the garage, he probably did the work in there—"

"Marshal Gamble?" A reporter at the end of the drive took an uncertain step forward.

There were too many things coming at Cort from all directions; he had to focus. "I've got to secure the scene and the vehicle. Can you keep the press off my back?"

"My pleasure." She headed for the reporter. "Hey, pal. Ever hear of private property? No? How about interfering with emergency services and an official police investigation?"

Cort retrieved his coat and goggles from his SUV before he approached the wreck. The crew had finished foaming down the car and the smoke had mostly dissipated. Three feet away, he could smell something in the air. Something that wasn't the burn-off from the gasoline. He looked down and saw that the tires had been burned away and all that was left were the rims and a tangle of wires that had once been the tires' steel belts.

Cort knew that tires hardly ever ignited during vehicle fires unless the car was left to burn. Because of the density of the material, it took a lot to start a tire burning. Unless someone had given it some help.

"Move the people off this block," he told one of the patrolmen. "I don't want anyone but service personnel in the immediate vicinity." He motioned back two firefighters working on the Mercedes. "Hold off opening the trunk and back doors until I give the all-clear."

Gil joined him. "We need the sniffer?"

"Not yet." He crouched down beside the front driver's-side rim and ignored the heat radiating from the wreck as he peered between it and the wheel well. The smell of burned rubber was strong, but there was something else. "Gil, come here." When his investigator bent down, he asked, "You smell that? Kerosene and gunpowder."

"Your nose is better than mine." He took a deep breath. "But yeah, I think I do."

"If all four tires blew at the same time, she couldn't move. She'd be stuck wherever he wanted her." And he had wanted her to burn right in front of her own home. In front of her family, her friends and her neighbors. *But why?*

"Boss, how could he shoot out all four tires simultaneously?"

"He couldn't, not without help." Cort stood up. "I want every inch of this car inspected. Take it apart by the seams."

"What are we looking for?" Gil asked.

"Transceivers, electronics, wiring. He rigged the tires and the firebomb to blow on a remote." Cort pulled off his goggles. "He was close by. He wanted to watch her burn."

"You want another refill?" the waitress asked Douglas. She looked impatient, but he had been occupying the booth at the Blue Primrose Café for well over an hour without ordering any food, and a cluster of people were waiting for tables.

His visitor, the cheerful giver, had never showed.

"No, thank you." He drank the last, watery inch from the glass before he paid for it with what coins he had in his pocket, and left the diner.

Outside, the sun struck his face like an interrogator's

spotlight, bright and indifferent. Douglas wished again that he had sunglasses; he had always been sensitive to daylight. Before he had gone to prison, he had owned seven pairs, and not one of them had cost less than three hundred dollars.

He had spent twenty-one hundred dollars on sunglasses and had never given it a second thought. Now he didn't have twenty-one cents to his name. There was a lesson in that; he should have worked harder to protect himself. Had he done so, his eyes certainly wouldn't have been filled with tears.

A police cruiser with lights and sirens on flashed by. Out of curiosity he turned, knuckled the wetness from his eyes, and saw it heading in the direction of a thick column of black smoke over on the next block. He had nothing better to do now, so he also walked in that direction. He got as far as three houses down from the smoldering car before he ran into the yellow-and-black-striped sawhorse barricades the police had set up to keep spectators away.

A woman and a young boy came to stand beside him. "You see the news spot on TV?" she asked Douglas.

"No, I saw the smoke." The fire disturbed him. It seemed too much of a coincidence, that the man who had come to see him at the hotel would want to meet him here, so close to it.

"Someone locked a girl in her car and set it on fire," the boy told him, his voice excited. "She got all burned up. I bet it was cool."

"Justin!" The woman looked mortified. "Don't ever say that. Someone getting killed is a *terrible* thing."

"Sorry, Ma." The boy looked anything but.

"Please excuse my son," the woman said to Douglas, and gave her child a hard look. "He watches a little too much violence on TV."

The boy shuffled his feet and stuck out his bottom lip. "You were watching it too."

"Well, keep talking that trash and I'll be watching nothing but the Disney Channel," his mother promised him.

Douglas wasn't upset by the argument. He envied the

woman and her son. All he had ever wanted was a loving wife and family, and that had been taken away from him. The sound of a camera snapping made him look up to see a man pointing a lens at him, the woman, and the boy. The man turned to take a photo of some people standing across the street from them, and Douglas saw the large yellow ATF letters on the back of his jacket.

Photographing witnesses was standard procedure at an arson scene, he recalled. Fire raisers liked to stay nearby so they could watch everything burn. For a moment he felt afraid. If someone recognized him from the photo, they'd put him on the top of the suspect list.

Maybe that was why he had been invited to the Blue Primrose Café. To distract the police from the arsonist who had done this. Another man with no alibi and no means with which to defend himself might be terrified at the prospect. Another man who had not quite yet hit rock bottom.

Douglas almost laughed.

"I can't believe this is happening. We waited two years to get an apartment here, where it's supposed to be safe." The woman put a protective arm around her son. "Come on, honey, I'll make you some lunch."

Douglas waited until they had gone around the corner before he casually walked back to the bus stop. Dinner at St. William's would be served at four p.m., and he wanted to be sure to get back in time to get at the front of the line. The front of the line meant he'd get more than a tablespoon of sauce on top of the overcooked spaghetti, and maybe even a slice of two-day-old bread spread with margarine and dusted with garlic powder, for that special authentic Italian touch.

A man had to keep his priorities straight.

Watching Terri Vincent fielding the press on the news at noon didn't surprise Ruel. Not everything about a crime could be held as privileged information; certain facts had to made available to the media. Terri had given the reporter only what would be a matter of public record; a non-specific description of the incident, the time and location at which it had happened, and the type of response emergency services had provided. His new transfer handled reporters as skillfully as she did suspects; she delivered all that using candor and charm while actually saying nothing concrete about the crime at all.

However, he hadn't put Terri on the Maskers case so she could serve as Gamble's personal press secretary.

"I'd like to have a word with Detective Vincent," he told the unit secretary on the way into his office. "Make sure she sees me when she reports in."

The secretary never paused in her machine-gun-fire-rapid typing. "Yes, Chief."

He went into his office and closed the door. A stack of reports was waiting to be reviewed; he also had three requisitions to write for new monitoring equipment. He ignored them and punched in an unlisted number on the telephone.

The line to his informant still rang with no answer.

This was the third day of silence. Ruel knew that his only trustworthy source of information had gone to Maskers on the night it had burned down. In fact, he had the uneasy suspicion that his informant may have been the arsonist who had set fire to the place.

He dismissed his guilt with the same deliberate blindness that he had employed to walk away from a promising career with the Bureau. Sometimes to catch a mass murderer and cop killer, one had to employ unorthodox methods. He had promised no immunity. If he was still alive, Ruel's informant was going to death row, and could occupy the cell right next to Belafini's.

A single knock on his door made Ruel realize he was sitting and listening to the unanswered phone line ring. "Come in."

Terri Vincent entered, carrying a wide folder crammed with computer printouts. "You needed to see me, Chief?"

"Sit down, Terri." Knowing that they shared one weakness, he took out the ashtray and the pack of Marlboros that he kept in a side drawer. "Does cigarette smoke bother you?"

"Only when I don't suck in enough secondhand." She gave him a wry smile and produced her own pack.

He reached over the desk to light her cigarette before his own. "What progress have you made on Gamble?"

"I've put the word out to some sources and researched his financial records." She held up the folder. "For a man who's supposed to be on the take, he's pretty spotless."

"We've already found a payoff," he said.

"That's the thing, Chief. That fifty thousand was deposited in cash through a drop box. No PIN number required to access the box." She pulled out a sheet. "I've contacted his bank's security department and asked them to turn over their security tapes for the day the deposit was made. There's an ATM right next to the drop box; could be the camera caught whoever dumped the money in his account."

He wondered how shocked she'd be when she saw it was Gamble on the tape. "I caught the car fire on the noon report." He exhaled a stream of smoke. "You handled Patricia Brown admirably."

"Reporters will buy anything on a breaking story, as long as the tag looks genuine." As he'd thought it would, the cigarette made her relax a little. "It's the follow-up we've got to worry about."

"Why is that?"

"Ashleigh Bouchard, the victim, was a socialite. Pretty, rich, very high-profile. She burns to death in front of twenty people two days after the fifteen are flash-fried at Maskers." She flipped her hand in a seesaw motion. "Two attention-screaming arson murders two days apart aren't good."

"You think it's the same arsonist." He studied her face. She also didn't want to tell him why.

Her relaxation disappeared. "I don't know for sure. It may be nothing."

"What is it, Terri?"

"Ashleigh Bouchard. A photo of her and Marshal Gamble was run in all the papers immediately after the Maskers fire." She reached over and ground out her cigarette. "He sees a lot of women, though, so that probably doesn't pan out."

Would Gamble have murdered his own girlfriend to silence her? Ruel couldn't pose it that way to Terri, she'd only go on the defensive. "How are you looking at it? A revenge killing, to get to Gamble?"

She stared impassively at him. "It feels more like a fluke, Chief. Bad luck, coincidence, whatever you want to call it. I'm sure it has nothing to do with the marshal personally."

Her predilection for finding new ways to defend Gamble was starting to seriously annoy him. "Do you know the last time the marshal saw Bouchard?"

She lost her poise for a moment and bit her lower lip. "January, I think. Just before the LeClare murder."

Ruel didn't let the triumph show on his face. "Perhaps the Bouchard killing was a warning from the mob."

"Marshal Gamble isn't dirty, Chief. I'd stake my career—hell, my life—on that."

He thought of Tom and Marianne, and felt the weight of their deaths grinding down on him. They were the only thing keeping him on the path to taking down Gamble, and through him to crucifying Belafini. "I hope you never have to."

Terri had been assigned to the evidence team, and spent the rest of the day pulling files from OCU's database on all arsonists within the region known to be involved with the mob. Once the unit secretary had given her a crash course in using the sophisticated computer, she'd found it was actually easier to use than a typewriter.

There was a connection, she just wasn't seeing it yet. Stephen Belafini, killed at Maskers. Cort at the scene the day after, asking about Belafini. The accident with the kerosene. Bouchard murdered the day after her photo with Cort appeared in the paper.

Maybe something linking the murders through the bodies. Terri picked up the phone and dialed the morgue, but was told Gray Huitt had worked the previous night shift and was off duty. "Ask him to give me a call when he has a chance, will you?"

She brought her list of potential suspects with her to the next morning briefing, hoping to compare them with Lawson Hazenel's lists. Before she entered the conference room, a secretary she didn't know intercepted her.

"Excuse me, Detective Vincent? Would you come with me, please?"

Terri followed the older woman down the hall and saw that they were headed for Cort's office. "Something wrong?"

"No, Detective. The marshal requested you join the meeting in his office." The woman gave her an uncertain look. "I'm a little behind on the routine here. I'm filling in for Sally while she's on leave."

"Sally took the call from the victim yesterday."

The older woman nodded. "It was such a horrible thing. She heard . . ." She made a quick gesture.

Terri knew that Sally had heard Ashleigh burning alive. It must have been like listening to a murder victim die on a 911 recording. She could still remember the first one she had heard, a teenager being stabbed to death by a drug-crazed boyfriend. She still had nightmares about that young girl's voice, screaming for help that hadn't gotten there in time.

"Sometimes we have to deal with things that are unspeakable," she told the secretary. "We do it so that we can protect people, but no one really protects us. That's why we have to look out for each other." She smiled. "Sally will have a tough time with this. It would be good if some of her friends from work stopped by to see her, keep her talking."

"I was thinking that I would." The older woman nodded. "Thank you, Detective."

Cort and Gil McCarthy were alone in his office going over a set of eight-by-ten photographs.

"It's not him," Cort was telling the other man. "There are too many inconsistencies."

"The remote wiring was identical. So was the catalyst." The investigator took a moment to smile at Terri, but Cort only gave her a brief glance before he nodded toward the empty chair beside Gil's.

"What's up?"

"We spent the night stripping down the Mercedes," Gil told her. "We found traces of six separate detonators, four on the rims, one on the trunk latch, and one under the driver's seat."

"Did he blow the tires?" Terri asked.

"He did." Gil passed her one of the photos. "After he filled them with kerosene."

"Why the fu—" she cut herself off and took a breath. "The fire came from the *tires?*"

"It's overkill. We think he put a slow burner—a device that doesn't ignite everything immediately—under the driver's seat. He triggered that on a separate remote. The tires were to . . . stop the car, I guess."

"What if he blew the tires after the interior fire started?" she asked. "When people were trying to help?"

"She's right." Cort looked furious. "He wanted to keep anyone from getting Ashleigh out of the car."

"She couldn't have escaped anyway. The car's security system was triggered by the remote on the trunk latch. It broke the circuit, which automatically locks down all the doors and windows. The locks then can't be released by anyone but the security company that originally installed the system. It's an antitheft measure, like the reinforced glass."

"He had to know about it." She sat back. "Damn, he really did his homework, didn't he?"

"We figure he spent a couple of hours in the garage, working on it." Gil shook his head as he put the photo back with the others on Cort's desk. "My wife says cars are death traps, but this one really was."

"Gil, would you excuse us for a minute?" Cort asked.

The investigator collected his photos and, after nodding to Terri, left the office.

"Before you start ragging my ass for whatever I did wrong," Terri said, "you handling this okay?"

He gave her a long, silent look before he said, "I'm getting there. Thank you."

She nodded. "So, what did I do now?"

"We're meeting with your bosses this afternoon," Cort told her. "Ruel and Pellerin."

"We." Terri frowned. "For what?"

"That's my question. Ruel told me he wanted to discuss some information that you gave to him." He eyed her. "Information you apparently didn't give to *me*."

"I briefed Ruel on the Bouchard murder." She thought back to the conversation she'd had with the OCU chief the day before. "I told him I thought it might be a connection between the two cases. The papers ran a photo of you and Ashleigh the day after the tavern fire."

"There is no connection."

"The girl was murdered less than twenty-four hours after that photo made the front page." She watched his expression, but it didn't change. "She was a young, wealthy woman but had no enemies to speak of. No threats were made, no warning was given. Yet she's killed in such a way to draw a huge amount of attention."

"The fires were coincidental."

She was hoping that they were. "But what about the photo? The timing? Doesn't it bother you?"

Cort's eyes narrowed. "And this is what you told Ruel."

"He asked, and I mentioned it."

"Beautiful." He sat back and rubbed his eyes with a big hand before he dropped it and glared. "Do you have any idea of what you've done?"

"Give me a sec." She rested her cheek against her hand. "I've made a connection between the two fires. Which, according to the all those classes I took on criminal theory and analysis at the academy, is what I'm supposed to do." She smiled brightly. "Guess that would be doing, uh, my job."

"Wrong. You've jumped to a ridiculous, erroneous conclusion and single-handedly compromised both cases."

"Seems to me like you're the one jumping, Marshal." She waved a hand. "Come on. I mean, you've dated dozens of women." *More like hundreds.* "It doesn't make you responsible for Ashleigh's death." She hesitated, and then plunged on. "It may make you a target, though."

"Whom I've dated is no reason to torch a bar or burn a woman alive in her own car."

"Not to a normal person, but this guy's cylinders aren't all firing." She watched him get to his feet and turn his back on her to look out the window. "It's a reasonable assumption, Cort. I have to look into it."

"Is this how you work? Does J. D. end up solving all the cases while you hunt for red herrings?"

Of course he'd think his brother was a superior cop. It was fraternal loyalty. That didn't mean she had to like it. What would he say if he knew how she'd been busting her ass, trying to clear his name? "We don't discount anything in regard to murder, and neither should you. It's a legitimate link. I'm going to check it out."

"You'll do no such thing." He swiveled around. "When we meet with Ruel and Pellerin, you'll tell them that you were wrong."

"I'm sorry you feel guilty about Ashleigh. I do, too, and I didn't even know her." She was standing now, and leaning over his desk. "But if this dirtbag is a repeater and he has an agenda and you're part of it, we've got to know."

"My private life isn't feeding headlines," he said, his voice low and threatening.

"Wake up, Cortland. It already is."

He propped his hands on the desk and leaned over. "Maybe you should think about your future with the department, Detective."

She didn't back down. "Maybe you shouldn't have banged half the women in the goddamn city."

The door behind Terri opened while she was in midsentence.

"The nice lady outside wanted me to wait," Grayson Huitt said as he came in, "but I couldn't hear too clearly out there. What I caught was pretty good, though." He looked from Cort to Terri. "Don't let me stop you guys."

"What do you want, Doctor?" Cort demanded.

"I got a call from Terri and I had to come over here, so I thought I'd use one stone, you know, kill two birds. My techs worked with your guys on the Mercedes last night. They recovered all the personal effects and brought them down to the lab for analysis." He sat down and propped one of his sneakers on the edge of Cort's desk. "Guess what we found."

Now Terri wanted to hit him. "What, Gray?"

"Ms. Bouchard was evidently a little precognitive. We recovered a fireproof pouch hidden inside the spare tire well." He waited a beat. "There was an unmarked cassette tape inside the pouch."

8

Cort knew OCU maintained a better sound lab than the medical examiner, so he contacted Ruel and Pellerin and changed the meeting location. Before he hung up the phone, Terri slipped out of his office with Huitt, ostensibly to pick up the recording for the meeting.

He fully intended to confront Ruel about OCU's involvement in his case. If Belafini was at the heart of it—which Cort suspected more each day—then OCU could provide some inter-departmental cooperation. He wasn't through with Terri yet, either, but he could wait. For a little while, until he could get her alone again. When he did, God help her.

Cort noted the cool reception he received from the OCU chief upon arriving at the sound lab. Ruel was rumored to be an excellent department head but a man who didn't bother to make friends or enemies.

He must have gotten a call from the mayor's office. "Chief. I appreciate you letting us borrow your equipment."

"I'm happy to make it available, Marshal Gamble." Ruel turned to greet Pellerin, and a minute later Terri and Huitt came in with the tape.

Ruel's sound technician examined the cassette. "The tape is a little rippled." He popped it into a player. "It may have some heat damage." He pressed a button and static came over the console's speakers. "Yeah, there you go.

Those pouches don't burn but they heat up, and audiotape is wafer-thin."

"Clean it up if you can, Jim," Ruel said.

Cort watched the technician adjust the console controls before he glanced over at Terri. Huitt was standing beside her, both of them listening as well, and the ME had his hand resting on the desk behind Terri. As Cort watched, Huitt ran his thumb in a circle on the small of her back.

It wasn't obvious, and no one could see it except Cort. Seeing it, however, convinced him that Terri was doing more than simply dating the pathologist.

How far has this thing between them gone? Terri showed no sign of any particular infatuation, but she wasn't the type to put her emotions on display. He had no idea how she felt toward Huitt. The ME's attitude was only too evident; he used any excuse to touch her.

It was none of his business, and he should have felt glad that Terri had someone to make her happy. That didn't get rid of an underlying urge Cort felt, watching Huitt's small, intimate caress. The urge to reach over, grab the other man's hand, and break each and every one of his fingers.

"This message is for Fire Marshal Cortland Gamble," a high, eerie voice said from the speakers.

"He's using a distortion unit," the technician muttered as he put the tape on pause for a few seconds and turned another dial. "Maybe a synthesizer. That's not his voice." He pressed a switch.

"You've been looking for the Torcher, haven't you, Marshal? I'm the one you haven't been able to find." Distant bells rang in the background noise of the tape. "You don't believe me. Some proof would be the remotes. I build them myself. The transceiver components are manufactured by Gold Electronics, and the wiring is shielded fiber-optic."

"Stop the tape," Ruel said to Jim, and then turned to Cort. "Is this information of his relative to the Torcher case?"

"It's correct, but he could be guessing. Gold is the largest components manufacturer in the south, and fiber-optic is standard now." He didn't know if he was trying to convince Ruel or himself, but it sounded reasonable.

The OCU chief nodded. "Restart the tape, Jim."

The voice continued. "Right now you're deciding the components are too common a denominator. Very well, I also used gunpowder and gasoline—such an effective combination—but I did the bar and the girl with kerosene and ammonium nitrate. I wanted more fireworks. More bang for the buck."

Cort closed his eyes for a moment, fighting a surge of outrage. "That's him."

"So now that we've established that I'm the fire-raiser you've been chasing," the voice taunted, "let me also inform you that I did these last two jobs a little differently for a reason. Specifically, so that I could kill the marshal's lovely ladies."

"Jesus Christ," Pellerin muttered, giving Cort an appalled look.

"You need to understand that what you sow, you must also reap," the distorted voice continued. "Both women loved you, Gamble, but you know that. You knew it the whole time you were laying them. You enjoyed their love. You wallowed in it."

"Shut it off," Cort heard Terri say.

"No." He stared blindly at the console. All this time he had figured Belafini as the cause, when all along it had been some nutjob, looking to avenge himself because of something he imagined Cort had done. "Play it through to the end."

"It's harvest time, Gamble. You sowed the seeds of betrayal, and now the fields belong to me. I'm setting them to burn. I'm going to kill everyone you've ever loved. I'm going to take my time and do it slowly. You'll never know who until the fire takes them. It's your turn to suffer the torments of hell." The voice uttered a raw, horrific sound. "Watch me burn them all, Gamble. Watch them die and know that you can do nothing to stop it."

The speakers went silent but for the crackle of distortion, and the technician turned the cassette off after a minute. No one said anything, but everyone was watching Cort. Waiting for Cort to say something.

He said what first came to mind. "I owe you an apology, Detective Vincent."

"Don't." Her eyes were as fierce as her voice. "Not for this. Not ever."

The technician removed the tape and regarded it with visible disgust. "Like burning women at the stake."

"Sick son of a bitch," Pellerin muttered.

"We'd better jump on this," Ruel said. "Jim, I'll need a full transcript and clean audio copies of it right away. Send one over to Psych and Profile for immediate review. I'd like Agent Josephine Edgeway in the Atlanta FBI office to look this over, too. Jo's profiled a lot of serial killers." He turned to Pellerin. "Captain, we'll need protection for the marshal's friends and family."

"We should safeguard his current girlfriend first," Pellerin said. "Marshal, if you'll give me a name and address, I'll send a unit to pick her up."

"That's not necessary," Cort told him. "I'm not seeing anyone." He hadn't touched another woman since he'd been with Terri. He couldn't grab her now and hold on to her, and he wanted to. More than he wanted to admit. "I haven't been with anyone since . . . Ashleigh."

Terri shot him a quick, unreadable look.

"Well, he's evidently gone after two of your exes, so we'll need a list of the others," Ruel said. "Let's go over to my office, I can coordinate things better from there. Dr. Huitt, I'll need a recheck on absolutely everything you recovered along with this tape. Fragments, fibers, hair, anything that could help us identify him."

"I've still got an unidentified Jane Doe," Gray said. "She could be the other woman he refers to in the tape."

"I'll make some calls," Cort said. "It shouldn't take me long."

"Thanks. I'll get back to you if I identify her first." Gray departed.

Once they had moved to Ruel's office, Cort absently accepted a cup of coffee and stared into it. There was no doubt in his mind that the serial arsonist was the Torcher, or that he was completely serious. The voice might have been distorted, but the words rang with utter, lethal intent.

He tried to wrap his mind around the idea that someone would want to kill everyone he had ever loved. The motive had to be more than simple revenge. The killer was both vicious and obsessed beyond all rationality.

"Now that we know you're the target," Ruel was saying to him, "we'll need protection for you as well."

"No." Cort made a bitter sound. "You heard him. He wants to kill everyone I've ever loved, not me. Me, he'll keep alive. At this point, I'm the safest man in the city."

"He might not try to do you at first, but he's heading there. The psych jobs always do." Pellerin sighed. "We need a decoy, but aside from J. D., I don't have an officer who resembles you enough to pass."

Cort shook his head. "My brother is on his honeymoon. He stays out of this."

"Perhaps instead of replacing the marshal, we can take an alternative approach. Use the target already specified by the killer and put a female officer in place. Someone who is already known as a family friend"—Ruel turned to Terri—"and who can pose as the new woman in his life."

Terri's composure never slipped an inch. "Not me."

"Not her," Cort said at the same time.

Ruel lifted one dark brow. "Terri, you're the logical choice."

"Chief, you want anyone but me for this duty." Her voice went flat. *"Anyone."*

"I disagree," Pellerin said. "We can't risk having any civilians near Marshal Gamble. You can provide protection and help draw this screwy bastard out into the open."

"It's too dangerous," Cort said at once. "He's already admitted to killing twice. Any woman close to me is going to be risking her life on a daily basis."

"That's what a cop does, Marshal," the Homicide Chief told him. "Terri's an experienced officer and knows how to handle herself."

"With all due respect, sir, I can't handle this one," Terri

said. At Pellerin's blank look, she added, "No one is going to buy me being the marshal's new girlfriend."

Ruel frowned and said what Cort was thinking. "Why not?"

Terri uttered a short laugh. "Well, for one thing, I'm not a deb." Ruel and Pellerin gave her blank looks. "I can't pass for the kind of woman the marshal usually, uh, dates."

Cort didn't miss the quick word change she'd made. Is that what she thought? That he went to bed with every woman he dated? *Of course she did.* She'd said as much before, when she'd accused him of screwing half the women in the city. She probably thought he preferred to skip the date and simply take a woman to bed.

He wouldn't defend himself. He couldn't. Because no matter how he had behaved with every other woman in his life, that was exactly what he'd done to Terri.

"We have to use an undercover officer, and you're already involved in the case. You're well known as his brother's partner. There's no time to set up another female for the duty." Pellerin sounded adamant.

"You'll need to be more than a casual girlfriend," Ruel said, his expression growing thoughtful. "If the Torcher thinks you're deeply involved, that would make him play moth to the flame."

"How involved?" Terri almost choked on the final word.

Ruel shrugged. "Lovers, at the very least. Maybe you could fake an engagement."

Cort wasn't going to use Terri as a body shield and he certainly wasn't presenting her to anyone as his fiancée. "The Torcher will know it's a setup. He sent the tape so I would know who he was targeting, and why. He'll expect a decoy."

"So, we leak to the press that the tape was destroyed during the gas-tank explosion," was Pellerin's solution. "We publicly admit that all we got were pieces and no way to recover what was on it."

"In the meantime, you two can capitalize on what happened at the car fire," Ruel added. "Terri was filmed offering you comfort at the time—"

"Excuse me?" She looked appalled. "I was *briefing* the marshal on the incident, not throwing myself all over him."

"I have no doubt that you were, but the different spin will convince the perp that you were involved before we ever recovered the tape," Ruel said. "In the event he doesn't believe it was destroyed."

"What do you expect me to do?" Terri demanded. "Sit on his lap and whisper shit in his ear during the morning briefings?"

"That would do no good; the briefings are closed. The relationship will have to be played out on your own personal time. It needs to be open and very public." Ruel thought for a moment. "The marshal attends numerous social functions; the papers ran a photo of him with the Bouchard girl yesterday. Terri, you'll have to be seen out with him at every event for the next week. You make the rounds and act like new lovers. Make sure you're photographed. If the Torcher doesn't crawl out of the woodwork by the end of the month, you announce your engagement in the papers."

"This won't work. Not with him." Terri flung a hand toward Cort. "No one is going to believe that a man like *him* is marrying someone like *me*."

"Then I suggest you find a way to make it work, Vincent," Pellerin told her, "because if you don't, other innocent women are going to burn."

Terri waited until Pellerin and Cort left Ruel's office before she confronted her boss about her new assignment.

She didn't bother to mince words this time. "You might as well start filling out the suspension papers on me now, Chief, because I'm not doing this."

Ruel didn't seem angry or surprised. "I understand your hesitation, Terri, but you have to see how ideal this is for our investigation. You can't get any closer to Gamble than posing as his fiancée."

Actually, I've been a lot closer to him. Butt-naked-and-sweaty closer. "You obviously haven't met any of the marshal's women."

"Women are women." He arched one dark brow. "I think you're reaching for an excuse."

"You don't understand. Marshal Gamble is a member of a very prominent society family as well as one of the most eligible bachelors in the city. Ashleigh Bouchard, you saw her photo, right?"

"She was a beautiful woman."

"Yeah, and they're all like that." She made a broad gesture. "Young, gorgeous, loaded, and with designer wardrobes the size of Nebraska."

He inclined his head. "Gamble has excellent taste."

"Bingo. Now, look at me." She turned around slowly to give him a three-sixty. "We'll agree that I'm not any of that. I don't own a dress or a single skirt. Off duty, I hang out in bars, target-shoot, sail, and fish. The only thing I have in common with those women is the same plumbing, and most of that"—she tugged at the front of her jacket—"doesn't measure up to the marshal's standards, either."

"I still don't see the problem." He made a negligent gesture. "We'll fix you up with the right clothes. You can have your hair and makeup done. Stuff your bra, if you have to."

"Oh yeah, there's a thought." She sighed. "Chief, you've got to let me out of this."

"I can't, Terri. Being Gamble's fiancée will give you access to his personal life, which you didn't have before. If he's on the mob's payroll, you'll be in the perfect position to secure evidence." Ruel eyed her. "You really don't own a dress or skirt?"

"No, I don't. And before you ask,"—she held up a hand—"I'm not a dyke. I dress for the job, not for glamour. It's a little hard to run after a fleeing suspect when you're in a dress and pumps."

The side of his mouth curled. "Remind me to introduce you to Jo Edgeway the next time she's in town. She's five-four and maybe weighs a hundred pounds. I've seen her take down a six-foot-five, two-hundred-fifty-pound bond jumper with a two-minute head start while she was in stiletto heels and a pencil skirt. *Without* firing a shot."

"See? That's the kind of woman you want to assign to

this gig. I know plenty of female officers over in Vice who—"

"No, Terri. I want you next to Gamble. Whatever you have to do in order to make yourself presentable, I'll approve the expense vouchers." His phone rang. "I need to take this. I want daily progress reports from here on out."

She headed for the door.

"Terri." He waited until she looked back at him. "Watch yourself."

"Watch me make a total jackass out of myself, more like," she muttered as she stalked down the hallway.

"Detective," a dour male voice called out from behind her.

"Now for Act Two of our comedic farce. The Reluctant Bride Faces the Unwilling Groom. Sparks fly." She turned around to see Cort headed her way. "Marshal Gamble." When he reached her, she produced a bland smile. "Or should I start calling you *honey* now?"

"In here." He took her arm and guided her into an office, where a secretary was making photocopies on an immense machine. "Would you excuse us, please?"

The secretary gave Terri an uncertain look before she edged around them and left the room. When she was gone, Cort released his grip on her arm and went over to flip the lock on the door.

"I'm not going to make a break for it," she said. The way he was looking at her made her add, "Am I?"

He leaned against the door and pushed his hands into his trouser pockets. "You have any vacation time saved up?"

That wasn't the question she was expecting. She'd been waiting for *Are you mentally ill?* or *How soon can you resign from the force?*

"Three weeks." She pushed her hands into her trouser pockets. "He won't let me take it."

"Ruel."

She nodded. "And Pellerin. They're like a tag team now." Cort swore under his breath. "Hey, I don't like it any more than you do."

"I doubt that." The glare he gave her was diamond-hard.

"Rest assured, Marshal, it's not going to take that long for me to fuck up." She personally gave herself forty-eight hours, tops. "When I do, Ruel will pull me off and assign someone else to be the love of your life, and we can go our separate ways, happy at last."

"It's just another joke to you, isn't it?" He came across the room so fast she bumped into the copy machine out of reaction. "One more hilarious story to tell the boys over a beer and a game of pool at the roadhouse."

He was angry, but under it, he was hurting. After what they'd heard on that tape, who could blame him?

"What happened to Ashleigh and this other woman was not a joke. This *guy* is not a joke." She put a hand on his arm without thinking about it. Beneath her fingers, his muscles tensed. "I can't imagine how you feel, but I would never make fun of it. Or you."

He stared down at her hand so hard that she snatched it back. "No."

Terri frowned. No, he didn't believe her, or no, he did? This was pitiful. Here was the man she loved and she couldn't even figure out what he meant.

She needed him to tell her, though. She needed that, big time. "What do you want me to do, Cort? If I can, I'll do whatever you say."

His head snapped up. "No, you won't," he told her, his voice raw. "You'll love this. The same way you loved shoving Huitt in my face."   .

She was confused again. "I didn't shove Gray—"

He yanked her up against him, so hard and sudden that it nearly knocked the breath out of her. "I want you out of my life," he said through clenched teeth. "Out of my head."

"Quit trying to fracture the bones in my arms, and I'll—"

Before she could utter another syllable, he seized the handful of hair she'd clipped up off her neck, angled her face up, and brought his head down.

The copy machine rocked behind her and bounced into the wall.

Cort had his mouth on hers, but he wasn't kissing her. Kissing was sweet and tender and pleasant; this was hot and angry and wet and hungry. His tongue was in her mouth, his fingers were in her hair, and his thigh was between her legs. It felt like the rest of him was all over her, plastering her on him like a poultice over a wound.

Terri hung on, telling herself it was still okay. Cort was simply reacting to the horror of Ashleigh's death and the obscene threats made by the killer. He'd just been through hell, and the man needed an outlet. *Let him get out his frustrations, and then he'll apologize and it'll be over.*

Except he wasn't the only one in that condition.

Heat kicked in, shut off her brain, and started working its way down her body. Her skin flushed, so suddenly and so hard that she shivered uncontrollably. Her breasts turned to hard, aching stone that want only to embed themselves in his chest. Her clothes felt heavy, smothering; like an elaborate straitjacket. Her thighs became shaky and everything beneath them simply disappeared. Between them, the crotch of her panties was suddenly and instantly soaked.

He might be hurting, but what he was doing to her mouth redefined oral sex.

Her knees buckled, and she grabbed handfuls of his shirt to steady herself. What had started angry was now snowballing into greedy, clothes-ripping sexual starvation. Somehow she had to get him off her before she lost it and one of their bosses walked in and found them going at it on top of the copy machine.

She tried to say *stop* without moaning it. And failed. Still, he heard the strangled sound and broke off the kiss.

Being an inch from his face wasn't helping. In fact, it was going to make her cave.

"Don't think." He bent again and settled his mouth over hers, not as hard or roughly now. His hands splayed over her hips as he moved and pressed her with the same steady rhythm with which he was kissing her. She let him do what he wanted, but she didn't participate. He lifted his mouth again, long enough to mutter, "Give it to me."

Terri caved.

She gave it to him, gave it with interest. Her tongue was in his mouth, her fingers in his hair, her leg wrapped around his. She had to go up on her toes to rub the tight, shrieking knot of her clit against the long curved ridge of his confined cock, the one he'd been grinding into her belly and was now sliding up and down.

One last shred of sanity tried to reason with her. This was Cort, the man she loved. The man who had occupied more fantasies and daydreams than she could count. The man for whom she had shed far too many bitter, impotent tears. He was also the cultured, privileged son of Creole society. The one man who didn't want her, was ashamed of her, and had done everything but use a stick to drive her away.

Terri's body didn't care. It had been kept in convent mode since the last time he'd touched her, and now he was touching her, and it wanted payback. Major payback. In fact, if he didn't tear off her clothes and spread her legs and put the long, thick, stupendous erection to work where she needed it within the next ten seconds, she was pretty sure that she was going to shove him to the floor and take care of business.

The longing and wanting and hungering hadn't gone away. It hadn't gotten better since February. It had gotten worse. It had gone nuclear.

He wrenched his head back and stared down at her. There were twin washes of red color blazing over the top of his cheekbones, and sweat ran like tears over them. His chest worked against her breasts, swelling with each ragged breath. And in his eyes, the same horrified sexual shock she suspected was in hers.

How can I want you like this?

He eased away from her in slow, careful degrees, as if a sudden move might make one or both of them explode. He untangled his fingers from her hair and took his hand from the back of her head. He lowered the leg she had been riding and dropped his arms.

Finally they weren't touching, and she could breathe again. She still couldn't see straight and her ears were literally ringing, so she concentrated on taking in oxygen. She'd actually been in brawls that had been kinder to her body.

"Say something." His voice was shaky, hoarse.

"Can't." The way she was breathing, if she'd felt afraid she'd have called it a panic attack. But she wasn't afraid. She was ready to jump him. She *would* jump him, if he didn't get the hell away from her. "Move."

He moved, taking the heat with him. Terri wrapped her arms around herself as she leaned against the copy machine and shuddered. She'd never felt anything like this; it was as if he'd set her on fire and then put out the flames by dropping her in an ice machine. Unbearable desire, instant freeze-out. How could anyone live with something like this? How could she?

"Look at me."

She looked. He was standing at the door, his hands clenched at his sides, his face tired and drawn. Of course it was, he'd just put a lot of effort into that—whatever *that* had been.

One thing for damn sure she knew, it hadn't been love. "Go."

"Therese—"

"Get out of here!" she shouted.

Cort unlocked the door and left without another word. On his way out he passed the secretary who had been making copies, who came in and stopped short when she saw Terri.

"Ma'am, are you all right?"

"Fine. I'm fine." No, she wasn't. Terri ran a hand over her face and stared at her wet palm. "Is there a back way out of this place?"

"Through there. The first right goes to the employee parking lot." The secretary nodded toward the opposite door. "Are you sure you're okay?" When Terri nodded, the woman looked over her shoulder as if expecting to see Cort come charging back in. "Who was that man?"

"I don't know anymore." She ran.

Elizabet and Louis already knew about Ashleigh Bouchard's murder by the time Cort made it home that night. The tragedy shocked them, but perhaps not as much as it might have before what they had all endured in the aftermath of Marc LeClare's death at the hands of his wife.

Creole society had its fair share of scandals, but discovering that Laure LeClare, one of their oldest friends, was a cold-blooded killer had turned his parents' world upside down. They had not been the same since.

Dinner was a silent affair, after which the Gambles' housekeeper, Mae Wallace, served coffee and cognac for the three of them in the sitting room.

For once Elizabet didn't nag her husband about his drinking. "I can't believe it," she said in a hollow voice. "Ashleigh was a lovely young woman. She never did anything to harm anyone. How could this happen to her?"

"There's more." Cort told them about the tape left in Ashleigh's car, and that the unidentified victim from Maskers was possibly a woman he had been involved with.

"Father in Heaven." Elizabet turned white. "Have you called our friends?"

"I've called everyone I've dated for the last year," Cort assured her. "No one has turned missing yet. It may be someone from the past."

"He means to kill every woman you have loved?" His father, who until now had been quiet, got to his feet. "This is madness." He began to pace. "*Ce sont des conneries. Je n'y crois pas!* What are the police doing to stop this pig?"

"They're going to put the women I've been dating into protective custody. They'll provide security for you and Mother as well." Cort hesitated. "J. D.'s partner will be with me until we catch him."

"J. D.'s partner?" Elizabet frowned. She had never been very fond of Terri Vincent. "Why will she be with you?"

"She's going to pose as my fiancée." He explained Ruel's plan for him to escort Terri around town and make their relationship very public. "I thought I would escort her to Ashleigh's memorial service, then to dinner and a few other places before we make an announcement."

Elizabet digested this for a moment. "You intend to tell people that you are marrying J. D.'s partner?"

"Yeah." He could hear the disapproval in his mother's tone. "It's only to deceive the killer. After we make an arrest, we can end the pretense."

"You would use Terri like this? Like a walking target?" Louie sounded aghast.

"She's a trained police officer, Dad. She knows what she's doing." Cort hoped.

"This is—this is—I have to go and cook something." His father stomped out of the room.

Elizabet rose and came over to sit beside Cort. "I know this is official business and none of mine, but Cortland, no one is going to believe you would . . . be with Detective Vincent."

Terri's reluctance had stung his pride. His mother's perplexed him. "Why not?"

"She is not one of us, and from what I've observed, she's not very . . . refined." Elizabet made a vague gesture. "The first time you appear in public with her, she'll make some gaffe which will be written up in every society column from here to Savannah. Perhaps you should request someone else. Someone at least familiar with the demands of society."

He thought of the women he had dated over the last year. There hadn't been many, and none after Terri, but there had been enough. He had been photographed and seen dancing with even more women, women he had not been personally involved with. For the first time he realized just how many people were in danger.

He didn't want Terri in the line of fire—or anywhere near him, after what had happened between them in the copy room—but Pellerin was right. She could handle herself. "I have to do this, Mother. Terri knows how to do her job and she won't take any chances. I can't risk anyone else dying the way Ashleigh did."

"I understand, Cortland, and I sympathize, but consider what you are asking Detective Vincent to do. She would have to change literally everything about herself, including her speech and mannerisms."

Cort regarded her. "You could help her with that. Terri's going to need someone's guidance, and I don't think she has any female friends to give her advice."

"I doubt Detective Vincent would appreciate advice from me, but I will do what I can." The sound of pots rattling in the distance made Elizabet rise from the sofa. "We should go see what your father is doing in the kitchen, or we will soon be served with a seven-course late-night snack."

Cort went with her to the kitchen, where Louie was working at the stove. His father was sautéing snails in garlic and butter.

"You cannot eat those, Louie," Elizabet said sternly. "They give you terrible heartburn."

He flipped the snails with an expert jerk of one wrist. "*I* am cooking them. *You* are going to eat them." He looked sideways at Cort. "Has anyone asked Terri how she feels about this ruse of yours?"

"She wasn't happy about it, but she agreed to take the assignment." For reasons he still couldn't fathom. At first he'd thought she had been giving up a token protest and was delighted by the prospect of humiliating him. But after the meeting, she had been very convincing. She didn't want this any more than he did.

"I am calling her," Louie said as he removed the pan from the stovetop. He picked up the address book, went to the wall phone, and dialed. "Hello, Terri? It is Louie, *cherie*. You are working tomorrow? No? *Bien.* Come to the house for brunch at eleven and we will talk." He listened for a moment and glowered at Cort. "He does not like it, he will not eat. *Merci, cherie.* Until then." He hung up.

Cort caught his mother's angry gaze. "We need to take the phone out of the kitchen."

9

Terri parked on the street in front of the Gambles' home. The gate to the driveway was flanked by two uniformed officers, and a black-and-white unit sat at the end of the block. She checked her watch, saw that it was past eleven, and swore. She knew she shouldn't have changed her clothes three times.

"Come over, have brunch, we'll talk," she muttered in a falsetto as she took off her helmet and strapped it to the back of her bike. "Yeah, this ought to be cute."

One of the uniforms nodded to her as she approached the gate. "Good morning, Detective."

She checked his name tag. "Officer Schwinder." She waited, but he said nothing and made no move to stop her. "Do you know me?"

"Got an American Express card?" he joked. When she didn't laugh, he nodded toward the other officer, who was writing on a clipboard. "We were told a detective would be stopping by the house. You're expected."

"But you really don't know if I'm a detective or a killer in drag, do you?" She felt like clocking him as he gave her a blank look. "I don't care if Santa Claus's name is on the approved list, and a big fat bearded man in a red suit shows up, you ask for some fucking ID."

With a sheepish look he took her billfold, checked her badge and license, and handed it back to her. "Sorry, ma'am."

"Get your shit together." She stalked past him. "And don't call me *ma'am.*"

The Gambles' mansion was one of the oldest and most elaborate in the Garden District. J. D. had told her that it had been built by some famous New Orleans architect in the nineteenth century, but she couldn't remember the details. Cort had given her grief about that once, but to her houses were a place to sleep and keep a change of clothes.

A slim black woman in a dove-gray dress opened the door and smiled. "Good morning, Detective Vincent."

"That remains to be seen, Mrs. Wallace." Terri grimaced. "I'm here for brunch, apparently. You might want to save Mrs. Gamble some chest pains and throw a drop cloth under the dining-room table."

"I'm sure that won't be necessary," Mae said as she led her into the house. In a lower voice, she added, "The carpet is stain-protected."

Terri laughed. "Good." She put a hand out and stopped the housekeeper before they left the foyer. "Mae, can I ask you some questions?"

"Of course."

"Cort moved in here in December, didn't he?" When the other woman nodded, she asked, "Has anyone unusual come here to see him while he's been staying with his folks?"

Mae frowned. "I don't know what you mean by unusual."

"Anyone you and the Gambles don't know personally?" The housekeeper shook her head. "What about phone calls? Anyone strange call in the middle of the night, or call to check and see if he's home? Any hang-up calls?"

"Evan called at two a.m. to tell the family about Jamie's birth," Mae said, "but there have been no other unusual calls. Does this have to do with that killer who has made these terrible threats against Mr. Cortland?"

"Yes." It was partly true. "Cort's probably told you this already, but it would be a good idea to be careful with phone calls and visitors until we can make an arrest."

"I will." The housekeeper smiled. "I'm glad to know you are watching out for him, Detective."

If only Mae knew. "Just doing my job."

When Terri entered the family dining room, Cort's father rose and hurried over to give her a kiss on both cheeks. "You look tired. You look skinny."

"I *am* tired and skinny." Over his shoulder, she gave Elizabet a polite smile. "Morning, Mrs. Gamble."

"Terri. It was good of you to join us on such short notice." Elizabet gestured to the empty chair opposite her own. "Please, sit down."

"Thanks." She'd been to one party at the Gambles' home, and had eaten a number of times at Louie's restaurant, Krewe of Louis, but she had never actually sat down to a meal with Elizabet. J. D. had invited her for dinner with the family plenty of times, but she had always found an excuse to wriggle out of it.

She loved Louie, and J. D. was her best friend, but Cort's mother made her almost as nervous as Cort did.

Terri took a seat at the table and noted the extra empty place setting beside hers. It was better than trying to figure out what all the forks were for. "Is the marshal here?"

"He is on the phone in his office, as always. He lives for the phone." Louie filled an enormous glass with orange juice and set it by her hand. "You like crepes, yes? I have made four kinds: sausage, asparagus, ham and cheese. I kept them warm for you."

Which reminded her. She looked across the table at Elizabet. "I'm sorry I'm late. Traffic was a real bi—bear." Cort's mother didn't reply, so she glanced at Mae, who was standing waiting to serve her. "You know, I usually just have a cup of coffee in the morning. That holds me until lunchtime."

"This is brunch. Half lunch." Louie took the serving platter from Mae and piled four huge crepes on her plate. "Eat."

"Holy Toledo." She surveyed the mound. "Louie, they look great, but I'm skinny, not hollow."

"You won't be either after these. Elizabet, talk to her while I go and cut the phone line to our son's room." Louie left.

Terri took a sip of the orange juice before she noticed the linen napkin arranged like a flower beside the plate. It matched the real flowers in the centerpiece between her and Cort's mother, so maybe she wasn't supposed to use it.

"It's delightful to see you, Terri," Elizabet said.

Delightful? "Same here," she lied.

"I can't recall the last time we had the opportunity to chat."

"I guess it's been a while." *Chat? With you? Never in my lifetime, lady.* Now what was she supposed to say? "Have you heard from J. D. and Sable, Mrs. Gamble?"

"Jean-Delano called last week before he and Isabel went on an island cruise. They're having a lovely time." Elizabet's smile wavered. "I don't know how I'm going to tell him about Ashleigh."

"I wouldn't get into too many details. It was pretty awful." She picked up a fork, noticed it wasn't the same size as the one Elizabet was using, and put it back down.

"The news coverage was horrific. It was on every station." Elizabet gave a ladylike shudder.

"The press tends to be a pack of vultures." It was nice that Cort's mother was making the effort to be civil. Most of the time Terri felt that she could never talk openly to the other woman, but she hadn't exactly tried, either. "I'm just glad they got her body out of there before the press showed up. Those reporters will film anything." *Oh, great, Terri. Why don't you describe the condition of the remains for her?*

The older woman set down her coffee cup. "Yes, I imagine that they do. How is the investigation progressing?"

"We're working our ass—our butts off." She found what she hopes was the right fork and used it to cut off a corner of one crepe. "Sorry."

Elizabet cleared her throat. "Mayor Jarden seems to be very interested in providing aid to the investigation."

"Don't believe everything you see on TV; the mayor is being a jerk. He screwed up a lot of people's caseloads by demanding we form this community-response team. Still, we got some decent investigators out of it, and everyone's pulling together." She slid the crepe into her mouth before she added, "We'll nail this son—uh, arsonist, Mrs. Gamble."

"I see." Elizabet sat back in her chair. "Cortland tells us

that you're going to act the part of his fiancée so that no other women are harmed."

"That's the idea." Terri drank more of the juice and caught a stray drop from her bottom lip with her tongue. "Not sure how that's going to go." She did, but *a total fuckup* wasn't something that you said to Elizabet Gamble, even when you were trying to be friendly and open.

"Do you understand exactly what posing as Cortland's fiancée will entail?"

"You mean, me acting like a society chick? I tried to tell my boss no, but he blew me off." She shrugged and took another bite of the crepe. "We'll give it a shot, see what happens. Although to be honest, I haven't worn a dress since Mama made the one for my high-school graduation. That one was pink and had lace." She started to make a rude sound, and then caught herself. "Sorry. I hate dresses, and I *really* hate pink."

"I can see that you do. May I be frank with you for a moment, Terri?" When she nodded, Elizabet continued, "I don't want to seem overly critical, but in this situation with my son, your manners are a cause for serious concern."

She frowned. "What's wrong with my manners?"

"You don't have any."

"I remembered to say please and thank you, didn't I?" Sometimes she forgot, and Jeneane often rode her about it.

"It's not your speech, dear. Not entirely." Elizabet gestured toward her napkin. "For example, it's standard etiquette to place your napkin in your lap before you eat or drink."

"Oh. Sorry." Terri grabbed the napkin and, after figuring out how to unfold it, draped it over her lap. She made a face. "I didn't know that one."

"Yes. I know you didn't. The same way you didn't know which fork to use. It's the largest one near your left hand."

She'd almost grabbed that one before. "Okay."

"Also, if you must make a sound to describe your feelings, it's best not to imitate flatulence. Not while people are eating. It makes them sick."

"Right." Terri gritted her teeth. "Is there more?"

"Again, I don't wish to appear overly critical—"

"We've gone this far and I haven't started bawling yet, Mrs. G." She made the corners of her mouth bend up. "Knock yourself out."

"Well, you swear like a truck driver, even when you're making ordinary conversation, and you speak of topics which are completely inappropriate for the table."

"Like dead bodies."

"Yes." Elizabet gave her a pained smile. "The swearing is particularly offensive. I realize police officers are exposed to it on a daily basis, but in society, we don't use that kind of language."

"Damn. I mean, right. Okay."

"We ladies don't use that kind of language *at all*."

She stiffened. "I'll watch my mouth."

"So will other people, and when you talk it's almost always full of food. In polite company, you either chew and swallow, or you talk. Never do both at the same time." Elizabet looked her over. "Your appearance is on the same level as your table manners."

Terri had checked her blouse before she'd put it on this morning. It was a little wrinkled—they all were—but it had smelled clean. She resisted the urge to sniff and double-check.

"I'll get some better clothes." When Elizabet's expression didn't change, she tacked on, "And an iron."

"Clothes aren't the only issue." The elegant hand gestured again. "When was the last time you brushed your hair or had your eyebrows waxed? Put on lipstick? Do you even *own* any perfume?"

"My helmet always messes up my hair. I don't do makeup or perfume." She touched her forehead. "Why would I put wax on my eyebrows?"

"Not on them, to—" Elizabet drew in and let out a long breath. "This is exactly my point. You don't know enough to know what you're doing wrong."

"I can learn." Terri imagined people laughing at Cort because of some stupid shit that she did in public. No way was she letting that happen.

"This is rather a lot to assimilate in such a short period of time." Cort's mother smiled again, this time with a little more force. "Perhaps someone else could fill in."

Someone else meant anyone but Terri.

"I'll go to a beauty salon," she said, grimly determined now. "They can trowel on the cosmetics and the eyebrow wax. What else do I need?"

"It's not something I can so easily describe," Elizabet said. "Creole girls are very refined young women. They're raised to know how to talk and what to say. It's a natural part of their character."

Terri didn't like hearing that. "While Cajun girls are better off sticking to the swamp."

"I thought that once, but my daughter-in-law taught me differently." A look of sympathy replaced the indignation on the older woman's face. "I am sorry to be the one to say these things to you. I've been told that you're an excellent homicide detective. J. D. has always enjoyed having you as his partner at work, and of course he's very fond of you."

She was too polite to say it, but Terri could fill in the blanks. *You're a great cop, an okay buddy, but as a woman you're a disaster.* It had to be the same way that Cort felt, minus the uncontrollable sex-on-copy-machines thing.

This is hopeless.

"If you'll excuse me, I'll go and see what's keeping Cortland and Louie." Elizabet left the dining room.

"Dr. Huitt, forensics just came back with the metals test on the two lumps found in the Bouchard vehicle," Lawrence said from the doorway. "They're both pure twenty-four-karat gold."

"Call that over to OCU Chief Ruel for me, will you?" Gray didn't look up from the toxicology report he was studying. The lab slips spread out all over his desk were all parts of the puzzle, but try as he might, he couldn't piece together what they represented. What they were doing was giving him a damn headache.

"Uh, Doc, I finished all the dental comparisons, but we still need a cause of death on Jane Doe Four." His technician brought the victim's case file to him. "Jen is waiting to type up the certificate."

The lab slips that were bedeviling him belonged to Jane Doe Four. "Tell her that she'll have to wait on that one for now." Gray rose and walked past Lawrence into the central examination room. "I'm not done with the remains, and we're still trying to ID her."

Lawrence trotted after him. "But, Doctor, I thought the COD was pretty obvious." When Gray glanced back at him, he grimaced. "I mean, one look at her and you know that she burned to death."

"Never assume anything based on appearance." Gray gowned and gloved before he removed Jane Doe Four's remains from body storage and wheeled her over to an exam table. "Particularly with burned bodies. Fire destroys evidence."

"Evidence of what?"

"An underlying cause of death." Gray took a biopsy needle and slid it into the least burned portion of the torso, a section between her left third and fourth ribs. Carefully he drew out measured samples of blood, tissue, and fluid, which he transferred to a sterile container. Then he hunted for a hair sample. "Reese sent back her labs and Jane's blood is a nightmare. Low red-cell count, practically no white cells to speak of. She was carrying at least two major bacterial infections."

"Leukemia?"

"No abnormal leukocytes. None of the signs of blood disease." He labeled the sample containers. "Her pH screen came back showing a high level of an unidentified alkaloid."

"Poison?" Lawrence asked.

"Most poisons show as either highly acidic or alkaline on the pH, so it's a possibility." Her blood work didn't match the profile of a classic poisoning victim either, however, and the inconsistencies were starting to get on Gray's nerves.

"If the killer poisoned her, he might have set the fire at the bar to destroy the body." His technician, who was a big fan of mysteries, sounded excited now.

The killer's voice from the tape echoed in Gray's head. "No, we're fairly sure he had another motive." While he didn't like Gamble much, it was impossible not to feel sorry for the poor bastard. "I'm going over to talk to Reese. Hold down the fort."

Gray took the sample over to the lab. When he had taken over as medical examiner, he had insisted on updating Pathology's analytical systems and equipment, and had requisitioned equipment for measuring atomic absorption and analyzing gas chromatography/mass spectrophotometry, including what he thought of as his personal baby, a prototype supercritical fluid chromatographer.

The city manager had thrown a tantrum until Gray eliminated all the special subcontracted testing that had been done prior to the purchase of the equipment. Within the first six months, the money saved on outside services had covered the cost of the equipment.

Gray had hired his lab chief, Reese Arceneaux, because of his expertise with the new equipment. The fact that the chemist was also the best squash player he'd ever faced on a court helped keep him in shape; the two men had a standing morning match twice a week.

"Reese?" The lab was empty except for the hum of a centrifuge. "Where are you?"

The lab chief emerged from a back room. As tall as Gray but leaner, Reese flaunted the vivid red hair of his Scots ancestors by wearing it long, in a ponytail, paired with a full beard and mustache. His sleeves were rolled back, showing half of the twin black dragon tattoos he sported on the inside of each arm. "You bellowed?"

Gray passed him the biopsy container. "I need a rework, or if you know, tell me why a woman in her late twenties has enough alkaloid in her bloodstream to kill a horse but dies in a fire."

"It wasn't bad luck, I can tell you that." Reese read the name Gray had written on the container label. "Jane Doe Four, yeah, I remember her. How soon you need the rework?"

"Yesterday." He frowned. "You do the initial screen yourself?"

"Paula did. She asked me to have a look," he said, referring to one of his lab techs. "She'd never seen that combo of results; neither have I. I can tell you that whatever the alkaloid was, it was present in the blood, tissue, and bone. Nothing in the hair follicles."

"So she wasn't poisoned slowly." In such cases, traces of the poison almost always showed up in the hair.

"You say she was maybe in her late twenties?" When Gray nodded, he whistled. "Her hormone level was through the roof too. You generally only see that in certain types of glandular disorders and fifty- and sixty-year-old women on estrogen-replacement therapy."

Gray felt his headache swell. "If she was being poisoned with an alkaloid, what kind of symptoms would she have displayed?"

"Obvious ones. She'd have constant nausea, puke a lot, bring up some blood. Alkaloid poisons are hard on the gastrointestinal system and mucus membranes." Reese set the container aside. "You find any mouth sores?"

Gray thought for a moment. "Her membranes were pretty crispy, but I found two existing cankers on the inside of her lips. Her teeth were etched on the inside surfaces, too."

"That's pretty typical of poisoning." Reese nodded. "The stomach acid eats up the mouth."

Gray sighed. "I don't know. The body shows signs of long-term malnourishment, so she could have been bulimic."

"Well, you saw her blood count. Doesn't explain the hormone level, though." He scratched the side of his beard. "What do her organs look like?"

"I haven't cut into her. She was one of the vics from that bar fire, and I was hoping to ID her first." Gray's eyes narrowed. "What about the organs?"

"I'm thinking I need to run this through the chromatographer and nail down this alkaloid before I tell you to hack her up," Reese said. "I can have it for you in a couple of hours. If you do ID her in the meantime, check with her family practitioner; see if she came in complaining of allergies or the flu. A lot of time poison cases are misdiagnosed that way. And call her OB, if she had one. She might have been going through premature menopause."

"I'll check with Missing Persons again. Call me as soon as you've got results." Gray headed back to his office, but stopped to put away Jane Doe Four's remains.

The first time his instructor had wheeled out a dead body, Gray hadn't gotten sick like the other interns. He only felt a terrible pity, and a fierce sense of protectiveness. Death left no dignity behind, and as a pathologist, he was the only one left to provide it.

The only dignity he could give Jane was in discovering who she was, why she had lost her life, and, if someone else was responsible for that, providing the means to punish them for it.

"I'll find the answers, pretty lady," he said as he closed the stainless-steel door to the refrigerated compartment in which she rested. "I swear I will."

Cort finished his phone call to Sally, who still sounded distressed but insisted she was better off working, and heard his parents arguing in low voices in the hall outside his home office. Probably over Terri, whose motorcycle he'd heard arrive twenty minutes before. He considered bolting the door, but Louie would simply hammer on it until he came out. And as much as he would have liked to avoid Terri, leaving her in his parents' clutches likely qualified as cruel and unusual punishment.

He really, really needed to get his own place, and soon, he thought as he walked out to join them. "You two need a referee?"

"Your mother is on her high horse again." Louie glowered at his wife. "She is riding sidesaddle, like a proper lady."

"While your father is doing his excellent imitation of a jackass." His mother folded her arms. "As usual."

"She is a good woman, Elizabet." Louie wagged his finger at her. "You refuse to see that."

Elizabet sniffed. "Prove to me that she *is* a woman first."

"I take it Terri's here," Cort said.

"Yes, she is. If you wish to speak to her, just follow the sound of open-mouthed chewing. I am going to call Ashleigh's parents and find out what time her memorial service begins." His mother stalked away.

Cort saw the look in his father's eye. "You know better than to get on Mom's back again. The last time you did, she almost divorced you."

"That has been the story since the night we met." Louie made a rude gesture. "Come. She has made Terri unhappy."

"What did she do?" Cort asked as he followed his father to the dining room.

"She was trying to be helpful, and you know how your mother is when she tries. Poor Therese will need a tranquilizer now. I do." Louie nearly bumped into the subject of their conversation as he opened the dining-room door. "Ah, *cherie,* there you are."

Cort took in her rumpled appearance with a single glance. That in part explained why his mother had been so upset. "Detective."

"Marshal."

Louie's gaze went from the keys in her hand to the table behind her. "You cannot leave yet. You have not finished your crepes."

"That would take me a good month, I think." Terri gave him a crooked smile before looking at Cort. "Marshal, would you tell your mother that I appreciate her advice? I'll use it to convince Chief Ruel to have someone else assigned to you as soon as possible."

Cort heard the defeat in her voice, and it infuriated him. "That won't be necessary."

"Your mother said—" Terri lifted a hand and dropped it. "Look, she knows about this society-chick stuff, and she reminded me that I really don't. Let's call it quits now before you and I end up on some embarrassing reality TV show."

"My mother is wrong."

Her expression went from surprise to wariness. "Why are you suddenly my cheerleader?"

"Because if he is not, I will thrash him," Louie told her,

and put his arm around her narrow shoulders. "Of course you can do this, *cherie*. You only need a little coaching, that is all."

"Coaching." She dragged a hand through her hair. "I don't think there are tutors for this kind of thing."

Cort saw his father smile broadly. "Ah, but there is."

10

Terri didn't want to leave her motorcycle behind at the Gambles', and she definitely didn't want to be alone with Cort, so she refused his offer of a ride and instead followed him to Alexandre Moreau's downtown office. She had an easier time parking than he did—one reason she loved her bike—and waited in front of the office while Cort found a space for his SUV.

She took out a cigarette and lit it before examining Moreau's two big front display windows. "Some fix-it shop."

The photographs artfully arranged in the windows showed scenes from a dozen different social events: weddings, birthday parties, christenings, and formal dances. Everything depicted was grand, and everyone smiling at the camera looked like a well-paid model. Someone had painted a quote in black-and-gold calligraphy on the molding above his front entrance: ETIQUETTE REQUIRES US TO ADMIRE THE HUMAN RACE, and beneath that, MARK TWAIN.

"Well, that kills it for me," she muttered. As she spotted Cort walking toward her, she squared her shoulders. "This guy is, what again? Like Queer Eye for the Society Chick?"

"Andre is not gay." He plucked the cigarette from her fingers, dropped it, and ground it out under his shoe. "He is, however, one of my mother's oldest friends." Cort opened the door for her with a decided jerk. "Try to remember that."

"The last one of your Mom's oldest friends I met bashed

her husband's head in with an oyster pole," Terri reminded him, "and tried to kill your brother's wife more than once. You remember, that was just *before* she set J. D. and his wife's bed *on fire*. With them *in it*."

"I haven't killed anyone yet, Detective," a rich masculine voice drawled. "No matter how often I have been tempted."

The man who came out to greet them wasn't handsome or young, but what Terri thought of as beautifully aged. He had on a three-piece off-white linen suit with a light blue shirt and dark blue tie. A handkerchief, also blue, peeped out of his front breast pocket. His hair was so silver it glittered in the sunlight, and his face was wrinkled just enough to give him an air of wisdom and kindness instead of frailty and defeat.

I will not say anything stupid. I will think before I open my mouth. "Um, hi. How are you?"

The man looked at her as if she were a big cottonmouth that had slithered in under the door. "Cortland, would you introduce us, please?"

"Of course. Andre, this is Detective Terri Vincent. Detective Vincent, Alexandre Moreau, our family friend."

"Mr. Moreau." She held out her hand to shake his, and nearly pulled it back when he turned it sideways and bowed over it. He didn't kiss it the way weird guys did in the movies, but she felt him sniff her fingers. "Thanks for seeing me."

Andre straightened and held out his hand. "May I have your cigarettes, please?"

"Sure." She took the pack from her pocket and handed it to him. "You need a light?" She searched around for her lighter.

"No, thank you." He turned and tossed them into a small trash can behind the counter. "You no longer smoke, Detective."

She must have heard him wrong. "Excuse me?"

"Please don't speak, you'll distract me." He walked around her in a slow circle, studying. "You're five foot nine and one hundred thirty-six pounds. Too tall for petites and too thin for women's sizes." He removed the clip from her hair.

"Hey." She grabbed the back of her head to keep her hair in place. "I'm a hundred and thirty-two."

"God in Heaven." He tugged at some strands. "Have you been hacking at yourself with hedge trimmers?" He grabbed her hands and turned them over. "Ah. I see you've also been using them on your nails."

She frowned. "Now wait a minute."

"Shush." Andre took hold of her chin. "Your teeth are excellent. Good, we won't need a dentist, just a whitening treatment to get rid of that smoker's stain." He released her. "Where do you call home, Detective?"

"I wasn't raised in a barn, if that's what you mean."

"Please answer the question, if you would."

"I lived out on the Atchafalaya until I graduated the police academy. Now I live in the Quarter." She thrust her hands into her jacket pockets. Being her social groomer was one thing, but the man was treating her like an ugly horse. "So what's your deal? You don't like Cajuns, or what?"

"Born and raised in a swamp. That explains it." Andre sighed and turned away. "Cortland, this is going to take an incredible amount of work. How much time do I have to prepare her?"

"I'm escorting her to Ashleigh's memorial service tomorrow evening."

"Very well." He took off his jacket and rolled up his sleeves as he gave Terri another long, hard look. "I'll need a tailor, a hairdresser, a manicurist, a skin consultant, two personal shoppers and, quite possibly"—he eyed her head—"an exterminator."

"Oh, you're a riot." She started tapping her foot. "Look, old man, all you got to do is fix me up with some clothes and makeup, okay?"

"No, my dear. One cannot simply slap new paint on a condemned building. It must be torn down and rebuilt from the ground up. In your case, however, perhaps a judicious application of heavy stucco might work temporarily." To Cort, he said, "It would be best to leave her with me. I'll call you when she's in presentable shape, although my advice is to tell everyone she has laryngitis until we can tame her mouth. Which will likely be somewhere around Mardi Gras in 2010."

Cort nodded. "Thank you, Andre."

"Think of it as my tribute to Ashleigh, poor girl. Now, Detective." He took Terri by the elbow. "Come with me." He steered her toward the back room.

"Wait a minute." In a panic, she glanced over her shoulder and saw Cort walking out the door. "You're not going to leave me here alone, are you?"

He didn't even slow down. "I'll be back when you're ready."

A single match was all it took to light the newspaper clipping. The Torcher dropped it in the van's metal ashtray and watched the flame consume Ashleigh Bouchard's image. It did not give him the same sense of exhilaration, but he imagined few experiences compared to watching a living, breathing woman burn to death.

She had shrieked and clawed, scrabbling at the windows with her long nails, her pretty pink mouth distorted, her lovely golden hair flying. Then the fire had taken her into its deadly embrace, and eased her back against the shrinking leather, and remade her in its own image.

Ashleigh Bouchard had died with her eyes open, her gaze fixed on the rearview mirror.

For him, it had been an absolution, and a release. Not in a sexual sense—he had never taken that particular pleasure from his work—but more a penance wrought of dealing out justice.

"As it says in Exodus," he told the ashtray. " '. . . If there is serious injury, you are to take life for life, eye for eye, tooth for tooth, hand for hand, foot for foot, burn for burn . . .' "

He understood that Gamble would not learn from this one lesson. Not now, not with the shock of loss. At this moment the fire marshal only felt the rage and impotence after passing through the fires of initiation, as he himself had felt. But soon he would come to understand.

Soon Gamble would reap what he had sown.

The flame in the ashtray died, and the clipping had been reduced to a frail grayish-black curl of ash. When he touched it, it disintegrated, leaving nothing behind.

He smiled as he put the van into drive. "Burn for burn."

As he drove out of the Garden District he turned on a local, all-new radio station. The top-of-the-hour broadcast began, leading with a story about yet another conflict in the Middle East, which confused him. He had placed the tape in plain view in the trunk, and by now Gamble should have heard it, and yet there was no mention of it.

Perhaps he should have sent copies of the tape to all the newspapers. That way the police could not suppress it. He braked for a bus, and saw a three-foot-tall ad for Live Spot Eight's news team. At the front of the handsome group of anchormen was a single woman dressed in a conservative white linen suit. Patricia Brown, he recalled, whom he had seen broadcasting from Maskers.

Patricia wore too much makeup, and her dark eyes were a hair too close together. He could see that a scalpel had reshaped her nose and chin—they didn't fit her face—but the elongated, silky bell of her hair was the color of new fire.

Surely it had to be a sign from God.

He stopped at a pay phone at a convenience store, and after a glance through the battered yellow pages hanging in a stained plastic guard bolted to the base, dialed the number for Live Spot Eight CrimeBuster Tips.

"I'd like to speak to Patricia Brown," he told the operator who answered.

"Ms. Brown doesn't take calls personally," he was told, "but I can pass along any information you have to her."

It was irritating, what he had to endure on his mission for God. He often wished he had some superhuman power, so he could strike down whoever stood in his way.

Patience. A man cannot reap what he does not sow. "I refuse to speak to anyone else but Ms. Brown. You can tell her this is about evidence the police are suppressing in the Ashleigh Bouchard case. A statement from the killer himself."

He was put on hold for three minutes, and was about to hang up when a breathless woman answered the line. "This is Patricia Brown. You said you have some information about Ashleigh Bouchard's killer?"

"Yes, Ms. Brown." He smiled. "I'm the man who killed her."

Several hours later Terri was ready. Ready to transfer to Traffic, type out every parking ticket issued in the city, hand in her badge, or shoot out Andre Moreau's kneecaps, if necessary.

Anything to end the torment.

"Hold still, please," the Chinese woman shoving wooden sticks under her fingernails said, for the fifth or sixth time.

Terri stopped squirming. Andre had put her in some sort of dentist's chair two hours ago, and sent in two women and a man to work her over. Or that was what it felt like.

"What are you doing?" she asked the manicurist, who had begun doing something that looked a lot like she was sanding off the pads of Terri's fingers.

"You have calluses."

"Yeah, and I need them for—ow!" The man was yanking her hair again. He'd already painted it with something that stunk to high heaven and put strip things in it. "Will you cut that out?"

"I'll cut it after I'm done tinting," he informed her in a snooty voice. "Don't talk, your treatment will crack." He tested the thick muck he'd smeared all over her face by poking his finger into her cheek.

"That's not all that's going to crack, pal." Something hot and rough touched her toes, and Terri jerked her foot. "What the hell is that?"

"Pumice stone," the second woman said, and clamped her hand around Terri's ankle. "Your feet are a nightmare. Have you gone barefoot your *entire* life?"

That does it. She couldn't see Andre but she heard his

voice close by. He was bickering with someone over hem-
lines and bodices.

"Yo, Andre," Terri called out. "I need a cigarette break."

He stopped arguing and let out a gusty sound. "I told you,
Detective, no breaks, and no cigarettes."

"Well, then I need to pee."

Andre appeared over her, his face as scrooged as if he'd
been sucking on a green lemon. "A lady does not announce
her bathroom needs to the world. She excuses herself politely from company."

He had been doing that all afternoon—telling her how a
lady was supposed to say something—every time she
opened her mouth. She was sick and tired of it.

"Oh, sorry. Excuse the hell out of me." She jerked her
hands and feet free of her personal torturers and sat up.
"Where's the john?"

The older man pressed his fingers against the top of the
bridge of his nose. "Would you direct me to the powder
room, please?"

"What, you don't know where it is?" She climbed out of
the chair and tugged off the plastic drape in which they'd
practically cocooned her.

"That is how you ask for directions."

"That's how *you* ask for directions. I don't need powder-
ing. Where is it?"

"Do you know what the attributes of a beautiful woman
are, Detective?" Andre demanded. "Sincerity, simplicity,
sympathy, and serenity. Emily Post."

More Emily crap. The old man had been spouting her like
she'd written the gospel, too.

She could play along. "I *sincerely* have to pee. It's that
simple. And *sorry* as I am to wreck everyone's *serenity,* if
you don't tell me where the john is, real fast, you'll be mop-
ping the goddamn floor."

He sighed and pointed across the room. "The powder
room is to the left, behind the rack of ball gowns. Do remember to flush."

Terri stomped back to the dainty, feminine restroom and
slammed the door shut behind her. And shrieked.

"What is it?" Andre was there a second later. "Are you hurt? Did you fall?"

"Jesus freaking Christ, what did you do to me?" Her eyes as if like they would pop out of her head as she stared at her reflection in the gilt-framed oval. Her hair was filled with multicolored tinfoil strips and her face was covered with green mud that had dried and was starting to crack. "I'm supposed to look like a society chick, not Swamp Thing!"

"For goodness' sake." He sagged against the door. "You'd think you'd never seen a highlights treatment or a facial mask."

"A *what?*"

"Don't touch anything. Just hurry up and p—use the facilities." Andre walked out.

As Terri used the facilities, she stared at her hands. The Chinese woman had totally wrecked her nails with her sticks and sandpaper; the tops were all rough now. She didn't want to look at her feet. She had liked her feet.

Women actually pay money for people to do this to them. She needed a cigarette, bad, but her spare pack was out with her bike.

This wasn't going to work. She had to get out of here before they did permanent damage.

When she finished in the bathroom, she went out and found Andre, who was sitting in his office. On his desk stood a full glass of water and a bottle of aspirin.

She wondered if she could cop one of the pills. "I need some air. Tell them to wash this shit off me so I can go outside without causing a riot."

"You're not going outside, and you're not smoking." He took two pills and chased them with the water. "You'll stay until we're finished."

"Bullshit I am."

He thumped down the glass. "Please stop using the word *shit,* or the innumerable variations thereof, in every other sentence that comes out of your mouth. It is not a synonym for everything you can't identify or don't understand, which is apparently everything outside the realm of law enforcement."

She grabbed the bottle and dry-swallowed two aspirin. "Look, old man, I appreciate the effort—"

He gave her a supremely ironic look.

"Okay, so I don't appreciate the effort." She reached into her jacket. "But if I don't have a cigarette in the next five minutes, I may shoot . . . some . . . one . . ." she halted and jerked open her jacket to look at her empty shoulder holster. "Where the hell is my gun?"

"Merely a safety precaution." Andre rose and pointed to where his makeover artists were waiting. "If you're a good girl, you can have it back when we're finished."

"Safety precaution." She stalked out of the office. "After this, I'm going to shoot *you*, then *him*."

Andre followed her out. "When this is over, my dear Detective, you may have to."

Because Cort's task force handled over ten thousand cases of arson every year, it was impossible for him to personally review every single file. Since taking over as fire marshal he had overseen the installation of a massive database, which now contained over forty years of records, governed by a sophisticated cross-indexing program that could search and compile records based on specific queries.

The list on his desk had been generated by that program, and listed the names of every convicted arson offender in the region who had been released from prison within the last thirty-six months. Each convict's present whereabouts, if known, were listed. Many had been returned to prison—arsonists were some of the worst repeat offenders—and others had relocated. The task force was now bringing in the remaining convicts to be questioned, and each day Cort received a highlighted list for his review.

Seven convicts were scheduled for interviews, but one name and date jumped out at him: Douglas Simon, released from Angola two weeks ago.

Cort remembered the case only too well. Like the Torcher, Simon had been involved in burning down business establishments. As the insurance-company investigator sent to determine if the fires were accidental or deliberate, he had provided information to the arson task force. Due to the sheer numbers, there was no way the task force could investigate every single incident of fire in the city, and Cort's department often relied heavily on insurance companies to cover the more routine cases.

Simon had taken advantage of his position and used it to obtain kickbacks for fraudulent claims. Cort also suspected he had been protecting Frank Belafini's operation, falsifying arson fires as accidental and cleaning up any residual evidence that might link the fires to the mob. There had been no evidence linking Simon to Belafini, however, and Simon had flatly refused to testify against the mob boss.

As it was Saturday and his assistant was off, Cort went to the records room himself to pull the file. On the way back, the shift supervisor asked him if he wanted to order in dinner.

"No, thanks, Warren." He glanced at the clock. "Who is conducting the interview with Douglas Simon?"

The other man checked his list. "Lawson Hazenel pulled that one. He's scheduled to come in at five."

He nodded. "Let me know when he comes in. If Detective Vincent or Andre Moreau call, put them through to my office."

"You got it, boss."

Reading over the case file refreshed his memory of the details. He'd been the lead arson investigator at the time, and had uncovered Simon's involvement mainly through the man's greed. Although they worked with insurance companies, they still kept a close eye on the adjusters and investigators, and Simon's financials had sent up a red flag. Douglas Simon's bank activity had been heavier than his modest salary justified, so Cort had made some inquiries and discovered that the investigator was living far above his means.

Cort could still picture Simon in his head. The man himself had been forgettable, but the tantrum his wife had thrown after his arrest had been long and loud. Mrs. Simon had demanded to see Cort, had demanded he arrange her husband's release, and had claimed it was all a conspiracy.

Only when confronted with the evidence of Simon's involvement did she turn on her husband.

"You idiot!" she had screamed. "How could you do this to me?"

Cort never forgot how meek Simon had been, sitting and cringing while his wife screamed at him, not for accepting kickbacks, but for getting caught at it. She'd become so violent that Cort had been forced to have her dragged from the interview room by two female officers.

When his wife had gone, Simon looked at him with his meek, mild eyes. "I won't go to prison forever."

"No." After seeing the wife, Cort almost felt sorry for the man. "With good behavior, you'll be out in three to five years to start making restitution."

Simon nodded. "You should remember that."

"You won't be setting up any more scams after this, Simon. You're done." He motioned to the detainment officer to remove him from the room.

"That's not what I mean." He rose and held out his wrists to be cuffed. The look he gave Cort was oddly chilling. "You've ruined my family and my life. When I'm released, I'm going to get even with you for this."

"You'd better hire someone to do it, then, little man." The guard hauled him out of the room.

Cort had been shouted at and threatened hundreds of times, so at the time he had dismissed it. Now he wondered if Simon was making good on his word.

He studied the file until Warren informed him that Hazenel had arrived with Simon, and then he went to the observation room, where he could watch and listen to the interview without Simon being aware of his presence.

Cort only vaguely remembered the man he had sent to prison as being heavier and having more hair, but the meek, mild look about him hadn't changed. Detective Hazenel offered him coffee, which he refused, before beginning the interview.

"You were released two weeks ago, is that right, Doug?" the homicide cop asked as he sat down across from the ex-con.

"Yes." Simon folded his hands in his lap like a polite child. "That is correct."

"What have you been doing since your release?"

"I've reported for my weekly parole checks and searched for employment," he said, his voice colorless. "Am I here as a suspect, Detective?"

"I don't know, Doug." Law regarded him steadily. "Have you been a good boy, or a bad one?"

"I'm not a boy." He smiled. "If I'm being charged, you must read me my rights, and give me the opportunity to speak with counsel."

Law smiled back. "You're not being charged. This is just a friendly chat. Where were you yesterday at two p.m.?"

"I was at the Blue Primrose Café in the Garden District." He recited the address.

It was only a block away from Ashleigh's home. Cort got to his feet and stared through the one-way glass of the observation panel.

On the other side, Law didn't bat an eyelash. "You must have seen the car fire, then."

"Yes, I did. I was told that a young woman was trapped and killed in that car." Simon still didn't show any emotion. "I believe I was photographed at the scene by one of your forensic technicians."

"Is that why you went to the Garden District, Doug?" the homicide detective's voice softened, became more entreating. "To see the fire?"

"No, I went to have lunch, but my dining companion never kept our appointment. After I drank several iced teas at the café, I followed the smoke and the sirens to the scene."

Cort was struck by how controlled Simon was. As if he expected every question Law asked him.

"Did you walk by the Bouchards' residence before the fire started?"

"No. I took the bus from my motel to Magazine Street and walked to the café from there. I did not pass the Bouchard residence at any time."

"Did anyone see you walking to the café?"

Simon's thin shoulders moved. "Not that I'm aware."

"Not much of an alibi, is it, Doug."

"I didn't know that I would require one, Detective." A small smile appeared on his colorless lips. "Will this take much longer?"

"Why, are you in a hurry?"

"I hate to miss the sermon on Saturday night." He turned and looked directly at Cort. "They give out free milk and cookies at St. William's to everyone who stays through until the end."

Ashleigh had worked at St. William's, delivering clothing and food for the homeless. Cort knew because she had talked him into making a donation back when they were been dating.

Cort strode out of the room and into the adjoining one. "Did you kill her, Simon?"

Simon's smile widened. "Why, hello, Marshal. It's a pleasure to see you again."

Cort stared down at him. "Did you kill her?"

"A direct question. How refreshing." He smirked at Law. "No, I did not kill the young lady. As you know, I was never a murderer, and the state of Louisiana will assure you that in regard to my other felonious activities, I am considered rehabilitated."

"Who were you meeting for lunch?"

"I wasn't given a name by the gentleman who invited me. Since my present circumstances require a creative approach to obtaining my daily bread, I was more than happy to accept the mysterious offer." He studied Cort. "You do look tired, Marshal. Tired and somewhat frustrated."

"And?"

"Simply an observation, nothing more. I read about the difficulty you're having, apprehending this arsonist known as the Torcher." Simon patted the thin layer of hair covering his balding crown. "Some of the newspapers are even calling for your resignation."

Law leaned in. "What do you know about the Torcher?"

"I know that the marshal hasn't been able to stop him." Simon looked smug now. "I wonder why. He's had nearly six months to investigate the case. He only took three to gather enough evidence to convict me." He turned to Cort. "Why is that, Marshal? Do you have some conflicting interest in this case?"

"Keep him here," Cort told Law as he went to the door.

"Do take care," Simon called after him.

Cort went to his office to call the assistant district attorney and found Chief Pellerin waiting for him. After reciting the facts on Simon, he asked, "Can you charge him?"

"Not unless you have a witness or evidence that places him in the Bouchards' garage or at the tavern."

"He knows something about the Torcher."

"Put Hazenel on it." Pellerin took out a roll of antacid tablets. "Have him tail Simon. He'll stick to him like dog shit on a shoe."

"All right. What can I do for you?"

"I dropped in to give you a friendly warning." He popped two tablets in his mouth. "Sebastien Ruel is gunning to take you down."

Cort remembered that the OCU chief had watched him throughout their meeting, and while he had been friendly, his eyes hadn't. In fact, he'd looked like a cop whose rock-solid case had just fallen to pieces. *Maybe Belafini still figures into this.* "How do you know?"

"Gut feeling. That and he seemed a little too eager to put Vincent in your side pocket."

Pellerin's instincts were honed by thirty years in Homicide, so Cort didn't question them. "Why me?" Had he done something to put a wrench into Ruel's investigation of Belafini? How, when Cort was the one being targeted by the Torcher?

"I don't know, and he hasn't said. He won't, either." The older man got to his feet. "Just watch your back, Gamble. If anyone slips a knife into it, it'll be Ruel."

"When he calls in, tell him it's urgent he return my call," Gray said as he left a third message with the answering service for Stephen Belafini's personal physician. "Thank you."

He hung up the phone. "What does it take to get a GP off the freaking golf course long enough to pick up his calls?"

"More money than you got," Reese Arceneaux said from the doorway. He lifted a stack of lab result slips. "I come bearing some good news, and some bad news."

"Bring it on in here."

Reese passed him the slips before he helped himself to Gray's coffee. "Bad news first: Your vic was poisoned. Good news is that she wasn't murdered. Someone was trying to save her life."

"Okay. How do you work poison into a lifesaving scenario?"

"When I examined the hair sample, it started to click. This one had no follicle and a blob of acrylic on one end. It also didn't match the length or thickness of the hair you sent in the first sample." Reese sipped and sighed. "I'll run a DNA comparison if you want, but my guess is that she was wearing a wig made of human hair."

"A wig?"

"She had to, because nearly all of her natural hair would have fallen out. I'd been suspicious before—the reduced white-blood-cell count and the mouth sores were telling— but the hair loss clinched it. I ran a comparative and identified the alkaloid as anthracycline aminoglycoside."

Gray frowned. "An antibiotic?"

"It's a component of Adriamycin, or doxorubicin, to be exact." Reese set aside the coffee and reached over to sort out one of the lab slips. "It's taken in combination with Cytoxan, or cyclophosphamide"—he pulled out a second slip—"high levels of which your vic also had present in her bloodstream. It causes severe hair loss and occasionally some damage to the heart and other organs."

His Jane Doe hadn't been poisoned. She'd been taking a poisonous treatment, because she was very, very sick. "Why was she having chemotherapy?"

"I called an oncologist friend of mine. Adriamycin and Cytoxan are the standard adjuvant regimen for advanced, node-positive breast cancer. You can open her up to confirm." Reese's voice softened with pity. "She was likely rid-dled with it."

Gray tried to turn it around in his head, but it didn't make sense. "If she was dying, why would the Torcher kill her? Why not just wait for her to go?"

Reese shrugged. "Could be he had a timetable, but more like he didn't know. The wig covered the hair loss, and she'd have looked thin but otherwise relatively normal. Were you able to get an ID on her?"

"Not yet."

His lab chief sat back. "This type of chemo treatment causes severe side effects and compromises the immune system. She might have been hospitalized while she was receiving it."

"I'll check with the oncology clinics at the local hos-pitals, see if any of their patients haven't turned up for a treatment."

Reese nodded and rose. "Check hospice, too. If she did manage to stay home, she'd have needed full-time nursing care."

"Why wouldn't someone report her missing?" Gray asked. "Woman like this, this sick? If she was my wife or my sister or my daughter, I'd be frantic. I'd be on TV, beg-ging people to tell me where she was."

"Me, too." His lab chief frowned. "Then again, maybe her people wanted something else."

"Like what?"

"Maybe they wanted her to disappear."

11

Cort asked Lawson Hazenel to release Douglas Simon but to keep him under surveillance, and left to pick up Terri from Andre's. By the time he arrived there, however, she was gone.

"Detective Vincent left thirty minutes ago," Andre told him as he sipped from a glass filled with an amber liquid. "She said something about picking up paperwork at police headquarters."

He glanced at the ornate silver flask the older man had left out on the desk. "It's a little early for cocktail hour, Andre."

"Cortland, you know how fond I am of you and your brothers, and how much I adore your mother." Andre drained the glass. "Nothing else could have seen me through this afternoon." He glared. *"Nothing."*

"I did warn you that she might give you a hard time." Cort would chew her out for it anyway.

"A hard time, in comparison, might have been enjoyable." He pressed a hand against his sternum. "I believe I'm having chest pains," he said with a tone of appalled wonder. "That woman has inflicted permanent cardiac damage."

"She's not that bad."

"She is a pit bull. With cleats." Andre leaned forward. "Her dress sense apparently encompasses not much beyond the visual delights of potato sacks and jute cord. Do you know how she sorts out her clothes? By *smell*."

He suppressed a smile. "Terri's never been a very feminine woman."

"I want to see a DNA test." The older man sighed. "And that mouth of hers. Good God, she'd make a merchant marine quail. Whatever you do, feed her, make her drink, give her chewing gum—no, don't do that, she'll stick the wad behind her ear—but try to keep her from speaking at all times."

"What else does she need?"

"The list is endless." Andre thought for a moment. "You'll be eating and dancing with her for the next week, is that correct? Elizabet already told me about her table manners. I imagine she can dance." He propped his forehead against his hand. "The cavemen could."

"Would you meet us over at the house tonight?" Cort asked. "We won't have time to do this during the week, so we should walk her through dinner and work on the dancing."

The older man sighed. "I don't know that I adore your mother this much."

On his way from Andre's to the police station, Cort's cell phone rang. "Gamble."

"You've been all over the television, but I haven't seen an arrest yet," Frank Belafini said. "Did you forget what I told you?"

"I remember." His threats had never been far from Cort's thoughts. "You having a problem with OCU these days?"

"I only have one problem." Belafini made the sucking sound of a man lighting an expensive cigar. "Where's this dead man who killed my son?"

"We'll find him, and he'll get the death penalty. I guarantee it."

"I know he will. I'll see to that."

He pulled into NOPD's visitor parking lot. "I understand how you feel, but not even you can take the law into your own hands. Taking down this arsonist won't get OCU off your back, either."

"You understand nothing, Gamble. If you don't bring the Torcher to me, maybe I'll give you some motivation. Like those big houses in the Garden District. Old wood burns so easy, but you know that."

"I've told you before, don't threaten me."

"You I need, Gamble. You I'm not threatening. But what about your friends, your neighbors? Your mother and father? I don't need them, now do I?" The line went dead.

Cort shut off the phone and shoved it in his pocket on his way into the station. The Torcher's threat was sickening, but now he had to worry about Belafini going after his parents. He couldn't trust Ruel enough to tell him about the mob boss's threats. Ruel had his own agenda, and he probably wouldn't hesitate to use Cort's parents if he thought it would help his case.

Terri Vincent was going to have to tell him what the hell was going on at OCU, and fast.

Inside the station, the desk sergeant couldn't tell him where Terri was.

"Haven't seen her come in, Marshal. I can leave a note in her old box, if you want, but she's been reassigned to OCU. Best try over there."

"If she checks in, tell her I'm looking for her." On the way to the door, Cort was distracted by shouts from an angry, heavyset man dressed in a florid purple pimp's suit, who was being brought into booking by two patrolmen. As he looked over at the trio, Cort bumped into someone coming out of the elevator.

He turned to apologize, but the woman he'd brushed shoulders with walked right past him, leaving a trace of light, enticing perfume in her wake.

"I want my lawyer!" the pimp shouted. "I ain't gwan nowheres 'til I get my lawyer!"

Cort was no longer looking at the pimp. Although he'd never seen her before, the woman from the elevator had captured his full attention.

From behind she was gorgeous—tall and slender, with a thick leonine mane of golden-streaked chestnut hair—and she wore a simple dark red sleeveless sheath that hugged her body in all the right places. Her legs seemed to go on forever, with slim thighs and tight calves above the skinny, sexy straps of her high-heeled crimson sandals. Around one tanned ankle was a thin chain of golden butterflies.

The entire package hit Cort like a baseball bat to the belly, and he started after her without thinking about it.

"I done told you," the pimp shrieked as he struggled, "I doan know no Aneeka. She done lied to you if she say I hit on her!"

She probably has a face like a horse, Cort told himself, but didn't care. He was mesmerized by the faint sway of her hips, and what had to be the tightest, best-looking ass in the state of Louisiana.

More shouts, this time from the patrolmen as the pimp wriggled out of their hold and made a dash for the door, heading straight for the woman in red as he did. Cort ran forward, only to come to a halt as the woman dropped her purse, hiked up her skirt and delivered a beautiful side kick to the pimp's knees, knocking his legs out from under him and sending him facedown on the floor.

"Now, now," she said in a terribly familiar voice as she straddled the would-be escapee and seized the back of his neck. "We brought you all the way down here, you can stay until the party's over." When he jerked under her, she pressed a knee into his spine to hold him in place.

Cort walked around them and looked down at the woman's face. The silky mane framed glowing skin, big green eyes and luscious, full red lips. She didn't resemble a horse; she looked like a cat. A sensual, dangerous tigress.

The beauty would have made him reel, but for her features. They were unmistakable. "Terri?"

"Yeah." She looked up and frowned. "What?"

Now he reeled. "It is you."

"Last time I checked." She glanced down at herself. "Oh, right. The dress was your pal Andre's idea. I didn't have time to change before I came over."

The pimp turned his head to look up at her with one eye. "You kicked me!"

"I quit smoking today," she told him in a conversational tone. "Give me any more lip and I'll rip your damn head off." She reached back to adjust one of her ankle straps. "These freaking heels are killing me."

"Come work for me, baby," the pimp said, and grinned. "I'll buy you better shoes."

"That's *Detective* Baby, you nitwit." She jammed her knee in harder, making him wheeze, and turned her head to look at the gaping patrolmen. "Well? Do I have to sit on him all day? Get the hell over here."

Cort reached to help her. "Are you all right?"

"Just peachy." Terri ignored his hand and hauled the pimp to his feet. She held him by the neck and arm until she could pass him off to the arresting officers, who were also staring wide-eyed at her, as was every other cop in the lobby. "Keep a better grip on him this time, huh?"

"Uh, right," one of them said as he stared at the triangles of fabric clinging to her breasts. "Thanks."

Terri finally noticed the other stares and swung around to scan the room. "What, you guys never saw a female officer in a dress before? Pick up your chins and get back to work." She retrieved her purse from where she had dropped it.

Someone wolf-whistled.

"Oh, shut up." To Cort she said, "You can cut it out, too."

"Sorry." He couldn't help the grin. "God, it's amazing."

"The dress?" She snorted and yanked at the hemline. "It's too damn short. I know I flashed half the city with my panties, riding over here on my bike."

He thought of her astride the Harley in that dress and nearly groaned. "You don't even look like the same person."

"I'm not the same person. Those people Andre brought in to work me over scraped off at least three layers of skin and yanked out half my hair. And these." She held up her hand to show him long fingers with perfectly shaped red-tinted nails. "Do you know I almost poked my eye out with these frigging things? How do I get them off?"

She could stop a burly, angry pimp trying to evade custody, but she couldn't handle a manicure.

Cort shook his head. "You don't."

"Shi—you want to know why there's no good word substitute for shit? Because shit is shit. *That's* why." She tried to push a hand through her hair, and then grimaced. "Like all the stuff they put in my hair. I'll never get it washed out. I think I saw that guy actually put shaving cream in it or something. And these fucking shoes have *got* to go." She teetered a little as she bent down to adjust another strap.

What had Andre called her? *A pit bull with cleats.*

"Come on." He took her arm and led her to the entrance. "We've got a lot more work to do before tomorrow night."

After two hours of being beautiful, Terri was tired of it. Her head hurt, her feet hurt, and she was pretty sure some of the crap Andre and the Beauty Inquisition had brushed and dabbed and worked into her face wasn't going to come off. Ever.

And the rules. Jesus, Mary, and Joseph, all the things she had to remember to do. Or not to do. Smooth her skirt down when she sat, but she couldn't scratch where it itched. Keep a scarf over her hair outside, but she wasn't to brush it, only fluff it with her fingers. She absolutely positively couldn't do anything with her hands, because she might chip her nails, and she'd sworn she would never endure that Chinese woman's version of fingernail torture, ever, ever again.

She also smelled like a walking air freshener and she had to carry her gun in a stupid little purse. And then carry the purse.

Being beautiful not only sucked, it rendered her useless. Which was the point, she supposed.

Now she was sitting back at the Gamble mansion, waiting to be tortured again. As if the beauty-o-rama hadn't been enough, now she had to do dinner and dancing lessons. When she could be back at the station, reviewing the bank's security tapes to see who had made Cort fifty thousand dollars richer.

"Can't we pick this up tomorrow?" she asked. "I need to go home and chain-smoke for a few hours." She might have to resort to sandpaper to get her face clean. Maybe she could call the Chinese woman and borrow some.

"We have the memorial service tomorrow." Cort looked

over the bar where he was mixing something in a silver container. "I thought you said that you quit smoking today."

She wanted a cigarette so much her lungs felt like they were turning inside out. "Like the pimp is going to come over and sniff my breath?"

"Andre will."

"I'm armed." She opened her purse to display her weapon. "I'll shoot him."

"No, you will not." Cort walked over and handed her a pretty glass filled with a greenish liquid. "Here. This should soothe the pain."

The only green things she consumed were salads, tart apples and bar ale on St. Patrick's Day. "What is this?"

"It's a daiquiri. You drink it."

"*You* drink it." She offered it back to him. "I want a beer."

"You don't get a beer. Ladies drink cocktails. Slowly," he added when she took a test sip. "You haven't had anything to eat yet."

"Good." It wasn't too horrible, so she took a bigger swallow and let the warmth spread through her belly. "Make me a couple more. I'll get shit-faced before dinner. It'll keep Andre alive and help me handle your mother."

"No drinking." He sat down beside her. "I need you sober and alert now."

She glanced sideways at him. "You think he'll make a move tomorrow?"

"I'm not assuming anything." He was staring at her face again. "I still can't get over the difference." He reached out and lifted her chin.

She may not have enjoyed the Beauty Inquisition, but she couldn't deny the final results were pretty impressive.

"Cool, huh?" She turned her head from side to side. "See the eye shadow? It's got teeny sparkles in it. So does the lip stuff. Hang me from a ceiling and spin me around, and I could double as a disco ball."

He shook his head. "I can't understand it. It's as if you've been hiding the way you look, all these years."

"I have been." She liked seeing the surprise show on his face. "Come on, Cort, you think that I never once put on makeup in my life? I didn't trowel it on like this, but I've worn some, just like any other female." A long, long time ago, in that happy carefree time of life she thought of as *Before Cortland*.

Now he looked suspicious. "I've never seen you like this. Not once."

"You've only known me since I became a cop. Back in high school I had long hair, the heels, the dresses, the jewelry, the works." She smiled, remembering how she and her mother had gone shopping. Jeneane and she had been a lot closer, that last year before she'd gone into the academy.

"What changed, Terri?"

Less happy memories crowded to the forefront. The taunts, the ragging, and the flat insults thrown in her face. She sorted through them for a moment, trying to remember the early, worst ones. "It was something that one of my academy instructors said to me, my first week in training. I had some trouble on the fitness course with the bar work, and he said, 'We'll get you into shape, Vincent. You'll need it to carry around the mattress.' Every guy in my class—except your brother—laughed at me."

His eyes narrowed. "Did they harass the other female students that way?"

"They don't harp on how the *guys* looked, if that's what you mean." She cradled the daiquiri glass between her hands and studied the miniature, transparent reflection of her face on the liquid's surface. "After a week of nonstop sex jokes I quit wearing makeup, and I never put it on again."

"You could have after graduation."

Typical man, oblivious to what it was like for a woman to work in a male-dominated field.

"Hardly. Even when I was in uniform, guys in the department constantly said things." She touched the fluffy, streaky mane framing her face. "I cut this short after one asshole shift supervisor over at the Seventh said something to J. D. about using the length to hold my head."

"Why would he need to—" he stopped and then swore under his breath.

"Exactly." Her mouth hitched. "That was why J. D. got

written up, our second year on the street. He hit the guy who said it with a beautiful roundhouse punch. Broke his nose. Blood everywhere." She made a wide gesture with one hand. "I loved it."

"J. D. took a fine and a three-day suspension for that incident, but he never told me why." He didn't sound resentful, only thoughtful.

"I think he knew it was my battle, not his. It was nice of him to back me up whenever it got especially nasty." She set aside the daiquiri glass. "You know, all I ever wanted to be was a cop. I knew I'd be a minority, but I wasn't afraid to fight for it."

"So you fought."

She shrugged. "I did when I had to. Most of the time I just tried to fit in. Over the years I guess I got used to all the stuff I did to make the guys forget I was female." She smoothed a palm over her skirt. "I really haven't worn a dress since high school. It's kind of weird. I forgot how you have to remember to keep your knees together all the time and not bend over too far."

"You're doing fine." As Mae looked in on them, he rose and held out his hand. "Time for dinner."

After a brief hesitation, Terri took his hand and carefully curled her fingers around his. "I'm not responsible if I stab you anywhere with these nails. Just FYI."

He gave her an odd look. "I'll remember that."

Andre and the Gambles were already seated at the table. Remembering how awful brunch had been, Terri stopped in the doorway.

The old man was bad enough, but seeing Elizabet made her cheeks grow hot. She didn't want to go through another lecture on what a baboon she was at the table. "I can't do this."

Cort leaned close. "Did you ever play tea party when you were a little girl?" he asked, his breath warm against her ear.

"Yeah, my cousin Olympia used to make me." Olympia, who had four kids and was working on number five, the cousin who Jeneane and Con often wished had been switched with Terri at birth.

"It's the same thing, only with grown-ups."

She turned her head but saw only reassurance in his cool eyes. "Don't be nice to me. It makes me nervous."

"Don't be nervous." He led her over to a chair and pulled it out for her, and then sat down beside her.

Okay, round two. Terri looked to the head of the table, where Louie sat staring at her. "Good evening, Lou—" A sharp look from Andre made her substitute, "Mr. Gamble."

Cort's father gave her a wide smile. "You have always been lovely to me, *cherie*. But tonight, you are . . . radiant."

Louie was such a charmer. He always knew how to make a woman feel uber-feminine. Maybe she'd ditch Cort and see if she could hang out with his dad at the social shindigs next week.

Terri braced herself as she turned to look across the table at Elizabet. "Thank you for your advice earlier today, Mrs. Gamble." She checked out the utensils, which had a few new additions. "I'll try to do better."

Elizabet looked disconcerted for a moment before she produced a strained smile. "I'm sure you will, Terri."

Finally she turned to Andre. "Mr. Moreau, after dinner, we have to talk about these shoes. They're . . ." she trailed off, groping for a description.

"Yes, Detective? What are they?"

Cort put his hand over hers. "Easy."

Easy my ass, you don't have to wear them. Terri thought it over and finally knew what to say. "I'm a lady, Andre." She darted a glance at Elizabet. "I'm told that we don't use that kind of language."

As Andre applauded, Louie laughed. "This is going to be wonderful."

Dinner was awkward, but not because Terri had difficulty with her manners. The concentration she gave to eating, drinking, and speaking politely was unwavering and at times ferocious. She also asked Andre questions in a low voice when she wasn't sure of something, and after some initial surprise, he made gently worded suggestions. Elizabet remained silent and watchful, while Louie spent most of the meal either complimenting Terri or beaming at her.

No, as meals went, it was a very successful one. It was sitting next to Terri and watching her that kept Cort on edge. Only a short gap separated their chairs, and if he had shifted his thigh slightly to the left, he could have pressed it against hers. He didn't attempt to touch her, but when she reached for something, the side of her arm touched his. Despite the perfume, the makeup, the hair, and the dress, he could still smell the scent of her skin.

Yet while all this was going on, she seemed completely oblivious to him and the fact that she was driving him out of his skull.

"You didn't eat very much, Cortland," Elizabet said when Mae had cleared their plates and brought coffee and dessert. "Are you feeling all right?"

"I'm fine." He had the dancing lesson still to face. "Terri and I will be in the music room when you're ready, Andre." To Terri, he said, "Come on."

"Can I take these shoes off?" she asked as he led her down the hall. "My toes are cramping."

"No." He had a semipermanent knot in his groin; let her limp a little.

She trotted to keep up with him. "Okay, but I'm not responsible if I stumble, fall, or break any of your toes."

Cort took her by the wrist and changed direction. "Let's get some fresh air." He hauled her outside onto the marble deck that his mother had framed in enormous rosebushes. The outside air was damp and warm as opposed to the air-conditioned house, but the scent of the red, pink, and white roses obliterated everything else.

"Nice flowers." She bent over to sniff an American Beauty in full bloom, presenting him with another excellent view of her tight little backside. "Your mom grow these?"

"Yeah." He started to pace. "She breeds them, too."

"You mean, like puppies?" She laughed at her own joke and wandered over to another cluster of blooms. "My mama loves flowers. She loves all the girly stuff. I was a huge disappointment, believe me."

He stopped and watched her. "What about your father?"

"Him, too." She didn't sound so happy now.

Her father was a sensitive subject; J. D. had told him once that Con Vincent had done a real number on Terri's head after his conviction on bribery charges. His brother had refused to say any more, and when Cort had pressed the issue said only that she had told him in confidence.

He knew that Terri didn't just trust J. D. She loved him. The way she had worried about him during the LeClare case had convinced Cort that J. D. was sleeping with her. So much so that he'd gone out, tried to get drunk, and then gone looking for her.

"We should go back in," she said, still trailing her fingers over the soft-petaled faces of his mother's roses. "Andre's probably up way past his bedtime."

"Andre will wait." Cort moved up behind her. "Why do you always avoid talking to me?"

"I talk to you all the time at work." Her voice became guarded. "Let's take it inside, huh?"

"Wait." The heated air suddenly felt cool against his face as he rested his hands on her shoulders. He thought of how he had grabbed her in the copy room, and how explosive the results had been. "We're not at work."

"You're not, but I am." She glided out from under his touch. "How about we forget the dancing lesson? You can say I'm shy or I have a bum knee. Tell the folks I said thanks for everything."

"There you go, running away again." He placed himself between her and the door to the house. The look on her face made him want to shake her, hard. "When are you going to trust me, Therese?"

Clouds drifted across the moon, stealing the light and casting shadows over her face. "The last time I trusted you, Cortland, I woke up alone."

It wasn't the sex that bothered her, it was the memory of the morning after. It stunned him to realize that she considered their encounter a matter of trust. Of course she did, and she was right. He had taken her and left her without ever once considering her feelings.

"I shouldn't have done that. I shouldn't have come to you in the first place." He took her hand between his. "Forgive me, Terri."

"You're sorry now that I look like this." She extracted her hand. "Don't let the high-priced buff and polish fool you, Marshal. Underneath, I'm still the same woman."

He was tired of her pushing him away whenever he tried to talk to her, particularly when he was trying to apologize. "I know who you are."

"Do you? Maybe we need a visual aid." She reached over and yanked one of the roses from the bush, then waved it under his nose. "This flower is beautiful and elegant and knowing your Mom, probably has a fucking pedigree a mile long."

Her voice shook, and brought out something dark inside him. "And?"

"I'm not. I don't."

He had to kiss her again, Cort decided. He'd take his time and not maul her, the way he had before. A little mauling would come later, when he had her naked and under him. "Is that all?"

"No." She grimaced and dropped the rose. "Now I have thorns in my hand. *Shit.*"

He grabbed her wrist and pulled her over so that the light shining through the windows illuminated her bleeding hand. Three greenish-black thorns were deeply embedded in her palm.

When she tried to pull away, he clamped his fist around her wrist. "Hold still."

"I'm bleeding. *You* hold still."

He bent and tugged out the first thorn with his teeth, turning his head to spit it away.

"Ow!" She held still until he had gotten the other two out. "Did you have to do that?"

"Yes." Using his mouth to pull the thorns from the soft palm of her hand had exercised some of his demons, even as the knot in his groin grew tighter. "Were you trying to hurt yourself, to impress me with how tough you are?"

"No, but I'm hoping I get hit by a car on the way home,"

she said, her voice blithe. "Would save me all kinds of aggravation, and I'll finally get to take my vacation days, even if it is while I'm in traction."

He was back to wanting to shake her again. "That's not funny."

"I'm not kidding."

"Children," Andre said from the doorway. "Stop squabbling and come inside before you become covered with sweat."

Terri sighed before she turned to the old man and produced a brilliant smile. "Andre, I've had a tiny little mishap. Would you please direct me to the powder room?"

12

"The navy blue suit." Terri cradled the phone between her cheek and shoulder and sorted through the garment bags Andre had sent over to her apartment. Luckily they were see-through, or she'd have been yanking zippers all day. "The white and navy or the navy and navy?"

"The solid navy."

"Got it." She removed the suit from her closet and studied it. "Shoes?"

"The navy-and-black pumps in the red shoebox," Andre told her. "I put your accessories in a black velvet case in the jacket's right hip pocket."

She kicked the specified shoebox out of the stack by the closet and watched the shoes fall out. The heels promised to realign her spine, but at least they didn't have straps.

"Navy and black pumps, check." With one hand she retrieved the case from the jacket and opened it to find a flat gold necklace and matching disc earrings. "Jewelry, check." The heavy, gleaming chain made her frown. "This looks real."

"We don't buy our accessories at the dollar store, Detective. Are you smoking?"

She reached over and stubbed out the cigarette she had forgotten to smoke. "No."

"I heard the ashtray rattle." He sighed. "Brush your teeth, use mouthwash, clean your hands, and don't light another one or I will beat you."

She bristled. "Assaulting a police officer is a felony, old man."

"Prison will be a vacation. Now, make up your face before you dress, and you're to only use the lightweight foundation, the translucent setting powder, the dark mocha lipstick, and just a whisk of the cinnamon blush over each cheekbone."

"Hang on, hang on." She took the cordless into the bathroom and sifted through the cosmetics bag he had given her last night.

When a phone call to Cort from the mayor had postponed the dancing lesson, she'd spent an hour in one of the Gambles' bathrooms so that Andre could show her how to remove and put on the makeup. Bickering with the old man had made her feel better, but not enough to face Cort again. As soon as Andre had left her, she'd slipped out of the house and taken off.

"God, look at all this shi—stuff." She checked a label. "How come this one says for cheeks, lips, *and* eyes? When did they become interchangeable?"

"It's a highlighter, and they're not."

She stopped sorting. "I can't do this." She dropped the blush. "I'm going to look like a clown. Can I meet you an hour early and you put it on me?"

"There isn't time for that. You'll do well, just remember your mantra: 'I am sincere, simple, sympathetic, and serene.' I will see you at the church, Detective. Be beautiful."

"Beautiful. Yeah." She turned off the phone and regarded the scattered cosmetics as she would the components of a ticking bomb. "God, I am so screwed."

There was a knock at her front door an hour later, and she hopped out of the bathroom, still in the process of putting on one shoe.

"Hold your horses," she called out. When she had the shoe on, she glanced down at herself. *Jewelry and watch, check. No runs in the hose or wrinkles in the skirt, check. Hair, check.* She almost used her teeth on her lower lip before she remembered her lipstick and bit the inside of her cheek instead. *Something's missing.*

A louder knock sounded on the door.

"All right, all right." She strode over and opened it to see Cort standing just outside, tall and handsome in a dark gray suit. "I'm not ready."

His gaze went from her nose to her toes. "You look ready."

The way he said that made her stomach clench. The last time he had shown up on her doorstep . . . no, she wasn't going to go there. She had to focus.

"I forgot to do something. I know it." She grabbed his arm and pulled him inside, then turned around in front of him. "What looks wrong?"

"Nothing." He sounded as if that were the problem.

She paced. "I did the face stuff. Well, just the foundation and the lipstick." She'd given up on doing her eyes after nearly blinding herself with the bristly end of the mascara brush. "Got the stockings, the hair spray, the earrings . . ."

His mouth curled. "Calm down. This isn't protocol for disarming a suspect."

"That would be easier." He was wearing his favorite aftershave, the one that smelled like an ocean breeze and made her nuts. She started to breathe through her mouth so she could concentrate, then froze. "Perfume." She was supposed to have put it on before dressing. "I need five minutes. I have to strip and spritz."

"Terri." He caught her arm as she whirled to run into the bathroom. "You don't need it."

"But Andre said—"

"Andre doesn't have to sit next to you in church." A muscle on the side of his jaw twitched. "I do."

"Oh." Maybe she'd worn too much yesterday. "Okay by me." She grabbed her purse and checked to make sure she'd stowed her weapon inside. "Let's go."

The trip to the memorial service was mostly a silent one. Terri knew how upset Cort was over Ashleigh's murder and gave herself permission not to chat. She sat still so she wouldn't wrinkle her suit and ran through everything Andre had told her last night.

"Watch the entrances and exits," Cort said as they pulled

into the church parking lot. "Let me walk a little ahead of you when we come out of the service."

"I'm the only one with the gun," she reminded him.

"No, you're not." He parked and shut off the engine.

Terri checked the line of his jacket and saw the bulge of a holster. "You're carrying concealed? Since when?"

"Since 1995," he said as he put on a pair of sunglasses. "I have a license for it, and yes, I know how to use it."

She sighed. "Good, then I won't have to bust you after church."

The memorial service for Ashleigh Bouchard was held at the Bouchards' church, St. Catherine's, which had been built in the nineteenth century on the outskirts of the Garden District.

Terri had expected it to be quiet, respectful, and well attended, which it was. There were countless solemn arrangements of flowers, sent from all over the country, and they made the old church smell like a hothouse. She sat with Cort and his parents in one of the front rows and watched Ashleigh's parents stare numbly at the photo of their beautiful dead daughter, which was surrounded by a wreath of rare white orchids.

There was no casket, Cort told her earlier, as the family had decided to keep the funeral private.

Several people rose and gave short eulogies about the young woman, including Andre Moreau. The fact that Ashleigh had been one of the privileged members of Creole society didn't matter to anyone. Instead, her friends told anecdotes about her childhood escapades, her love of travel and good times, her generosity and sweetness.

Terri was surprised to see Moriah Navarre walk up to the podium reserved for speakers. The young blonde appeared pale, drawn, and nothing like the confident, superior woman who once had sniped at Terri whenever chance permitted.

"Ashleigh was one of my best friends," Moriah said unsteadily. "We roomed together at Tulane, and we were both cheerleaders, so we swapped clothes and double-dated and worked on our high kicks together. I had to learn to deal with Ash's quirks, like the way she made promises." She demonstrated a girlish gesture of hooking her little fingers together. "But any sorority sister will tell you, there is nothing more reliable than an Ashleigh Bouchard pinkie promise."

Soft chuckles of agreement drifted from some of the young female mourners.

"The last time I saw Ashleigh was at her house, just the other day. She was trying on a new outfit and wanted to know what I thought of it." Moriah looked at Cort for a moment before averting her gaze. "I was in a bad mood and I know I wasn't very helpful. She asked me to have lunch but I sort of ran out on her. I drove really fast, or I think I would have seen the smoke in my rearview mirror."

Terri quietly took out her notebook and checked her witness list. No one at the Bouchard house had mentioned Moriah being there that day. She'd have to talk to her; it was possible she had seen something.

"Not today," Cort murmured, looking from her notebook to Moriah.

Does he really think I'm that unfeeling? Terri clamped down on her temper and gave him a small nod.

Moriah left the podium and walked down to stand before Ashleigh's photograph. "If I'd said yes, if I'd stayed, I would have been in the car with you, Ash. You wouldn't have been alone. I would have gotten you out somehow." Her voice broke as she curled her little finger against the glass over the frame. "Pinkie promise."

Mrs. Bouchard turned her face against her husband's shoulder and sobbed.

Cort silently rose and went to Moriah, who gazed up at him with the blank blindness of a woman in light shock. He leaned over to murmur something to her, and then gently guided her back to where her family was seated.

Terri's irritation faded as she watched him sit down beside Moriah and slip his arm around her hunched shoulders. She had never liked J. D.'s former girlfriend, especially as Moriah had dated Cort before J. D., but the old jealousy settled into an aching wistfulness. She knew that no matter what she did or how she looked, Cort would never treat her with such tenderness.

Good thing, she thought as she stared at the collar of the man sitting in front of her. *Because if he ever did, I'd show Moriah just how badly a woman can fall to pieces.*

Douglas stepped off the cable car and onto the grass median, waiting for several cars to pass before he crossed the street and walked down the block to St. Catherine's. News vans were parked up and down the perimeter, so he sat on a bus-stop bench at the corner where he could watch the mourners exiting the church without attracting attention.

He had followed the story of the Bouchard murder on the TV set in his room all week. When the memorial service was announced he had decided he had to go, if only to watch Gamble mourn for what he had lost. It was not a violation of his parole, and perhaps if he could somehow show himself to Gamble after the service, he might incite the fire marshal to become reckless.

He wanted Cort Gamble to hit him. He fully intended to provoke the man until he did.

The Gamble family was wealthy; perhaps one punch would be sufficient for a sizeable lawsuit, or serve as good reason for the mayor to fire Gamble. After all, what city wanted a fire marshal who used his fists on an innocent man?

He didn't feel guilty about what he was doing. Gamble had everything. Douglas had lost everything, including his family. No one should take a man's family away from him.

A small weight dropped down beside him on the bench. "What are you doing here?"

At first the girl's face didn't register, so caught up was he in his fantasy of triumphing over Gamble. Then he realized it was Caitlin, the girl from the hotel. "I could ask the same of you."

"I followed you," the girl said bluntly. "Like the girls on 'Totally Spies!' do on TV."

"That is a cartoon." He gazed across the street to the church. "You're old enough to know that cartoons aren't real. You shouldn't be out here by yourself, either. It isn't proper for a girl your age to run around the city alone."

"I'm not alone. I'm here with you." She drew her knees up so that her dirty sneakers rested against the edge of the bench. "You're in trouble, Mister, aren't you?"

"Not anymore, and my name is Douglas." He saw Cort Gamble walk out with his arm around a petite blonde woman, and thought of the man who had come to visit him—the cheerful giver—and the empty promises he had made. "You should go home now. I am serious, Caitlin, it's not safe for you here."

"I'm safe. *You're* the one who's being followed."

That tore his attention away from the fire marshal. "I beg your pardon?"

"There's a man following you. In the brown car, over my right shoulder. Don't look straight at him," she whispered fiercely. "Then he'll know that you know."

Douglas pretended to inspect a clump of weeds growing around the base of the bus-stop bench and darted a quick glance to the right. A brown Chevy sedan was idling by the curb where he had gotten off the cable car. Behind the wheel sat a pale-haired man with dark sunglasses.

"He was outside the motel this morning, and didn't leave until you did." Caitlin rested her chin against her knees. "He's a cop."

So he was under surveillance. He had expected as much. Yet this girl had discovered his tail before he had. "How do you know that he's a police officer?"

"He has one of those attachable red lights they stick to the roof when they gotta go fast. I saw it when I walked by the car." She peered at him. "Did you kill someone?"

It hadn't shocked Douglas when Gamble had asked him that question, but a child as young as Caitlin shouldn't even be thinking such things. "No."

"But you were in prison. For a while, right?"

A while. He imagined the seemingly endless procession of the days working over ledgers and the nights pacing a nine-by-twelve-foot cell. "Three years."

"Thought so." She nodded. "Daddy had the same look in his eyes, last time he got out. He did eighteen months on a weapons charge." She said it as if it were as insignificant as a parking ticket. "So what are you going to do?"

"I'm not doing anything. I'm only sitting here."

"I can keep a secret, you know. I never tell on Daddy when he brings home stuff from the store without a receipt," she assured him.

Douglas looked over at the church and tried to formulate a reasonable response. As he did, he saw a dark van parked at the corner. *So I'm not the only one under surveillance.* Was it the cheerful giver? Would he see Douglas? Would he see Caitlin? "I really think you should go home now."

"Aw, come on, Mister. Tell me what's going on," the girl urged.

"There is nothing to tell. I have no job, no family, no money, no friends." In a few days, he would have no motel room.

"You got me." Caitlin nudged him with an elbow. "You want to know how to ditch that cop? Clover did it a really sweet way with this bad guy on the last episode."

"Clover?"

She nodded enthusiastically. "See, what we need is a distraction." She bent over and plucked a squirming gecko out of the grass. "Ever see what a guy does when you drop a lizard down the back of his shirt?"

"I don't think the officer will allow me to do that."

"You won't." Caitlin closed her small hand over the gecko until it was completely concealed, and gave him an angelic smile. "I will."

Cort stayed with Moriah through the remainder of the service, and escorted her and her family outside to where the private limousines were lined up waiting. Mr. and Mrs. Navarre thanked him for his assistance before climbing into their car, but Moriah hung back.

"Mother helped me write something for this," she muttered, looking at her folded, twisting hands. "It was beautiful and appropriate, but when I got up there, I couldn't remember the words. I couldn't talk about her like that." Her pain-filled eyes stared down the line of cars. "I should have been with her. I should have died with her."

"Ashleigh would never have wanted that, honey." He cradled her face and wiped away the tears spilling down her cheeks. "She loved you."

"No." Moriah drew back. "She loved *you*, Cortland. That day, when she . . . she was trying on clothes for you. She wanted to impress you. She had it all worked out, you'd get back together, get married, have babies and live happily ever after."

He looked out at the street, and saw a dark van parked at the corner. "I never led her to believe—"

"I know. I've been there, remember?" Moriah reached up and kissed him on the cheek. Her lips were cold. "She knew, and still she was going to try. That was Ash. Nothing stopped her." She smiled miserably before she climbed into the limo.

Cort stood watching the car drive away. He had had no idea of Ashleigh's intentions or feelings, and now the weight of her death seemed to double. It wasn't the assumption of a crazed killer. Ashleigh *had* been in love with him.

Terri came to stand beside him. "She going to be all right?"

"Not for some time, I think." Neither was he, but he couldn't stand here all day brooding over a love he hadn't wanted, sought, or deserved.

"It was a nice service." A slim, warm hand curled around his. "Want to take a walk?"

He walked with her. Behind St. Catherine's, there was a small private cemetery that provided the final resting place for many of the priests who had served the parish. Because the high water table made it impossible to bury the dead, their remains lay entombed in marble and stone vaults, each carved with the name of the deceased. Willows had been planted around the wrought-iron gate of the cemetery, and shaded the plain wooden prayer benches provided for visitors.

"There was this poem they made us read in school once," she said as they followed the square-stoned path that paralleled the gates. "It was about death, but it was like being on a ship, sailing away."

"I didn't know you liked poetry." He didn't know anything about what she liked, outside of police work and guns. It made him feel unsettled and angry, as it had to learn why she had cut off her hair.

"I don't, usually, but this one . . . it was sad, but it was right. You know?" She glanced at him, and then shrugged as if she were embarrassed. "Doesn't matter, I guess. I can't remember all the words anymore."

" 'And just at the moment when some one at my side says: "There, she is gone," there are other eyes watching her coming, and other voices ready to take up the glad shout: "Here she comes!" ' " he said. "Henry Van Dyke."

"Yeah, that's the one." She stopped by the gate and looked down at the front of one vault, where the chiseled image of an angel spread its wings. "Do they make you memorize poetry or something in private school?"

"I read it at my grandmother's funeral last summer." At the time Elizabet had wanted him to read a psalm from the Bible, but Van Dyke's verse had better expressed his feelings. *Like Moriah's pinkie promise to Ashleigh.* "I didn't go to private school."

"You didn't?"

He shook his head. "My father insisted that my brothers and I go to public school. He said it would keep us from becoming spoiled, and he was right." He glanced at her. "You were pretty scarce last summer, if I remember correctly."

"J. D. and I were working a hit and run on a three-year-old boy named Bryan Couday. We took the call to the scene, and when we got there, Bryan looked like he'd just lain down and taken a nap, right there on the road." Her voice went low and sad. "He was so damn little."

Absently he threaded his fingers through hers. "Did you catch the driver?"

Terri nodded. "Businessman, claimed he never saw the kid run into the street. Told his mechanic and his golf buddies a different story, though. He got ten years upstate for manslaughter. Putting him away was Bryan's ship." She glanced up at him. "We're going to catch this lunatic and give Ashleigh hers."

Sitting by Terri in church had been a subtle ordeal, and he had gone to Moriah partly to get away from her. He couldn't exorcise the guilt he felt over Ashleigh's death, however, and it had only expanded after what Moriah had told him.

Yet some of the weight lifted from inside him now as he looked into Terri's eyes. "You seem so sure that we will."

"We make a good team." She went back to studying the vault fronts. "When we're not bitching at each other, or . . . doing other stuff."

She had a point. "I didn't think of how awkward this might be for you." Although he didn't feel uneasy with her. Quite the contrary, which is why he had left her alone in the church. "I'll do whatever I can to make you comfortable."

"You can't wear these shoes, so let's just do our jobs, okay?" She squeezed his hand. "Ashleigh and those people from the bar, they need that. They need us."

He looked down at her face. There was steadiness there, and a strength he hadn't realized that she possessed. Strength tempered by what drove her to pursue murderers and bring them to justice. She had the kind of resolve that only the worst of experiences could bring.

J. D. had always said that he trusted Terri without reservation, and never worried when she was there to watch his back. Now Cort could see why.

"Excuse me, Marshal." Lawson Hazenel said as he walked up to them.

Terri frowned. "Haze? What are you doing here?" She glanced at the front of him. Huge splatters of caramel-colored liquid soaked the front of his shirt and pants. "And why are you covered in latte?"

"If I ever talk about wanting kids, remind me of this, will you?" He turned to Cort. "I tailed Simon here. He was sitting watching the front of the church from a bench at the end of the block. He seemed very interested in you and that blonde you walked out with."

Cort swung around. The dark van that had been parked at the corner was gone. "Where is he?"

"That's the thing. A girl came up to my car and asked if I'd seen her little brother. When I looked around, she dropped a damn lizard down the back of my shirt. End result was this." Law pulled the latte-soaked material away from his chest. "The kid ran off, and when I looked for Simon, he was gone. I lost him."

Gray's receptionist looked around the edge of the door into his office. "I downloaded those files you wanted, Doc." She brought in a CD and handed it to him. "There's a Paul Taravelle holding on line four, says you called him?"

"Yeah, I did. Appreciate it, Jen." He punched the blinking button on his phone. "Dr. Taravelle, thanks for returning my call." Finally.

"Dr. Huitt," a deep, gravelly voice replied. "My service said it was an emergency."

"I'm trying to identify a victim from the Maskers fire." He picked up his call list and checked Taravelle's name. "You were Stephen Belafini's personal physician."

"That's correct."

"My Jane Doe was in the last stages of breast cancer, and she was undergoing radical chemo. She was approximately twenty-eight years old, five foot eight inches tall, and weighed between ninety-five and a hundred and ten pounds. She had lost most of her hair."

"I can't positively identify a woman from such a general description, Doctor."

General? He'd all but given him fingerprints. "I understand that, but does this description fit any member of Stephen Belafini's family? A wife, perhaps, or a sister?"

The older man's voice went flat. "That is confidential patient information."

"Your patient is dead, sir. So is mine, but she doesn't have a name. Help me to give her one."

There was a long silence on the other end of the line. At last Taravelle said, "I diagnosed Mr. Belafini's wife, Luciana, with breast cancer last year. Your Jane Doe could be her."

"Luciana Belafini," he repeated, writing down the name. "Did you refer her to an oncologist?"

"Of course I did, immediately." Taravelle gave him the other doctor's information.

"Thank you." Gray checked his MPR list. "Mrs. Belafini wasn't reported missing by the family. Why was that?"

"I don't know. Now, if we're finished—"

Gray thought of the thin, emaciated body. "Why did Stephen Belafini take her with him to that bar? Didn't he know how sick she was? Didn't he care?"

"I was Mr. Belafini's physician, Dr. Huitt, not his therapist. Good day." The line was disconnected.

Slamming down the phone gave him a little satisfaction, but not much. He glanced at the CD Jen had brought him and put it into his computer drive. The files she had downloaded for him from the Harvard medical database covered the latest treatments available for patients with advanced breast cancer. As he skimmed the information, he dialed the number for Luciana Belafini's oncologist.

"I called Stephen Belafini myself two weeks ago, when she didn't show up for her treatment," the specialist told him. "He told me he and his wife were separated, and he didn't know where she was."

"Did you see her after that?"

"Let me check my appointment book." There was a brief pause. "No, Dr. Huitt, according to my records, she never came back. Do you want me to send over what X-rays I have? They should confirm her identity."

"Yes, I'd appreciate it." He sat back and rubbed his eyes. "She wasn't going to make it, was she?"

"No, she was definitely on her way out. I was planning to hospitalize her after the last treatment." The specialist sighed. "She was a lovely woman, but I can't say I'm sorry she's dead. She was in an unbelievable amount of pain, but she refused morphine and there was very little else I could do about it."

"Why put her on chemo, then?"

"That was actually her idea. I advised against it—by the time I saw her, her liver, lungs, and kidneys were compromised—

but she insisted." The specialist uttered a sad chuckle. "Told me that she had everything to live for and didn't want to give up fighting."

Gray frowned. "That doesn't sound like a woman preparing to leave her husband."

"Leave him?" The oncologist echoed, incredulous now. "Dr. Huitt, Luciana Belafini was utterly *devoted* to her husband. She believed that the chemo would buy her a few more months, and she took her treatments through my outpatient clinic so that she could stay at home with him. If you ask me, her love for Mr. Belafini was really the only thing keeping her alive."

13

The day after Ashleigh Bouchard's funeral, Terri reviewed the outside ATM security tapes from the bank. Not one of them showed a clear shot of the patrons who used the drop box, which was just out of range of the camera lens. At best she had a few shots of some shoes and occasionally the patron's leg from the knee down. None of the shoes looked like anything Cort Gamble would wear, but that didn't mean anything.

What she needed was the cash that had been deposited, Terri thought as she stowed the tapes in their cases. Which had already been run through the banking system and distributed to other customers. That or . . .

Terri grabbed the phone and called the branch manager who had provided her with Cort's financial records. "How long do you keep the envelopes used to make deposits?"

"We dispose of them every thirty days," he said.

"Great. I need the envelope used to make the fifty-thousand-dollar deposit into Cort Gamble's account."

"I'm sorry, but they're thrown in a discard bin, Detective. We would have to sort through literally thousands of envelopes to find the one you want."

Terri thought of telling him how many dumpsters and landfills she and J. D. had crawled through, looking for evidence, but decided to use some bait. "The person who made that deposit could be a murderer, and you know how important fingerprint evidence is during trial. You'd be an instant hero for helping us nail this guy."

"It might even make it on Court TV," the manager said, sounding more enthusiastic.

"Exactly." She didn't wait for him to agree or disagree, but pressed on. "Have your people wear gloves and handle the envelopes carefully. Oh, and I'll need fingerprint records on every employee who might have handled the envelope. Thanks so much for your cooperation."

After she marked the case of security tapes for return to the bank and dropped them, Terri left the station and headed for the Italian-American Club downtown. The manager, Carlo Mancetti, was a stout former New Yorker who regarded her badge without surprise. Unlike the bank manager, Mancetti was less than cooperative.

"I wouldn't know the names of Mr. Belafini's guests," he told her. "As a member of the club, he is permitted to bring anyone he wishes to dine here."

"What about the rest of your staff?"

He looked down to adjust the little carnation in his lapel. "There is no reason for them to know that information."

"Really. One of your people reported a meeting between Frank Belafini and Fire Marshal Cortland Gamble. A guy named"—she checked her notes—"Santino. I'll need to talk to him."

"Santino is no longer employed here."

Hounds chasing their tails made more progress than she was with this case. "You got a home address on him?"

"He moved to Naples."

"In Florida?"

"In Italy." Mancetti stared down his faintly bulbous nose at her. "Is that all, Detective?"

"No, it isn't." She examined the different doors leading off from the lobby. Each was marked for the different sections of the club: kitchen, assembly room, dining room, and business office. One was marked PRIVATE. "What's in there?" She nodded toward it.

He smirked. "As soon as you produce a search warrant, I'll give you a personal tour."

Terri checked her watch and saw she only had five minutes left before she had to face the Society Girl Sadists. "I'll work on that." She fished out a business card and handed it to him. "In the meantime, if anyone around here suddenly emerges from the attack of mass amnesia, give me a call."

Terri walked out of the club and nearly collided with Gray Huitt, who was coming around the corner. "Hey, Doc. What are you doing over here? Following me?"

"Not just following you." He crooked his hands into menacing claws and hulked over her. "Stalking you."

"I'm irritable." She patted her purse. "I'm also carrying a fully loaded weapon."

"Okay, so we'll just be good friends." He dropped his hands. "What's got you irritable?"

"Having to report to Andre's House of Torture in four minutes." She inspected the tailored suit he was wearing. "You look nice. Why?"

"God, you're such a cop sometimes." Gray laughed. "I came down here to do a notification. I try to look official when I do those." He in turn inspected her creased trousers and leather jacket. "You?"

"I had to check out a lead. My lead moved back to Italy." Terri shrugged. "I'd better take off. See you, Gray."

He hesitated, and then nodded. "Call me later."

Gray watched Terri roar off on her Harley before entering the club. He had intended to tell her about Luciana Belafini, but she was in a hurry, and he wanted to get his facts straight.

An overweight Italian in a black suit met him in the lobby. A discreet gold pin listed his name as Mancetti with the word MANAGER beneath it. "May I help you?"

"I'm Dr. Huitt. I'm here to see Frank Belafini."

Mancetti's expression soured. "Do you have an appointment?"

"I have his dead daughter-in-law lying on a table in my morgue," Gray said politely. "Does that qualify?"

"Wait here." Mancetti disappeared into a room marked PRIVATE.

Gray waited ten seconds and followed him. The room behind the door was a combination bar and dining room, with room for at least two hundred guests. Four men occupied one table situated in a corner, and three of them looked like hired muscle. Mancetti was speaking to the fourth, a thin, balding man with thick glasses and a heavy gray mustache.

Gray strolled over, ignored the manager's sputtered protest and addressed the only one without muscles. "Are you Mr. Frank Belafini?"

"I am." Belafini waved away Mancetti. "You're the one who did the autopsy on my son, Stephen?"

"Yes." Gray casually pulled out a chair and sat down. "I'm not here to talk about him. It's about his wife."

Belafini chuckled. "What wife? They were getting a divorce." He picked up his wineglass and drank from it. "What does she want now, more money to fix her tits? That'll take more than I got, Doc."

The other men chuckled.

"Your daughter-in-law was receiving cancer treatment." Gray waited for a reaction, but Stephen's father didn't bat an eyelash. "You knew that, didn't you?"

Belafini uttered a few words in Italian, and the three men rose from the table and went to the bar. To Gray he said, "I know. So?"

"She was killed in the Maskers fire."

The news had an extraordinary effect on Belafini. His hand contracted around the crystal glass until the stem snapped and wine spilled all over the tablecloth. "What the fuck was she doing there?"

"I came to ask you that."

"I threw that bitch out of my house two weeks ago. She was making Stephen sick with her bullshit."

"She had breast cancer. She was entitled."

"She was dead anyway, but she tried to make my boy nuts, trying to get her cured. Had her tits cut off, couldn't have no kids, what use was she if he had?" He made a disgusted sound. "Stephen was better off without her hanging from his neck and crying on him." He gave Gray a narrow look. "She the reason he was there? That diseased bitch get him killed?"

Gray suspected if he threw a punch at Belafini, one or more of the three thugs would shoot him and dump his body in the river. Still, he considered smashing in the old man's face. "I don't know." He wasn't going to ask Belafini what to do with Luciana's remains. "Did she have any family I should contact?"

"No, they're all dead, too. You want to know what to do with the body, eh? For what she did to my boy, she should keep burning for eternity in Hell." Belafini absently wiped the wine from his hand. "Why would he go to her, after what I told him?"

"What did you tell your son, Mr. Belafini?"

"None of your fucking business." He nodded to one of his men, who came over to stand beside Gray. "You should leave now, and don't let me see you around here again."

"I'm not coming back." If he did, he'd have to test his theory of what would happen if he belted the old man. Then he thought of something better. "One more thing you should know."

"What?" He took his water glass and drank from it.

"We found their bodies together. They were holding each other," he lied, and smiled down into the old man's face. "Your son died in her arms."

Walking away gave Gray almost as much satisfaction as hearing Belafini choke and cough.

"Do you intend to spend the rest of the summer in your room?" Claire Navarre called through the door. "If you do, I can have a slot installed for your dinner trays. It will be much easier on the servants if they can simply slide them through."

"You don't have to do that. I'm not hungry." The thought of food made Moriah bury her face against her pillow.

"Oh, Moriah." Claire's voice softened. "I know you're still upset about poor dear Ashleigh, darling, but you can't wall yourself away from the world like this."

The world had become a terrifying place, where cars burned with friends inside them. *Oh yes, I can.*

"The Polstons are coming for dinner," her mother said. "You do remember their son, Lewis, don't you? He was quite taken with you."

Lewis Polston was a short, asthmatic pervert who had tried to slip his sweaty hand up Moriah's skirt the last time he had sat beside her while dining with his parents at the Navarres'. Ashleigh had called him the Clammy Pincher, and they had giggled together over his repeated attempts to cop a feel during any given social situation.

"Moriah, please, answer me."

"I can't see the Pinch—anyone now, Mother."

"At least come down and see the flowers that just arrived," Claire insisted. "I suspect Cortland Gamble sent them. He was so kind to you at the service, wasn't he? You should call and thank him."

Guilt made her roll over and stare at the ceiling. Cort *had* been wonderful, but seeing him only made her think of Ashleigh's promise to snare him.

"Well, darling, I have to go if I'm to have my hair done before dinner. Think about joining us tonight. Lewis will be so disappointed if you're not there." The sound of her footsteps retreated.

Moriah pulled off the covers and sat up, shivering as the air conditioning, which Claire kept at icebox temperature, struck her face. She hadn't bothered to take off the remains of her ruined makeup after the service, and there was a horrible taste in her mouth. Brushing her teeth and washing her face in her private bathroom filled up five minutes, and then she had to dress. She couldn't open her closet without thinking of Ashleigh, though, so she walked downstairs in her robe and slippers.

"Miss Moriah." One of the maids met her at the bottom of the stairs. "Would you like some breakfast?"

"No, thank you." Moriah looked at the enormous bouquet of exotic flowers occupying the center table in entry room. It wasn't like Cort to make such a gesture, but she *had* been weeping all over him yesterday. "Just some coffee and the newspaper out on the terrace, if you would." She felt she had to follow the details of the murder investigation, for Ashleigh's sake, but couldn't bring herself to watch television. The local stations replayed video of the car fire over and over.

The article on the memorial service made the front of the society page, but more was written about who had attended than about Ashleigh herself. As Moriah read it, her fingers curled into the printed page. Everything was written politely, but the underlying gossipy tone made her want to tear the article to shreds.

Yes, Ashleigh had been young and beautiful, and she had dated some gorgeous men, but that was not all she had been. She had had so much potential. She might have done great things with her life, and now would never have the chance.

But would she have? Moriah set down the paper. *Not like I'm any different. A few months ago, all I could think about was what I'd wear when I married J. D.*

The maid brought the phone out to her. "It's a Detective Vincent for you, Miss Moriah."

She hadn't taken any calls since the day Ashleigh died, but J. D.'s partner wouldn't phone unless it was official business. Terri Vincent had very little patience for anything but police work.

She'd always thought Terri Vincent was rude and often crass. Ashleigh had seen her once with J. D. and marveled at the female cop's dismal garments. "I think a homeless person has more style," she had remarked.

Moriah had never really noticed Terri's clothes. Usually she had been too busy feeling frivolous and foolish around the older, shrewd-eyed woman. She'd also deeply resented the amount of time J. D. had spent with her, and how he constantly referred to her as his best friend—and meant it.

Terri Vincent might not know how to dress, but she didn't seem to care. She was smart, perceptive and, according to Moriah's former fiancé, the best homicide cop on the force. She'd always made Moriah feel like a complete twit.

She took the phone from the maid. *This should make my humiliation complete.* "Hello, Detective Vincent."

"Ms. Navarre. I'm sorry for disturbing you at home."

"I'm just sitting around in my bathrobe, feeling useless." That sounded pathetic, and she forced a more brisk tone. "What can I do for you?"

"I'd like to come by today and ask you some questions about Ashleigh Bouchard. I've got a thing now, but what would be a good time?"

Moriah wondered what the "thing" was that made Terri sound so disgusted. *Maybe it's not this "thing," maybe it's just me.* "Anytime, really, I'm not going anywhere." She glanced at the paper. "Is something wrong?"

"No, just some routine questions. Would three p.m. be all right?"

"Okay."

"There's something else. The man who killed Ashleigh has made some threats, and it's possible that you could be in danger. Did Marshal Gamble speak to you about this?"

She frowned, trying to remember. Everything after that day had become something of a numbing blur. "Cort called and said something, but you know that he and I only dated a few times before J. D. and I became involved. I told him no one would even remember that."

"You should still be very cautious, Ms. Navarre. Watch your vehicles, and if you receive any strange calls or packages, let us know immediately. I'll see you at three."

Moriah ended the call and finished her coffee as she recalled the specifics of the conversation with Cort. The killer was evidently targeting women with whom Cort had been involved. It was ridiculous to think that the killer would come after her, however. She and Cort had barely seen each other a half dozen times, and they had certainly never been in love.

At the time, Moriah had felt he was too controlled and remote to suit her, although now she felt she understood him a little better. Ashleigh's murder was only one case. Cort likely had to deal with men who set things on fire and killed innocent people every day.

Moriah brought the phone in with her from the terrace and stopped to examine the flowers. It was an expensive arrangement, but she didn't like orchids and tiger lilies. They had no fragrance, and seemed oversized and almost plastic. She much preferred the pretty red tea roses he had sent her after their first date.

"You've got a terrible memory," she murmured as she set down the phone and reached for the card. It was marked on the front with her name, but it was spelled incorrectly: *Mariah* instead of *Moriah*.

That had to be the florist's fault. Cortland knew how to spell her name.

. . . *If you receive any strange calls or packages, let us know immediately.*

Her hand hesitated, and then she stepped to one side, peering at the stems of the big bird of paradise blooms. The florist had used oddly thick wire—silver instead of the usual green—and the water in the vase was almost yellow.

Her heart began to pound, and she took a deep breath. "So he ran out of green, and the water's old." But the arrangement did smell odd, as if it had been saturated with some sort of artificial flower fragrance.

Moriah went to take the card out, and felt a slight resistance. She pulled it forward and saw two golden hoop earrings had been taped to the back, along with a thin red wire that ran up under the sealed flap.

The world *was* a terrifying place.

"Oh, God." She backed away from the arrangement, then remembered the phone and carefully took it from the table. She dialed 911, and when the emergency operator answered, she backed away. "This is going to sound really stupid, but I think . . . hold on." She saw the maid about to walk around the corner and moved to give her a hard push back into the hall. "Lisette, get out of here."

"What's wrong, Ms. Moriah?"

Something sizzled and snapped, and a wall of sound and fire flung Moriah across the room.

After a terse voice-mail message from Terri, demanding that he come over to Andre's office, Cort cancelled his afternoon meetings and drove over. He heard them shouting at each other as soon as he walked in.

"It is appropriate for the occasion."

"I don't care. I'm not wearing it."

"Yes, you will."

"No, I won't." Something thumped onto the floor. "What are these damn things . . . sticking in my . . ."

"Don't touch your hair!"

"It's *my* hair and I'll touch it any way I damn well please."

"No, no—don't do that, you're tearing out the flowers!"

"He put *flowers*? On my *head*?"

Cort went to the back room, where Terri and Andre stood toe to toe, with a garment bag between them. Ivory beads glittered under the plastic. "Is there a problem here?"

"Yeah." Terri was searching through her hair with one hand and gripping the garment bag as if it were filled with heroin. "Professor Higgins here wants to dress me up like a Playboy bunny"—she pushed the garment at Andre—"and I'm not doing it."

"It's a Versace evening gown," Andre said, shoving the bag back at her, "not a bunny suit. Will you for God's sake stop that! You're ruining your hairstyle!"

"I don't need a damn hairstyle. I'm not wearing a dress so short that I can't bend over in it without flashing the entire city."

"A lady does not bend over!" Andre snapped.

"Oh gee, I didn't have the stick-up-the-ass treatment," she snarled back. "Want to lend me yours?"

"Terri." Cort went over and took the bag from her. "Go outside and have a cigarette."

"I quit smoking, damn it." She dragged her hand through her hair, pulling out sequined flowers and throwing them to the floor. "Flowers in my damn hair. I am *done* with this shit. You hear me, old man? *Done*." She stalked out of the room.

"You see? *That* is what I have to deal with." Andre threw out a hand. "Foul-mouthed, vulgar, prudish—did you see how she deliberately ruined her hair?—abusive, unnatural, obtuse, blundering, flat-footed, narrow-minded monster.

She complained the *entire* time that Pierre worked on her, and when he did her wax, she nearly broke his wrist."

"Her wax?"

Andre sighed. "For God's sake, Cortland. It's a depilatory treatment for her legs and bikini area. He was simply trying to tidy her up a bit."

Cort could well imagine Terri's reaction to that. "Andre, she's trying."

"To do what? Drive me insane? It's working!" The old man dropped into the stylist's chair and pressed a hand to his forehead. "If I have to spend one more hour with that woman, I will end my golden years in an asylum, eating Jell-O and weaving baskets while I watch reruns of 'The Price is Right' and drool along with the other inmates."

"I'll talk to her."

"Talk as much as you wish. God knows I have." Andre took out his flask, unscrewed the top, and took a long swallow before slumping back in the chair. "I can't turn a sack into a silk purse, Cortland. And under that beautiful but grossly neglected skin, that girl is one hundred percent pure *burlap*."

"Stay here." Cort went outside to find Terri climbing onto her motorcycle. "Wait a minute."

"Do you know what they did to me? That hair sadist smeared wax on my—"

"I know." He already had a visual, he didn't need her enhancing it.

"Then he let it harden and ripped it off!"

He cleared his throat. "I've heard it can be painful, the first time."

"Painful? Why don't you try getting your balls waxed, see how you like it?" She rammed her helmet over her head. "He's lucky I don't bring him and Moreau up on charges."

He reached over and took the keys out of the ignition. "You're going to go in and apologize to Andre."

She glared at him. "In what universe do you exist? Cause it sure as hell ain't mine. Give me back my keys." Her cell phone began to ring, as did his, and she took the phone out of her pocket. "Vincent."

He slipped her keys into his jacket and answered his. "Gamble." He listened as the 911 dispatcher described the bombing, and saw Terri's eyes widen. "I'll be right there."

As soon as he hung up, she asked, "Moriah?"

She had gotten the same call he had. "She's still alive." He handed her back her keys and climbed onto the back of her motorcycle. "Go."

Terri started up the engine and flicked on the emergency lights before she flipped down her faceplate. It muffled her voice as she said, "Hang on."

She drove to the Garden District at breakneck speed, weaving in and out of traffic when it became backed up. Cort kept his hands on her hips and moved his weight with hers to keep from unbalancing them.

He saw the smoke column first and pointed to it. "There."

Terri saw that the damage to the Navarres' three-story home was restricted mainly to the front rooms. There were no flames, but firefighters were hanging back as the members of the bomb squad moved in and out of the house, looking for devices.

She drove up and parked off one side of the drive, where Cort climbed off the back of the Harley. He waited for her to do the same before heading for the fire chief supervising the scene.

"Everyone got out alive, but two women were caught in the initial blast," the chief told them, and pointed to a pair of paramedics working over a gurney on the ground next to one of the two ambulances. "One's okay, but the other's burned pretty bad."

Terri followed Cort to where the medics were treating the victim. A woman in a maid's uniform with her arm in a sling was being helped into one ambulance, but the other woman lay facedown on the gurney still on the lawn.

Terri caught her breath as she saw it was Moriah Navarre. "Oh, no."

Moriah's lovely golden hair was gone, singed down to the scalp. Soot and the remains of burned fabric blackened her badly burned back. Someone had doused her with water—probably the firefighters—and there was a pressure bandage around her head.

Terri flagged a couple of patrolman and instructed them to set up a perimeter. She looked up and down the streets, wondering if the Torcher was watching them even now. *He probably looks like everyone else. Nice and normal.*

She rejoined Cort, who was watching the medics work on Moriah. He was standing so still he could have been a statue. "What else can I do?"

He rested a hand on her shoulder for a moment. "Stay with me."

One of the medics was on a handheld radio, speaking with a doctor. "We've got carotid and radial pulses present and equal, airway open, clear equal lung sounds with slight wheezing in the bases on expiration only. Prep for MCI." He fitted a nasal cannula to her face and began administering oxygen.

"Does she have inhalation injuries?" Terri asked him.

"She took in some smoke and heat, but it's not as serious as these burns." The second medic removed his stethoscope and bent down. "Ms. Navarre, can you hear me?"

Moriah's eyelids fluttered, and she made a low sound.

On the radio, the other medic said, "Female is approximately twenty-five years old, one hundred fifteen pounds, removed unconscious from residential fire involving an explosion, now semi-responsive. Patient sustained second-degree burns to the back and outer extremities, six-inch shallow laceration to the forehead, significant amount of glass shards embedded along the back and legs. One chunk's real close to her femoral artery. Bob, get the Water-Jel blanket from the unit." He applied a bulky, loose dressing over the back of her left thigh before carefully starting an IV in an unburned area on the back of her hand.

Terri had seen enough burn victims to know that Moriah was in serious trouble. "I just spoke to her an hour ago. I was coming over this afternoon to talk to her about Ashleigh."

Cort crouched down beside the gurney. "Moriah?" The injured woman opened her eyes to slits and tried to lift her head. "No, honey, stay still. They're taking you to the hospital. You're going to be okay."

"Flowers," she whispered. "Was . . . flowers."

"The bomb was in some flowers?"

She managed a nod. "Lisette?"

Cort looked up at the medic. "How is the other woman?"

"She has a broken arm and some superficial burns, but she'll be fine." The medic injected morphine into the IV line. "She told me that Ms. Navarre pushed her out of the way just before the bomb went off."

"Fleur D'amour." Moriah's eyelids were slowly closing. "Gold. On . . . card."

Terri pulled out her cell and made a quick call. "There's a *Fleur D'amour* florist shop on Long Street," she told Cort. "Maybe the lettering was gold."

"Moriah?" a woman shrieked.

Cort caught Mrs. Navarre as she ran up and nearly hurled herself on top of the injured girl. "Claire, you can't touch her."

The medic carefully secured Moriah, the IV bag, and the oxygen tank before elevating the gurney. "We have to take her now, ma'am."

"I have to go with her," Claire sobbed. "This is my daughter."

"You can ride over to the hospital with us," the medic told her as he pushed the gurney to the back of the ambulance.

"She's strong, Claire," Cort said as he walked with Moriah's mother to the front of the unit. "She'll get through this."

"She's all burned up." Claire pulled away from him, and swiped at her tears before she looked up at him. Hatred glittered in her eyes. "Because of you."

"Ma'am, you're wrong." Terri took a step forward, reaching out to the other woman. "The marshal isn't responsible for what's happened. A very sick man did this to your daughter."

Moriah's mother lunged at Terri, trying to hit her, but Cort caught her by the arms. "Claire, calm down."

"Don't you touch me, Cortland Gamble." The older woman wrenched away from him. "*You* did this to her."

He nodded. "Yes. This is my fault."

"You say it like it was nothing, you heartless bastard." Claire slapped his face. "I hope he kills you next. Do you hear me? *I hope you burn.*"

The medic put an arm around the hysterical woman and helped her into the ambulance.

Cort watched the unit depart before he turned to look at the scorched front of the Navarre house. The red imprint of Claire's hand blazed across his face.

Terri couldn't put her arms around him, couldn't press her mouth to the hurtful mark. Still, she put her hand on his arm. "Mrs. Navarre's upset, Cort. She didn't know what she was saying."

"He must have seen us," he said, his voice toneless. "Moriah kissed me outside the church, before she left." His gaze turned on her. "If she hadn't, this would have been you."

After Ruel received the report of the firebombing attack on Moriah Navarre from Pellerin, he went directly to Mercy Hospital's burn unit. He wasn't surprised to see Terri Vincent in the waiting room with Gamble and Pellerin, but stayed out of sight for a few minutes to observe them.

Gamble looked as grim as usual. Terri spoke to Pellerin now and then, going over some detail about the case. Gamble didn't comment or join in the discussion at all, but when Terri rose to get a cup of coffee from a vending machine out in the hall, he never took his eyes off her.

Things were progressing nicely, Ruel decided as he walked over to the vending machine. "I came as soon as I heard. How is she?"

"Ms. Navarre's got second-degree burns on her back and embedded glass all over the back of her body," Terri said. "They're going to operate on her leg in the morning, but the doc said she's in stable condition."

"Will she live?"

"Looks that way." She took the Styrofoam coffee cup from the machine.

Ruel took some change from his pocket and fed it to the machine. "Was Ms. Navarre a former lover of his?"

"No, they only dated a couple of times, years ago. Cort thinks the Torcher saw her kiss him at the church after Bouchard's memorial service and made the wrong assumption." Terri sipped from her cup and grimaced. "I've got to stick closer to him in public."

"What did he use for the bomb?"

"Prelim search turned up the same ingredients as the Bouchard murder. We think it was placed inside the residence and remote-detonated." She glanced past him into the waiting room. "Marshal Gamble was downtown with me when he got the call on the fire." She met his gaze. "So there's your proof: He's not involved."

"Not necessarily. You know as well as I do that Gamble could have paid someone to throw the switch. Or perhaps this is Belafini's idea of how to keep Gamble in line." Given the theatrical threat on the tape, Ruel was leaning more toward the latter theory now. "Has he said anything to you about it?"

"He hasn't said a word to anyone since we left the scene," Terri said through gritted teeth. "He's blaming himself for it, and he's not the only one. The victim's mother went crazy and hauled off and *hit* him."

"Then it's the ideal time to work him for information," Ruel told her. "He's emotional, so he won't be as guarded."

"You think?" She turned on her heel and strode back into the waiting room.

Ruel followed her in and greeted the other men. "Terri told me about Ms. Navarre. I'm sorry, Marshal."

Cort rose and went to the window to stare out at the parking lot below. "We have to set up protection for Moriah. When he finds out that she survived, he'll try to kill her again."

"How do you know that?" Ruel asked softly.

Cort swung around. "He's a repeater on a mission. Arsonists like this don't do things halfway. He didn't kill her this time, so he'll try again."

Ruel noted the subtle change in the other man's voice.

You know I'm on to you, but you don't know how much. Terri would have to work quickly now, and Ruel intended to pour the pressure on her until she got what he needed.

"This nutcase doesn't do anything in a small way, either," Pellerin said, his forehead creasing. "Having her here will put the entire hospital at risk."

"Not if we let him think that he succeeded," Terri said. She went over to Cort. "If the Torcher believes that Moriah is dead, he'll move on to the next target. We'll make sure he thinks it's me."

Ruel saw how Gamble wavered. He wanted to protect the Navarre girl and Terri. *This is Belafini's work, then. Gamble will crack under the pressure, soon enough.*

The chief of Homicide nodded. "We've relocated endangered witnesses before. If she's stable enough, I can arrange to transport her over to the burn unit in Atlanta tonight. I can move the family, too, so they don't blow the story."

"Everyone else will have to think she's dead," Terri said.

"Yes, that's the only way it will work. Marshal, you'll have to give a press conference, to get the word out right away," Ruel suggested.

"Call the mayor," Cort said. "Acting is his job."

The marshal was good, Ruel acknowledged. He knew just how to deflect responsibility for his actions onto someone else. Only Ruel wasn't going to let him. "The Torcher will get off hearing it from you. Unless you have some other means with which to stop these attacks."

The look Gamble gave him was lethal. "What other means?"

"Well, you've got Vincent," Pellerin said.

Ruel smiled. "Yes, you do."

14

Cort left Terri at the hospital and returned to the scene. His task force was busy searching through the rubble that had been the Navarres' entry hall, but little evidence had been turned up.

"We've got kerosene and gunpowder residue, along with some plastic explosive this time," Gil said. "Definitely went off a remote trigger."

"He needed it to be small but powerful." Cort turned around, assessing the damage. "That way he only had to use a single device."

"That fits. According to the housekeeper, the only delivery to the house was a flower arrangement for Ms. Navarre," his investigator told him. "Thirty minutes later, the bomb went off. Good thing these are structure-support walls, or it might have blown out the whole front of the house."

The plastic explosive would be traceable, unless the Torcher had obtained it illegally. "Moriah Navarre said that the bomb was in the flowers. Detective Vincent has the name of the shop."

"I know, she called from the hospital, and I checked it out," Gil said. "Wasn't delivered by the store, but the owner remembers selling a big bouquet yesterday."

"So he bought it, rigged it, and delivered it himself." Cort walked through the open front doorway, from which the door had been blasted off its hinges. "Did we get a description of the buyer or the delivery man?"

"Shop owner's an older lady, says she can't remember much about him." Gil grimaced. "White guy, late thirties to early forties, ball cap, sunglasses. Housekeeper here stated that someone rang the doorbell but all she found were the flowers on the doorstep."

Cort examined the arrangement of the hall, which was enclosed on three sides and had no windows. "How did he know when to trigger it? He couldn't see inside the house."

"One of the bomb-squad guys thought it might be timed or voice-activated." Gil scratched his head. "Couldn't have known when she'd be near them, though, and anyone's voice would have set it off."

"No, he wanted Moriah. He needed to know it was her." Cort moved through the hall, looking at every inch of the soaked, scorched flooring. He spotted something sticking out from under a collapsed tabletop. "Gil, got a bag and some tongs?"

When his investigator handed him the clear plastic tongs, Cort bent down and carefully picked up the edge of the table-top. Holding it aloft, he used the tongs to gently retrieve a short length of burnt black cable and two lumps of black-ened, twisted metal. He dropped them one by one into the evidence bag Gil held out for him.

The investigator held it up to the light. "Wire's a little thick for a remote. Metal could be brass."

"It's audio cable." He shifted some of the debris and found the remains of a tiny microphone. "That's how he knew it was her. He was listening in." He took the bag and examined the metal. "Brass doesn't look like this when it melts. This is gold."

"Transmitter would have a limited range." Gil tagged the spot with evidence markers. "I've never heard of a firebug using gold in a bomb except in the movies."

"Who's been taking statements from eyewitnesses?"

"That would be me, Marshal." Law Hazenel gingerly picked his way around the working techs over to them. "One of the neighbors reported seeing a man walking around in the neighborhood early this morning. The description fit Douglas Simon, but when I called the motel where he's been staying, the manager said that he'd checked out. His parole officer doesn't know where he is."

"Put out an APB on him." He thought of how Ruel had spoken to Terri back at the hospital. He hadn't been able to overhear their conversation, but it was obvious that the OCU chief was putting some pressure on her. It didn't matter. He'd already made up his mind about what to do about Terri. "Keep Detective Vincent out of the loop on this one."

Law frowned. "But I copy Terri on everything."

"Not anymore." By the end of the day Cort intended to have Terri off the case and reassigned to another department.

Moriah Navarre was moved to Atlanta along with her family and, as Cort disappeared and couldn't be reached, Pellerin made the announcement to the media.

Ruel ordered Terri to stay away from the impromptu press conference. "You're not a cop, you're Gamble's girl-friend. Go find him and stay with him." He gave her the once-over. "And do something with yourself. You look like hell."

It was the long, grueling hours at the hospital paired with the phony press conference that made Terri disobey her new boss's orders and ride home. All she wanted was a long hot shower and a few hours of peace and quiet in order to collect herself before she saw Cort again.

The phone began ringing two minutes after Terri stepped under the spray. She got shampoo in her eyes, trying to rinse out fast, and nearly slipped on the damp floor getting out.

"Vincent," she snapped into the phone.

"Is my son there?" Elizabet Gamble asked.

"No." Terri knuckled her stinging eyes. "Uh, sorry, Mrs. G., I don't know where he is. Have you tried his cell?"

"Yes. He's not answering it. Louie and I just saw the news about Moriah on television." She cleared her throat. "Why didn't Cortland call us about this?"

Terri was tempted to tell her about the ruse, but she didn't know if Elizabet would keep it to herself. Also, it wasn't her decision to make.

"You'd have to ask him, Mrs. Gamble." She grabbed her sagging towel. "I'm, uh, sorry for your loss."

"I don't believe that." Elizabet's voice rose an octave. "You never liked Moriah."

True, she never had. Any girl Cort had been involved with had stuck in her craw, and she'd never thought Moriah was good enough for J. D., either. There was a healthy amount of envy mixed in with that as well, something that she'd thought about plenty today.

Moriah Navarre might survive the attack, but the beautiful girl was going to carry scars from it, inside and out, for the rest of her life.

"You were supposed to prevent something like this from happening." Unaware that she was practically reading Terri's mind, Elizabet sounded wretched and tearful now. "Why didn't you?"

Terri thought about the call she had made to Moriah, just before the firebombing. She had gone over it in her head a thousand times while waiting at the hospital. If she had said more, or urged the other woman to be more cautious, none of this might have happened. "If I could have stopped it, I would have."

"Who else is going to suffer because of your ignorance? How many more people are going to die?" A sob burst from the older woman. "If you had been doing your job correctly, Moriah would still be alive."

Would you cry for me like this? If you knew how I felt about your son, would you even be sorry? "You're right. Moriah would be alive, and *I'd* be dead."

"I didn't mean . . ." Elizabet fell silent.

"If I hear from the marshal, I'll ask him to call you. Good-bye, Mrs. Gamble." Terri set down the receiver gently.

She went back and finished her shower, moving mechanically, as if all her nerves had been disconnected. She heard the phone ring several times, but ignored it and let the answering machine pick it up. She'd had her fill of guilt trips for one day.

She reached for a pair of jeans and a T-shirt, hesitated, and instead pulled out one of the garment bags. The dress inside it was black silk, simply cut, and didn't have a single flower, sequin, or bead attached to it. She took out the dress and held it up to check the length. It fluttered just above her knee.

"Now why couldn't I wear something like this?" she asked her reflection.

She slipped on a black bra, but she had no matching underwear. Instead, Andre had sent over some G-strings, and she sorted through them until she found a black one to match. It had ties on the sides, but it felt more comfortable than her more staid cotton panties.

"No wonder strippers like these things." She pulled on the dress and turned from side to side in front of the mirror to inspect it. "Yeah, this is definitely me."

Would Cort think the same thing? Did the clothes really make the woman? Part of her felt like ripping off the dress and tearing it to shreds. Another part, which had been locked up in a dark corner of her head for a long, long time, wanted to go play with Andre's makeup and see what she could do with her face.

If he was here, I could make him want me again. The knock at her front door made Terri tense and glance up at the ceiling. "Don't be funny, God."

A quick check through the narrow window slot by the door made her relax. "Grayson," she said as she swung the door open. "What are you doing here?"

"I needed to talk to you. I tried calling a few times, but I just got your machine." He let his gaze wander down, then up. "Going somewhere, and want to give me directions?"

"No, just messing with the girl stuff. Come on in."

The pathologist had never been to her apartment, and looked around with interest. "Nice place, for a closet. Plus you don't have leaks." Gray was forever patching up the ancient hull of his houseboat.

"I don't need much, I'm never here." She looped the towel around her shoulders. "Want something cold?"

"I brought you a present instead. IDed our Jane Doe Four and did an autopsy on her." He handed her a folder. "X-rays confirm she was Luciana Belafini, wife of one of the victims."

"Luciana." Terri rocked on her heels as she remembered the tall, handsome brunette. Cort had brought her to the ceremony when J. D. and Terri got their shields, and she had teased Cort's brother unmercifully. She had been one of the few women Cort had dated that Terri had ever liked. "You went to the Italian-American Club today to see Belafini? Are you out of your mind?"

"Generally. Know if she's an old girlfriend?"

"Yeah, she was." Terri sat down on the edge of her sofa and opened the file. "Have you told him?"

"I left a voice mail, but no details. I figured they might have been involved."

"Yeah. You might want to wait on it until tomorrow." She dropped the file onto her coffee table. "He'll be more receptive."

"That's why you look so pale." Gray sat down beside her. "Is he ragging on you?"

"No, I'm fine." Cort was the one who had suffered, just as the Torcher had predicted. All she'd had to do was watch and feel utterly useless.

"In that case, want to put that dress through its paces and have wild monkey sex with me?" He fluttered his eyelashes at her.

An unwilling laugh burst from her. "Not tonight, Tarzan."

He put an arm around her shoulders and gave her a half hug. "Then let's go get something to eat and we'll talk."

The only thing she'd had all day was bad coffee, and the mention of food made her stomach wake up and growl. "Okay, let me grab some shoes."

She went into the bedroom and started to slide her feet into her favorite sneakers before she eyed the stack of shoeboxes.

"Oh, all right." She took out a pair of black leather slides and shoved her feet into them. "Walk slow. Don't shuffle."

She stopped in the bathroom and whisked on some makeup. If she did it very fast, and didn't use much, it looked all right. Her mouth looked nice with the fire-engine-red stuff that never, ever came off, even if you ate or drank, according to Andre, until you used the liquid remover.

"Shit, I'm turning into a girl again," she said to the mirror over the sink. She made a hideous face, and laughed at herself.

"What's so funny?" Gray called from the living room.

She turned her back on the reflection. "Me."

Terri followed Gray to the restaurant on her bike, so she could practice riding with a dress on again. If she kept her knees in and the sides of the skirt tucked under her thighs, the hem stayed put.

The restaurant was small and crowded, but the seafood was fresh and the beer Gray ordered was dark and had a nice bite to it. They swapped crawfish and crab from their plates while Gray filled her in on what he had learned about Luciana Belafini.

"The thing that still bothers me is the different stories I got on her," Gray said. "The oncologist says she's madly in love with her husband, but the housekeeper claims she left him. Belafini said he threw her out."

"I could see Belafini doing that." Terri snapped open a crab leg and dug out the steaming white meat inside. "Then again, maybe she knew she was on her way out and wanted to spare Stephen that."

"Don't think so." Gray snitched a French fry from her plate. "She took the chemo outpatient, so she could be home with him. With the dosage she was taking, she had severe side effects. He had to see her hair fall out, daily vomiting, the works. Why would she bail on him or let the old man chase her off at the end?"

She thought of Cort and picked up her drink. "Maybe she wanted him to remember her as alive instead of being with her when she died. Sometimes we do things we don't want to, to protect the people we love."

"Like you working for Ruel."

She nearly choked on her beer. "Excuse me?"

"Word has it that Chief Ruel has pulled every file that exists in the department on the marshal. Old case work, personnel, training, all the way back to when he was a firefighter.

Then he brings you over to OCU and assigns you to the Maskers fire. You bring me in to play boyfriend, but suddenly Ruel has you playing Mrs. Marshal-to-be. I mention Luciana Belafini, wife of a mob boss's son *and* Gamble's ex-girlfriend, and you nearly pass out." He looked steadily across the table at her. "I'm no genius, Ter, but the addition's not that hard."

She thought about lying to him. Yet Gray already knew most of it, and she could really use some friendly advice, at which he was excellent. "If I tell you, it can't go any further."

He raised three fingers. "Former Scout's honor."

"I'm running an independent investigation for Ruel. He thinks Cort is working for Frank Belafini." She gave him the background information, the anonymous deposit, and the meeting between Belafini and Cort. "Ruel is wrong, but I'm the only who can prove it."

"Gamble doesn't know?"

She shook her head.

"You should tell him, or at least have me around when he finds out." Something beeped, and Gray removed a pager from his pocket. "I'm on call tonight. Sorry, but I've got to go." He waved down the waitress and asked for the check.

The thought of riding off alone had lost its appeal. She didn't want to be alone, and if she couldn't be with Cort, Gray was the next best thing. "Mind if I tag along?"

"Not at all." He grinned at her. "I stopped polishing my desk, you know. I might get one of those nonslip blotters, too."

She chuckled and shook her head. "Keep dreaming, pal."

Cort spent two frustrating hours trying to have Terri Vincent removed from the Torcher case. Pellerin had been more interested in bitching him out over not showing at the press conference, and then claimed he didn't know where she was. After five terse voice-mail messages, Ruel called Cort back and blandly said the same.

To his surprise, it was the mayor who finally agreed to

intercede on his behalf with Chief Ruel, but only if Terri agreed to be removed from the case.

"You said she's done nothing wrong," Jarden told him. "If you're not bringing her up on charges, then it has to be voluntary."

Cort felt certain that after what had happened to Moriah he could convince Terri to take her vacation time. That was when he discovered that she wasn't answering her cell or her pager, and he couldn't find her.

Cort sat outside her apartment and tried to think of where she could be. Driving to her duplex did no good. The windows were dark, the Harley was gone, and Cort could hear her cell phone and pager going off inside. He'd already checked her favorite watering hole, and she wasn't at the lake cottage. J. D. had always said she had no friends and only visited family once every blue moon. That left her boyfriend Huitt or the Torcher.

She's not in any danger, Cort told himself as he put the SUV into gear and drove over to the morgue.

The night-shift technician on duty didn't have an address for Huitt. "He's got a houseboat, Marshal, but he moves it around a lot. Says he gets tired of his neighbors."

Did he have to get a brace of bloodhounds to find the damn woman? "I need to get in touch with him tonight." And if Terri wasn't with him, he'd recall the entire task force to hunt her down.

"Doc's on his way in now," the tech said. "You want to wait in his office?"

Cort went and paced the confines of the pathologist's office. The desk was a mess of files, lab slips, and specimen containers. There were Springsteen posters on the wall, tacked up beside dissection charts. An anonymous chunk of some unidentifiable organ floated in a glass jar filled with clear liquid set on top of a surfing magazine. Ten ceramic canisters lined the top of the filing cabinet, and Cort saw dark grounds in one that had been left open. The place smelled like a cross between a Columbian coffee plantation and Dr. Frankenstein's laboratory.

He moved the glass jar to pick up the magazine. Huitt

was on the front cover, poised on his board, riding the curl of a perfect wave. *And this is what she wants.* Disgusted, he tossed the magazine back on the desk. *Golden Boy.* The sound of Terri's laughter made him wonder if he was losing his mind, until he saw her and Huitt stroll in.

Cort hadn't prayed in years, but he did now. *She's safe. Thank you.*

She was more than safe. She was arm in arm with the blond doctor, smiling up at him, and looking as if she didn't have a care in the world.

Seeing Terri with Huitt didn't make Cort angry. Neither did the glossy red color on her lips or the tousled condition of her hair. The skimpy black dress and high-heeled slides, however, made him consider putting his fist through the wall.

Cort didn't kick the door open or shout as he walked out to confront her. "Detective Vincent, I've been trying to contact you for several hours."

Terri's smile vanished and she let go of Huitt's arm. "Is it Moriah? Is she all right?"

"She's stable. She and her family are in Atlanta by now." Cort gestured toward the hall. "I need a word with you."

Huitt looked puzzled. "Did something happen to Ms. Navarre?"

"It's a little complicated," she said to the pathologist. "I'll just be a minute."

As soon as they were alone, Cort asked, "Were you out in public like that?"

"Uh, yeah. Gray and I went to get something to eat." She glanced down at herself. "I like this one better. Can I wear it the next time I play Marshal's Girlfriend?"

Had she been drinking? "It will be difficult to convince the Torcher that you're mine if you're out running around with Dr. Huitt."

"It was just a little seafood place," she said. "No one saw us."

"You could have been followed." He didn't look at the dress, it only made his blood pressure spike. "Please remember that you are to wear the clothes Andre has provided for work, not to get laid."

"Duly noted." Anger glittered in her eyes. "I'll change as soon as I get home."

Now he'd tell her that she needed to quit the case, so that she wouldn't end up like Moriah. But what came out of his mouth was, "I don't want you seeing Huitt again."

Her dark brows arched. "I beg your pardon?"

"Your personal life is interfering with this investigation." That sounded reasonable.

"Is it?" She folded her arms. "That manger comfortable, Marshal?"

"Don't start with me," he warned her. "I am *not* in the mood."

"You're never in the mood. Go get drunk. You're nicer when you're drunk." She swung away from him. "But don't come to my place after." She glanced back over her shoulder. "I'll be busy."

Cort stood out in the hall for several minutes after Terri returned to the morgue. He had no claim on her, and what she did on her own time was none of his business. He could call her in the morning and tell her everything over the phone. He looked through the square window into the morgue, where Terri was standing with Huitt, talking to his technician. The pathologist lifted his hand and casually rested it on the back of her neck.

The *hell* he would.

Terri looked over as Cort walked in. "Was there something else, Marshal?"

"We have a seven a.m. briefing in the morning," he lied. "I'm taking you home."

She faced him. "I've got my own wheels, thanks."

"Maybe you should head out, Ter," Huitt said. "We can get together about the autopsy reports tomorrow."

"She won't be available," Cort told him, and took hold of her wrist. "Let's go."

"I'll go when I'm ready." Terri tugged her arm.

Tightening his grip on her felt good. Throwing her over his shoulder would feel better, and he was about ten seconds away from doing that. "You'll leave when I tell you to, Detective. Now say good night."

Huitt moved forward. "That's enough, Gamble."

So Golden Boy has a backbone. "I've had an ugly day." Cort released Terri and regarded the other man. "Don't give me an outlet."

The pathologist smiled. "But it would be my pleasure."

"Hey." Terri tried to get between them. "You're not going to start pounding each other. I'll cuff both of you."

"You're not carrying your handcuffs." Cort didn't look away from the other man's eyes.

Huitt's gaze shifted. "Save them for later, sweetheart."

Cort would have thrown the first punch, but Terri stepped in front of him and planted both hands on his chest. "Stop it."

"You don't have to do anything he says, Terri," the pathologist said. "He doesn't own you."

Setting her aside was proving impossible. "Neither do you, Huitt." Cort encircled her wrists with his hands and looked down at her. "Decide."

She took in a sharp breath. "All right, I'm leaving." To the pathologist, she said, "I'll talk to you later, Gray."

"Good night, Doctor." Cort hauled her out of the office.

Terri nearly fell twice, trying to keep up with Cort's long-legged strides out of the morgue. He wouldn't let go of her, and trying to wriggle free wasn't working. Her slides skidded on the slippery floor. "Would you slow down?"

"No."

Once they were outside, the soles of her slides hit the dew-soaked grass and she teetered again. "I'm going to break an ankle in these things."

"Good."

He was *really* steaming this time. All at once she was tired, tired of hiding the investigation she was doing for Ruel and using Gray as a wall between her and Cort. If they were going to solve this case, she needed to come clean. "Look, I need to clear up some things between you and me."

"So do I."

She saw he was leading her to his SUV, and glanced over at the Harley. "I can't leave my bike here overnight. It won't be here in the morning."

Cort changed direction and headed for the motorcycle.

Terri fumbled, getting the keys out of the little purse she brought. "I'm sorry I wasn't available when you needed me, and I know you're upset about Moriah. But don't be mad at me. We're both under too much stress to be expected to act like rational human beings."

He looked down at her with a strange expression. "Get on."

She straddled the bike, and felt the tires compress a moment later as he swung on behind her. So he was riding with her. To her apartment? "What about your car?"

His big hands clamped on her hips. "It will be here in the morning."

"Where am I taking you?" Not to her place, not with the way he'd been acting, or the way she was feeling.

His fingers dug in, hard enough to make her flinch. "Just drive."

15

Terri started up the Harley's engine and pulled away from the curb. She'd take Cort home. It was a short ride, and by the time they got there both of them would be calmer. He'd probably invite her in to have a drink and want to be all civilized again. Not like he was going to jump on her in his parents' house.

She hoped.

Although Cort was barely touching her, she could feel the heat of his body all along her back. The wind caught the hem of her skirt, flipping it up on her thighs and, remembering the G-string, she swore under her breath and reached down to tuck it in. Cort beat her to it, spreading his fingers over her leg and preventing the hem from creeping up any farther.

Feeling his callused palm against her bare thigh made the muscles in her stomach knot. Reaching around her to hold down her skirt brought Cort's upper body in contact with her back. The thin black silk of her dress and the fine cotton of his shirt weren't much of a barrier. She could feel every breath he took, every beat of his heart.

She'd been this close to him before, but not being able to see his face was making her uneasy. She couldn't tell if his temper was cooling off or getting hotter.

Glancing down at his long, solid thighs and seeing the way they pressed along the outside of hers made Terri scoot forward. He simply shifted his weight to compensate, which ended with his crotch nestled right up against her backside.

Now she was the one who was getting hotter.

This was a really, really a bad idea. She focused on the deserted roads and took the fastest route she knew from downtown to the Garden District.

She had to brake when she came to a flashing red traffic light, and rolled to a stop. As she braced the bike with her feet, she realized she hadn't bothered to put her helmet on. That was how rattled he had her back at the morgue.

She gave the hand he was using to hold down her skirt an awkward pat. "I've got it now, thanks."

His fingers clenched for a moment before his palm slid back over the skirt to rest on the curve of her waist. He didn't ease his chest off her back, however, and she could feel him watching over her shoulder as she secured the sides of the dress. After checking the intersection, Terri released the foot brake and shifted into first.

As soon as the Harley was moving again, Cort put his mouth next to her ear. "Don't stop again."

His temper hadn't disappeared yet. "Why not?"

Cort didn't answer her. His hand glided back down her thigh, but instead of pressing down her skirt he tugged the fold under her right thigh loose and slipped his fingers beneath it from the side.

Terri was sure he had a perfectly acceptable reason for sticking his hand under her dress. Maybe he'd seen a bug crawl up her leg, and was just trying to get it without startling her. That's why he was moving his fingers up the soft skin of her inner thigh. He was hunting around for it.

The bug theory went out the window when his fingers moved to the abbreviated band of the G-string.

He isn't feeling me up. He wouldn't do that. Terri looked down to see his hand moving under the black silk, and felt his fingers push under the front of the G-string. *Oh Christ, he is.*

Terri loved riding the Harley because it made her feel strong, sexy, and in control of her life. Nothing was like sitting astride the bike, feeling the powerful vibrations of the engine, and knowing how fast it would take her. She loved the wildness of it, of handling such a sleek, beautiful machine.

Now and then she'd even indulged in a sensual fantasy, imagining what it would be like to do something sinful and shameless like making love on the back of her motorcycle. Not while it was in motion, of course, but maybe while it was parked under one of the big trees down by the lake. Right out in the open, where she could feel the wind and the sun on her body. Every time she imagined that, it was always Cort who undressed her, and Cort who had sex with her.

What the real Cort was doing to her now totally blew away that little illicit daydream.

His hand was between her legs now. She should hit the brake, stop the bike, make him get off, or do *something* to keep him from touching her like this. He had no right, not after the way he'd treated her, and not when her emotions were this wobbly. Terri started to brake, and then felt his fingers part her and curl over to probe. He said something, but it was too low for her to make out.

Does he want me to stop? He'd said not to, and she didn't want to stop. She didn't want him to stop.

The road ahead was clear of traffic, and she shifted from first into second. At the same time, she tilted her hips, letting him sink two fingers into her, clenching herself around them.

Her limbs felt like melting. The way he was stroking her felt so good, so sweet. She could ride like this all night.

"You like that?" Cort asked, his mouth just next to her ear as he worked his hand against her, pushing his fingers in deeper.

Terri hoped *Mmmmm* was an acceptable answer. That was the only sound she could get out of her mouth.

He moved the pad of his thumb over her clit, pressing against it. "Did you fuck him?"

The harsh question jerked her out of her daze. He was talking about Gray. About her and Gray. "No."

"Don't lie to me." His hand moved, rougher and more insistent. "Have you ever fucked him?"

Cort wasn't angry. He was jealous. Over *her.* The shock of it forced the truth out. "No."

He wasn't through interrogating her. "You haven't been with anyone since me, have you?"

Was this why he was playing with her? Just because his pride was bruised? And here she was, letting him. She was pathetic. "A dozen guys. Maybe more."

"I told you not to lie to me." Oddly, his hand gentled, and the sweetness returned. "You're as tight as you were that night. No one's had you since. I can feel it."

Terri shuddered. She was so wet now that she could hear everything that she felt him doing to her. She had to turn a corner, and downshifted. She'd be at his house in two minutes. She could stand this for two more minutes.

Cort's mouth touched a spot under her left ear. "Turn left."

She had to turn right to take him home. Which is where she was taking him, where she would dump him, and then she'd go back to the duplex and have a good cry and tomorrow the universe would right itself.

Terri turned left.

His fingers twisted inside her, nudging a spot that made her groan. "Go to the highway."

The highway, where she wouldn't have to brake or turn. She slowed down. "Cort—"

He put his free hand over hers on the accelerator and increased their speed. Terri had to concentrate on driving and the road to keep from losing control of the bike, but pressed her thighs together to hold his hand against her. Wind rushed over her hot face and her bare thighs. The slick flesh cradled by his palm and tightening around his fingers pulsed with aching delight.

If he stopped touching her, she'd scream.

She took the entry ramp onto the highway and automatically shifted into third, opening up the Harley. There were only a few cars around them, and she moved into the far left lane, away from illuminating flashes of the highway lights.

Cort took his hand from the accelerator and pressed it against her ribs, directly under her left breast. He brought his knuckles up over her nipple and then caught it between the backs of two fingers, squeezing it between them. At the same time, he stroked her clit.

The double sensation made Terri jolt back against him. "Jesus, Cort, I'll crash us." Her voice shook with fear and excitement.

"No, you won't." He slowly eased his fingers out of her body and used them on the tie on her right hip, then her left. "Lift up."

Her breath went ragged as she rose off the seat an inch and felt Cort pull the G-string away from her body. She couldn't believe he'd taken it off until she saw a faint dark blur as he pulled it from under her skirt and tossed it to the wind. She couldn't turn and look at his face, couldn't speak as she felt his hand draw back and work between her backside and his crotch.

He's unzipping his pants. She shivered as she felt his penis, hard and erect, the blunt head pushing against the black silk. A speeding car blew past them, and instinctively she moved back, trying to conceal him. She felt his hands slide under the curves of her buttocks.

"Lift up," he said again, his breath harsh against her ear.

They couldn't do this. Not on the back of the Harley, not when they were doing seventy on the highway. Neither of them had helmets on. One mistake and they'd both be smeared all over the wall that separated the north and south lanes. It was stupid and reckless and dangerous.

Adrenaline surged in her veins. Nothing so wild or erotic came without risk, and she was tired of being a good girl. She needed this.

She needed him.

Her heart thundered in her chest as he urged her up, guiding himself under the fluttering skirt and between the back of her thighs. She felt him graze the tightly puckered orifice that was more readily accessible, and gulped in a breath at the dark, foreign sensation.

Was that what he wanted?

Terri had experience, but not this much. Feeling him there was as thrilling as riding the Harley this way; it was outrageous and risky and she wanted more.

She wanted everything.

For a moment he pressed in, enough to make her drag in a deep, bracing breath. Then his free hand gripped her thigh painfully as he shifted under her, pushing forward until he was directly under her, breaching the drenched, engorged folds until the tight ring of her vagina began to stretch over the smooth head of his cock.

"Oh, God." She felt herself convulse around him. The orgasm that hit her was hard and fast and savage. She was completely unprepared, and as she peaked the bike wobbled slightly.

"Easy." The heated flow allowed him to sink in another inch, and his arms came around her, supporting her while his big hands covered hers on the handle bars. "Push down on me. Take me inside you."

He was giving her control now. He had to, there was no other way.

Terri couldn't take him all at once, he was too wide, too long, and every muscle between her legs had tensed. The burning ache that taking the head of his cock had caused was already receding, but she couldn't stay like this. She had to have him, the full length of him, buried deep inside her.

She rocked forward and pushed back, taking him in another inch. Coming had made her even wetter, which helped a little. The tight wedge of their bodies and driving the bike made it difficult to gain the leverage she needed.

"I can't do this," she told him. "Help me."

He pressed his mouth to the side of her neck, biting down hard enough to sting. "Move your feet."

The toes of his shoes nudged the back of her heels, and when she lifted them, he slid his feet under hers, taking control of the bike's brake and gear shift. She hooked her heels on the foot pegs and took control of him.

She rocked, worked herself over him, rocking him into her. Her whole body shook with the effort, until their body hair meshed and a deep, wrenching sound came out of her throat. Then she felt his thighs press in, lifting her higher, settling her back so that her weight rested against him. The movement shifted him inside her, making their fit easier even as she felt him growing harder and becoming more distended.

"Go on, Therese," he whispered against her hair. "Ride me."

The Harley flew down the highway, skimming the shadows of the retaining wall, the engine purring smoothly as Cort shifted gears. Terri propped her hands against the center of the steering column and clutched it as she rose, feeling him slide out of her almost to the tip before she reached between her legs to wrap her fingers around his shaft. Holding him, she slowly lowered herself, impaling her body on his.

As she squeezed him with her hand and her body, she felt her back grow damp. Sweat glistened on the corded muscles of his arms, the rush of his breath was hot against her neck. Moving on him was making her sweat, too, the wind pasted her dress against the trickles running between her breasts. But it was the slow, delicious slide of him into her body, the long, deep penetrations that held her in a vise grip of unbearable tension.

Pleasure returned, so hot and heavy and thick that it swamped her senses and made her writhe atop him.

But it wasn't enough. Not for her.

"Faster," he said, his voice hoarse now. "Harder."

She braced her arms and did what she had wanted to do at first, jamming herself down on him, crying out at the shock of the suddenness and a near-electric shock that sizzled through her womb. Cort's thighs lifted as he ground himself inside her, trying to squeeze himself deeper before she lifted away.

Terri rode him, stroking him with the narrow glove of her vagina, pushing back and forth as hard as she could stand. Her thighs burned, and his penis was so hard and swollen now that it dragged on her with every thrust, but she couldn't slow down and wouldn't stop.

"Yes, like that," he urged her on, his deep, beautiful voice reduced to a ragged growl. "Make me come, Therese. Make me come with you."

She was so close, so ready, but it wasn't enough this time. She wanted to kiss him, she needed to see his eyes. "I can't."

Cort turned the bike, crossing three lanes and shifting down until they were on the shoulder, away from the lights, coasting to a stop under the shade of a huge dark tree. He hit the kickstand and lifted her up with him, disengaging their bodies as he swung around.

"What are you doing?" Disoriented now, she clutched at him.

His arms eased her back. "The ride's not over."

The daydream became reality. Terri found herself on her back, spread-eagled across the Harley's seat, with Cort straddling the bike and pushing her thighs apart. Before she could make a move he slipped his hands under her hips and lifted her, thrusting himself in deep.

"Yes, please." She heard herself sobbing those two words over and over as she gripped his sleeves and wrapped her legs around his waist.

Cars passed them, and on one level Terri knew someone had to see what they were doing. Yet Cort never hesitated, never stopped pushing in and out of her.

"Bring it to me, now," he told her, burying himself so deep inside her that she could do nothing else but look into his eyes as the shattering wave of incredible joy burst inside her and spread over her.

Cort stayed inside her, holding her and stroking her with his hands. It wasn't until she felt the warmth spurting inside her and the clench of his hands that she realized that he was coming, too, so hard that his body jerked with the force of it.

He lifted her into his arms and held her but said nothing. They were both out of breath. Aftershocks ran through her, making it impossible to speak.

Not that she had anything to say. There was nothing to say.

As he cradled her, Terri closed her eyes. She'd given him what he wanted, as she had before. He'd demanded, and she'd surrendered, end of story.

Cort pressed something into her hand—a handkerchief—

and set her on the ground. He held her until she was steady, and then turned away.

Terri heard him zipping up his fly as she used the handkerchief between her thighs. They were on the side of the road, where anyone and everyone could see them. Cort Gamble had taken her on top of a motorcycle on the highway and finished her off on the side of the road, all because he was jealous.

Or was he? She'd been here before. Tomorrow he'd go back to treating her like she was invisible. Or worse, like she'd given him a disease.

Dear God, what have I done?

He walked over to her and reached out to touch her hair. She dodged him. "Don't."

Her legs were shaky as she climbed back on the Harley. She put on her helmet, tucked down her skirt, and started the engine. Cort stood watching her for a long moment before moving toward the bike. She waited until he was on and had his hands on her waist before she drove onto the empty right lane.

Say something. Tell me it was fun. Anything.

Cort remained silent on the ride back to the Garden District, and his hands stayed light and impersonal. Terri had never been happier to see the Gamble mansion, but the black-and-white unit parked by the curb made her cruise to a stop at the end of the block.

She wasn't taking the chance of flashing her bare ass in front of a couple of uniforms.

The Harley rose an inch as Cort climbed off and turned to look at her. The dark made his expression unreadable, but his frame was tense.

Regret. He was going to tell her he was sorry, and then she'd break his jaw.

Terri released the foot brake and took off before he could say a word.

Gray set one of the two Styrofoam cups he carried on the marshal's assistant's desk. "Café au lait, with two sugars. Right?"

"Oh, Dr. Huitt, you shouldn't have." Sally gave him an uncertain smile before shuffling some paperwork on her desk. "Is there a briefing this morning? I've been out and I'm a little behind on the schedule."

"No, I brought the café strictly as a bribe." He noted the faint shadows under her eyes and the visible weight loss, and remembered that the marshal's assistant had been the one to take the call from Ashleigh Bouchard. "How are you doing?"

"Better," Sally admitted. "Detective Vincent called me a couple of days ago, and we talked for hours. It really helped."

"Terri's why I'm here." He glanced at the marshal's closed door. "But officially, I've identified the Jane Doe from Maskers."

"Let me check with him." Sally picked up the phone. After she announced Gray, she listened for a moment, and then gently eased down the receiver. "The marshal is . . . busy. May I have him call you?"

Gray knew Gamble wasn't on the phone; all the line buttons were dark. "Anyone in there with him?" She shook her head. "If this was a movie, I'd burst in through the door while you run after me and tell me I can't go in there. Want to do that?"

She picked up some sealed envelopes. "I think I should run mail downstairs." She gave him a fleeting smile and left the office.

Gray walked into Gamble's office and closed the door behind him. "I love your assistant, who is on her way to the mail room now, by the way. When Jen goes back to college in the fall, I'm going to steal your Sally away from you."

Cort closed a file he was reading and regarded him with a distinctly hostile expression. "I'm very busy, Doctor. Would you make this quick?"

No, he wouldn't. "You'll get a copy of the report, but the Jane Doe from Maskers has been identified as Luciana Belafini, wife of Stephen Belafini, one of the other victims." He saw the recognition flicker in Gamble's cold eyes. "I understand you and she were close at one time."

"We were."

"I've found physical evidence which links the Bouchard and Navarre murders. Two lumps of gold were recovered from both sites. The gold from both is identical: Italian, twenty-four karat, very fine quality. Probably from some type of jewelry."

"Tributes." When Gray raised his eyebrows, the marshal added, "He's leaving tributes at the scenes. Burning items of importance is a ritual that certain types of arsonists perform."

"Very interesting. It's probably not Frank Belafini, though; he hated Luciana and drove her away from his son. There's only one more thing." Gray removed a folded printout from his pocket. "You're being investigated by OCU for possible connections to Belafini's organization."

"What?"

Gray smiled. "You can thank Chief Ruel, next time you see him. He's bound and determined to personally escort you to the penitentiary."

"How did you get this information?"

"Terri told me. She's the one investigating you." He tossed the folded printout on the desk between them. "I also hacked into Ruel's system. He's got an anonymous deposit and some witness statements. Not enough for an indictment, but he can take it to the mayor and have you fired pretty much any time he wants."

The marshal unfolded the paper and read over the data. "Why are you telling me this?"

"I don't believe in keeping secrets. I also don't give a shit about you, Gamble, but Terri's my friend." He watched the marshal crumple the printout in his fist. "She's putting her career on the line for you."

"By investigating me."

"She believes you're innocent and wants to clear your name. Ruel is using that, and her, to get close to you. If she does anything to protect you, which you and I know that she will, he's going to bust her." Gray let his voice go flat. "She'll lose her badge."

The marshal shoved his chair away from his desk and

stood. "You should stay out of department business, and stick to autopsies, Doctor."

"Frank Belafini had Terri's father on his payroll for years. He used him to get rid of evidence when it was inconvenient, and plant it where it was needed." He enjoyed seeing the shock on the other man's face. "How do you think it makes her feel to hear you being accused of working for the same man, Marshal?"

Gamble shook his head slowly. "She never told me," he muttered, almost to himself.

"Why should she?" Gray leaned over the desk. "You should try talking to her occasionally. Maybe during that nice little quiet time after you screw her. Women love that, don't they?"

The marshal's gaze turned lethal. "Forget about her, Huitt. She's mine."

Gray straightened. "Then I suggest you hold on, Gamble. If she comes to me, you're not getting her back." He went to the door. "Have a nice day."

Ruel took off the headphones and handed them to the agent supervising the monitoring equipment. "Where did you plant the mike?"

"We switched out the telephone on the marshal's desk," the agent told him. "Along with the wire tap, the voice-activated transmitter in the base picks up conversations in the office area nice and clear."

"Keep recording everything."

Ruel waited until he was back in his office before he let the anger surge through him. He had known about Terri's friendship with Grayson Huitt, but he never suspected she would confide in him, or that the pathologist would try to protect her by dropping everything in Gamble's lap. He could bust the pathologist for hacking into his system, but the damage was done. Now that Gamble knew about the investigation, he'd cover his tracks and make peace with Belafini.

It wasn't necessarily a bad thing. No more women would die.

His sound technician had left copies of the Torcher's tape in a padded envelope on top of his "in" basket. Ruel took out one and turned it over in his hands.

Patricia Brown had called him earlier, claiming that the Torcher had contacted her directly. At the time Ruel had brushed her off, but now he saw an opportunity where none had existed before.

Professional pressure was one thing, personal was another. Terri wasn't the only woman he could use to get to Gamble. Patricia would be so grateful for the exclusive that he could get her to present it exactly as he wanted.

By the time the reporter was done milking what was on the tape, Gamble's own mother wouldn't be speaking to him.

He picked up the phone and dialed a private number. "Patricia, this is Sebastien Ruel. I have something that you might be interested in hearing. What are you doing for lunch today?"

16

"That cop came here," Caitlin told Douglas as she entered the utility shed.

He sat up. "The one who was following me?"

"Uh-huh. I had to duck out of the office real fast before he saw me." She handed him her flashlight and placed a tray on the gas can he had been using as a table. The tray contained a paper plate with two sandwiches and a large glass of milk. "I think my dad is starting to get suspicious about the food. We need to find you another place to stay."

Caitlin had been hiding Douglas—and feeding him—since Moriah Navarre's murder.

"I'll go to the homeless shelter," he told her. He was charmed to discover the sandwiches were peanut butter and jelly, something he hadn't eaten since he was a boy. Camping out in Caitlin's shed and using her Totally Spies! sleeping bag had also been something of an adventure back into childhood, but he did not want to put her in any danger. "The police won't look for me there."

"Yeah, they will." Caitlin took back the flashlight and held it up so he could see as he ate. "The cop asked my dad, and he told him how you were getting food from there. They've probably got wanted posters up all over the place."

He imagined a poster with his image. DOUGLAS SIMON, WANTED DEAD OR ALIVE. There was a certain romance to it, although no one would ever take it seriously.

Caitlin dug a paper napkin out of her jeans pocket and

handed it to him. "You should forget about getting even with this marshal guy and maybe beat it out of Nawlins."

Since learning that there was an APB issued for him, thanks to Caitlin, who listened in on every phone call her father received, Douglas had reconsidered his master plan. "I don't have the money to leave town."

"I'd borrow some from the register, but my dad counts it every night." The girl made a face. "Once he had a conniption fit because I used fifty cents for a Coke." Her face brightened. "Hey, I know. You could rob us. I'll make you a mask, and I've got this water pistol that looks like a real gun."

The little girl evidently didn't know that her father kept a sawed-off shotgun in a locked box under the counter. "No, my dear. My criminal days are over." As were his family-man days. A man couldn't be that unless he had a family.

They fell into silence as Caitlin thought and Douglas ate. When he finished, he tidied up and collect his meager belongings. "I'd better go now. Thank you for taking care of me."

"I don't want you to go back to jail, Douglas." The little girl threw her arms around his waist and began to cry. "It's not fair, you didn't do anything wrong."

"It's all right, Caitlin." He had only shown her a pitiful amount of attention, and here she was, weeping for him. "Remember, I haven't done anything wrong."

"That won't matter to the cops," she said through her sobs. "That nasty marshal man—he should go to prison, not you."

"If he's guilty, he will." Douglas might even occupy the cell next to his. He crouched down and looked into the child's tear-wet eyes. "Caitlin, listen to me. I want you to keep working on your math, and going to school every day. You're very smart and you can do anything you want with your life."

"Could I be a spy?"

He nodded.

"What about you? That marshal man thinks you set the

fires, and they said on television that whoever did could get the death penalty."

He frowned. "Who said that?"

"The red-haired lady on Channel Eight. She's been talking about it every single night." Caitlin swiped at her face with her hand. "I watch her because she's the only one who says bad things about that marshal man."

"Does she." Douglas sat back on his heels. He had seen Patricia Brown on television, of course. There was something very special about her, although he couldn't say what it was. "Is your father home now?"

The child shook her head. "He went out drinking. He won't be home until after midnight."

He rasped a hand over his beard stubble. "I have an idea, but I'll need to use the shower and shave."

"Sure, but why?"

He smiled. "I want to look good. I have to if I'm going to be on TV."

Grayson Huitt's revelations stayed with Cort for the rest of the day. As he reviewed his daily reports and issued several bulletins to the local departments about the Torcher and Douglas Simon, the conversation looped in his head, interspersed with the memories from the wild ride he'd taken on Terri's Harley.

She's putting her career on the line for you.

Terri's head, resting against his shoulder as he sank deep and hard into her. He'd almost come a dozen times, just being inside her.

She'll lose her badge.

He'd lost control. All he could think of was taking her and destroying her affair with Huitt, but her body had told him a different story. Then she admitted that she'd never been the pathologist's lover, and that she hadn't been with anyone since Mardi Gras. Since him.

She's reliving that nightmare all over again.

She'd felt so wet and silky. It had blown his mind and erased any thought of restraint. All he could think when he pulled off the road was taking her over and over. Never stopping again, not for anything.

If she comes to me, you're not getting her back.

But Cort had pushed her too hard. Terri wouldn't look at him after they were finished. When he'd tried to touch her, she'd cringed, as if what they'd done made her ashamed. He didn't feel the same, but he couldn't blame her. He'd gone too far this time, done things to her that he would have never done with another woman. He'd been too rough, too demanding, and it had driven her from him.

He would have said something, found some words that made sense of it, but she'd taken off as if she were being chased by a demon.

Or she'd been taken by one.

Cort didn't trust himself to call her, and considered forgetting about taking her to the charity dinner and auction being held at his father's restaurant. After last night, she wouldn't want to see him again. She'd probably jump at the chance to be taken off the case.

The only thing that bothered him was what she'd said, coming out of the morgue. *I need to clear up some things between you and me.*

So do I.

Terri had wanted to talk to him, but he'd been too angry, and he'd shut her down.

You should try talking to her occasionally.

He hated to admit it, but Huitt was right. He'd done everything to Terri but talk to her. And whether she wanted to listen to him now or not, he needed to settle things between them. He wasn't going to walk away and pretend it had never happened this time, and she owed him some answers, too.

"Sally, call Detective Vincent and remind her we have a dinner tonight," Cort told his assistant as he left the office. "I'll pick her up at seven."

"Yes, sir. Marshal, I'm sorry." When he looked back, she grimaced. "About Dr. Huitt barging in on you. I kind of . . . let him."

He studied her. "He's going to offer you a job. Tell him no and I'll give you that raise."

Her cheeks dimpled. "That I can do."

To allow time to talk to her, Cort arrived a half hour early at Terri's. She had parked the Harley in front of the porch, and he stopped next to it. Running his hand over the seat seemed juvenile, but he couldn't help it, any more than he could help getting hard, looking at it and remembering her on top of him and under him as they rode it.

He wanted to do it again. Soon.

When he knocked on the door, she called out for him to come in, but the front of the apartment was empty. "Where are you?"

"Back here. Sit down. You're early."

Terri didn't sound angry, which dispersed some of his tension. He saw that the door to her tiny bathroom was open, and went to look in on her. "Hi."

"Hi, yourself."

Terri was standing in front of the sink, which was covered with cosmetics, and struggling with her arms behind her back. The blue satin dress buttoned up the length of her back with tiny, loop-fastened knots, and she'd only done up half of them.

He looked away from the golden stretch of bare skin. "I thought I'd drop by early so we could talk."

"Talking I can do." She gave the mirror a look of disgust. "It's dressing that's not working out too well."

She wasn't behaving as if things had changed between them or she was upset for what had happened. Which, after last night, didn't seem possible.

"Let me help." He stepped in behind her.

She dropped her arms with a sigh of relief and picked up a lipstick. "Does Andre even know about the invention of the zipper?"

"Probably." The back straps of her bra were the same blue satin as the dress, and one was twisted. He turned it and smoothed it out. "What happened to the ivory beaded dress?"

She started to apply the lipstick to her mouth. "Ugh, too

red." She discarded it and wiped off the color with a tissue. "I told Andre that if he made me wear it, I'd drive out to the swamp after and roll around in the mud." She smirked at her reflection. "And he believed me."

She wasn't upset. She was smiling. Happy. It confused him on one level and aroused him on another.

As Terri put on her makeup, Cort fastened the buttons. He was halfway to her neck before he realized something. "You can't wear a bra with this. The back is too low."

"I have to." She twisted and looked over her shoulder. "I'll show through the front without one."

"Let me see." He put his hands on her shoulders and turned her back toward the mirror. The dress wasn't low-cut, but there were diamond-shaped inserts of blue organza that ran in diagonal lines across the bodice down to the waist. He could see her skin through the semitransparent fabric, and he found himself looking for the shadows of bruises. "Did I hurt you last night? I didn't intend to."

Her shoulders became rigid under his hands for a split second. "I was a little stiff this morning, but it's been a while for me." She cocked her head to one side. "You did give me a thing."

"A thing?" He'd given her more than that, and why was she laughing about it?

"You know." She flicked her fingers at her neck, and he saw a cleverly applied patch of concealer. "A love bite."

Like a teenager. He met her eyes in the mirror. "You were angry with me last night, but now you're not." She shrugged. "What's changed between now and then?"

"Me, maybe. I did some thinking." Her mouth curved. "I'm a big girl, Cortland. I can handle what happened."

"Can you?" He found himself wanting to test that, and reached for the back fastener of her bra. "What if things get out of control again?"

"I'll do what I did last night." The smile she gave him as her bra fastener separated made his cock stiffen again. "I'm also supposed to be *getting* dressed."

"In a minute." He reached around and tugged the cups up and away from her breasts. Her nipples didn't show through, but some of the curves did. The hard peaks were clearly delineated by the soft, clinging satin as well. "You need something covering your breasts."

She lifted her hands and placed them on the outside of the bodice over his. She pushed his hands until he was cupping her under the dress. "We could stay like this, and you could cover me."

He pulled her back against him as he used his hands to caress and squeeze her. Watching it in the mirror made him groan. "Your breasts are perfect."

"When you can find them." She looked down. "I've been told a magnifying glass helps."

"I can find them. I can take them in my mouth," he muttered, feeling the slow rub of her bottom against his restricted erection.

She was doing it, not him. She wanted him.

"You'll just have to prove that, Marshal," she teased.

"I wanted to last night." He heard something ringing but ignored it. "I want to now."

Terri turned and peeled down the front of her dress, taking off the bra with it. "You really like these little things?" she teased, cupping them with her own hands.

Cort had never seen her like this, but he loved it and he wasn't questioning it. Not when it meant that he could put his mouth on her and suck on her.

He went down on one knee and splayed his hands over her bottom. Her nipples hardened even more as he laved his tongue over them, and when he sucked her hands glided into his hair and curled tight against his scalp.

"Oops. I think they're getting bigger," she said.

"So am I." He lifted his mouth and blew on her, watching the small, rosy aureole crinkle. "I could play with you like this all night." All week. All month.

He'd never get tired of her.

"No fair." She sounded breathless. "I want my turn."

He focused on her mouth. "I'll let you. Later."

"What's the male version of a dominatrix?" She shook her head as if confused. "And what is that ringing?"

He listened and reached into his pocket. "My cell." He

stood and checked the display. "It's from the restaurant. I'll tell them we're not going to make it."

"Oh yeah, we are," she said, and gave him a slow smile that made him want to toss her on the floor. "Just not there."

"Gamble," he said into the phone.

"Cortland, where are you?" his mother asked. "Your father and I were worried. We're waiting at the house for you."

He remembered that he had promised to take his parents over to the restaurant. Terri's hand tugged at the cummerbund of his tux. "There's been a change of plans. Can Dad drive you over?"

"Of course. Is it Terri? Is she being difficult again?" His mother sighed. "I can't say that I blame her, after what I said to her last night. I'd like to speak to her now, if she's with you."

"She's busy." He felt her cool fingers slip into his clothes. "Another time, Mother."

Elizabet wasn't through fretting. "You don't understand, Cortland. I couldn't reach you, and I was so upset. I implied that it would have been better if Terri had died instead of poor Moriah. Please tell her that I truly never thought that for an instant."

Cort gritted his teeth as Terri's hand closed over him and stroked lightly. "I'll tell her."

"Your father says he has outdone himself with the menu tonight, so you may wish to change your mind," Elizabet said brightly.

"I think I have. Give me twenty minutes."

"If you're sure, darling."

He switched off the phone and set it on the sink. Terri was going down on her knees, but he stopped her and helped her back up.

"What's wrong?" she asked. "Not my turn yet?"

He eased her hand out of his pants. "I came here to talk to you, not to have sex with you."

She grinned. "We can do both."

Cort adjusted her bra and dress so that she was covered.

"Let's talk first." He led her out of the bathroom and into the living room.

She sat down on the sofa. "So what's on your mind?" She eyed his erection. "Besides the obvious, which I should mention I'm hoping we'll get back to, like, right away?"

He joined her and took one of her hands in his. "Why are you doing this?"

"I've done a couple of things since you got here," she told him. "Be more specific."

"The way you've been acting: playful and sexy and happy." It was driving him out of his skull, too. "You're treating me like a lover."

She snuggled up against him and played with the buttons on his shirt. "Well, I guess it's not official, but I'd like you to be my lover." She gave him a hopeful look.

He didn't buy that. "Since when?"

"Man, you're one hard sell." She sat up and sighed. "Look, it's really very simple. You want me, and I want you. I mean, correct me if I'm wrong, but we've got a lot of mutual lust going on here, right?"

He nodded, still watching her eyes. She was rushing her words, almost tripping over them. She'd been like this after she'd pulled him out of the mechanical room at Maskers. *She's not kidding around. She's scared, and she's trying to cover it up.*

"Okay. So we're mature, responsible adults, both sexually active, and what have we been doing with all this lovely lust?" She tossed up her hands. "We've danced around it and snarled at each other and pretended like it wasn't there. I even got Gray to be my fake boyfriend so I wouldn't be tempted to jump back in the sack with you."

"That's why you've been hanging all over Huitt?" To keep him away.

Just as he'd tried to keep her at a distance.

"A girl has her pride. So we do everything we can to ignore this thing, and what happens? We end up doing it on a bike going eighty down the highway." She inched closer and trailed her fingertips over his mouth. "I think we need to get this out of our systems, Cort. For reasons of self-preservation, if nothing else."

He'd learned more about Terri Vincent in the last ten minutes than he had in eight years. And it was going to bother him for a long, long time. "You think we can do that by being lovers."

"I know we can. We have sex—lots of sex—until we get sick of each other and it goes away and we can get on with our lives." She spread her hand out. "Simple."

Just like the constant joking, she was using sex to gloss over her fear. Making it sound casual and meaningless when it wasn't. Terri was running from him again, this time in her heart.

"There's another way," he said.

"Does this way include me and you getting naked on a bed?" she asked, looking suspicious.

"It does."

Her eyebrows rose. "A lot?"

"As often as you like."

She chuckled. "Sounds like my idea."

"Not exactly." He touched her face. "We have a staged relationship. We can make into a real one."

"A real relationship." Terri stared at him. "You and me. That's your idea."

"That's it."

She burst out laughing, and laughed so hard she nearly fell off the sofa. When she could speak, she said, "Oh, that's good. That's really great. You and me, for real." She laughed again.

He frowned, watching her. "It's not that funny."

"Oh, but it is. Think of the headlines." She was wiping tears from her face. "Rich Creole society boy with political ambitions falls in love with swamp-bred Cajun butch cop. It's like 'Green Acres' for the new millennium. People will pee their pants when they hear this."

"It isn't a joke," he said, getting angry now.

"Are you kidding? Leno will do a monologue on it. Hell, they'll probably make a Lifetime movie out of it. Call it 'The Prince and the Coon-Ass.'" She gasped for breath for a minute, and added, "Thanks, Cort. I needed a good chuckle."

Cort wanted to drag Terri back to the bedroom, where he could show her exactly how real it could be, but decided it was better to wait. He had to rethink everything he had assumed about her, and plan out how to get around her formidable defenses.

After last night, he wasn't settling for anything less than the whole woman: body, mind, and soul.

"Change your dress. We're going to dinner."

"Aw, gee." She stretched lazily. "You sure you don't want to stay here? I can make it worth your while."

He wasn't even touching her again until he cooled down and sorted this out. "I'm sure."

Although she had been presented with several awards and trophies during her career, Terri felt that her personal performance tonight should have earned her an Oscar. Especially when she had managed to come off sexy and sweet and full of fun, when all she had wanted to do was curl up into a ball at Cort's feet and weep like a baby.

Cort had no idea of what he had put her through. None. And that was exactly how things between them were going to stay.

"That dress looks lovely, Terri," Elizabet said from the back seat of Cort's SUV. She had been making an effort to talk to her since they'd picked up Cort's parents from the house. "Golden brown is so flattering on you."

Terri didn't look down at the velvet sheath that she had put on instead of the blue satin. Velvet always made her feel a little like a teddy bear. "Thanks, Mrs. G."

Krewe of Louis was located just off Jackson Square, in one of the oldest and most historic areas of the French Quarter. Originally built to serve as a small trading house, the long, narrow building had been carefully preserved and restored to look as it had when built by a plantation owner back in the eighteenth century.

"Reporters are like mosquitoes," Louie grumbled as Cort pulled up to the valet station, which was hemmed in on two sides by the waiting press. "You swat one, two more take its place."

Cort helped his mother and Terri out of the SUV as cameras flashed and reporters called out questions. Terri pasted a bright smile on her face and kept her hand in Cort's.

"Who's the unlucky lady?" a crass voice shouted.

"Marshal, so you like extra crispy or original recipe?" another called.

Terri felt like telling them to shut up, but concentrated on keeping her head high and not tripping over her heels.

Another couple arrived just after them, and Cort turned. "Simone and Jacque Maveilot, some friends of the family," he said to Terri before he greeted them.

The Maveilots ignored Cort and merely nodded to Louie and Elizabet as they walked into the restaurant.

"*Friends* of the family?" Terri murmured, disturbed by the show of blatant rudeness.

"I thought so." Cort tucked her arm over his and led her into the restaurant.

Krewe of Louis was famous in New Orleans for classic Creole cuisine and for authentic atmosphere, for which Louie had spared no expense. Passing over the threshold was like stepping back in time and into a ballroom where wealthy men in top hats and coats lifted monocles to inspect ladies in gorgeous pastel gowns with full, floating skirts that swept like flower bells over waxed hardwood floors.

Terri loved coming here. Although her people had come to Louisiana by way of Canada, after being driven from Acadia by the English, this was her history, too.

The furnishings were all reproductions of exquisite French antiques, from the grand baroque tables to the finely gilded white tapestry chairs. Immense needlework wall hangings, gifts from a convent in Provence that Louie's family had supported for centuries, depicted in intricate detail the rich history of France, from the time of the Romans to the decadent courts of the last of its kings. The old trading-house gaslights, converted to electric, still illuminated the walls, while four enormous crystal chandeliers shed glittering light on the diners.

Their entrance seemed to create a stir, which Terri thought at first was due to the arrival of the owner. Louie was well known and much loved in the Creole community, and had never been one to ignore attention. Even now he was making the rounds, shaking hands and kissing cheeks, always with one arm around his wife.

However, it became very apparent that the two hundred people attending the private function weren't interested in Louie and Elizabet as much as in their son. The looks they gave Cort and the murmurs that filled the air weren't of the friendly variety, either.

"Why is everyone staring at us?" she whispered.

"I don't know." Cort scanned the room and nodded. "Let's go talk to Andre."

The old man was seated at a table with a pair of ladies who, when they saw Cort and Terri approaching, rose and walked away. Terri remembered to wait for Cort to pull out her chair before she sat down.

"My dear boy." Andre gave him a pained smile. "I'm so sorry about this. You'd think people would have better sense."

"What happened?"

Andre looked startled. "You mean, you haven't seen the report on Channel Eight? That wretched Brown woman and her exposé?"

In this era of camcorders and digital cameras, no one had any privacy. Terri thought of the number of cars that had passed her and Cort last night and cringed inside.

"I haven't seen it. Neither has Terri."

"Patricia Brown obtained a copy of a recording. The man on it said terrible things about you." Andre pulled his silk handkerchief from his jacket and blotted his forehead. "I know it must be an obscene hoax, but I can hardly bear repeating it. He confessed to setting the fires to murder two women you were involved with. He threatened to kill every woman you've ever loved."

"I'll call Chief Ruel," Terri said, rising from her chair. "We'll find out who leaked the tape to the press."

"Wait," Cort said. "What else, Andre?"

"The wretched woman interviewed some horrible little man who was just released from prison." He sighed. "He has some sort of experience with arson cases and he apparently knows you very well."

That snagged Terri's full attention. "What horrible little man?"

"Douglas Simon, an insurance investigator on the take who I busted," Cort told her. "What did he say, Andre?"

The old man took a sip of his water before he looked directly at Cort. "He told Ms. Brown that he believes that you're corrupt. That you're working for some mob family and that you're protecting this Torcher lunatic for them. I'm afraid he sounded very convincing."

Terri felt her skin grow cold. "That's slander."

"Not the way he said it," Andre insisted. "They must have coached him. He was very careful not to make any direct accusations."

Elizabet and Louie joined them.

"Cortland, a woman from some television station is making the most outrageous accusations about you," his mother said. "She has everyone believing you're involved with some kind of gangster."

"Mobster," he corrected. A waiter came up to him and handed him a folded note. "Would you stay with Terri? I have to take a call."

Andre watched him go and turned to Terri. "You were to wear the blue dress tonight." He peered at her face. "Where is your blush?"

"I lost it when I was sixteen." She rose from the table and bent to speak to Elizabet in a low voice. "He doesn't deserve to be treated like this. Not like some kind of leper."

"I agree." Cort's mother gazed around the room. "But what can we do?"

"Tell these friends of yours that you know Cort better than some bimbo on TV," Terri suggested. "If that doesn't work, have Louie kick their asses out of here."

"I may just do that." Elizabet gave her a grim smile. "Thank you, my dear."

Terri went back to the kitchen, and wove through a gauntlet of busy waiters, chefs, and prep cooks until she found Louie's head chef, Herlain. J. D. had introduced her years ago, and they'd hit it off from the moment Terri had tasted his *Lapin au vin* and told the chef that she didn't need to die to go to Heaven. "Hey, Harry."

"Therese!" He set aside a saucepan and embraced her. "It has been too long, *cherie*."

"Have you seen Cortland?"

"He go into his father's office." Herlain nodded in that direction, and pouted. "I tell him I will bring him food, but he ignores me. He does not look happy."

"Thanks, Harry. Save some of that gorgeous *glacée* for me." She headed for the office.

17

"I'm tired of waiting, Gamble," Frank Belafini said over the phone line in Louie's office. "I don't appreciate your medical examiner coming over to my club and harassing me, either."

Cort dragged a hand through his hair. "Find something else to do besides call me, Belafini. It's unproductive and boring, and I'm not on your payroll."

"I'm so sorry I'm not entertaining enough for you," Belafini said. "Maybe I'll send a couple of my men over to show you a good time."

"Send them. I haven't gotten to the gym this week."

"We can make noise at each other all night, Gamble, and it'll only make things worse for you." The older man's tone changed. "You know where this Simon character is, and you're going to tell me. Now."

"Douglas Simon is only wanted for questioning," Cort told him. "We have no proof that he set the fires, and I don't know where he is."

"He's on the fucking television, that's where he is. Telling everyone what a lousy human being you are." Belafini exhaled heavily. "Got people thinking you're one of mine now, too."

"You know that I didn't set the fires, and I don't work for you."

"Don't torch those bridges, Gamble. Your parents, they

having a good time tonight? I want them to. Could be the last time they do."

"You go to Hell." He slammed down the phone.

"How long has Frank Belafini been threatening you?" Terri asked from behind him.

He turned around slowly. "About as long as you've been investigating me for Ruel."

"Nice comeback." She wandered over to his father's desk and picked up one of the old silver saltcellars he used as paperweights. "It seems like we've both been keeping a lot of secrets."

"Not after tonight." He turned on the little black-and-white set Louie kept on his credenza and switched it to Channel Eight. Patricia Brown appeared in some sort of meeting room, with Douglas Simon sitting across from her. "That should get me fired by tomorrow morning."

She reached over and shut off the set. "I have to know everything. Tell me."

Cort told her. He recounted Belafini's threats, how Huitt had told him about her, and what he knew of the grudge Ruel had against him. "I spoke to a friend up in D.C. Belafini murdered Ruel's partner when he was working for the Bureau. It's Belafini he wants to nail, not me. Me he thinks he can use to get to Frank, no doubt."

"Someone has been feeding Ruel false information in order to frame you. He's got a bogus deposit of fifty grand to your savings account, and a phony statement about you meeting with Frank at his club downtown. Only the deposit envelope had no handwriting or fingerprints on it."

"That doesn't mean anything."

"You always type your deposit envelopes and wear gloves when you drop them off at the bank?" she countered. "The witness who claimed to have seen you with Frank quit his job to move to Italy. One day after he gave the statement to Ruel."

"Convenient." Fifty thousand dollars was chump change for Belafini, and the mob boss had sent other employees out of the country to keep them from being questioned. "Belafini is playing Ruel."

A faint line appeared between her eyebrows. "Why?"

"I don't know. He has the resources, but this started before Maskers, right? So no motive." He sat down in his father's chair, put his head back, and closed his eyes.

"So what do we do?"

"We don't do anything. I have to concentrate on protecting this idiot Simon and my parents." He looked at her. "You have to quit the case."

"Ruel won't let me go."

He felt a small, savage satisfaction in knowing that even if he couldn't save himself, he could at least protect her. "Ruel won't have anything to say about it; Jarden guaranteed that."

"You hit the mayor up for a favor?"

"He owes me several. It was the only way to get you out before I destroy your career along with my own." He picked up the phone. "Pellerin will help; he doesn't like Ruel either."

Terri jerked the receiver out of his hand and slammed it down. "No."

"There's nothing else I can do for you." He reached for the phone again.

She put her hand on the receiver, holding it down. "I don't care. I'm not quitting. Ruel's evidence against you is falling apart. I just need a little more time."

The show of faith made his throat tight. "I'm not watching you go down with me."

She waved a hand in front of his face. "Hello, it's *my* job, not yours. Besides, you're a fireman. I'm the cop. Leave the criminal investigation up to me."

"If you were thinking like a cop, you'd report the conversation you overheard between me and Belafini to Ruel." He would have said more, but he saw his mother open the door. "Terri—"

"Shut up." She planted her hands on her hips. "You just don't get it, do you? I don't care about Ruel's bullshit evidence against you. I don't care what Simon or Patricia Brown say on TV." She threw out an arm. "If I'd walked in

here and watched you take an envelope of hundreds from
Frank Belafini, it wouldn't convince me."

So much for keeping his mother in the dark. "Why?"

She made a sound of supreme frustration. "Because I *believe* in you, you stubborn, oversized, thickheaded jerk."

She did. It was shining in her eyes, it was vibrant in her
voice. It made him feel stronger than he thought possible.

"Thank you." Cort looked over her shoulder. "Mother,
Terri and I need some time."

"I can see that." Elizabet smiled as Terri whirled around.
"Your father has the kitchen staff out eating with the guests,
but if you get hungry, you know what to raid." To Terri, she
said, "I'm very glad my son has you on his side." She quietly withdrew and closed the door.

"Great." Terri rubbed the back of her neck. "Now Mom's
in the middle of this."

"She won't interfere. My mother is an expert at biding
her time."

"So what's our next move?"

There was nothing more Cort could do about Ruel or
Belafini tonight, and no point in returning to the dinner to
face more condemnation and censure. He was alone with
Terri, and still aching from the erotic embrace they'd shared
back at her apartment.

He rose, came around the desk, and took her by the hand.
"Come on, I'm hungry."

"We should work out a strategy to deal with Ruel," she
said as she followed him out of the office. "I can put the word
out to my snitches, see if any of them know if Frank's got it
in for him. We might be able to get a nice little turnaround
on this thing and get his ass booted out to the unemployment
line."

Cort looked at the east pantry and smiled a little. "Tomorrow." He tugged her over to the door and guided her
inside.

"I can't eat anything now, I'm too upset." Terri sucked in
a breath as he switched on the light and closed the door.
"Wait. I lied."

Louie's staff used the east pantry mainly to store the

ingredients for his exclusive desserts, as well as finished dishes that could be served for a number of days. Cort remembered his own reaction as a boy, sneaking into the east pantry to look up at shelf after shelf filled with incredibly elaborate French desserts.

During the summer months, however, Louie's dessert chef made hundreds of *sotelties,* sculpting sugar and chocolate into fanciful shapes. There were baskets woven out of spun sugar and filled with crystallized flowers, life-sized chocolate mice nibbling at chunks of real cheese, and delicate hummingbirds made of tinted marzipan hovering over toasted coconut nests. The *sotelties* were one of the reasons summer tourists flooded Krewe of Louis each year, because not only could they be eaten, they could also be packed and shipped home.

"The next time I get PMS, will you lock me in here for a couple of hours?" Terri asked him.

He turned and locked the door. "Why wait?"

"They're so beautiful." She moved away from him, inspecting a shelf filled with marzipan children making snow angels in pans of white chocolate. "How do you eat something so pretty?" She straightened. "Um, that didn't come out right."

She could ride him like a mare in heat on a public highway but became embarrassed over some innocently risqué words.

"You want it more than you want to look at it," he told her, reaching up to take a plain white dish from an upper shelf. "You feel as if you're going to go mad unless you have a taste, and then you know you'll go insane unless you fill yourself with it." He held out his hand. "Come here and I'll show you."

She eyed the locked door. "I said I'm not hungry."

"You will be." He set down the dish on the small prep table and moved toward her. "Don't be afraid of me, Therese."

"Hey, you turned down sex two hours ago, I didn't." She met him halfway and came into his arms. "So what are you going to do with the"—she glanced around him—"oh, man, that is not fair."

"It's only crème brûlée." He ran a fingertip over the heart-shaped top of her bodice. "My father has made it for you before, hasn't he?"

"Yeah. It's one of the reasons I've seriously considered breaking up your parents' marriage." She shivered as he skimmed his hand up the side of her neck. "Just what did you have in mind?"

"I want something sweet." He bent and brushed her lips with his. "Sweet and soft and very rich."

She uttered a shaky laugh. "You don't want me, then."

"Wrong." Cort dipped one finger into the dish, breaking through the caramelized sugar to scoop up a little of the yellow custard beneath it. He brought it to her mouth, but when her lips parted he skimmed it along the curve of her bottom lip. "It's not for you." He licked the creamy line away. "You're not hungry."

She braced herself against him and shuddered as he cupped the back of her head and kissed her slowly and thoroughly. When he lifted his mouth, she opened dazed eyes. "Do that again."

"Be patient. The presentation is as important as the ingredients." Cort painted the exposed top of her breast with crème brûlée in the shape of a heart before laving it with his tongue. The front of her dress was held in place by two body-conforming wires, and peeled down easily. She wasn't wearing a bra this time, so there was nothing to keep his mouth from her breasts.

Cort lifted her up, nuzzling her for a moment before he set her down on the table and pushed her skirt up with his hands. She wore stockings and a beige garter belt with matching panties. "Contrasting textures are essential as well."

"Are they?"

He tugged her panties down and looked at her. She had a small mons and the triangle of dark curls over it was now trimmed and tidy, thanks to Andre's painful treatment. He wanted to see what she looked like as he pushed himself inside her, but not yet. He dipped two fingers into the dish and brought them between her legs, watching her face as he carefully spread the cool, creamy custard over and between her hot, flowering folds.

When he added a little more, completely covering her clit, Terri took in a sharp breath. "You're an evil, depraved man. I really like that about you."

"I'm glad." He dropped down between her knees and inspected his work. "How do you eat something so pretty? Like this."

He took his time and slowly licked until the crème brûlée was gone and she came against his tongue twice. Only then did he ease back and look up at her.

She was panting and shivering from the force of her last climax, and lifted her hand as if to say *stop*. Custard coated the tips of her fingers, and she wiggled them. "My turn."

Slipping into Louie Gamble's restaurant proved slightly harder than killing two of the women who had loved his son. There were the media to avoid, and some of the guests also presented the danger of unwanted recognition. Still, he was patient and waited for the right moment, which came when the lights were turned down and the charity auction began. Then he moved through the shadows, looking for his new target.

No, *target* was not the proper term. She was the beautiful fruit of love's vine, ripe and ready to be reaped.

He'd watched from the van as Gamble had walked in the place, and had closely inspected the lovely brunette escorting him. She seemed terribly familiar, but he was only able to see her from behind. Now neither Gamble or his new lady were anywhere to be seen.

It made him furious, but after one of the guests mistook him for a waiter and ordered a bottle of champagne, he was forced to return to the van.

He had planned Gamble's third lesson carefully, but would have delayed it in order to burn the brunette. Now he would have to allow her to be the fourth, or fifth. It depended on how successful his night proved to be.

Inside the van, he placed a duplicate of his warning to Gamble in the tape player and turned it on to listen to his own voice. Using the synthesizer had been an unfortunate necessity, but aside from the distortion of his natural voice he quite enjoyed listening to himself.

The police should never have lied about his warning to Gamble being destroyed in the car fire.

He was so grateful to Patricia Brown for exposing the truth, and for interviewing Douglas Simon. It warmed his heart to know that he was not the only one to see Gamble for what he was. It had utterly wiped out his poor opinion of network television.

A soft moan drifted to his ears, and he glanced back. His passenger was not quite conscious. The beating he had administered had been severe, but he would not have obtained the information any other way.

As he drove toward the Garden District, he called the motel where Douglas Simon had been staying. A young female voice answered the line.

"I have a message for Mr. Simon," he told her.

"He checked out, Mister."

He didn't like the obnoxious tone in her voice but let it pass. She sounded ridiculously young, and he was in the mood to be charitable. "I'd like to leave it anyway, in the event he returns."

The girl sighed. "Go ahead."

"I have left a very important package addressed to him in care of general delivery at this post office." He gave her the specific branch's address. "Tell Mr. Simon to call me at the number enclosed in the package."

The sound of a pencil scribbling stopped. "Is that it?"

"Yes, thank you."

"Don't you want to leave your name, Mister?"

"Tell him it's from a cheerful giver." He ended the call and turned up the drive of a house he knew was vacant before parking and killing the headlights.

Everything was in place, he had only to leave the message where Gamble could find it. He took out his knife and tested the blade before climbing into the back of the van and nudging the semiconscious, bound and gagged woman lying on the floor with his foot.

"Yoo-hoo, Patricia," the Torcher said softly as he brushed her hair back from her face. "Wake up, now, it's showtime."

Terri shifted over Cort, resting her hot cheek against his hip. Somehow they had ended up on the floor, with him on his back and her on top of him, their clothes half on, half off. Beside them the dish of custard sat, almost empty.

"I think I like crème de Cortland better than crème brûlée." She eyed her watch. "The auction should be in full swing by now. Want to go out and bid on some junk you don't need and support the genteel cause of the week?"

His hand caressed her hair. "No."

She moved up until they were on eye level, and felt his arm come up around her. "Want to take some of those strawberry éclairs back to my place?"

Cort's gaze moved over her face. "I'd like to know how you feel about this."

"A little sticky, but nothing a shower won't cure." She frowned. "I guess the shi—uh, circumstances could be better." A voice on the other side of the pantry's far wall made her lift her head. "Is that Harry?"

They both listened. The chef's voice was distant but what he was shouting was unmistakable.

"Fire!"

Terri scrambled to her feet and pulled up her bodice before grabbing her purse and taking out her gun.

"No, wait." Cort dragged her back from the door and pressed his hand against the knob—checking to see if it was hot, she realized. "Okay." He yanked it open and looked out into the kitchen. "Not in here."

They ran together out to the restaurant's dining room, where two hundred people were in various stages of hysteria. The front entrance was blocked by bodies fighting to exit through a door that swung in, people were coughing and gasping, and dozens of voices screamed for help.

Through the faint haze of smoke, Terry saw a table in flames. "There."

"I'll deal with it." Cort took a fire extinguisher from one of the walls. "Take the microphone and calm them down."

Terri went to the mike the auctioneer had been using and removed it from the stand. "Ladies and gentlemen, please listen up. I'm Detective Vincent of the New Orleans Police Department. Everyone, please quiet down and follow my instructions." She repeated this twice before the voices died down. "The entrance doorway will not open with everyone piled against it. The people standing at the entrance to the restaurant need to calm down and back up so that we can open the door."

She continued talking, projecting authority while reassuring the diners. "The situation is under control, ladies and gentlemen, and the fire is not spreading. I see a woman in a wheelchair over at the right back table, and a man with a cane by the fountain. Would someone give them a hand, please?"

Slowly the pack of bodies moved back into the restaurant while several people went to help the elderly.

"That's it," she said, encouraging the frightened guests at the rear of the bottleneck. "Keep backing up and let the people at the front open the door. You're doing fine. Don't push and don't run, and we'll all get out of here okay."

At last the people who had been pressed against the door were able to open it, and the flow reversed. This time no one ran or screamed, and the restaurant began to empty out.

"Don't worry about your belongings, please just leave the restaurant." Terri turned to see Cort dousing the last of the flames with the extinguisher's white chemical foam. "When you exit the building, move across the street. Please stay with anyone who needs medical assistance until medics arrive."

At last the restaurant was empty, except for a man and woman crouching beside a table.

Terri turned off the mike and hurried over to discover it was Andre and Cort's mother. "We need to get out of here, now." She looked down and saw Louie stretched out and still on the carpet. Elizabet was clutching his hand between hers, but his face was ashen and his chest wasn't moving. "My God, what happened?"

"Terri, I've called 911, but we need help." Andre looked up at her. "I think Louis is having a heart attack."

She bent down checked for a pulse and found none. "Do either of you know CPR?" she asked them as she tilted Louie's head back and checked his airways.

"I do," Andre said.

"Okay, you do the compressions." Terri watched as the older man placed his hands against Louie's sternum. "Remember, after every time I breathe for him, you're going to do five compressions. Count them out loud and press down as hard as you can."

Andre quickly nodded.

Terri pinched Louie's nose, covered his open mouth with her own, and used her breath to inflate his lungs. "Now, Andre."

Cort's mother counted along with Andre as he worked on her husband's chest. Terri checked for a pulse before she breathed for him again. Halfway through Andre's second set of compressions, Louie twitched and his legs jerked.

"Here we go." Terri found a weak pulse in his neck and heard him take in a shallow breath. Her own heart wanted to stop, the relief was so sudden and overwhelming. "We got him back, we got him back." She rolled him onto his side. "That's it, Louie, breathe for me."

Andre sat back on the floor, took out his flask and unscrewed the top. After taking a healthy swallow, he offered it to Terri. "Here, Detective. Cognac is good for the nerves."

"No, thanks." She kept her fingers pressed against on Louie's carotid and tried to feel if the beats were getting stronger and steadying out. She looked up at Elizabet. "You okay, Mrs. G.?"

Cort's mother took Andre's flask, which he was pressing into her hands, and sipped absently. "I despise cognac." She stared at the flask, carefully handed it back to her friend, and leaned down toward her husband. "If you die, Louis, I will give Andre all of yours. Do you hear me? Every bottle."

Louie groaned and his eyes opened. "No . . . you . . . will . . . not . . . *ma belle . . . fille . . .*"

Paramedics arrived and swiftly took over. Terri gently helped Elizabet to her feet and guided her back out of the way.

"They'll take care of him now, dearest," Andre told her, leaning heavily on his cane.

"He won't die, will he?" The thought filled Elizabet's eyes with horror as she watched the EMTs place Louis on a gurney and rush him out of the restaurant.

Terri put her arm around the older woman, unsure of what to say. Then she simply said what she felt. "Louie is stubborn as hell. He would never give up without a fight." She felt a hand touch hers, looked over and saw Cort standing on the other side of his mother. They both had their arms around her. "None of the Gambles do."

He nodded slowly.

Cort's father was transferred from Mercy ER to the cardiac intensive-care unit, where only Elizabet was allowed to remain with him. Andre obtained coffee for the three of them, but Terri never left Cort's side.

"He'll be okay," she said once. "I know he will."

The attending physician performed a thorough exam and several tests before coming out to the waiting room. "Your father's condition has stabilized for the moment," he told Cort. "However, he needs emergency bypass surgery."

As the physician went on to explain some details about Louis's condition, Cort felt Terri slip her hand from his. He wanted to grab on to her, but forced himself to focus on what the doctor was saying. Because Louis became agitated whenever Elizabet wasn't near, the hospital would allow Cort's mother to stay in the room with him until he was stable enough for the lifesaving operation.

Cort signed the necessary paperwork, and saw Terri leave the waiting room. As soon as he thanked the doctor, he went after her. She was walking up the corridor, looking into the patient rooms.

"Terri?" He caught up to her. "What is it?"

"I saw someone watching us through the window. A man, I think." She whirled around. "He got away from me. He wasn't a reporter, either."

"How do you know?"

"A reporter wouldn't run away. Plus it's eighty-five degrees outside and he was wearing a coat over a suit." She took her phone out of her purse. "I'll set up a police guard for your dad."

Cort's phone rang as she was speaking, and he took the call, which delivered the second shock of the night. "I'll be there in five minutes," he told the fire chief before he hung up.

Terri was already off the phone. "What now?"

"Someone set my parents' house on fire."

18

As Cort and Terri were en route to the Gambles' mansion, the fire chief from the scene at Krewe of Louis confirmed that the fire had been accidental. "One of the waiters said he had dropped a flaming orange rind onto a tablecloth instead of in the guest's *café brulot*."

"Sweep the restaurant to be sure there's nothing else," Cort ordered from the phone in his SUV. Terri had insisted on driving, and they were nearly to the house. "Call me if you find anything."

The SUV slowed down, and Terri made an odd sound. "Cort."

He switched off the phone and looked at his parents' home. The entire structure was ablaze, with high fountains of flame pouring from every window and door. Two teams of firefighters were attacking the fire from three sides, but the roof had already collapsed, and one wall appeared ready to do the same.

Mae Wallace, the Gambles' housekeeper, would have been inside. So would two of the maids who came three nights each week to help with the household cleaning.

Cort jumped out of the SUV and ran over to the captain organizing the fire crews. "Did you get the women out?"

"Yes, sir. The housekeeper managed to contain the fire on the first floor long enough to evacuate everyone. They breathed in a little smoke, but no injuries." The fire captain took off his hard hat to wipe blackened sweat from his brow.

"She reported hearing a woman screaming for help just before the first explosion. There were at least six throughout the structure."

"Who screamed?"

"Unknown, sir." The man looked at the inferno being driven back by the pressurized hoses. "We haven't been able to get inside yet."

Cort walked along the perimeter of the property. The Torcher had been inside his home. Had somehow planted incendiary devices in the house where Cort and his brothers had spent their childhood. Now there was nothing to do but watch the beautiful old nineteenth-century mansion that he and his parents had loved so much burn to the ground.

"Mr. Cortland!" Mae rushed over to him, and collapsed into his open arms. "I'm so sorry, I didn't see him get in the house. I don't know how he did."

"It's all right, Mae." He comforted her for a moment before easing her to arm's length. "You told the firefighters that you heard a woman screaming?"

She gave a jerky nod. "When I was in the kitchen, brewing some tea for your mama. She likes that chamomile before she goes to bed, you know?"

Cort checked his watch. If Louie hadn't had a heart attack, his parents would have been home by now. "What else happened?"

"A woman screamed." Mae's face crumpled. "I couldn't tell who it was, and it sounded close by, but not in the house. Like someone was in the yard. I walked out to look in the garden, and then there was this awful loud boom, and . . ." She covered her mouth with one hand to catch a sob.

"Don't cry, Mae. You got everyone out of the house safely." He pressed a kiss against her forehead before letting one of the maids lead her away.

Terri trotted up to him and handed him the flashlight from his glove compartment. "Neighbors reported hearing screams from the back of the house. If we go around through your neighbor's yard, we can get closer, have a look."

Cort went with her around the burning house and through his parents' neighbor's property. The fire at the back of the house was burning just as hot, and some of the mulch in the flower beds was smoldering. Elizabet's small greenhouse was still intact.

"In there," he said, shining the flashlight over the glass panes. "Watch for trip wires or motion sensors."

Terri drew out her weapon. "Long as you watch for guns and knives."

They circled around the greenhouse, which was quiet and still. Terri motioned for him to flank the other side of the entry door before she eased it open an inch. Cort checked the gap before nodding to her, and she flung it open and turned, her weapon ready.

Quickly she lowered the gun. "Shit." She checked for devices and rushed in.

"Terri!" Cort followed her, but came up short as the beam from the flashlight revealed the body of Patricia Brown, bloodied and bound with ropes, tied to his mother's workbench.

"She's been worked over pretty good, but she's alive," Terri said as she tucked away her gun and carefully loosened the silk scarf gagging the reporter. "Ms. Brown, can you hear me?" She reached up to brush the tangle of red hair back from her eyes, and then went still. "He left a message."

Cort moved the light to illuminate Patricia's face. Across her brow, words had been carved into her skin with the point of a knife. LOVE DIES. "Son of a bitch. That son of a *bitch*."

His voice roused Patricia, who opened her eyes and tried to scream, but only produced a raw croak of fear.

"It's okay, Ms. Brown," Terri murmured in a soothing voice. "We're getting you out of here. You're safe now." She glanced up at Cort. "Can you carry her?"

He lifted the petite woman carefully and followed Terri out of the greenhouse. Lawson Hazenel met them halfway, and Terri quickly filled him in.

"We had an MPR come in on Brown yesterday, when she didn't show up for work," Haze told them. "I'll go with her to the hospital, see if she can give us a description."

They had nearly made it to one of the ambulances when a group of Patricia's colleagues ran at them.

"Marshal Gamble, do you know who set fire to your home?" one demanded.

Another instantly recognized Patricia. "Was Ms. Brown attacked by the arsonist?"

Cort ignored that and the other, frantic questions hurled at him. As Terri tried to move the reporters back, a paramedic hurried over to help transfer the semiconscious Patricia onto a gurney.

"No pics, pal," he heard Terri saying, and saw she was fending off the Live Spot Eight cameraman. "The lady has been through enough."

The male reporter with the Channel Eight cameraman maneuvered past Terri and strode up to Cort. "Did you do this to her, Marshal Gamble?"

Cort ignored him and instructed the medic to have photos taken of the reporter's injuries and the message carved on her skin tested for evidence. Lawson climbed into the back of the ambulance to help load the gurney in.

"Let these men do their job now," Terri said, tugging the reporter back.

"Hasn't he done enough?" the reporter demanded. "Sixteen people dead, and now Patricia's been assaulted." He lowered his voice. "She wasn't, you know, raped first, was she?"

"My boss was right," Terri said in a conversational tone. "You guys *are* nothing but bloodsucking leeches with legs. Why don't you go interview Anne Rice?" She looked across the block at the famous author's mansion. "Lights are on. I think she's home."

"Keep rolling, David," the reporter said to the cameraman. "Say whatever you like, Detective. It'll be on the eleven p.m. report."

She grinned at the camera. "Gotta tell you, Anne, *Queen of the Damned* was a way better book than the movie." When the reporter tried to dodge around her again, she pushed him back. "Hey, now. Don't make me call for backup. They're always bigger and meaner than me."

"Screw you, cop bitch." The aggressive reporter shoved

her back, and then looked at the fist curled around a handful of his shirt. "Huh?"

"Her name is Detective Vincent." Cort dragged the shorter man up on his toes. "Not cop bitch."

The reporter writhed like a hooked fish. "Let me go! I'll press charges! I'll sue you for assault!"

"Then you'll need some evidence." He drew back his fist.

"God, Cort, no!" Terri grabbed his arm and tried to push the reporter away.

"Mr. Bouvais, isn't it?" Andre was suddenly there, stepping between the two men. "I knew your mother Julie when she was a girl. In fact, I almost married her." As Cort released the reporter, Andre put an arm around the younger man's shoulders. "The only thing that made me hesitate was that unfortunate affair between her and those two strapping young sailors from Biloxi." He frowned. "Or perhaps was it three. She was such an energetic young woman."

The reporter seemed dazed. "But no one knows about . . . there were *three?*" His voice squeaked on the last word.

"I believe one was your father, but perhaps we should compare notes. You do know how fond your mother was of large men in uniform . . ." Andre led him away.

Cort would have followed, but Terri blocked his path. "Let him handle it. We should go."

"Go where?" He turned back to blackened, fiery skeleton of his home. "The hospital, I suppose." He didn't know what to do.

"They won't let you see Louie until he's out of intensive care, and your mom is there with him. Come on." She put her hand in his. "Let's just go."

Terri had never seen Cort lose control as he had with the reporter. It frightened her, and yet she understood how his father's heart attack and the Torcher getting into his home had pushed him into lashing out. Admitting that she had been investigating him for Ruel hadn't helped, either. Any other man would have reached the breaking point long before now.

She considered returning to her apartment, but after her part in the tussle with the reporter, it would likely be under siege by morning. Instead she drove him in his SUV out to the cottage on the lake, where it was quiet and peaceful, and no one would bother them.

"You and J. D. haven't been out here since last winter," Terri said as she parked by the small cabin facing Lake Pontchartrain. "Well, J. D. has, for about ten minutes when he was running around trying to hide Sable."

"You knew where he was that entire time, didn't you?" Cort asked.

"Some of the time," she corrected as she unlocked the door and turned on the lights. "Your brother can be a real enigmatic pain in the ass when he wants to be."

The McCarthys had left a note on the coffee table, thanking her for lending them the cabin the weekend before. Jack wrote that they had also deposited some of the bass they had caught in her freezer.

"Why did you bring me here?"

"We should go over things. You know, review the case, see if we can figure out who the hell this guy is." She glanced at him. "Or we could go skinny-dipping and chase each other around down by the lake, butt naked." Her cell rang, but when she took it out to switch it off the caller ID made her hesitate. "It's Ruel."

"Answer it." Cort went to look out the front windows at the lake.

She considered yanking out the battery, then pressed the talk button. "Detective Vincent."

"Where are you, Terri?"

"I'm on my way home, Chief." She wished she could spit in his face. "It's been kind of a long night."

"Frank Belafini called me. He's made several statements in regard to Marshal Gamble. He acknowledges that Gamble is the Torcher, and has in the past set fire to the property of owners who refused to pay protection money. He also indicates that Gamble deliberately created the Torcher's threats against him to divert attention from himself. Evidently he burned down his own home tonight to reinforce the hoax."

Terri's jaw sagged. "You *arrested* Frank Belafini?"

"I have the statements on tape, and he's turning himself in tomorrow. In the meantime, you are to arrest Marshal Gamble immediately. The charges are felony arson and first-degree murder."

Here it was. Her worst nightmare, coming around for a second shot at her.

"I'd be happy to, except I don't where he is." It wasn't a lie. She had her back turned toward Cort, so she couldn't see his exact position. "I'll keep an eye out, though."

"You're to bring him and book him on these charges, Terri," Ruel snapped. "Call me the minute you have him in custody. Is that clear?"

"Yes, sir." She switched off the phone and looked at Cort. "Great news. Frank Belafini now says that you're the Torcher, and you've been faking all these death threats to cover your ass. I've been ordered to bring you in. Is that not like the perfect end to this fucking day?"

"I warned you that this would happen."

"That you did." Because she was tempted to throw it across the room, she carefully set down her cell phone and went to stand beside him. "Did you know that I was at the academy when I found out about my dad?"

"J. D. never talked about it."

"Couple of IA agents came to see me, pulled me out of morning warm-ups. Real jerks. When they said that my dad was on the take, screwing with evidence to protect the mob, I almost punched out one of them. J. D. held me back that time." She opened the window to let the breeze from the lake come in. "I got permission to go home that night, and after my parents went to bed, I picked the lock on my dad's desk. You know, I was so sure that they were wrong."

His arm came up around her waist. "What did you find?"

"Airline tickets for trips to Las Vegas, Reno, and some Caribbean islands. My parents went to visit relatives upstate a couple times a year, but they never left Louisiana." She leaned against his shoulder. "I knew because I went with them."

She told Cort how she'd found other, unexplained

purchases for things that had never come into the Vincent household. The receipts for other things her father had never sold to anyone. It was the bill of sale for the lake cottage, however, that had tied it all up for her.

"The bill of sale showed that my father had bought it for cash." She looked around them. "Want to guess who sold it to him, and for how much?"

"Frank Belafini."

"Yep. A half-million-dollar property, sold to my daddy for one hundred and fifty dollars." The laugh that came from her was bitter. "I took everything to my father the next morning. Set it right there in front of him on his desk at the station. There had to be some logical explanation for it. Like he was working a secret undercover job or something.

"He dragged me into an interrogation room and shouted at me. When I shouted back, he hit me and told me I couldn't live with him and Mama anymore, and then he just left me there, wiping the blood off my mouth. After I cleaned up, I came back out. He was gone, and so were all the papers."

Cort's hand tightened on her waist. "What did you do?"

"I went back to the academy and called IA. When they came to see me, I gave them the copies I'd made of all of Daddy's papers."

"You turned him in."

She nodded. "They told me that I'd helped them so much that I wouldn't be required to testify at his trial." Her eyes stung. "My mother never knew, but I made them tell my father that it was me." She rubbed her eyes. "In a way, he was my first collar."

"Ruel must know all of this." Cort's voice went flat. "He used it to manipulate you."

"He made one huge mistake: He doesn't know you. He doesn't know the kind of man you are. I do. I know you'd rather put a bullet through your own skull than hurt anyone." She took in a quick breath. "But the evidence . . . with Belafini's statements, he's got enough now to have you held without bond. If he does that, Belafini only has to make one phone call to have you killed inside." Her hands clenched.

"Ruel wants Belafini for killing his partner, and to get him, he's going to let him kill you."

"Ruel wants Belafini, period. Belafini wants the Torcher." He moved his shoulders. "They're only playing each other, and using me to get what they want."

She wanted to shoot both men, but that wouldn't help Cort. *Would make me feel better, though.* "We'll go to the mayor in the morning. He'll listen."

"It's better that I turn myself in. My attorney will handle Ruel, and I'll be put into protective custody while I'm in prison." He released her and walked back to the center of the living room.

She felt like putting her fist through the window. "You're not going to prison. It's an automatic death sentence. I won't allow it."

"It's not your choice, Therese." He picked up the phone and dialed a number. "Lawson Hazenel, please." He waited a moment. "Detective, this is Marshal Gamble. I understand there's a warrant out for my arrest."

"Stop it!" She nearly jumped on him.

He pulled her against him and held her there. After listening for several moments, he said, "Please let the desk sergeant know that I'll report to the station in the morning. Yes, to turn myself in. Thanks." He switched off the phone. "The mayor just called another press conference, and fired me. Hazenel says every cop in town is looking for me."

Things had not worked out according to plan. Gamble's parents were alive instead of dead. The old man's heart attack had kept them from returning to the mansion in time for the lovely fire he had made for them, and now the couple was together at Mercy Hospital.

The Torcher had tried again. Gaining access to the cardiac intensive-care unit had seemed easy enough, until one shrew of a nurse had noticed him. Being caught watching and chased by Gamble's lovely brunette might have worked out better—he had planned to pull her into one of the rooms and do her there—but Gamble had come after her and spoiled everything.

The anger had built up inside the Torcher from there, becoming as volatile as a pile of gasoline-soaked rags. He needed to burn it away, or soon it would smother him.

He went to St. Louis Cathedral to pray, and then across one corner of Jackson Square to a row of historic buildings that had been turned into high-end art shops for tourists with slightly deeper pockets. The owners had pooled their resources and bought a central alarm system, which was financially smart but practically foolish. He disabled it from the electrical box in the alley and began quietly carrying the seven heavy duffle bags from his van into the stairway. From there he made four trips up to the top floor, which ran the length of the row, and began to set up his pièce dé résistance.

The last items he took from the bag were two beautiful golden hoop earrings, etched with flowers that had tiny diamond-chip centers. He laid them out on his palm and turned it slightly in the dim light from the window to see the sparkle of the stones and the gleam of the gold.

What are you doing, you silly man?

"Being a cheerful giver," he murmured. It didn't frighten him to hear her voice; she was always with him now.

He could remember other things, too: the smell of lilacs, the gentle whisper of her long, dark hair as she turned her head from side to side, admiring herself. *Do you like these?*

"Very much." He would have bought her a hundred pairs of them, if he had known. He would have made her change them every hour.

A sweet, high giggle. *They make me feel like a peasant girl. I should take off my shoes and mash some grapes under my bare feet.*

"Grapes." He curled his fingers over the gold. "Grapes from the vine."

The memories were not all precious. Some ate into his mind, like hungry rats. The other things the old man had said. Things that he had never known. *She's gone. She's gone back to Gamble. Yeah, Cort Gamble. The silly bitch is still in love with him.*

He hadn't believed it at first. He'd gone after her, hoping

to reason with her. He'd stood outside the doctor's office, gathering his courage, and then he'd heard what she said to the oncologist about her chemotherapy, and about Gamble.

It will work, it has to work. I love him. I've moved out of that bastard's house, and he can't stop me. I'm going to be with him. I'm going to live for him.

Something stabbed into his palm. He opened his hand to see that he had driven the sharp posts of the earrings into his flesh. "Hand for hand."

The only love of his life had never loved him. Would never love him. He'd known that from the day he met her. Luciana's heart belonged to Cortland Gamble.

He walked slowly down to the center of the building to set the last of the remotes. He tested the battery, taped it down into place, and raised the antenna. His hands were slick once he had finished, but he didn't wipe them off on the sides of his trousers.

It was his finest creation, his greatest lesson. It had only had to be taught.

He caressed the mound of plastic explosive, painting the outside of it with a palm print made of sweat and blood. "Burn for burn."

19

Terri looked up at the ceiling and watched the faint patterns of light glittering off the lake made on it. Beside her, Cort was breathing slow and steady.

He'd been exhausted, but when she'd brought him to her bed, he'd pulled her down with him.

Holding back was hard, but he'd been through enough. "You're tired."

"I need you." He framed her face between his hands. "Come here."

They'd made love this time, the way they had back in February, and he had held her after for a long time before finally falling asleep.

The way he'd taken her had wrenched Terri's heart almost in two; the way he'd concentrated on her pleasure, the way he'd kept kissing her. Everything he had done was silent and gentle, but tinged with desperation. With the soul-deep despair of a condemned man.

When she was sure he wouldn't wake, Terri moved out from under the heavy arm he'd put across her waist and rose silently from the bed. She had to do something tonight to prove Cort's innocence, and there was only one person she could trust to help her do that.

She found her cell and carried it out to the back porch, where her voice wouldn't disturb Cort. The voice that answered her call was sleepy. "Grayson, I'm sorry to wake you up. You remember that truckload of shit I told you about? It just hit the fan."

"What can I do?"

She swiftly filled him in on the events of the night. "We're staying at my cabin on the lake tonight, but Cort's going to surrender in the morning. I need to prove that he isn't the Torcher before then."

"I still think my Jane has something to do with this," he said.

"Your Jane?"

"Sorry, I mean Luciana Belafini. Her story just doesn't add up."

Terri recalled the crime-scene details. "Her body was found right next to Stephen's, wasn't it?"

"Yeah, and yet she was so sick she couldn't have stood up straight. Why was she there? What did he do to make her go there, in her condition?" He made a disgusted sound. "At least she died quickly. That fire was so hot that even her jewelry melted onto her."

"She always wore beautiful jewelry," she said, and sighed, thinking how much she had envied the Italian woman. "I used to covet her earrings."

"What kind did she wear?" Gray asked, his voice sounding odd.

"Big gold hoops. They were sort of her trademark." Terri flashed on what she had seen in Patricia Brown's ears when she had brushed back the hair from her bloody face. "Wait a minute. That reporter was wearing gold hoops when we pulled her out of Mrs. Gamble's greenhouse."

"Melted gold was found in Bouchard's trunk and at Navarre's house," Gray told her. "The marshal thought that the arsonist might have been leaving some jewelry as a kind of ritual tribute, to be burned in the fire."

"Or to mark these women as a sacrifice. For Luciana." She grew cautiously excited. "This could be it. Can you come and pick me up?"

Gray groaned. "I'm already wide awake. Where are we going and what are we looking for?"

"Hospital, then the forensics lab," Terri said. "The earrings the Torcher put on Patricia Brown didn't burn."

Douglas used the money that Patricia Brown had given him for their exclusive interview to relocate to another motel. The BoJangles Motor Lodge was not as clean as the Big Easy Sleep Motel, and was located a quarter mile from the city's largest landfill. And smelled like it.

However, once Douglas had paid for his room, the desk clerk promptly went back to solving the *Tribune*'s crossword puzzle and paid no more attention to him.

There was no telephone in his room, but Douglas would not have used it anyway. He walked down four blocks to use a pay phone to keep his promise to Caitlin.

"I saw you on television!" she squealed when he called her. "Just like Clover and Alex and Sam, only for real!"

He was rather pleased with his performance, too. He had taken great pains with his appearance. "Your father did not notice my use of his toiletries, I hope."

"Nah, Daddy just passed out on the living-room carpet when he got home. That's better than when he ralphs all over the toilet." Caitlin sighed. "So are you going to hide out until the heat is off, or are you going after the marshal man?"

"Ms. Brown promised me another interview, but I have been unable to reach her." He wondered why. She had promised him a follow-up within a few days.

"Oh, that reminds me." Paper rustled. "A man called and said he left a package for you at the P.O. He said it was real important." She read him the information.

Douglas frowned. "Did he leave his name?"

"No, he just said something weird. He said he was a happy something. It wasn't charity worker."

His blood ran cold. "Did he call himself a cheerful giver?"

"That's it! Is he a friend of yours?"

"No, and if he calls again, I don't want you to speak to him. Tell him I checked out and hang up."

"Okay. I got a B on my math test today."

He smiled. "I knew you could do it."

"I didn't." Caitlin sniffed. "I miss you, Douglas. Am I ever going to see you again?"

"When this is over, and I have a nicer place to live, you can come over for a visit." He thought of a little ranch house out in Metairie, with a picket fence and perhaps a dog for Caitlin to chase around the yard. "I'll find a place where you can meet some other children your age and make new friends." It would almost be like having his own family again.

"You'll call me again, won't you?"

"I will. Remember what I said about talking to that man."

Douglas took care to go to the post office branch at noon, when it was busiest, and retrieved the package without being questioned. From there he took a bus to the airport, and went to the nearest gate.

"Excuse me," he asked one of the security guards manning the metal detector. "I was wondering if I could run this package through your machine."

The old man frowned. "Why?"

"I received this at the post office, but there's no return address." He lowered his voice. "You know what they say; we're supposed to be extra vigilant about unmarked packages these days."

"You got that right, my friend." The old guard put it on the conveyor belt and watched his monitor. "Nothing metal inside. Looks like an envelope full of paper to me."

"Thank you so much." Douglas retrieved the box and carried it into the men's room, and locked himself in the stall before tearing open the package.

There was a plain envelope inside, with a single folded sheet of paper and a thick bundle of five-hundred-dollar bills. The sheet of paper had instructions for another meeting. It was signed with a single word.

Torcher.

Douglas sat and thought for a very long time. It was enough money to give him a fresh start, but the instructions said he would be given another ten thousand if he attended the meeting. The only job offer he had received since leaving jail was to work for minimum wage at a local fast-food restaurant, and that offer had been withdrawn when he admitted during the interview to being a convicted felon.

Was the cheerful giver the Torcher?

Douglas found that he didn't care. Ten thousand dollars would give him a start, but twenty thousand would give him the down payment on a house in the suburbs. A house where Caitlin could come and watch her cartoons and be safe. After she finished her homework, of course. He'd marry again, and have his own children, and Caitlin could babysit for him and his new wife.

To have that kind of life, he would do almost anything.

Douglas called the number on the paper and left a message on the Torcher's anonymous voice mail. He took the bus back into the city, and made the long trek over to St. William's Mission, where they were to meet at last.

He had not felt this good since appearing on the news.

A tall, dark-skinned man with a shaved head came and sat next to him at his table. He reminded Douglas so much of the cheerful giver that he nearly jumped up.

"Douglas Simon?"

He tried to produce a confident smile. "Yes."

"Sebastien Ruel, Organized Crime Unit." He produced identification. "You're under arrest."

Douglas had not expected him to be a cop. "I am?"

Ruel patted him down before securing his wrists behind him with handcuffs. "I tapped the phone at the motel, and I had the package at the post office switched. The money is real, the instructions were changed. I also had you followed from the moment you left the post office, in the event you tried to run with the money."

So it had been another sting operation. "Very clever, Mr. Ruel." A curious sensation, one he had never experienced before, began twisting inside him. It was as if his insides wanted to split apart.

Had he developed an ulcer? Should he ask to be taken to the hospital?

"I know you're not the Torcher," Ruel told him. "However, given your record, it's going to be very difficult to convince the DA of that."

The unnatural position the cuffs put his arms in were making his muscles ache. It was not fair, and he told Ruel that. "I haven't done anything wrong."

"I believe you, and I think we can work this out, if you're willing to cooperate."

Douglas listened as Ruel told him what he wanted. The tearing sensation inside him grew stronger, but he resisted it. "This Frank Belafini won't tell me anything. He doesn't know me. He won't even see someone like me."

"He wants to use you to get to Gamble. He's had his men out combing the streets for you for days." Ruel showed him the envelope of money he had taken from him. "Wear the wire, get Belafini to admit that Gamble is protecting the mob, and you can keep the ten grand and leave New Orleans a free man."

"I want to stay in New Orleans," Douglas told him. "In a little house in the suburbs. I want to start over." With luck, he might meet a kind woman who would be willing to start a new family with him. Someone who wanted the same kind of quiet, peaceful life that he did.

"I don't care what you do, Simon, as long as you nail Gamble and Belafini for me."

Douglas thought of Caitlin, and Cort Gamble, and returning to the monotony of prison. If he cooperated, he could take his revenge, avoid incarceration, and help the little girl who had done so much for him. If he didn't, everything would be ruined.

"Very well, I will do it. Would you please take off these handcuffs now?"

Sebastien was pleased. He had sent Douglas to meet with Belafini, and now all he had left to do was wait for Cort Gamble to show up at police headquarters, as the marshal had promised Lawson Hazenel that he would.

Everything had come together perfectly.

"Chief Ruel," Grayson Huitt said, joining him at the booking desk. "We need to talk."

"Maybe another time, Doctor." He checked the front lobby again. "I've got a suspect to process."

"Do you know what you're doing? Or is sending an innocent man to jail your side hobby?"

Ruel gave him a bland look. "Gamble's dirty, and he's going to give me Frank Belafini on a silver platter."

"Forensics just gave me a print comparison that says different." Gray shoved a paper into his hands. "These prints were lifted off the gold earrings the Torcher left on Patricia Brown. They ran them, and they don't match Gamble's prints. They do match another set of prints on the database, however."

Ruel looked down at two sets of identical fingerprints, and the name typed in below the second set. "This isn't possible."

"I pulled the medical file on him and compared it to the autopsy report. It didn't match. Detective Vincent had a little chat with my tech, Lawrence. Turns out someone paid him to switch records." Gray's voice turned flinty. "Now what are you going to do about it?"

"I need to speak with Terri Vincent."

The pathologist shook his head. "She's gone over to the hospital to check on Louie Gamble."

A flood of patrolmen came out of the morning brief room, scrambling past the people in the lobby as they hurried out to their cars.

Ruel turned to the desk sergeant, who was trying to answer a dozen lines, which had started ringing simultaneously. "What is it?"

The officer looked up impatiently. "Firebombing over in the French Quarter. The Torcher says he's going to take out one whole side of Jackson Square."

Cort discovered that he didn't like waking up alone. He checked the cabin, and then looked outside to see his SUV where Terri had parked it the night before.

She had no transportation. How had she left him, then? On foot?

Feeling uneasy, he took a quick shower before he dressed and went to look for his keys. The blinking message light on her answering machine caught his eye, and he pressed the play button, hoping to hear her voice.

"Gamble," a distorted voice said. "Are you there? I've been trying to get hold of you all night. Got hold of your pretty new girlfriend." He laughed.

Cort froze and looked at the front door. Terri hadn't locked it last night. He'd gotten in. He'd taken her.

"I'm taking her down to the French Quarter for a little morning tête-à-tête on Art Row," the Torcher told him. "The timers are set for nine a.m., don't be late. You can't reap what you don't sow." The tape stopped.

Cort snatched up the phone and called the emergency line to the Arson Task Force. "Gil, I need every truck we can roll down at Jackson Square."

"Company 21 is on their way now," his investigator told him. "He's threatening to burn out an entire block of buildings."

"He's also got a hostage—Detective Vincent. Relay this to NOPD and tell them I'm going directly to the scene to coordinate." Before Gil could say anything in response, Cort dropped the phone and ran out the door.

Terri felt no shame in using her badge to get in to see Louie. "I need to ask Mr. Gamble some questions," she told the disgruntled nurse who had stopped her on the way in. "I'll keep it short and sweet."

Cort's father was sitting up in his bed, and while he looked tired and somewhat haggard, his smile was still as warm and wonderful as ever. "*Cherie!* You have come to rescue me from this torture chamber?"

Terri bent over to kiss him on each side of his face. "Officially, I'm here to question you," she told him in a stage whisper, "just in case the nurse comes in and starts yelling." She turned to smile at Elizabet. "Morning, Mrs. G."

"Hello, Terri." Cort's mother rose and came around the end of the bed to give her a gentle hug. "It's so good to see you."

"Um, you, too." Awkward now, she patted the older

woman's back. In a whisper, she said, "I'm afraid I've brought some bad news. Can we step outside for a minute?"

"We already know about the house," Louie told her, and gestured toward the small TV hanging above the bed. "It did not give me another heart attack."

"Lay back, Louie, or I'll tell the nurse to give you another shot." Elizabet sighed, and said to Terri, "I would like to speak to you for a moment."

"I want you back in three minutes," Louie said to his wife. "I cannot live without you near me."

"You're going to put me in the next bed," his wife told him as she leaned over to give him a kiss. "Now, behave until I come back."

Terri walked with Cort's mother until they were out of earshot. "Have they scheduled the surgery?"

"If he continues to improve, it should be in the next day or so." Elizabet's cheerful expression vanished. "At least he has a good chance. I hope I never have to see him collapse like that again." She forced a smile. "I owe you a great deal for what you did."

Terri shook her head. "I did what anyone would have done."

"You didn't tell Cortland what I said to you, that day Moriah was injured."

"You were upset."

"I was a screaming bitch," the older woman told her flatly. "You would have been completely justified in telling Cortland everything. But you didn't. I heard everything you said to him last night, too."

"It doesn't matter." Terri eyed the exit door. "I really should be going . . ."

"He doesn't know that you're in love with him, does he? You should tell him." Elizabet leaned over and kissed her on one cheek and then the other. "If you don't, I believe I will."

Terri was dumbfounded. "You will? And not run me down in the street beforehand?"

Cort's mother laughed. "I am not quite the insensitive virago I sometimes appear to be."

"Detective Vincent." A patrolman hurried down the corridor toward them. "Thank God you're safe."

"Of course I'm safe. Why wouldn't I be?"

"You haven't heard?" He looked stunned. "There's a bad situation down in the Quarter, ma'am. You need to come with me, right away."

Blocking off and evacuating Jackson Square took time, but every available squad car and law-enforcement officer in the city converged on the French Quarter to lend a hand. Tourists and locals were moved back too far to see what was happening, but the arrival of every truck from three fire companies indicated the gravity of the situation.

"Because the buildings here are so old," one reporter told the camera filming the scene, "and St. Louis Cathedral is in such close proximity, officials are not taking any chances with this bomb threat. Back to you, Bruce and Candy."

Art Row was surrounded by fire trucks, and bomb squad and fire crews geared up to enter each of the shops through the first floor.

Sebastien Ruel arrived on the scene with Gray Huitt in time to see the multiple explosions and the black smoke billowing from the top floor windows. As men dodged the flying glass, the sound of people screaming erupted from the broken windows. Seeing that he was ranking officer at the site, Ruel went and obtained a quick briefing from the fire captain.

"We think he's got people trapped upstairs," Ruel was told. "We haven't been able to get a positive ID on how many. If we're going in, we need to do it now."

The top floor wasn't yet engulfed in flames. "Get the people out."

The fire captain barked out orders, and teams of firefighters rushed in through the front of each shop. The fire captain switched on a handheld radio. "Crew chiefs, I want status."

"First floor is clear," one called back.

"Same here," another reported. "We're moving upstairs."

Ruel listened as the five teams reported no fire on the

lower floors and worked their way up to the source of the smoke and screams. The radio went silent for a long, ominous moment, and then one of the crew chief said, "What the hell?"

"Status!" the fire captain snapped over the radio.

"Captain, you're not going to believe this, but there's no fire. All we got is a tape recorder, some speakers, and smudge pots all over the place. Wait, here's something." There was a pause. "Mary Mother of God."

Ruel took the radio from the fire captain. "What is it?"

"It's a note, sir. It says the whole place is wired to blow if we try to leave."

Another crew chief interrupted by swearing. "There are motion sensors planted on the doors and windows. We tripped them coming in."

"I can see it," another, shaky voice said. "Through a gap in the floor. Looks like a block of plastic explosive on the floor beneath us."

"How much?" Ruel demanded.

"A lot. Maybe ten, fifteen pounds of it."

The fire captain turned pale. "That's enough to vaporize the entire Row."

Douglas walked into the lobby of the motel and was relieved to see Caitlin at the front desk.

"Douglas!" She came around and hugged him, then pulled back. "What's this thing under your shirt?" She prodded the hidden wire.

"It's something I said I would do for the police." He smiled down at her. "Can you sneak away for a few minutes?"

Her face fell. "My dad's not here. I'm not supposed to."

"It'll just be for a quick ride," he promised. "We'll get some ice cream, would you like that?"

Her little forehead creased. "Do you have enough money?"

"Oh, yes." He took out the bills he had found in his coat pocket and showed them to her. "Plenty."

Her eyes rounded. "Wow, you're rich!"

Douglas was careful to observe the speed limit as he

drove from the motel into the city. "I'm going to buy a house out in the suburbs soon," he told her. "Would you like to come and stay with me when I do?"

"I guess." Caitlin looked around her. "Where are we going now? I don't see any ice-cream parlors."

"There's this lovely little place I found down by the water." He changed lanes and took the lake exit.

"I don't know, Douglas. My dad is going to be really mad if I don't get back soon."

"Do you have to go back to that place?" he asked her.

She giggled. "Well, yeah. I live there."

"You shouldn't have to."

"It's not so bad." She frowned at him. "Douglas, are you okay? You're acting kind of funny."

He felt nauseated, but he didn't want to alarm her. "I'm fine, my dear."

Cort arrived at Jackson Square and found Ruel and Huitt talking to several officials. Smoke was pouring from the top floor windows of every shop on Art Row, but not a single hose was being used to put out the fire.

"What the hell are you doing?" he shouted at the fire captain. "Get this fire out!" He started to head for one of the hose rigs.

"Gamble." Huitt caught his arm. "There's no fire up there, just smudge pots. He set it up to look like it was burning."

"What?"

"The Torcher's wired the whole top floor with plastic explosives," Ruel told him. "The device triggered as soon as the men entered the floor, and it's live now. If they try to leave, the real bombs will explode."

"How many?"

"Two that we know of, with ten pounds of explosive each."

He ignored the clench of fear in his gut and turned to Gray. "Did they find Terri up there?"

The pathologist shook his head. "Terri's at the hospital with your parents. She wanted to tell them about the house."

"You're sure."

"No, he's wrong," a breathless Terri said as she joined them. "What did I miss?"

Cort ignored the men and grabbed her up into his arms. "You're safe."

"Yeah." She hugged him back. "Sorry I left you last night. Gray and I had some work to do." She glanced at Sebastien Ruel. "Did he tell you?"

Ruel nodded.

She turned back to Cort. "We're pretty sure we know who the Torcher is." The sound of his cell phone ringing made her frown. "If that's your mother, call her back."

Cort took out the phone and answered it. "Gamble."

"Are you at Jackson Square?" the Torcher asked.

"I'm here. So is Detective Vincent."

"Oh dear, you've caught me out in a lie. Still, there should be at least twenty firefighters trapped in those buildings by now."

"What do you want?"

"Have I not made myself clear to you yet?" He made a *tsk*ing sound. "The men you've worked with, men you've loved like brothers, are now trapped. If they try to leave the top floor, sensors will activate the detonators and Art Row and your fire crews will be scattered in little pieces all over the city."

"You can have me."

"I already have you." The Torcher's voice turned cold. "The bombs are on a timer, which will go off at precisely nine a.m. I also have a remote transmitter which will blow the building any time I want. But I suppose I could take something in trade."

"Me."

"You, and Detective Vincent, I think. Bring her to her cabin on the lake. Just you two. If I see you arrive alone, or anyone else besides the lovely detective with you, I'll trigger the bombs."

Cort glanced at Terri. "She's a phony. A decoy."

"She does resemble my beautiful Luciana a little. Tall, dark, and so lively." The Torcher sighed. "Do take care and hurry. The clock is ticking, and so are my bombs." The line clicked.

"He wants a face-to-face out at the lake." Cort pocketed the phone and looked up at the building. "It's timed to blow at nine a.m. We have to get the men out of there."

"We'll handle it here," Ruel told him. "Go."

Cort went to Terri, who was taking something from the trunk of a squad car. "He's out at your cabin. He wants us there."

Terri handed him a Kevlar vest and a helmet. "Then let's go get him."

20

"They'll be here any minute," the Torcher snarled. "Get your brat inside before someone sees her."

Douglas was tired. From the first time the Torcher had visited him, Douglas had done everything he had asked of him. Yet no matter what Douglas sacrificed, it never seemed to satisfy him. This unexpected visit was frightening, too. How had the Torcher known they would be here?

"I will, but I don't want you to scare her." Douglas straightened his shoulders. "She's only a little girl."

The other man's face twisted with contempt. "You don't want me to go out there and get her, do you?"

"Very well. I'll bring her in. But you have to stay in here until they arrive." Before the Torcher could argue with him, Douglas walked out of the bedroom and closed the door behind him.

Terri Vincent's cabin was such a pretty place. Perhaps after this was over, he could make an offer to buy it. It was more suitable for a family than a single woman, anyway.

Douglas found the little girl standing down by the water, tossing pebbles at the gently lapping waves. "Come inside, Caitlin."

"I don't want to." She threw a round, flat rock and watched it skip two times before it sank.

Douglas frowned. "Are you hungry? You hardly touched your ice cream on the way over." She had fussed so much that he had made a special stop for it.

"I have a tummy ache now." She turned around. "Am I being kidnapped?"

He chuckled. "Of course not. I just thought you'd enjoy seeing how pretty the lake is." He didn't understand why the Torcher had come here, but he had given up asking the other man for explanations. Very little he did made any sense to Douglas at all.

"Who's that man in the bedroom I heard you talking to?"

"He's my friend. He was just saying how much he'd like to meet you." He held out his hand. "Come inside and I'll introduce you."

She drew back. "I don't want to. He sounds mean. I want to go home, Douglas."

"He isn't really mean. He's very sad, and he hides it by being . . . mean," Douglas explained. "He lost someone he loved in a terrible fire. Being around you might make him feel better."

Caitlin shook her head. "I can't stay here. My dad's going to be worried."

He felt something twist inside him. "My dear, he never knows where you are."

"He does, too." Tears welled up in her eyes. "He loves me."

"Your father is a drunk," Douglas snapped. "The only time he even notices you is when he needs you to cover the desk or get him a beer." He watched the tears slide down her cheeks and felt immediately contrite. "Oh, Caitlin, I'm sorry. You should just face the truth about him. He's a very bad parent and you deserve better."

"He only drinks because my mom's dead." She wiped her nose with the back of her hand. "It's not his fault. He's sad, too."

Douglas sighed. "Well, if you really want to go back, I'll take you. Let's just go inside and say good-bye to my friend." The Torcher would simply have to do this without him, this one time.

"I'm sorry I'm being such a brat." She slipped her small hand into his.

"You're not, my dear." He held her hand as they walked back to the cabin. "You're my reason for living."

Cort approached the cabin from the wooded side, stopped the motorcycle four hundred yards away from it, and parked Terri's Harley behind a fallen scrub pine.

"We'll have to go the rest of the way on foot." She climbed off and turned to see Cort sitting on the bike, checking the clip from his gun. "You're sure you know how to handle that thing."

"I made one hundred out of one hundred from three hundred yards on a moving target at the range." He slid the clip back in with a smooth, practiced motion before climbing off the seat.

"That qualifies you to shoot against me, any time you want." She glanced at the cottage. "We want to take him alive if we can. He may be the only person who can defuse those bombs."

"I'll go around to the front, you come up through the back door. Try to get behind him." He put his hand on her arm. "If he has any kind of a device in his hands, or if he's strapped it to himself, don't grab it. Let me handle that."

"How are you going to do that?"

"I know who he is."

She hesitated, thinking of the phone call she'd overheard him making before they'd left the city. "Why did you tell Frank Belafini he's here? He's just going to come over here and kill him. And probably us."

"No, that's the one thing Frank won't do." Cort smiled and touched her cheek. "Do you trust me?"

"Didn't I let you drive my Harley?"

He bent over and brushed his mouth over hers. "Stay behind him."

They approached the cabin silently, and as Cort circled around to the front Terri used her key to let herself in through the back door. She eased the door shut and then went still as she heard the sound of a child laughing.

Maybe it was the television.

She checked around the corner of the utility room before

moving out into the hall. At the other end, she saw the trousers of someone sitting on her living-room sofa with his back toward her. She lifted her gun so that the barrel pointed directly at the intruder's heart as she advanced to the end of the hall.

The man was balding and wore a shabby jacket. On the floor in front of him, a little girl was curled up on a pillow on the floor, watching cartoons.

Oh, no. Terri's heart sank. The kid changed everything.

The man was reading one of her books of poetry, but he didn't appear armed. He didn't appear threatening at all. Terri would have moved forward, but Cort stepped inside and leveled his weapon at the man.

"Come in, Marshal Gamble," the man said. He turned his head and smiled at Terri. "Detective Vincent, our lovely hostess. We've been waiting for you."

Terri walked into the room opposite Cort and immediately went for the girl. "Hi there," she said as she crouched next to her, using her body as a shield between the child and the man. "What's your name?"

"Caitlin." The girl frowned at Cort before rolling over to look around Terri. "What's the marshal man doing here, Douglas? He's not going to shoot you, is he?"

"My friend asked him to come and visit," the man told her. He rose and held out a hand to Terri. "I don't believe we've been introduced. Douglas Simon."

She didn't shake his hand or move an inch away from the child. "*You're* Douglas Simon."

"I am." He lifted his ignored hand and used it to pat his thinning hair. "Not quite what you expected, I imagine. My friend was very upset when he called you. I should apologize for him. He's been suffering a great deal since the fire at Maskers."

"We'd like to talk to him about that fire," Cort said. "Right now."

"I'm afraid that's not possible. He was angry and I didn't want him to upset Caitlin, so I made him leave." Douglas moved around the coffee table. "Would you like something cold to drink? There seems to be quite a lot of beer in the refrigerator."

Terri stood and pointed her gun at his heart. "You're not going anywhere." She looked down at the little girl. "Honey, I need you to run down to my neighbors. They have a pink house, and a big white boat with green sails docked in front of it. Tell them to call 911."

The girl snorted. "I'm not going anywhere. Douglas said I could watch my show before I go home." She turned back to stare at the television.

Terri felt like snatching up the little girl and running out, but she couldn't see under Simon's jacket. If he had rigged something to himself, such a move might make him trigger something.

"Come into the kitchen," Douglas suggested. "We can talk there without disturbing Caitlin."

Cort nodded to Terri and lowered his gun. "Douglas, how long have you known this friend of yours?" he asked as he followed the man into the kitchen.

"It seems like forever, but not long." He went to the sink and turned on the faucet. "Stephen was the only one who ever visited me in prison, you know. My wife and daughter never did."

Terri watched him fill the sink and begin washing some glasses. "What did he want?"

"He offered me a great deal of money to give him some of my medical records. I can't imagine why." He rinsed off one glass and placed it on the dry rack. "I didn't receive the money, but it doesn't matter. I'll still get what I want."

"What's that?"

He turned off the faucet. "A chance to start over."

"That's going to be a little hard," Terri said. "Seeing as Douglas Simon burned to death at Maskers tavern."

"Obviously, you're mistaken. I'm right here." He looked around the counter. "Did I leave my watch in the bedroom?" He wandered out of the kitchen.

Terri and Cort followed him into Terri's bedroom. With a glance at Cort, Terri shut the door.

"Here it is." Douglas retrieved his watch from the bureau,

and then studied it and frowned. "I thought I needed a new battery for this." With a shrug he put it on his wrist.

"It's not your watch," Cort said.

He stared at Cort, and then at the watch. "You're right, it isn't. How strange." He ran a finger over the watch's face. "I must have picked it up somewhere."

"Did you know that Douglas Simon was the same height, weight, and blood type as Stephen Belafini?" Terri asked softly.

"No, I didn't."

"With a little work," Cort added, "Stephen could look just like Douglas."

"I don't know what you mean, Marshal." He gave the mirror a desperate look. "Why would someone want to look like me?"

"The dead man from Maskers was positively identified as Douglas Simon last night." Terri came to stand beside him. "We compared medical files this time. Douglas broke his left arm in two places while he was in prison. We found the same breaks on the left arm of the corpse."

"No, you're wrong." He looked at himself, and extended his left arm. "I never broke this. It's fine. Don't you see?"

"You invited Simon to Maskers that night to pick up his money. He never knew what you had planned." Cort paused. "But Luciana did. She must have. She went there to stop you, didn't she?"

Douglas's mild face flooded with dark color. "She didn't love Stephen. She felt nothing but contempt for him. I heard her on the phone, talking about me."

Me, Terri thought. *Not about Stephen.* "Do you know who you are?"

"I'm Douglas Simon. I told you that already, several times." His voice changed, became deeper. "Do you have some sort of hearing deficiency?"

"Did you see Luciana walk into the bar?" Cort persisted.

"I didn't see anyone walk in. I was waiting where he told me to. He was getting my money." A confused frown appeared on his face. "No, I wasn't there. I was at the window.

At the hotel." He stared at his reflection. "You ran down. You tried to stop her."

Cort blocked the doorway to the front room. "Is that why you killed the other women?"

A strange shift swept over Douglas Simon's reflection. As Terri watched, his bewildered expression slowly faded. His mild eyes narrowed and his brows drew together. Lines appeared around his lips, which thinned and flattened. Even his posture changed, with him straightening his spine and throwing back his hunched shoulders.

"No, Gamble," he said, his voice lower and deeper. "I killed them for you. So you would finally learn to reap what you have sown."

Cort took out his gun and pointed it at the man standing in front of the mirror. "Hello, Stephen."

Gil McCarthy spread out six different sets of blueprints on the hood of a squad car. "I got these from the courthouse."

"We only need one," Ruel told him.

"There isn't just one," the investigator snapped. "The buildings down here have been rebuilt and renovated a dozen times since the Civil War. The row started out as warehouses for cotton and salt." He looked up at the top floor and muttered something.

"What's wrong, Gil?" Gray asked.

"My son. He's up there." The arson investigator turned back to the drawings and pulled out one on yellowed paper. "This is the original building plan, I think. It predates everything else."

Gray leaned over to study it. The design was so old that all the labels were in French, and the black ink used to draw it had faded to a pale brown. "What's this?" He pointed to a square shaft running from the top floor into the basement. "It's labeled *descend*-something."

"Descendeur," Ruel told him. "It means *chute*. Probably a bale chute." He stared at the drawing. "Slaves would work here"—he pointed to the top floor—"packing and binding cotton for shipment. The finished bales were dropped down

the chute to the basement level, where they were sacked and picked up."

Gil peered over his shoulder. "They would have sealed it off."

"Maybe." Ruel shuffled the blueprints. "It shows up in all the other prints, see? They may have sealed it off by putting new interior walls in front of it."

Gil called for a radio, and spoke into it. "Chief, I need you to check the south interior wall. Four feet north of the last window, there should be a hollow space behind it."

"What are we supposed do if we find it?"

"There's an old bale chute that goes down to the basement," he told the crew chief. "Chop a hole big enough for you and your men to climb into it. Rig some ropes in case it's blocked."

Gray directed the paramedics to go around to the open side of the building, where a sloped drive ran directly down to the basement level, and wait to provide assistance. "Any word from Gamble or Terri?" he asked Ruel when he returned.

"None." The OCU chief took out a cigarette and lit it. "Do me a favor, Doc."

"What's that?"

"Tell Gamble I'm sorry for the trouble."

"How do I always end up being Cort Gamble's gofer?" Gray complained. "Tell him yourself."

"I'm turning in my resignation and I'm leaving New Orleans." Ruel blew out a stream of smoke and watched the top floor. "Soon as we get these men out of there."

"Giving up on Belafini? Just like that?"

"Someone else will pick up where I left off." The sound of the trapped company calling Gil over the radio made him toss away the cigarette.

"Go ahead, Chief," Gil said.

"We've cut through the wall, and we're lowering the first man through the chute."

Ruel borrowed the radio. "Have your man take a flashlight and check for wires. If it's rigged, pull him out of there."

"Stand by," the chief said.

After a moment, the sound of vicious swearing came over the radio.

Gil paled. "Say again, Chief."

"The eagle has landed," the chief said, and uttered a weak laugh. "You might want to hit him with some bug spray, though, Gil. I think your kid picked up a few spiders on the way down."

Terri stared as the man claiming to be Douglas Simon pulled the toupee from his head, revealing the black stubble on his shaven skull. "You know that you're Stephen Belafini."

"Of course I know who I am. I like being called the Torcher more," Stephen told her. "Torcher, torture. Kind of poetic, don't you think?" He glanced at Cort's gun and tugged open one side of his jacket, revealing a vest with a number of transmitters attached to it. "Put it away, Marshal, or I'll start flipping switches, and vaporize your firemen."

Cort lowered the gun. "I'm the one you wanted all along, Belafini. Why don't you and I finish it?"

"Look under your pillow, Detective. Go ahead, it's not going to blow up in your face. Not yet, anyway." Stephen watched as Terri lifted the pillow from her bed. Beneath it was an detonator wired to a large gray brick of plastic explosive. "That's enough to take out this entire cabin."

Terri glanced toward the front room. "What about the little girl? She isn't part of this."

"Simon made her part of it. He told her too much, and now she's a liability." He leaned back against the counter. "Don't worry, she's just some white-trash kid. No one will miss her." He let his gaze wander over Terri. "You were better looking last night."

"You were better looking five minutes ago," she said. "Why kill Simon and fake your own death?"

"I was going to use Maskers to fake my death and frame Gamble as the Torcher. I thought it would show the old man that I had some initiative, getting rid of your boyfriend here by making him take the blame for what I'd done." He glowered. "I've done enough shit jobs for my father over the years. It was time to move up."

Cort shifted to the right. "Luciana found out what you planned."

He made an ugly sound. "Stupid bitch shouldn't have interfered. But she couldn't stand the idea of you taking the fall for me."

"So you killed her," Terri said.

"No. I took out Simon and a few barflies. She walked in there and killed herself. I paid the ME's tech to switch the dental records and identify Douglas as me." Stephen caressed one of the transmitter switches. "Then Douglas showed up again. Who'd have guessed a little shit like him would survive that inferno?"

Terri exchanged a look with Cort. "Mr. Belafini, you've been through enough. Let's end this now, and we can get you some help."

"I don't need your fucking help." Stephen sneered at her. "I still have lessons to teach. Pain to give. God loves a cheerful giver." His face contorted, and he bent over slightly and stared into the mirror. "No. You stay out of this, Simon."

"Douglas," Cort said. "Help us."

"Shut the fuck up," Stephen shouted, turning his back on his reflection. "I loved her. I stayed with her the whole time she was sick. I never left her side for more than a few hours. But it didn't matter. She never loved me. She only married me because you wouldn't have her. My father told me everything." His eyes lost their focus. "Do you know what it's like, to know the only person you'll ever love is going to die? To take care of her and hold her and know she still wants another man? To watch her leave you for another man?"

"Luciana and I only saw each other a few times," Cort told him. "She was never in love with me."

"She took the chemo hoping it would cure her. She didn't do that for me. It was all for you. I heard her tell her doctor." Stephen put his hand on one of the transmitters. "Get away from the door or I'll blow everything."

Cort backed away, and Stephen strode out.

"Get your ass—" he looked around. "Where is that scrawny little bitch?" He turned toward Cort and Terri. "Where is she?"

The front door opened, and a thin, balding man with a heavy gray mustache came in. He was carrying a shotgun, and pumped the slide before lifting it and aiming.

"Frank, no!" Cort shouted.

Frank Belafini fired. The blast hit Stephen in the back, and propelled him forward. Cort caught him and kept him from falling onto the transmitters.

"He . . . will . . . reap . . ." Stephen sagged and hung limp.

Cort eased him over onto his back and began yanking wires from the transmitters.

Terri trained her gun on the shooter. "Put the weapon on the floor in front of you. Hands behind your head. Do it or I'll fire."

Frank tossed the shotgun onto the floor. "He killed my son! He deserved it!"

Terri went over and retrieved the shotgun. "You might want to take another look, Mr. Belafini." She went to the window and saw Caitlin out on the pier, being taken onto a Coast Guard patrol cutter. "The kid's okay," she told Cort.

Frank walked over, drawing back his leg to kick the fallen man in the face. Then he nearly fell over himself. "Stephen?"

Cort stood and walked around the two men to join Terri at the window. "Is she okay?"

"Yeah." She glanced back.

Frank was on his knees beside his son. "Stephen? Dear God, you were dead. I thought that bitch killed you!"

"Luci . . . not a . . . bitch."

"She was. She was dragging you down with her, son. Remember how you were? You couldn't eat, couldn't sleep, couldn't work. I had to get rid of her."

"So you threw her out and lied to him," Terri said. "You told him that she was in love with Cort."

"I'd have told him anything to get him away from her,"

Frank snarled. "You see what she did to him?" His expression turned hopeless as he regarded his son. "She made him like this. She drove him out of his mind."

"Reap . . ." Stephen Belafini's eyes had opened to slits, and blood bubbled from his mouth as he spoke. ". . . what . . . you . . . sow . . ." He lifted his right hand, in which he held the remote control for Terri's television. With his thumb, he began blindly pressing keys.

Frank reared back. "No, son. Don't do it."

Terri tried to pull the mob boss away, but he wouldn't budge. She grabbed Cort instead and hauled him through the open front door. "Run!"

A hundred feet later, the cabin exploded.

The final briefing for the Torcher case was conducted after the press conference at the mayor's office the following day.

"The child at the scene escaped without injury," Gil McCarthy said. "She's undergoing some counseling—Belafini did quite a number on her head—but she's a good kid. She'll be okay."

"So this Belafini thought he was two people?" the mayor asked.

"The profiler from Atlanta, Agent Edgeway, believes that Stephen Belafini suffered a psychotic break immediately after the Maskers arson," Cort told him. "Assuming Douglas Simon's identity had been part of his original plan. It was the shock and guilt over killing Luciana that drove him over the edge to actually believe that he was Douglas Simon."

"Stephen was also the informant who contacted me," Ruel added. "He claimed that Marshal Gamble was the Torcher and had threatened to kill him in order to move up within the Belafini organization. He made the phony deposit, and had Santino lie about Gamble meeting his father."

Cort looked at the OCU chief. "He must have been convincing."

"I was a little too receptive." Ruel's gaze remained steady. "Next time I won't be. My apologies, Marshal."

Mayor Jarden looked at the report in front of him. "There is no question now that Belafini was the Torcher."

Ruel nodded. "He planned to fake his own death to protect himself as well as frame Gamble for his crimes. He had a long-standing grudge over the marshal's former relationship with his wife as well, one that his father knew about. Frank used it to split them up. When Luciana was caught in the Maskers blaze, our profiler believes that he focused on Gamble to keep from facing what he had done."

"All right. I want copies of this report sent to all the agencies involved in the community response teams." Jarden turned to Pellerin. "Your Detective Vincent should be recognized for her work on this case."

"As should Dr. Huitt," Ruel said, "and Chief Investigator McCarthy."

As the men discussed which commendations would be appropriate, Cort excused himself from the meeting. Outside the mayor's office, Elizabet was waiting along with J. D. and Sable.

"Cortland!" His mother rushed to embrace him before drawing back. "I've been so worried. The nagging will be endless this time."

As he held his mother, Cort smiled at his new sister-in-law and extended a hand to his younger brother. "You see Dad?"

Louie Gamble had undergone bypass surgery the day before, and the operation had been a complete success.

"He's already sitting up and demanding better food," his brother told him with a grin. "He even gave Evan a hard time for flying down from Montana to be here for the surgery, and then nagged him for not visiting sooner. If Jamie hadn't needed a nap, Evan would still be in there, arguing with the old man." J. D.'s expression turned serious. "Mom was telling me about Moriah. Have you heard how's she doing?"

"I got a call from Atlanta after her surgery, and she came through it fine," Cort said. "She'll need some more skin grafts and cosmetic surgery, but the doctors are optimistic about her chances for a full recovery."

"Thank God." His brother let out a sigh of relief. "Dad will want a cigar when he hears that."

"Terri said she'd beat him if she ever sees him with a cigar again, remember? And she's quit smoking, too," Sable said. She was as tanned as J. D., and short, dark red curls framed her beautiful face. "Did you have something to do with that, Cort?"

"It's a long story." He glanced down at his mother. "Is Terri with you?"

Elizabet shook her head. "She came here with us, but I think all the reporters downstairs made her nervous. She said she was going back to the police station. Captain Pellerin has moved her back to Homicide."

"Where she's staying," his brother added.

Cort clamped an internal hand down on his temper. Terri had been actively avoiding him since the final confrontation at the lake cabin. Why, he didn't know, but he intended to find out.

"I told her we were going over to the restaurant and celebrate," J. D. said, putting his arm around his wife. "But you know how Terri is. She didn't want to intrude on family time. She just took off."

"That's nonsense. Terri is family now." Elizabet looked up at her son. "You'll simply have to go and collect her, Cortland."

"The cabin completely burned to the ground," Terri told her mother over the phone. "So tell Daddy that I'm sorry and I'll see what I can work out with the insurance company."

"No, you will not. I never liked that cabin," Jeneane said. "I'm glad it was blown up."

She rubbed her eyes. "Is he really pissed off at me?"

"Ask him yourself."

A moment later, a gruff voice said, "I saw you on the TV, girl. You looked like hell."

"I sure did." Terri glanced down at her rumpled suit. So much for her temporary glamour. "I'm sorry about the cabin. If I could have stopped him, I would have." She was just glad she and Cort and the child had gotten out alive.

"They say your work was what stopped this Torcher," Con Vincent continued.

"I had plenty of help, but yeah, I did my part." Terri closed her eyes for a moment, remembering how she'd felt as the blast went off and she'd been knocked to the ground. The only thing that had kept her sane was feeling Cort's hand in hers. Then the fire crews, Coast Guard, and local police had pulled them away from the burning ruins and taken them to the hospital.

He cleared his throat. "Lotta people coulda been hurt. You did good, Therese. Real good."

His praise made her throat feel tight. "Thanks, Dad."

"You should come on out next weekend," her father said. "We're having the cousins over for a crab boil."

Her father hadn't invited her to visit since he'd left prison. She tried to think of what to say. *Men are proud,* her mother claimed, but so was she.

She remembered Frank Belafini, and how he had looked down at his dying son. Her father was at least making an effort. "I'd like that."

"You might bring back them trophies your mama hauled outta here, too. Hutch looks empty without 'em. We'll see you next weekend."

Terri put down the phone. She wanted a cigarette, a beer, and a dark place to sit and brood. She wanted to see Cort. She wanted to dig a hole in the ground and bury herself.

She picked up the phone and dialed Andre Moreau's number. "This is Terri Vincent."

"Detective, what a lovely surprise," Andre said. "Have I mentioned that I am completely booked for the next six months? As is my staff?"

"Relax, old man. I'm not coming over for you to trowel on the glop." She sat down. "I just wanted to thank you for putting up with my . . . that four-letter word I'm not supposed to use."

"You're very welcome." The sound of liquid pouring came over the receiver. "I saw the reports about your confrontation at the lake on television; you weren't hurt, were you?"

"No, I just got a face full of dirt and grass. The marshal's okay, too." She hesitated. "Andre, do you think there's any hope for me? With all this girl stuff, I mean?"

"You have everything you need to be a vibrant and attractive woman, Detective. You only require the desire to make the most of it." His voice softened. "I would say that being in love with Cortland Gamble is some excellent motivation."

"I'm that obvious?"

"Imagine a sign painted on a barn in three-foot-high hot pink letters."

"Uh-huh."

"Your love for him outshines that."

She flushed. "Yeah, okay, so I'm head over heels. But it's not that simple. He only wants me because we have this one thing going for us."

"Indeed. Would that be your dedication to your work, or great sex?"

"Great sex."

"I thought as much. The air around the two of you when you're together positively hums with it." Andre sighed. "What is it that you want from Cortland, Terri? Outside of the bedroom."

"I'd like everything," she found herself telling him, quite candidly. "Marriage, kids, until death do us part, all that junk. But you know how I am. I'm a cop, and I'm always going to be a cop. Fitting in the wife and mother stuff will be hard enough. How do I make that work for him?"

"There comes a time in everyone's life when compromises must be made," the old man said. "Are you quite certain that Cortland is who you want?"

Cort was all she wanted. "Yeah."

He drank something. "Then come over here and let's get to work."

Terri had not gone from the mayor's office to the station, and her apartment was deserted. Cort returned to the house his parents had temporarily rented and spent the afternoon on the phone, trying to track her down. No one knew where she had gone off to, not even her family.

Where was she? Why was she hiding from him again?

Elizabet arrived home from visiting Louie at the hospital and suggested he get ready for the concert they had planned to attend.

"I know you don't feel like going, dear, but your presence will be appreciated." She laid a gentle hand on his shoulder. "I put your clothes in the second bedroom on the left."

Cort went to dress, and emerged a moment later carrying the plaid shirt, faded blue jeans, and ball cap he'd found on the bed. "Mother, are these J. D.'s?"

"Yes, he's lending them to you. They're what you're wearing to the concert." Elizabet handed him two tickets to see a popular local swamp-pop band performing at an outdoor arena. "I'm told that there will be a tractor pull immediately after the concert. I'm not sure exactly what that is, but it should be quite entertaining."

"I don't understand."

"You will, dear. Your date is waiting over at Andre's office. You'll want to give her this at some point in the evening, too." She put a ring box on top of the tickets.

He opened it. His great-grandmother's engagement ring, a family heirloom that went to the bride of the oldest son in the family, gleamed against the bed of black velvet.

"A winter wedding would be very nice," his mother said, and gave him a kiss on the cheek. "Hurry along now. And Cortland," she said as he walked back toward the bedroom, "don't mess this up."

He dressed in the clothes, which were clean but comfortably shabby, and eyed himself in the mirror. "A tractor pull." He put the ring box in his front pocket and placed the ball cap on his head. "Whatever it takes."

He arrived at Andre's office thirty minutes later, and followed the arguing voices.

"I can't wear this."

"Tugging will not make the hemline any longer."

"He didn't put flowers in my hair again, did he?" A pause. "He did, damn it. Where's my gun?"

"I have it. Now stand still or I'll shoot you myself."

He looked in the back room and saw Terri standing in front of a full-length mirror, with Andre behind her fastening a strand of crystals around her throat. She wore the ivory Versace evening dress, which sparkled and showed off nearly every inch of her long, golden legs.

Andre glanced at him, smiled, and backed away. "There. You look magnificent."

"I look like a goddamn Christmas ornament." She turned and glanced at him. "Don't say a word, J. D., or I'll sock you in the mouth, I swear to God." She went over to the vanity table and picked up a wide brush. "I have to do this to show your brother I can look like this whenever I want." She swiped the brush at her cheeks. "It's supposed to make him want to marry me. Think it'll work?"

"I want to marry you," he said.

"You're already married, and don't be gross." She turned around. "Did you see him at . . ." She stopped and stared. "Oh, shit."

Andre tossed his hands in the air. "All my hard work, up in flames. Please, God, let me be retired by the time they have children." He stalked out.

Terri ignored him. "Cortland?"

He tugged at the front of his shirt. "This was my mother's idea. It's supposed to make you want to marry me. Think it'll work?"

She walked to him, and then around him. "Damn, you look so great in jeans. I knew you would."

"I was going to wait to do this until after the tractor pull." He took out the ring box, and looked down at her. The most beautiful thing about her was what he saw shining in her eyes. "I love you, Therese. Marry me."

She hooked her finger in the belt loop of his jeans. "Can you wear these to the wedding?"

He took out the ring and slid it onto her finger. "If you wear that dress." He put his arms around her.

She curled her hand over the back of his neck to tug his head down to hers. "No flowers in my hair."

"I heard that," Andre called from the next room.

Cort smiled. "As long as we take the Harley on the honeymoon."

"Oh yeah," she said, and grinned back. "Definitely."

Into the Fire

by Jessica Hall

0-451-41130-7

A warehouse fire in New Orleans' French Quarter
kills a local politician—and ignites intrigue and
pent-up passion between former lovers.

PRAISE FOR THE NOVELS OF JESSICA HALL:

"JESSICA HALL HAS SOMETHING MAGICAL."
—LINDA HOWARD

"DO NOT MISS READING THIS RIVETING,
PASSIONATE NOVEL. IT'S FANTASTIC!"
—BEST REVIEWS

"A FAST-PACED SERPENTINE OF HIGH TENSION,
STEAMY SEX AND JUST THE RIGHT TOUCH OF ROMANCE."
—LISA JACKSON

Available wherever books are sold or at
www.penguin.com

The White Tiger Sword Trilogy
by
Jessica Hall

The Deepest Edge 0-451-20796-3

While in Paris, Valence St. Charles, an expert on antique Asian swords, inadvertently saves the lives of the reclusive collector T'ang Jian-Shan and his daughter. Now, caught between a Chinese tong's assassins and U.S. government agents, Jian-Shan and Val have nowhere to turn but to each other.

The Steel Caress 0-451-20852-8

Raven never doubted that years ago she'd be betrayed by the agency she worked for—and by her handsome boss, General Kalen Grady. Now, Raven has launched a new career—and a new life. But just when she's certain the past is behind her, Kalen turns up on her doorstep with one final and crucial assignment.

The Kissing Blades 0-451-20946-X

Los Angeles-based jewelry designer Kameko Sayura thought she had managed to steer clear of the criminal world inhabited by her father and brothers. But when her 16-year-old shop assistant is abducted, Kameko is drawn into a perilous search for a priceless sword collection. Now, with a young woman's life at stake, Kameko must turn to the one man she vowed never to see again.